New York Times Bestselling Author

SHERRYL WOODS

Catching Fireflies

HARLEQUIN®

entertain, enrich, inspire™

ISBN-13: 978-1-62090-262-2

CATCHING FIREFLIES

Copyright © 2012 by Sherryl Woods

Printed in U.S.A.

Dear Friends,

Unfortunately these days, hardly a day goes by without news of an incident of childhood bullying. Some of these are so horrific or tragic that they defy understanding. Those really grab our attention. Others are all too easily dismissed as some sort of rite of passage, an acceptable part of growing up.

The truth, though, is that bullying of any kind has the power to change who a child is, the kind of person he or she grows up to be. When ignored, the victim can be scarred for life, emotionally, if not physically. The perpetrator grows up with a skewed value system that suggests it's perfectly okay to make another person's life miserable, to feel powerful, even for a moment, at the expense of someone weaker.

It's up to adults—parents, teachers, entire communities—to take a stand, to say bullying is not okay, not ever, not by anyone! And that's exactly what happens in Serenity when schoolteacher Laura Reed and pediatrician J. C. Fullerton realize a student is being bullied. Both Laura and J.C. have experienced the damaging effects of bullying, so what's happening to Misty Dawson is personal and unacceptable.

While there are often subtle messages tucked away in my stories, I hope the message in *Catching Fireflies* is loud and clear. There is nothing cute or normal or acceptable about bullying, whether it's a toddler on the playground or a teenager using the internet to torment a classmate. Pay attention to what may be happening to your children, no matter how young or how old. Pay even closer attention to how they're treating others. Bullying is wrong. It needs to stop. And alert parents and teachers and a united community can make that happen.

I hope you'll enjoy spending time with all the Sweet Magnolias once more, and that you'll take their message—and mine—to heart.

All best,

Sherryl

For all the young people
who feel as if no one's paying attention, I wish you
at least one person who will listen and make your life better.

1

It was little more than six weeks into the new school year, and already Serenity High School English teacher Laura Reed was seeing signs of a potential problem with one of her juniors. Misty Dawson had been skipping class for the past week. Attendance records showed she was in school, but when it came time for English, she disappeared off the radar.

"Was Misty in your class today?" she asked Nancy Logan, who taught history and current affairs.

"Front and center," Nancy confirmed. "I wish I had a dozen students like her. She's smart and she's always prepared. Why? Don't tell me she skipped English again?"

Laura nodded. "Afraid so, and I just don't get it. All of her class records suggest that she's one of the brightest English students in the school. She belongs in my advanced placement class. The first papers she turned in were excellent. She's definitely not having trouble with the material. That's what makes this so frustrating. It's as if she simply vanishes during third period every day."

Physical education teacher and longtime coach Cal

Maddox, who'd come in to grab some bottled water from the refrigerator, joined them at the conference table set up in the teachers' lounge.

"Sorry to eavesdrop, but have you mentioned this to Betty?" he asked, referring to their principal. "She needs to know if a kid's not showing up for class."

Just the thought of going to Betty Donovan with this made Laura shudder. A problem with a potentially simple solution would wind up being blown out of all proportion. Cal, of all people, should know that. Betty had gone after him for a violation of the morals clause in the teacher contract and created a whole hoopla that had required school board intervention before being resolved in Cal's favor.

She looked him in the eye and shook her head. "Not yet," she confessed. "Which means I'm breaking all sorts of rules myself, but frankly, I'm less concerned about Misty skipping than I am about why she's doing it, and why just *my* class."

Cal frowned. "Are you sure it's only your class?"

"You heard Nancy. Misty's been in her class every day. I've checked with Misty's other teachers, and most of them say she's had perfect attendance all year. She started out okay in my class, too. Then she missed a day here or there, but a week ago she simply stopped coming. That tells me something's going on in my class that upsets her. Or maybe she's having a problem with another student who's in there. I can't figure it out."

"But aren't most of the juniors taking the same courses?" Nancy asked. "If Misty's got a problem with another student, English wouldn't be the only class where they'd cross paths."

That wasn't as true now as it had once been, Laura thought. Serenity High School wasn't exactly huge. In fact, until the past few years, when developments had begun popping up on the fringes of town, the school had barely had five hundred students in grades nine through twelve.

Over the ten years that Laura had been working here, though, that number had started to climb. Classrooms were more crowded, and most core courses had to be taught multiple times during the day to accommodate the growth. Last year they'd had to add portable class-rooms for the first time to accommodate the overflow until money could be allocated for new construction. However, there were comparatively few advanced place-ment students, and they did wind up in many of the same classrooms.

"You know I'm not a big fan of Betty's," Cal said, drawing her back to the problem at hand.

"An understatement, I'm sure," Laura replied, not allowing herself even a tiny smile over Betty's futile attempt to get Cal fired several years earlier for dating the older, divorced mother of one of the baseball play-ers he coached. Most of the community and the school board had rallied behind Cal. He and Maddie were now happily married and the parents of two kids of their own. The son who'd brought them together was a star pitcher for Atlanta.

"Definitely an understatement," he agreed. "My point is that she needs to know when there's a problem like this. As I know all too well, she's a stickler for the rules, including a few that are more in her head than on the books. Despite our issues, I do know she cares about the kids. If Misty's in some kind of trouble, she'd want to help, not just rush to judgment."

"I suppose I know that, too," Laura admitted grudgingly. "And if I can't sit down with Misty and straighten this out, I'll go to Betty. Bottom line, though, I'd rather not involve her if I can avoid it. I don't want this girl suspended because Betty's intent on making an example of her." She gave Cal a wry look. "You know firsthand that's her style. Isn't that what she did to your stepdaughter?"

Cal winced. "Oh, yeah. She came down on Katie like a ton of bricks right after the school year started. Believe me, it was not fun around our house when Maddie found out. She grounded Katie, too. It'll be a while before Katie pulls another stunt like that."

"Then you know what I mean," Laura said, pleading for understanding.

"I also know Katie deserved the punishment she got," he said.

Laura sighed. "On some level I know you're right, but something makes me believe there's more to this, and that I need to understand what that is." She knew firsthand what a rush to judgment could do to damage an already fragile teen. If she hadn't had a teacher on her side years ago, she'd have been a high school dropout herself. That teacher's mentoring and faith in her had driven Laura into teaching herself.

She met Cal's gaze. "I swear to you, though, I won't wait much longer before talking to Betty."

"Fair enough," Cal agreed. "I'll talk to Katie when I get home tonight. Maybe she'll have some ideas. She's in that same AP class, right?"

"She is," Laura confirmed. "And doing very well, by the way."

Cal hesitated, his expression thoughtful. "You know, I can't help wondering if it's just some weird coincidence that Katie was caught skipping and suspended. At the time she flatly refused to say why she was doing it, but she must know if there's some sort of dare the girls are taking to see if they can skip without getting caught."

"I remember being shocked about Katie's behavior, but I hadn't put it together with what's going on with Misty," Laura said, intrigued by the possibility. "Do you really think it could be a game to them, even with suspension as a consequence?"

Cal shrugged. "Kids that age don't always look ahead to the consequences. I doubt that Katie did. I can think of a few times over the years when the seniors have dared the younger students to do some pretty crazy stuff. Usually, though, it happens at the end of the year, when they figure the rules are more relaxed and graduation's just around the corner. Still, I wouldn't rule out some kind of informal hazing activity."

Laura shook her head. "I'd expect this kind of behavior from the usual troublemakers, but kids like Katie and Misty? It's a shock."

"I'll do what I can to help you get to the bottom of it," Cal offered. "Kids tend to see and hear things we miss. If Katie's picked up on something, I'll let you know. The guys in the locker room occasionally let something slip, too, so if there are rumors around here, I eventually hear most of them."

Laura nodded. "Thanks, Cal. I'd appreciate it."

"I'll keep my eyes and ears open, too," Nancy promised.

"Any insights would definitely be welcome. I know I can't put off talking to Betty forever," Laura said. "I think I'll scout around right now and see if I can find Misty. She's the one with all the answers. If I have to, first thing next week I'll have her called out of one of the classes she *is* attending."

She really hoped to solve this before a very bright student landed in the kind of trouble that could wind up hurting her very promising future, just the way Vicki Kincaid had kept her from making the second biggest mistake of her life.

Misty Dawson had waited until after the bell, then taken refuge in the stairwell for the second time that day. She'd been there only a few minutes when Katie Townsend opened the door, heaved a sigh at the sight of her, then came and sat shoulder to shoulder beside her.

"You're going to get thrown out of school if you don't stop this," Katie warned her, giving her a nudge.

"What about you?" Misty responded. "You're here, too. And you've already been suspended for skipping class once because of me. They'll probably expel you next time."

"I knew you'd be hiding out again. You have math this period and I know you haven't been going. I only have study hall right now and I told the teacher I needed to use the restroom," she said, holding up her hall pass. She gave Misty a worried look. "You can't keep skipping classes just because Annabelle's a total jerk. Don't you think Ms. Reed and Mr. Jamison are going to notice?"

"Mr. Jamison never takes attendance," Misty replied. "And I don't think he can see past the end of his nose, so he has no idea whether I'm in class or not. As long as you let me know when the tests are coming up and I show up to take those, he won't have a clue."

"We're not in the same AP math class, though," Katie protested. "They had to divide us into two groups, re- member? One of these days he'll give the tests on dif- ferent days, and then what?"

"I'll deal with that if it happens," Misty insisted.

"Well, Ms. Reed is neither blind nor dumb," Katie told her. "She's bound to notice. Just tell her what's going on, Misty. She's pretty cool. I think she'd get it. Maybe she could even help."

Misty shook her head. "I can't take the chance, Katie. Who knows what Ms. Reed would do? Whatever it is, it will just make things worse with Annabelle. They're bad enough already."

She gave Katie a pleading look. "You know I'm right. You know how mean Annabelle can be. And that mother of hers is this overprotective grizzly bear who's count- ing on her little darlin' to propel them into the enter- tainment big time one of these days. Mrs. Litchfield will tell everyone it's my fault, that I must have done something just awful to her precious darlin' for her to do these horrible things."

"I still say Ms. Reed would believe you," Katie countered, not relenting. "Or why don't you tell your mom and dad and let them handle it?"

Katie made it sound so simple, as if the whole world would be ready to leap to Misty's defense. Misty knew, though, that nothing in her life these days was simple.

"Come on, Katie. I can't do that," she replied wearily. "My parents are barely speaking to each other. Mom's so mad at Dad, she doesn't care about anything else that's going on. She just wants me and my brother to be invisible. She seems to have this crazy idea that if the house is perfect and Jake and I are little angels, Dad will change his mind about wanting a divorce."

Katie nodded, her expression filled with understanding. "I remember what that was like. I was only six when my mom and dad got divorced, and I didn't totally get what was going on, but there was way too much fighting that made my mom cry all the time. Even though I hated it when my dad moved out, things got so much better after that. And once my mom started seeing Coach Maddox and they got married, everything's, like, a thousand times better at home."

Misty sighed. "I wish someone like that would come along and sweep my mom off her feet. I don't think it's going to happen, though. She's going to hang on to my dad for dear life, even though it's so over for the two of them. I don't even think she loves him anymore. I think she's just scared to let go."

They sat side by side in silence for a few minutes. Then Katie glanced at her. "What if I said something to my stepdad? I know he'd help."

Misty's eyes widened with alarm. "Coach Maddox? No way. Leave it alone, Katie. It's my problem. I'll figure something out."

"You need to do it soon, Misty. You're gonna get caught. Look what happened to me. Mom and Cal came down on me even harder than Mrs. Donovan did. I've never seen my mom so furious. She even made me scrub the whole locker room at The Corner Spa, and believe me, that was gross. Women are really messy, even in a classy place like that."

"Suspension actually sounds good to me," Misty admitted, unable to keep a wistful note out of her voice. It was almost hard to remember what it had been like when she'd loved coming to school, loved learning and books and hanging with her friends. These days the only time she even saw her friends was if she hooked up with them after school at Wharton's, and even that was tense because Annabelle showed up every now and then and set out to make her life miserable.

Katie looked shocked. "You don't mean that. You love school! You're on track to get a scholarship, Misty. It'll be on your transcript if you're suspended. Believe me, I heard all about how it was going to ruin my future."

"I know. I'm just saying, it sounds better than being here and hiding in the stairwell during English and math. I can't even go to the cafeteria for lunch anymore. That's the one good thing about this daze my mom is in. She hasn't noticed I'm bringing my lunch to school all of a sudden, instead of buying it here."

She gave her friend a weary look. "I just wish I could figure out why Annabelle hates me so much. She's beautiful. She's got this incredible voice that will get her onto *American Idol* someday, just the way Travis McDonald said on the radio on the Fourth of July. And she's dating the most popular boy in school."

Katie regarded her incredulously. "Come on. I know you can't be that clueless, Misty. This is because super jock Greg Bennett, the most popular guy in school, is crazy about *you*. He'd dump Annabelle in a minute if he thought you'd go out with him. And worst of all, she knows it."

"But I *won't* go out with him," Misty said with frustration. "I've turned him down. Annabelle knows that, too. It's not my fault if he can't take no for an answer. It ought to show her what a sleaze he is for being with her and asking me out at the same time."

"The most popular boy in school," Katie repeated with emphasis. "Annabelle feels she's entitled to the best. And since she can't blame him without losing him, she blames you."

"I guess," Misty said with a shrug. "I sure don't get it, though. I'd have kicked him to the curb the second I found out he was hitting on another girl."

"Because you're smart and have it together," Katie said loyally.

Misty sighed heavily. "If only that were true."

The truth was that every single day she felt more and more as if her life were falling completely apart and Annabelle Litchfield was at the controls.

After fending off his nurse's latest attempt to fix him up, pediatrician J. C. Fullerton was pondering the tendency of Serenity residents to meddle in other people's lives when the door to his office opened a crack.

"Is it okay if I come in?" Misty Dawson asked hesitantly. "Everyone's gone out front, but the lights were still on and the door was open. I thought you might still be here."

"Sure. Come on in," he said, regarding the teen worriedly. This kind of after-hours visit usually spelled trouble. With a sixteen-year-old girl, an unplanned pregnancy came immediately to mind.

"Everything okay?" he asked.

Misty sat gingerly on the edge of the chair across from him, her schoolbooks in her lap. "Not really." She sucked in a deep breath, then blurted, "Could you write me some kind of note to get out of school?"

Over the years, J.C. had worked hard not to react visibly to anything patients said to him. Teens, especially, had tender feelings and could easily be scared into silence if their physician said the wrong thing. It usually worked best to listen and ask questions very, very carefully.

He studied Misty closely. Other than looking nervous and maybe a little pale, she appeared to be as healthy as she had been when she'd had her annual physical before the school year started. Her straight blond hair was shiny, her bright blue eyes clear. Looks, though, could be deceiving.

"Aren't you feeling well?" he asked, treading carefully.

"Not really."

He took the response at face value. "What seems to be the problem? Is something going on at school?"

"I just can't go anymore, okay?" she said, instantly defensive. "And I know they'll need some kind of an excuse if I stop showing up. I figured a note from you would work. You could tell 'em I have something really, really contagious, right?"

He held her gaze. "Do you have something really, really contagious?"

"No, but—"

"Then you know I can't do it," he said, his tone gentle but firm. "Talk to me, Misty. What's really going on?"

"I'm not going back, that's all," she said stubbornly.

J.C.'s antennae went on full alert. He had seen this kind of thing before, kids who were good students who suddenly didn't want to go to school. He'd seen it in a way that was up close and way too personal. He was instantly determined to get to the bottom of whatever was on this young girl's mind.

"Is there a specific reason you don't want to be in school, Misty?" he prodded gently. "The way I heard it from your mom, you're an outstanding student, taking all sorts of advanced placement classes."

She shrugged. "Doesn't matter. I don't want to be there anymore."

"What will you do if you don't go?" he asked reasonably. "I thought when we did your physical you mentioned something about wanting to be a broadcast journalist someday. You'll need a high school diploma and college for that. You were all excited about the possibility of a scholarship."

"Like you said, I'm smart. I'll take the GED and ace it, then get into college someplace far away from Serenity. It might not be a fancy Ivy League school like I was hoping, but that's okay. It's a trade-off, but it'll be worth it. I can do it," she said earnestly. "Please, Dr. Fullerton. You've got to help me out."

He leveled a look into her troubled eyes. "You know I can't do that, Misty. Now, why don't you tell me what's really going on? Maybe I *can* help with that."

Tears rolled down her cheeks, but she stood up,

squared her shoulders and headed for the door, her disappointment unmistakable. "Sorry I bothered you."

"Misty, wait. Let's talk about this," he pleaded, not wanting to be one more adult who let her down. She might not be physically ill, but she was clearly deeply disturbed about something. The fact that she'd come to him gave him a responsibility to help in any way he could.

"It's okay. I knew it was a long shot." She held his gaze, her expression pleading. "You won't tell my mom about this, will you? I mean you didn't really treat me, so it's not like you'd have to tell her, right?"

J.C. was torn. It was true that there'd been no medical issues discussed, but he wasn't sure he should promise to keep silent when she was obviously in some kind of distress.

"How about we make a deal?" he said eventually.

Her gaze narrowed suspiciously. "What kind of deal?"

"You pick an adult—preferably your mom or dad, but any adult you trust will do—talk to them about what's going on, and I won't say anything about this visit."

She immediately shook her head. "It's not something I can talk about," she insisted.

He shrugged off the excuse. "That's the deal. Take it or leave it," he replied, his gaze unrelenting. "And I want this person to let me know you've talked. I don't need to know what you said. That can be totally confidential, but I want to know you've confided in someone who can help."

To his surprise, the corners of her mouth lifted ever so slightly.

"What ever made me think you were going to be easy?" she asked ruefully.

"It's all the lollipops and teddy bears around here," he said. "A lot of people mistake me for a softie."

"Boy, do you have them fooled," she said, though there was a note of admiration in her tone. "How long do I have before you rat me out?"

He thought it over, weighing the risks of waiting against the value of allowing her to get the help she needed on her own. "Twenty-four hours seems reasonable to me. This time tomorrow."

"And if you don't hear from someone by then? What happens? Will alarms go off all over town? Is Chief Rollins going to hunt me down and drag me off to jail?"

He smiled at her. "Nothing that dramatic. Just expect me to drop by your house around dinnertime to have that talk with your folks." He held her gaze. "So, do we have a deal?"

"I'd rather have that note for school," she said regretfully, "but, yeah, I guess we have a deal."

J.C. watched her leave his office and prayed he'd done the right thing. If she'd seemed even a tiny bit depressed, he wouldn't have given her the leeway to work this out for herself. He'd have been all over it. Misty struck him as a kid who just needed a bit of a shove to solve this problem for herself. And, in his experience, the sense of empowerment that came from that could go a long way toward healing whatever issues a teen might be facing.

He'd just spend the next twenty-four hours praying his instincts in this instance had been right.

2

Since he'd sworn off dating, J.C. tended to spend a portion of most evenings at Fit for Anything, the new gym for men that had just opened in town. An hour-long workout before he headed home for dinner constituted what passed for his sorry social life most of the time.

It was a lot easier to pretend working out was a good substitute for dating in this environment than it had been at Dexter's. Nobody had wanted to spend a minute longer than necessary in that dump. Here, he could even grab a bite to eat before heading home, and since the healthy food selections were supplied by Sullivan's, one of the region's best restaurants, they weren't half bad.

Though it had taken a while because of his working partnership with Bill Townsend—a pariah with some people since his very messy divorce from Maddie a number of years ago—J.C. had eventually become friendly with Cal Maddox, Ronnie Sullivan and a few of the other men involved with the gym. As long as he left Bill out of the conversation, they seemed to get along just fine.

Tonight he found Cal here, just finishing up his own workout.

"You're late," Cal noted. "Don't tell me you finally asked some woman out for coffee and broke the hearts of all the matchmakers in Serenity."

J.C. chuckled. "Sadly, no. I had an unexpected after-hours visit from a patient."

Cal immediately looked concerned. "An emergency? Was it a kid I might know?"

Though he wasn't about to violate Misty's confidence, he wondered if Cal would have any insights about what might be going on to make her dislike school so much she wanted to quit. "Do you know Misty Dawson?" he asked.

The look on Cal's face was answer enough.

"You do," J.C. concluded. "Any idea what's going on with her?"

"No, but you're the second person today who's expressed real concern about her. What did she tell you?" Cal asked, then instantly waved off the question. "Sorry, I know you can't say anything. I shouldn't have asked."

"It's okay. Actually, knowing that I'm not the only one who's worried is reassuring. If enough adults are paying attention, hopefully we'll figure this out and get things back on track. From everything I know, she's a bright girl with great potential."

"Laura Reed, Misty's English teacher, is all over it," Cal assured him. "I'm looking into a couple of things myself."

"Good to know," J.C. said, relieved. "Has anyone spoken to her parents?"

Cal shook his head. "Laura's trying to dig a little

deeper and figure out what's going on before she stirs things up by going to either her parents or the principal. Want me to have her give you a call, let you know if she finds out anything?"

"Absolutely," J.C. said. "And I'll get back to you or to her, if I come up with any answers."

Cal nodded. "I know living in a small town can have its drawbacks, but in situations like this, I see all the advantages. People genuinely care. They get involved. It's a great environment for raising kids."

J.C. grinned. "So there is a positive side to all that meddling, after all."

Cal laughed. "That's the way I see it, anyway." He glanced at his watch. "I'd better get home. Maddie's probably hit a wall and is ready for backup with handling the little kids' baths by now, and then I have some sleuthing to do with my stepdaughter."

"Good luck with that," J.C. said sincerely. He knew better than most what it was like trying to get information from a teenager. From what he'd observed, they were better at protecting their sources than any experienced journalist had ever been.

Laura had been feeling restless ever since her talk with Cal and Nancy and her failure to track down Misty before school let out. Over time she'd found that the two best solutions for this kind of mood were ice cream or what she liked to think of as shopping therapy. And she had a coupon in her purse for Raylene Rollins's boutique on Main Street that might satisfy at least one urge. If a shopping splurge didn't pan out, Wharton's was just across the town green and had the best hot-fudge sundaes around.

Inside the store, which was known for its smart fashions, she headed straight for the sale rack. On a teacher's salary, full price was out of the question.

"Looking for something special?" Adelia Hernandez asked her as Laura checked out what was available in a size eight. "Or are you just browsing, hoping for a great deal?"

Laura grinned. "You know me too well, Adelia. I can't resist a bargain, and I have a coupon from the paper burning a hole in my purse."

"Then let's find something to spend it on," Adelia said eagerly. "A pretty date dress, maybe?"

Laura rolled her eyes. "I can't even remember the last time I had a date that required anything fancier than jeans."

Even though she'd been drawn to teaching in a small town much like the one she'd grown up in halfway across the country, she'd suspected the lack of social life would be one of the disadvantages. At the time, fresh out of college and still deeply scarred by her first great love back in high school and its disastrous outcome, having a social life hadn't really mattered to her. These days, though, she was coming to regret the serious lack of available professional men. The men who asked her out, while perfectly nice, were, for the most part, not intellectually stimulating.

"You're obviously looking in all the wrong places," Adelia said, though even as she spoke, her expression turned rueful. "Not that I'd know. I only have one toe into the divorce process. Dating is way, way down the road, somewhere past never, for me."

"I was sorry to hear about your marriage breaking up," Laura said carefully, eager to change the subject but not sure if she was being too personal with a woman she knew only casually.

Adelia gave her a wry look. "But not surprised? I know everyone in town was aware that Ernesto was cheating on me, but they were all too polite to say anything."

"I'm not sure there's a good way to broach that particular subject," Laura told her. "What do you say, 'Hi, how are you? By the way I spotted your husband out with someone else last night.'"

Adelia chuckled. "You're right. I doubt Emily Post covered anything quite like that in her etiquette books."

"At least you can laugh about it now," Laura said approvingly. "That has to be progress."

"Yeah, on the days when I'm not furious, bitter and resentful, I'm a barrel of laughs," Adelia said, tempering the remark with a smile. "But the truth is, every day *is* better than the day before. I can thank my kids and this job for keeping me focused on the future, rather than the past. And my attorney has been a godsend. Helen's not letting Ernesto and his dirtbag lawyer pull anything."

Laura nodded. "I've heard Helen is an amazing ally in a situation like this."

"The best," Adelia confirmed as she plucked a dress out of the size-twelve section of the rack. "This is an eight, and it would look fantastic on you. This soft sage-green would be perfect with your coloring. It'll bring out the green in your eyes and the blond highlights in your hair."

Laura studied the simple, A-line design of the linen dress. On the hanger it didn't look like anything special, and she'd never before worn any shade of green. She'd always thought it would make her skin look sallow. "Are you sure?" she asked doubtfully.

"Trust me," Adelia said. "You'll thank me the minute you see yourself in the mirror. Go. I'll keep looking, in case there are more size eights that have been misplaced on the rack."

Two minutes later, Laura was gazing at herself in the dressing room mirror with astonishment. The dress skimmed over her curves, slimming her hips, caressing her breasts and showing off just the right amount of cleavage with the V-neckline. The sage-green did, indeed, turn her eyes emerald. Her cheeks bloomed with unexpected color.

"Holy cow," she murmured, just as Adelia arrived with the perfect flowered silk scarf to add a splash of extra sophistication and style.

"Told you so," Adelia said with a satisfied grin as she adjusted the scarf in various ways to demonstrate the possibilities.

"Could you come to my house and dress me all the time?" Laura asked, only half kidding. She never put outfits together with the pizzazz Adelia had accomplished in minutes. It seemed every time she complimented one of her friends on a new look, the credit always went to Adelia. No wonder Raylene's store was doing a booming business these days.

"Find yourself a hot date and I'm there," Adelia promised with a chuckle. "I yearn to live vicariously."

"I haven't even looked at the price tag," Laura lamented. "I'm going to cry if this is beyond my budget."

"It's on sale and you have a coupon," Adelia reminded her. "And who can put a price on looking as smashing as you do?"

"You're really good," Laura complimented her as she changed back into her clothes and then followed her to the register. Though she winced at the total, she handed over her credit card with barely a whimper.

She consoled herself with the thought that the shopping excursion had been so successful, she no longer needed that hot fudge sundae. Good thing, since to pay for this, she'd be dining on cereal or peanut-butter-and-jelly sandwiches for dinner for the next month.

After years of coaching and teaching at Serenity High School and a good long while being married to Maddie and dealing with stepchildren and their own two little ones, Cal thought he had some pretty finely tuned instincts when it came to those children lying to him as Katie was doing right now. He'd asked her to hang out with him in the kitchen after the dinner dishes had been put into the dishwasher. She'd reluctantly stayed behind.

They were sitting at the kitchen table now, and she was doing her best to avoid looking him in the eye as she skirted every question he'd asked so far.

"You're being very careful to sidestep what was a direct question," he told his stepdaughter eventually. "Let me try again. Do you have any idea why Misty is skipping Ms. Reed's English class?"

"Shouldn't Ms. Reed be asking Misty that?"

"Believe me, she will. I was just hoping you could fill me in before this whole thing blows up and Misty winds up being suspended. Ms. Reed doesn't want that. She's trying to help before Betty Donovan gets involved. You know for a fact that Mrs. Donovan has a zero-tolerance policy for skipping. Didn't you learn that the hard way all too recently?"

Katie squirmed uncomfortably. "Misty shouldn't get suspended," she protested weakly. "Not when there are, what do they call 'em, extenuating circumstances."

"Oh, why is that?" he asked, wondering at her logic and even more interested in those extenuating circumstances.

Katie looked as if she realized she'd already veered onto dangerous turf. "Come on," she said with a hint of belligerence clearly meant to cover her mistake. "She's only missing a class or two, not a whole day or anything."

Cal regarded her impatiently. "Don't play dumb, Katie. You know suspension is mandatory for a repeat offense, and apparently Misty has been skipping regularly."

"But…" she began, then fell silent.

"But what? If there's a good reason for her skipping class, fill me in."

Katie's chin set stubbornly. "I can't say anything."

"Because you don't know or because you've been sworn to secrecy?" he pressed.

"Because it's confidential," Katie said heatedly. "What kind of friend would I be if I blabbed someone else's secrets?"

"Maybe the kind who could keep a friend from getting in more trouble than she can handle," Cal told her. "I admire your loyalty. I really do."

"Then stop asking me all these questions," she pleaded, her eyes bright with unshed tears.

Cal held firm. "Sorry, I can't do that. Sometimes there are things that kids need adults to resolve. I suspect this is one of those times."

She regarded him thoughtfully. "You mean like when Sarah and Raylene kept quiet about Annie not eating back when I was little," she said, proving that she wasn't as naive as she'd been pretending to be. "They should have told."

Cal nodded. "Exactly like that."

Though Annie had survived her nearly fatal anorexia and was now happily married to Ty, Katie's older brother, what had happened to her back then had made an impression on all of them. It was a lesson Cal thought bore repeating now.

"There's nothing like that going on with Misty, is there?" he asked.

Katie's immediate shake of her head was reassuring.

"I'd never keep quiet about that, Cal. I promise. Every time I turn around either Mom or Annie or Ty is all over me about that kind of stuff. I probably know more warning signs of anorexia than any kid in school."

"Is this potentially as serious?" he asked, now that he had her full attention. "Is there some kind of situation that's getting out of hand?"

Again, Katie squirmed uncomfortably. "It's not like that," she said carefully. "If it were, I'd tell you, no matter what promise I made. I swear it."

"Okay, then," he said, relenting. "Just promise you'll come to me or your mom, if you think Misty's in any kind of danger, okay?"

Katie regarded him earnestly. "I already asked her to come talk to you herself, but she wouldn't," she said with unmistakable frustration. "It's not like I don't know there should be an adult involved."

Cal frowned at her tone. Clearly she was upset about whatever was going on. "Okay, what am I missing?" he asked more gently. "Isn't there something you'd feel comfortable sharing with me?"

"It's complicated," she told him, again looking near tears.

"But you believe with everything in you that Misty will ask for help if she needs it and you promise me if she doesn't, you'll come to me or your mom before this gets any worse?" Cal pressed.

She nodded. "Promise," she said, then all but ran from the room before he could try one last time for more information.

Sighing, Cal went into the living room to join Maddie on the sofa. She immediately snuggled in close.

"What was that about?" she asked. "Why did you want to speak to Katie? I figured it had something to do with school, so I left the two of you alone."

"Katie's friend Misty is in some kind of trouble. I'm trying to help one of her teachers put the pieces together. I thought maybe I could convince Katie to open up about whatever she knows. Those two kids spend a lot of time together. I'm sure Katie knows something."

"But she's not talking," Maddie concluded. "Want me to give it a try?"

He shook his head. "Maybe later. Hopefully I planted enough seeds that Katie will start to worry about whether keeping silent is doing Misty any favors."

"Do you have ideas about what might be going on?"

"I don't think she's anorexic or bulimic, which were my first concerns. From what Katie just said, she doesn't think so, either. I think she would say something about that after Annie wound up hospitalized. That made a real impression on her, even if she was so young when it happened. And she saw it happening again with Carrie Rollins just a few months ago, before Carter and Raylene got married."

"I agree. Katie would never let something like that slide. Annie's near miss scared all of us," Maddie said. "Which leaves what?"

"An unexpected bad grade, problems at home, boy troubles. It's hard to say. At that age, everything turns into high drama, doesn't it?" He sighed. "Remember when the toughest thing in a kid's life was catching fireflies on a summer night?"

"Those were the sweetly innocent days," Maddie confirmed, then added, "There are problems at home, by the way. I know because Misty's mom dropped her spa membership the other day. She said she couldn't afford any unnecessary expenses right now. Word around town is that her husband wants a divorce and she's fighting it. I don't know if that means money's at the root of their problems, or whether she's trying to sock away money in case of an eventual divorce or she needs it to pay an attorney."

"I suppose that could explain it," Cal said. He shook his head. "Somehow it doesn't feel right, though. Most of the time when things like that are happening at home, school becomes a refuge. It's the opposite with Misty."

Maddie nodded. "That makes sense."

"Besides," Cal said, sorting through his thoughts, trying to get a handle on what might be happening, "a lot of people go through divorces. Would Katie feel a need to keep quiet about that, especially if the news is all over town already anyway?"

"Good point," Maddie said. "That's one of the reasons I love you. You're so sensitive." She kissed his cheek. "And smart." The next kiss landed on his forehead. "And insightful." The final, lingering kiss was on his lips.

Cal grinned, then gave her a slow once-over that brought a blush to her cheeks. "Why do I get the feeling you're trying to seduce me, Mrs. Maddox?"

She gave him an innocent look. "And I thought I was being so subtle." Her expression turned hopeful. "The little ones are down for the night. Katie's locked in her room, either on the phone or hopefully doing homework and listening to her iPod. The timing seems excellent for a little alone time for you and me."

Cal grinned. "Well, why didn't you say so the minute you walked in here? We've already wasted a good fifteen minutes."

"Talking to you is never a waste of time," she replied. "It counts as foreplay."

Cal laughed. "And *that* is why I love you."

Marrying this woman, despite all the controversy it had stirred up all over town, was the smartest thing he'd ever done.

* * *

Misty had just finished her homework—all of it, even English and math—when Katie called.

"I just got the third degree from Cal," Katie announced. "I think he was only minutes away from using torture to get the truth out of me."

Misty's breath caught in her throat. "The truth about what?"

"You skipping class," Katie said impatiently. "What else? I told you it wasn't going to stay a secret for long."

"Who'd he hear it from?"

"Ms. Reed, of course. Like you said, Mr. Jamison is clueless. At least Cal never mentioned him."

Panic immediately set in. "What am I going to do now?"

"Go to class, for starters," Katie said as if it would be a breeze to walk in and face down Annabelle after all the nasty innuendoes she'd posted online and the sly little threats she'd muttered whenever she and Misty crossed paths. "I'll be there, too. If Annabelle so much as looks at you cross-eyed, we can punch her lights out."

Despite her dismay, Misty managed a faint chuckle. "Yeah, like that's gonna happen."

"I'm telling you, we could do it," Katie said. "Ty's taught me a couple of self-defense moves. He said I might need 'em if some guy gets out of line when I'm on a date. Taking Annabelle down would be a piece of cake. I've seen her in gym class. She's a wuss."

"I'm not sure getting kicked out of school for fighting would be much better than getting kicked out for skipping class," Misty told her. "And you can't afford to get suspended again at all."

"If we told the truth about why we did it, I'll bet it would be okay," Katie said.

"But then even more people would find out what Annabelle is saying about me," Misty protested.

"The kids at school already know," Katie reminded her. "It's online, Misty, remember? Everyone who knows you knows not a word of it is true."

Misty heaved a sigh. "I know, but there are plenty of kids who believe her filthy lies. I hear them whispering behind my back when they see me. Why do you think I stay out of the cafeteria? Walking in there just gives them a chance to spout all that stuff right to my face. At least in my classes there's a teacher around. That usually shuts them up, except for Annabelle, anyway. She doesn't care who's around. I wish just once Ms. Reed or Mr. Jamison had heard what she said to me."

"I've heard her," Katie said. "So have some other kids. We'd all back you up if you told someone."

Misty thought about it. Heck, she'd thought about little else since the school year had started and Greg had asked her out that first time. That's when the online posts had started, as well. It hadn't been a coincidence. Katie was right about that.

But even though she knew she needed help, she couldn't bring herself to ask for it. It would be humiliating if her teachers, especially the ones she really admired, like Ms. Reed, found out what Annabelle was saying about her. They'd think she was some degenerate sex maniac or something. If she'd done even a tenth of the things Annabelle had posted online about her, she'd have probably been knocked up by now. It was disgusting.

And then there was no question her mom and dad would find out. Things were bad enough between them as it was. She didn't want them fighting over her and maybe even believing those awful lies. She could hear her dad blaming her mother for allowing her to become some trashy kid with no morals. God, it was a nightmare. Her whole life was a nightmare.

"I gotta go," she told Katie. "I think my mom's calling me."

"No, she's not," Katie said knowingly. "You just don't want to talk about this anymore."

"No, I don't," Misty said candidly.

"Then we'll talk about something else," Katie said at once. "Want to see a movie this weekend?"

"I don't think so." The last time she'd gone to the movies, she'd run into Greg and Annabelle. Greg had looked at her with that knowing sneer that made her blood run cold and Annabelle had looked smug. She'd wanted to leave even before the opening credits rolled.

"I know there's no point in asking you to go to tomorrow night's football game," Katie said with regret.

"Not a chance," Misty said with feeling.

"How about this? We could go to Wharton's for a burger while the game's going on. There won't be any chance Annabelle will be there as long as Greg is playing. In fact, half the town will be at the game."

"But you shouldn't have to miss out on the game because of me," Misty protested, though she was touched by Katie's offer.

"Believe me, I'll hear every detail over breakfast," Katie assured her. "Kyle's coming home for the weekend. My big brother and Cal will do the entire play-by-play. It'll be like being there, but not as boring."

Misty chuckled. "With a baseball jock like Ty for a big brother and Coach Maddox as a stepdad, how did you wind up with such an aversion to sports? Even Kyle, who never played anything, at least goes nuts over the games."

Katie laughed. "Just lucky, I guess. But at least I know enough sports trivia to fake it with a date. No guy will ever believe I am totally clueless. So, are we on for tomorrow night?"

"If you're sure you don't care about going to the game, going to Wharton's would be great."

"Then it's a plan. And keep thinking about talking to Ms. Reed, okay?"

"Sure," Misty said, her mood sinking again. With Dr. Fullerton's ultimatum hanging over her head, too, she might not have much choice.

3

Most days J.C. had someone in the office pick up lunch for him while they were out, but his concern for Misty made him restless today. He decided a walk to Wharton's would relieve his stress and give him a much-needed change of scenery.

He'd just settled into a booth when he looked up and saw his nurse standing there with a statuesque, red-haired stranger beside her. She was attractive in a way that would have once appealed to him, but today he felt not a single spark. He congratulated himself on finally building up sufficient immunity to all women. It was something he'd worked hard to do ever since the disastrous and sadly predictable end of his marriage. He should have known before ever walking down the aisle that he, too, would fall victim to what he thought of as the Fullerton curse, an inability to choose women who wouldn't betray them.

"Isn't this a wonderful coincidence?" Debra said, beaming at him. "May we join you?"

Even though he saw this for exactly what it was—yet another of her very sneaky attempts to set him up—J.C.

couldn't think of a single gracious way to say no. "Of course," he said grudgingly, standing. "Have a seat."

As soon as they'd slid into the booth opposite him, Debra said, "J.C., this is my friend Linda's daughter, Janice Walker. She's visiting from California. Remember? I told you all about her yesterday. It's her first time in Serenity."

J.C. managed a smile. "And how are you liking it so far?"

"It's a lovely town," she said at once. "Call me Jan, please."

She gave him a commiserating look that suggested she understood his discomfort and shared it. That, at least, helped him relax.

"How long will you be here?"

"Only a few days," she said.

"Unless I can persuade her to stay longer," Debra chimed in. "Did I mention that Jan is a pediatric nurse practitioner? I've been talking to Bill for ages about adding to the staff. With the town growing so fast and all these young families, the two of you can barely keep up anymore, isn't that right?"

Though she had a point, J.C. was not about to encourage her scheme. "Bill makes the staffing decisions. It's up to him."

"But he'd listen to you," Debra pressed.

Jan chuckled. "You've made your point, Debra. Leave the poor man alone. I did not come here looking for a job."

"Maybe not, but you'd be the perfect addition to our team. I, for one, do not intend to let you get away."

Fortunately Grace Wharton bustled over just then

to take their orders. "Sorry, Doc Fullerton. We've been swamped. Apparently nobody in town decided to brown bag it today. They're all in here, and not a one of them can make a decision."

"Well, I don't have that problem," he assured her. "I'll take the chef's salad, Italian dressing on the side."

Grace rolled her eyes as she always did. "Big surprise. One of these days I'm going to convince you to eat a burger like a normal customer."

He laughed. "Someone besides me must eat the salad, or you wouldn't have it on the menu."

"How about a chocolate shake to go with it? Milk's good for you, right?" she taunted.

"Not with the amount of ice cream you add to it," he told her. "I've heard about those impossibly thick shakes you make. As delicious as they sound, I'll pass."

"You are so boring," she accused, turning to Debra and Jan. "I hope the two of you are a little more adventurous." She regarded Jan curiously. "You're new in town. I never forget a face."

"She's visiting me from California," Debra said. "Janice is the daughter of an old friend. I'm hoping to persuade her to move here."

"Well, good luck with that," Grace said. "Now, what can I get you?"

"Cheeseburger for me," Debra said at once.

"And I'll have the same," Jan said, a twinkle in her eyes. "I'll just run an extra mile this afternoon."

J.C. gave her another look. "You're a runner?"

"Not a marathoner, if that's what you mean," she said with a chuckle. "But I usually get in a few miles on a regular basis so I can justify all the terrible things I enjoy eating."

"Maybe the two of you could go for a run together," Debra suggested, clearly not giving up on her match-making scheme. "Jan mentioned just this morning that the track at the high school is starting to get boring. You could show her the route around the lake."

"It's not necessary," Jan said, clearly embarrassed by Debra's persistence.

"I'm going for a run first thing tomorrow morning," J.C. found himself saying. "I'd be happy to pick you up and take you along. The lake is a lovely setting, especially just after dawn."

Jan nodded. "Then I'd love it, if you're sure you don't mind."

"Is seven too early? Much later and it starts getting crowded."

"Absolutely not."

He noticed that Debra finally sat back looking like the very sated cat that had swallowed the canary. A part of him hoped she'd choke on it.

Five minutes after he returned to the office, J.C. called his nurse in.

"You ready for your first patient?" Debra inquired cheerfully.

"Not just yet," he said, trying to keep his expression stern. It was hard to do when she was so clearly pleased with herself. "Debra, have I not told you repeatedly that I'm not interested in dating?"

"You have," she said readily.

"And which part of that didn't you understand?"

"Oh, I heard all the words," she said. She beamed at him. "I just don't accept them."

"Debra," he began in frustration, then faltered. What could he say that he hadn't already said, especially if he had no intention of revealing all the sordid details about his divorce years ago? He heaved a sigh. "Never mind. Just put Mrs. Carson and Tommy in room two and tell them I'll be right there."

"Already done," she said, proving once more the sort of efficiency that would make her nearly impossible to replace. If she turned that same skill to his social life, he was probably doomed. The only way to beat her at that game would be to take charge of it himself.

"Have you spoken to Dr. Townsend about Jan?" he asked as she started to leave.

"Not just yet," she said. "I thought it would be more effective if you mentioned it."

He frowned at that. "The way I heard it straight from her lips, she's not really interested in moving here."

"Oh, I think she would if the right opportunity came along," she responded confidently.

"And you think working in a small town medical practice would be the right opportunity?"

She shrugged. "Maybe not, but I know working with you would be."

"Debra!"

She laughed at his discomfort. "I'm just saying, you could both do worse." Then she gave him a look that was all too knowing. "Something tells me you already have."

And that, J.C. thought, was the sad truth of things.

* * *

Laura was thoroughly frustrated by her inability to figure out what was going on with Misty. She'd been AWOL from class again today, and Cal had had nothing to report that might give her any insight beyond mentioning that Misty's pediatrician shared her concern. Time was running out. If she couldn't solve the mystery and get Misty back into class by Monday morning, she'd have no choice but to bring it to the principal's attention. Then it would be out of her hands. She'd take enough heat for having been silent for this long.

She'd just finished recording the grades from the last assignment when she looked up and saw Misty standing in the doorway to the classroom. She looked as if she might bolt at any second.

"There you are," Laura said, unable to keep a note of relief out of her voice. "I've missed you in class. I've asked your other teachers to let you know I wanted to see you, but you've been ignoring my messages."

"I'm sorry," Misty said, making her way into the room with unmistakable reluctance.

The poor child looked as if the weight of the world were on her shoulders.

"Do you have a minute now?" Misty asked hesitantly. "Or some other time?"

"Now's good," Laura assured her.

Misty sat down and looked everywhere but directly at her.

"Want to tell me what's been going on?" Laura asked eventually.

Misty shook her head. "Not really."

Laura bit back a smile. "Then why are you here?"

"I made a promise to somebody and I have to keep it or I'll be in big trouble."

"You're already in big trouble," Laura reminded her. "Skipping class is grounds for suspension."

Misty sighed, her expression oddly resigned. "Maybe that wouldn't be such a bad thing. I could just study at home and turn in my assignments."

Laura frowned at her. "What's wrong with school, Misty? You've always been an excellent student. The first papers you turned in for me were A-plus tests and essays, so I know you're not struggling with the material. Now you're skipping my class."

"And Mr. Jamison's," the teen admitted.

Laura wasn't all that surprised that he hadn't noticed. Dave knew his subjects—algebra and geometry—but beyond that he wasn't exactly a teacher who stayed on top of things. She wondered, though, what the common denominator was between those two classes.

"So it's not just my teaching style you don't like," she said, hoping to lighten the mood a little.

Misty looked appalled by the suggestion. "No, you're great! I love English. Math, too, for that matter. I just can't come to class."

"You need to explain that to me," Laura said firmly. "I can't help unless you do."

Misty shook her head. "It'll only get worse if I talk about it. Please, you've got to believe me. It's better if I'm not in class." Her expression brightened. "Maybe I could transfer back into the regular English and math classes or at least to the other section of AP math, the one Katie Townsend's in. That would be okay, wouldn't it?"

Laura immediately shook her head. "Not a good idea.

Of course, it would be up to Mr. Jamison if he allowed
you to change to his other AP class, but this English
class is the only choice and you need to stay in it. I could
understand you wanting to do that if you were having a
hard time with the material, but you're not. These classes
will be important on your transcripts for college, Misty.
I thought you were determined to try for a scholarship
to an Ivy League school."

"That's probably just a pipe dream, anyway," Misty
said, though there was an unmistakable hint of regret in
her voice. "I'll ace the other classes, and it'll be okay if I
only get into a state school or even community college."

"That doesn't sound like you," Laura said, more worried than ever by the regretful, defeated tone in the girl's
voice. Years ago, she'd probably sounded much the same
way to Vicki Kincaid. She'd been lost and overwhelmed
by a situation that had gotten out of control. Only Mrs.
Kincaid's kindness and guidance had gotten her through
that terrible time. She prayed she could provide the same
for Misty.

"I'm just facing reality," Misty told her earnestly.
"Please, Ms. Reed, let me transfer back. It's not such a
big deal, really."

Laura was not about to authorize a transfer without
a better reason than Misty was providing. Once more,
she shook her head. "Sorry, no. You might see it as a
quick and easy solution to whatever's going on, but there
are more important things at stake. This could change
your entire future."

Misty looked totally deflated. "If you won't okay that,
will you at least do one other thing for me?"

"What's that?"

"I went to see someone yesterday to try to get an excuse to get out of school. He said he wouldn't tell my mom, but only if I talked to another adult. That's you. All you'd need to do is call him and tell him I made good on my promise." She regarded Laura hopefully. "Can you do that?"

Laura suddenly had some inkling who had extracted such a promise from her. It had been rather cleverly done, though she doubted that she was one bit more enlightened about what was really going on with Misty than J. C. Fullerton had apparently been.

"Give me the name and phone number," she said just to be sure she had it right.

Misty handed her a business card for the pediatrician. Laura had seen J.C. around town, of course, but they'd never met, despite several well-meaning friends who'd offered to fix them up a couple of years ago. Apparently he hadn't been interested.

"I'll talk to him," Laura said, resolving to stop by his office, rather than phoning. She might learn more if they were face-to-face. In the meantime, she held Misty's gaze and said, "But you and I are going to keep talking about this, and I expect you in class next week. Understood? No more second chances."

Misty ignored her edict and said only, "Can you call him right now? He kind of gave me a deadline, and it's only an hour from now."

"A deadline? And then what?"

"He said he'd have to stop by the house to see my mom."

Laura's respect for the doctor climbed a notch. Clever and responsible. It was a good combination.

"I'll make the deadline," she promised Misty. "And I'll see you in here on Monday."

"Whatever," Misty said, which wasn't especially re-assuring.

At least she'd finally made contact, Laura thought. And that was due to J. C. Fullerton. For that alone, she owed the man a debt of gratitude.

J.C.'s gaze kept straying to the clock on the wall in his office. If his phone didn't ring in the next fifteen minutes, then he had an uncomfortable visit to pay to Misty Dawson's parents. When his phone buzzed, though, the medical records clerk who'd stayed to finish updating patient files advised him that Laura Reed was here to see him. It took him a second to recall that she was the teacher Cal had mentioned to him the night before.

"Great. Send her back."

"Will do, and then I'm gone for the weekend. I'll lock the door when I go."

"Thanks. Have a good weekend," he said, even as the door to his office swung open to reveal a pretty woman, probably in her early thirties, with soft clouds of highlighted brown curls framing her face. She was wearing one of those filmy skirts that seemed to be in style these days and a ruffled sweater. It all had the effect of softening her appearance. The effect was spoiled, though, by the no-nonsense glint in her eyes. He couldn't quite imagine Misty choosing her to speak to about her problems.

"Dr. Fullerton," she said briskly. "I'm Laura Reed, Misty Dawson's English teacher."

He stood and held out his hand. "Call me J.C. It's nice to meet you."

"Really? You didn't seem so enthusiastic when Maybelle Hawkins at the Serenity Inn wanted to fix us up."

He was about to sputter an embarrassed response when he caught the glint of real amusement in her eyes and realized she was actually teasing him, though he didn't doubt for a second that Maybelle had tried to set them up. Until he'd moved out of the inn, the innkeeper had been second only to Debra in her determination to find him a wife.

"Actually, Maybelle tried to fix me up with at least a dozen women while I was staying at the inn. Her choices ranged from wildly inappropriate to downright weird. Excuse me for being skeptical about her taste."

Laura laughed, and the tension in her face vanished. "But she does have the heart of a romantic," she said. "Must be all those trysts I hear were held at the inn over the years."

"That would definitely explain it," he agreed, thinking how much prettier she was with a smile on her face. "So you're here about Misty. Cal Maddox mentioned to me last night that you'd been concerned about her. Did she open up to you today about whatever's going on?"

"Not really," Laura admitted. "She did come to see me, though, and tried to convince me to let her transfer out of my advanced placement English class."

J.C. frowned. "Is she failing?"

"Far from it."

"Then why would she want to drop the class?"

"I have no idea. I was hoping, if you have the time, we could compare notes on what she said to each of us and see if we can figure this out. I'm worried she's in some kind of trouble. What was your perception?"

"The same thing," he admitted. Though it went against his gut instincts, he impulsively found himself asking, "Are you free for dinner? We could go to Rosalina's or Sullivan's and see if we can come up with any answers. Or did Maybelle find someone else who's now waiting impatiently at home for you?"

"Maybelle's matchmaking on my behalf was no more successful than hers was with you. And truthfully I'm starved, so dinner sounds great."

"Any preference?"

"Either place works for me."

"It'll be quieter at Sullivan's, and the service is fast. There's a game at the high school tonight. I assume you're going?"

"I usually meet a couple of other teachers there," she confirmed.

"Good, then we're both on a timetable. I'll tell the waitress. If we're lucky, the Friday-night special will be catfish. No one does it quite like Dana Sue."

"So I hear," she said.

He regarded her with surprise. "You haven't been there?"

"Just a few times, and I've never had the catfish. Sullivan's is a little beyond a teacher's salary except for rare special occasions. Once in a while several of the teachers get together there to celebrate a birthday, but we usually opt for the Sunday brunch."

"Then Sullivan's it is, and it's my treat."

Her green eyes sparkled with more of that unexpected

mirth. "Wouldn't that almost constitute a date? I thought you were opposed to dating. That's what Maybelle said."

He chuckled. "Maybelle has a big mouth, but to be honest, in this case, she wasn't far off the mark. Not that she or any of the other people I've tried to head off have paid a bit of attention to me. I must not sound as convincing as I've meant to."

Laura held his gaze. "Something else to discuss over dinner."

J.C. frowned. The last thing he wanted to do was give Laura Reed the wrong idea. She seemed like a lovely, thoughtful woman, but she needed to understand that this dinner was strictly business. They had a mystery to solve about a troubled teen, nothing more. He'd found that laying out the ground rules usually kept expectations in check and avoided unpleasantness later.

"Maybe we should stick to talking about Misty's problem." Even to his ears the comment sounded stuffy, but at least he'd made himself clear. He waited for her reaction. Her smile died along with the warmth in her eyes, but she merely shrugged.

"Whatever makes you comfortable, doctor," she said, suddenly sounding as distant and cool as he had. "Misty's my first priority, as well."

The relief he should have felt at her response didn't come. In fact, what he did feel was the faintest twinge of regret and disappointment. The sparks that had been missing during his lunch with Janice Walker reared up in *I-told-you-so* fashion, proving that his immunity sucked, after all.

That wasn't good, he thought, as he ushered her to the parking lot. It wasn't good at all.

He hoped he was just looking for a handy alternative who might get Debra to back off with her candidate, but he knew all too well that would be playing a dangerous and pretty selfish game. Tonight when he was home in his lonely bed, he'd have to examine his motives for inviting Laura Reed to dinner a little more closely…and then pray that the answers weren't too disturbing.

Laura saw the speculative looks when she walked into Sullivan's with J. C. Fullerton. Not only was she rarely seen around town with a date, but if he could be believed, neither was he. For a town that loved its gossip, their arrival together was bound to be big news.

"Are you sure this was a good idea?" she murmured as they were shown to a table.

J.C. frowned. "I thought you wanted to come here."

"I did until I realized that we were going to be on tonight's menu right along with the specials."

He glanced around, then sighed. "So we are. Too late to hide now, Laura. The cat's out of the bag."

She regarded him with surprise. "You think this is amusing? By tomorrow morning everyone in town will think we're dating."

"Anybody in your life going to be furious about that?" he inquired.

"Well, no, but…" She frowned. "It's not a good idea. I don't want to answer a million questions. Do you?"

"Hey, you're my second unplanned date of the day," he admitted with a rueful expression. "If anyone's going to be a hot topic over breakfast, it'll be me. They'll probably just feel sorry for you getting mixed up with an obvious scoundrel."

She stared at him incredulously. "What on earth are you talking about?"

He explained about his nurse and her apparent mission to set him up. "End result? First thing tomorrow I have a date to go for a run. I'm not a hundred percent sure how it happened. The words just came out of my mouth, and there I was with a date."

Laura couldn't help chuckling. "You're really bad at not dating, aren't you? Or is it that you're easily manipulated?"

"Not until recently. Debra's sneaky. And then you showed up in my office and before I knew it an innocent invitation came out of my mouth and here we are. Two dates today and one more in the morning. My extended track record as a total stick-in-the-mud has taken a real hit."

"You don't sound half as distressed as you should for a man who claims he doesn't want to date," she accused lightly.

He shrugged. "Maybe I'm tired of my own company, after all. And we're here to talk about Misty, so it's not as if this is a real date."

"Tell that to everyone in this room currently on their cell phones reporting the news far and wide," she said.

She could certainly understand why everyone in town would be fascinated with J.C. and consider him a hot prospect. Though he wore his light brown hair in a crew cut, it was evident that it would curl out of control if it grew longer. His compassionate brown eyes were exactly the sort to inspire young patients to confide in him, as Misty almost had. At least she'd sought him out as a trustworthy adult. That had to say a lot about his character.

When Laura glanced across the table, he was studying her, rather than the menu. The intensity of his gaze was disconcerting. She swallowed hard, then gestured toward the list of specials.

"No catfish, so what are you having?"

"The meatloaf's another favorite of mine," he said.

She nodded. "Sounds good. I'll have that," she said and set the menu aside. "Now tell me what Misty said to you."

He winced. "I can't. Doctor-patient confidentiality. I can tell you it was enough to worry me. How about you?"

"She's been skipping my class and one other."

He frowned. "But not all of them?"

She shook her head. "No, it seems her math class and mine are the only ones."

"What's the connection?"

"That's what I'm trying to figure out. My gut's telling me she has a problem with another student, and those are the only two classes they're both in. I'll compare notes with Dave Jamison to see if there's a student who's a common denominator, but I'd be very surprised if there aren't several. Small school, and only one AP English class, though there are two of the AP math classes. Not all advanced placement kids excel at both, but many of them do."

"So that's not going to narrow it down by much, is it?" he said. "And you haven't heard rumors about a problem with another student?"

"Cal's more likely to hear the school gossip than I am," she admitted. "But he hasn't heard a word."

"That's not good," J.C. said, his expression filled with unmistakable concern. "For Misty to reach out to me and want a note to get out of school, she's on edge. I don't like it."

"Neither do I," Laura admitted. "I insisted that she be in class on Monday morning. We'll see. Something tells me she won't be. If so, I'll have no choice but to go to the principal."

"And then?"

"She'll be suspended," Laura said, dismayed. "I was so hoping to avoid that. It's one thing when a kid breaks the rules for no good reason, but I don't think that's true in this instance. I think there's a real problem."

"My gut's telling me the same thing," J.C. said. "I could speak to the principal with you, even be there if Misty's called in. Maybe together we could convince the principal to hold off on suspension, try to find some other solution."

"Have you met Betty Donovan?" Laura inquired. "She doesn't bend the rules for anyone. I even have to say, I can't blame her. The next thing you know, every student and parent would be coming up with excuses that they think justify missing classes, that their little darling deserves an exception."

He smiled. "Definitely a slippery slope," he agreed. "But right now, I'm only concerned about Misty. She has to be my top priority."

When she looked into his eyes, she saw real worry there. The depth of his caring surprised—and impressed—her. Maybe a little too much. He was shattering all sorts of first impressions—mostly bad ones. If he wasn't careful, he was going to start sounding almost human.

4

Going online was a little like being unable to look away from some awful accident you drove past on the highway, Misty thought as she clicked on the social-networking site that Annabelle used to post her latest slurs against Misty. Sure enough, there were more, and they were just as ugly as the ones she'd posted two nights ago and a week before that. Tears stung Misty's eyes as she read them.

How on earth was she supposed to show her face at school at all? She knew that's exactly what Annabelle was hoping, that she'd be so humiliated she'd drop out. She also wanted to tarnish Misty's reputation so badly that it would make Greg look like an idiot if he kept asking her out.

What Annabelle didn't get was that Greg apparently got turned on by the idea of dating the school's biggest slut. These posts just made him more determined. He'd left half a dozen messages on her cell phone in the past week. She'd stopped answering and stopped listening to the messages. She just deleted them. She didn't even tell Katie about Greg's calls because she was afraid Katie would insist she keep them as some kind of evidence in case things got even nastier.

When she got to Wharton's Friday night, she could tell from the sympathetic expression on Katie's face that she'd seen the online posts.

"You looked, didn't you?" Katie asked.

"So did you," Misty accused, slipping into the booth.

She glanced around Wharton's and breathed a sigh of relief. There was no one in here except a couple of older ladies—Frances Wingate, a retired teacher, and Liz Johnson, who was practically a legend in town—eating ice cream. She doubted they paid any attention to the social-networking sites online.

"What did your mom say when you told her you weren't going to the game?" Misty asked Katie after they'd given their order for burgers and fries to the wait-ress.

"She was fine with it. I told her I was meeting you here and that I'd be home way before curfew." She rolled her eyes. "These days that's nine o'clock, if you can be-lieve it. She probably would have made me leave the stupid game at halftime. She's still punishing me for skipping school. The grounding ended last week, but I'm pretty sure I'm going to have a curfew till I leave for college." She gave Misty a warning look. "Let that be a lesson to you."

"You don't get it," Misty responded. "I'd love to be grounded. Suspension would be great, too."

"You don't mean that," Katie protested. "Did you talk to Ms. Reed?"

Misty nodded. "It didn't help. She just asked a bunch of questions I wouldn't answer. If I'm not in class Monday morning, it's all over. She made that pretty clear. She'll tell Mrs. Donovan."

"So, you're coming to class, right?" Katie pressed.

Misty felt tears welling up in her eyes. "How can I?"

Katie looked alarmed. "Misty, you don't have a choice. You're probably out of second chances."

"You saw those new posts online. I don't want to show my face at school ever again. Maybe I should just drop out, maybe even run away."

"No!" Katie said, looking shocked. "You can't do that. You'd be letting Annabelle win."

"She's already won. She's making my life miserable, which is exactly what she wants to do."

"You could fight back," Katie suggested. "She's not the only one who can post online. Turn the tables on her."

"A part of me would love to do that," Misty admitted. "Payback sounds great, but you know I'd be the one who'd wind up in trouble. Annabelle would claim I started it."

"But there's proof that she did," Katie insisted. "The posts are dated."

Misty shook her head. "I can't do it," she repeated. "It would all come out. It would kill my mom and dad. I don't want them to ever have to read that filth."

Silence fell as the waitress returned with their food and their diet colas. Thankfully, Grace Wharton, who seemed to be everywhere at once and heard everything, was at the game tonight. This waitress was fairly new to town and barely said two words to the customers.

"Thanks for meeting me here tonight," Misty said

eventually. "I don't know what I'd do if I didn't have at least one friend I could talk to about this."

"You have plenty of friends," Katie reminded her. "They're all just waiting for a signal from you that you want them around."

"I guess," Misty said. She couldn't help wondering, though, if real friends would have been waiting for some sign from her. Katie hadn't. She'd been in her face, outraged on her behalf, from the moment the first post had gone up online. If anyone else had reached out, maybe she wouldn't be feeling so isolated and alone. She had a hunch even the people who claimed to be on her side were wondering if what Annabelle was posting was true.

"What are you going to do this weekend?" Katie asked.

"Hang out at home, do my homework, nothing special," Misty said with a shrug.

"There's a fall festival close by. We could go to that. We probably wouldn't see anyone from here."

"How would we get there? Neither of us has a car."

"But Kyle's home and he does. I'll bet I could talk him into taking us."

Misty shook her head. She'd always had a secret crush on Kyle. She knew he wasn't half as hot as Katie's other brother, the sports superstar, but he was cute and smart and sweet. She was terrified someone in town would blab to him about the posts online, and he'd be totally disgusted with her. "No way," she told Katie.

"Okay, then you could come to my house for a sleepover tomorrow night," Katie suggested. "Mom wouldn't mind."

"Thanks, but I don't think so," Misty said. "Your stepdad knows about me skipping class. You said so yourself. I don't want him to start asking questions."

"Well, you can't spend the whole weekend stuck at home all alone," Katie protested. "How about I come over to your house? We could make popcorn and watch a bunch of romantic comedies."

"Absolutely not," Misty said, then blushed. "I didn't mean that like it sounded, like I don't want you there. It's just my mom and dad. If they're in the same room, they fight. You don't want to be in the middle of that. Heck, I don't want to be in the middle of that."

"We could take our books and go study by the lake," Katie suggested, clearly determined to be Misty's social director. "That could be fun."

Misty shook her head. "We might run into other kids from school." She gave Katie a look filled with regret. "I'm sorry I'm such a downer. I know it's no fun being around me right now."

"You're my friend, no matter what kind of mood you're in," Katie said loyally. "I learned all about what it means to be a good friend by watching my mom, Dana Sue and Helen. They were way younger than us when they first got to be friends, and they were our age when they started calling themselves the Sweet Magnolias. To this day nobody hurts one of them without answering to the others. I figure you and I are going to be just like that our whole lives."

Katie held up a hand, and after a few seconds, Misty actually managed a watery smile and gave her the expected high five. Maybe her life didn't totally suck, after all.

* * *

"Where's Katie tonight?" Dana Sue Sullivan asked as she and Ronnie joined Maddie, Cal and the kids in bleachers at the high school.

"She met her friend Misty at Wharton's for a burger," Maddie replied.

Dana Sue regarded her with surprise. "I thought family football nights were a command performance, especially these days."

Maddie shrugged. "Cal has me convinced that Misty needs a friend right now, and Katie's apparently appointed herself to that role."

"Leave it alone," Cal murmured from beside Maddie.

Dana Sue studied her two friends, who rarely showed any signs of dissension, at least in public. "What am I missing?" she asked.

Ronnie gave her a warning look. "Did you not just hear Cal indicate we all need to stay out of this?"

Dana Sue cast a dismissive look at both men. "When a teenage girl is in some kind of trouble, I'm sorry if my antennae go up. Since we almost lost Annie to anorexia, you'll have to pardon me if I'm concerned."

Cal leaned across his wife and lowered his voice. "Not the place or the time, okay? This doesn't involve an eating disorder, I can tell you that much."

Just then the play-by-play announcer introduced Annabelle Litchfield, who was going to sing the national anthem.

"Now, there's a girl who looks as if she has an eating disorder," Dana Sue murmured. "I hope Mariah is paying close attention to her."

Maddie smiled. "I think you can count on that.

Mariah is counting on Annabelle taking them to the top of the country charts in Nashville with that voice of hers. She still hasn't stopped talking about the *American Idol* judges who didn't give her a pass for Hollywood. She complains to everyone who'll listen that they must be tone-deaf. That won't stop her from pushing Annabelle front and center for the next auditions."

"I almost feel sorry for Annabelle," Dana Sue said. "That's a lot of pressure for a kid. And you know why Mariah's doing it, don't you? It's all because she lost her own big shot at stardom when she got pregnant with Annabelle and had to get married. Now she's living vicariously through her daughter."

Cal gave her a wry look. "Maybe Mariah is pushing her for her own selfish reasons, but I don't think you need to feel bad for Annabelle. She has more than her share of self-confidence. It's a little unnerving, actually, to watch all the kids at school circle around her like she's some diva with an entourage. I worry sometimes what will happen to her if that big break never materializes."

"Oh, it will materialize," Ronnie said. "Mariah's the kind of woman for whom failure's not an option. Not for her little girl. I'm not sure how Don Litchfield puts up with her."

Dana Sue shuddered. "I still say that's way too much pressure."

"I'm with you," Maddie said. "I saw my share of that kind of early adulation with Ty, when he was pitching right here at Serenity High and the pro scouts were hanging around."

"Not the same at all," Cal said. "Not only was Ty the

real deal, but you raised him to be a grounded kid. The proof of that is how well he's done as a pro."

"Not without his share of mistakes," Dana Sue commented, thinking of the way he'd nearly lost Annie by cheating on her before they were married. She squeezed Maddie's hand. "All in the past, though. He couldn't be a better husband and father now. My daughter's a lucky young woman."

"How on earth did we get so far off track, when there's a game already started on the field?" Maddie said. "Aren't we here for the football?"

Kyle leaned past Cal. "Since when, Mom? You know you're going to hear about every play again at breakfast. You could sleep through the actual game."

Maddie regarded him indignantly. "As if," she huffed. "I'm a fan."

Kyle's grin only spread. "Any idea what an I-formation is? Or where the tailback plays?"

As the others chuckled, Maddie regarded her son with a dismayed expression. "Did I raise you to have such a smart mouth?"

"You did," Kyle confirmed. "You always told me I was hilarious."

Maddie sighed. "Well, I was mistaken. You're just annoying."

Dana Sue grinned. So did Cal, though he tried really hard to hide it. Maddie caught him and scowled. "You, too?"

Cal held up his hands in a gesture of surrender. "Time for hot dogs. Who wants one?"

A chorus greeted the question, and he and Ronnie took off for the relative safety of the refreshment stands.

Dana Sue leaned closer to her friend. "Now you can tell me the real scoop about what's going on with Misty and Katie."

Maddie just gave her a weary look. "I wish I knew. I just know Cal's worried, and that's never good."

"Anything we should try to do to help?" Dana Sue asked.

Maddie shook her head. "If I think of anything, I'll let you know. From what I know, Misty's the one in real trouble. I just don't want it rubbing off on Katie. She's already had enough problems at school this year."

"Hey, we survived all the mistakes we made at that age," Dana Sue consoled her. "Katie will, too."

Maddie still looked unconvinced. "I hope you're right. I really do."

Dana Sue grinned. "Since we have no solutions for that, how about some hot gossip to chew on? You'll never guess who was having dinner at Sullivan's just now when I left."

"Who?"

"J. C. Fullerton and Laura Reed, the self-professed bachelor and the introvert teacher. Want to know the best part? They were actually laughing."

"Holy mackerel," Maddie said, obviously impressed. "J.C. is cute as can be, but this is the first I've heard of him going out with anyone in town. Even Bill's mentioned what a hermit he's been since he moved here. And Laura? She's absolutely lovely, but awfully quiet. Who would have imagined the two of them hitting it off?"

"All I know is what I saw with my own eyes," Dana Sue said. "They had their heads together and looked to me as if they were deep in conversation. I imagine it'll be tomorrow's headline at Wharton's. Everyone in the place was grabbing for a cell phone to make a call."

Maddie chuckled. "You gotta love the Serenity grapevine."

"At least as long as you're not the hot topic on it," Dana Sue agreed. "We've both been there, done that."

"Amen, sister!" Maddie said, just as the men returned with food and drinks.

Cal regarded them suspiciously. "Do we even want to know what you two had your heads together about?"

"I doubt it," Dana Sue said breezily. "You macho men never give two hoots about girl talk."

"I can always fill you in," Kyle said, giving them a wicked grin. "They forgot all about me being right here. They were never that careless when I was a kid. All Katie, Ty and I ever heard around the house when the Sweet Magnolias got together was 'little pitchers have big ears.' We missed all the good stuff."

"What's it going to cost for you to pretend you didn't hear any of this?" Dana Sue inquired.

Kyle's smile spread. "I could use a coupon for dinner at Sullivan's. I have a hot date tomorrow night."

"Don't you dare!" Maddie said to Dana Sue. "I will not have one of my children blackmailing you." She whirled on Kyle. "As for you, you're not too old for me to ground you."

"Mom, I don't live at home anymore," he reminded her patiently. "I can always head back to college."

Maddie buried her face in her hands. "What ever made me think that parenting would get easier with experience?"

Cal draped a comforting arm over her shoulders. "You were delusional, all right."

She turned an accusing look on him. "And just when I had three almost grown and out of the house, thanks to you I have two more little ones."

Cal laughed. "How can you complain when creating them was so much fun?"

Maddie shook her head. "Let's have this conversation again when they hit their teens."

"The teens," Ronnie said, nodding knowingly.

"Oh, don't even try to sound like you suffered through those years," Dana Sue said. "We were divorced most of the time when Annie was a teenager and you weren't even living here in Serenity."

Ronnie winced. "Probably best not to revisit that time right now. Sorry."

She pressed a kiss to his cheek. "It's okay. I've forgiven you. Mostly, anyway."

But an occasional reminder of that awful time did wonders to keep their marriage on track these days. Just like Maddie and Helen, she found herself counting her blessings when it came to love. Who could have imagined it would take the drastic step of a divorce to get her and Ronnie to such an incredible place?

J.C. glanced surreptitiously at his watch and realized that the football game at the high school would already be well under way. He enjoyed stopping by the games. The whole community usually attended, and he liked feeling a part of things. He should have noticed the time when Sullivan's had started emptying out a half hour ago.

"Am I keeping you from something?" Laura asked, studying him with concern. "I'm so sorry. It never occurred to me that you might have other plans. It's a Friday night. Of course you do."

He smiled, enjoying the flustered rise of color in her cheeks. "I mentioned before we came that I'd planned to stop by the game. You said you were planning on going, as well. I lost track of the time and just now realized it's probably started."

She looked even more nonplussed. "Oh, my gosh, we did talk about that. I need to make a call. The other teachers will wonder what on earth has happened to me."

"Why don't we drive over together? It'll be faster than going back to my office for your car."

"Are you sure you don't mind?"

"Of course not."

He quickly paid the check, then led the way to his car, which he'd wisely parked on the street, rather than in the crowded lot. Now that lot was almost empty.

Ten minutes later he found a parking space a block from the field. As soon as they got out, he could hear the shouts of the crowd and smell the aroma of popcorn.

"Sounds to me as if we just missed a great play," he said, as he helped Laura out of the car.

"Are you a big football fan?"

"Big enough," he said. "I played a couple of years in college, but it was tough to do that and keep my grades high enough in premed. Since I knew I'd never go pro, I dropped off the team. Let me tell you, it put a crimp in my social life."

She studied him curiously. "Then you weren't always averse to dating?"

"Not always," he said, leaving it at that.

"There's a story there," she said, holding his gaze. "Maybe you'll tell me sometime."

"Maybe," he said, evasively. Surprisingly, though, the thought of revealing that time of his life didn't seem as depressing as it usually did. The best thing about moving to Serenity had been the fact that not a soul in town knew a thing about his marriage to his childhood sweetheart or how it had blown up in his face.

When he'd paid for his ticket and Laura had shown her pass, they walked into the stadium just in time for the Serenity team to score a touchdown on a pass from quarterback Greg Bennett.

"That kid has an incredible arm," he commented.

Laura nodded, but there was something in her expression that suggested she wasn't half as impressed with him as J.C. was.

"You don't like him," he said intuitively.

"He's a good player," she said carefully.

"But you don't like him," he repeated. "Why?"

She hesitated, then said, "If you really want the truth, he has a massive ego and I've seen the careless way he treats the girls at school. It's a bad combination."

J.C. nodded. "I don't really know him personally. He's Bill's patient. All I know is what I see on the field."

"Lucky you," she said, then winced. "What is wrong with me? I'm not usually so indiscreet when it comes to students."

"I think we're past worrying about being careful with each other. If we're going to get to the bottom of what's happening with Misty, we need to trust each other enough to speak frankly."

"But one thing has nothing to do with the other," she said.

J.C. hesitated. It was a shot in the dark, but it was something worth considering. "You sure about that? You just said Greg's careless with the girls he dates. Could Misty be one of them?"

She shook her head at once. "I'd say she has better sense, but at that age, who knows? The problem with your theory, though, is that he's not in either of the classes she's been skipping. And the word around school is that he's seeing Annabelle Litchfield."

"Oh, well, it was a thought."

"And not a bad one," she said, then caught sight of her friends who were waving from the stands. "I see the other teachers. I should join them. If you're not meeting anyone, you could come along."

"And stir up even more talk?" he asked, grinning at her.

She smiled back at him. "That ship sailed long ago. First Sullivan's and then we walked in here together. Haven't you noticed that since the touchdown more eyes are on us than on the field? I can't imagine having you sit in the bleachers with a bunch of women would make anything worse."

"All women? Where are the men?"

"Sitting with their wives," she said. "There's not a bachelor on the faculty. Trust me, you'll feel like a king."

He laughed. "How can I possibly resist that? Lead the way."

They climbed up to the top row, where three women moved over to make room for them. He already knew all of them, at least by sight.

"You sly girl," Nancy Logan said in what was meant to be a whisper but was easily overheard. "How'd you snag the hottie?"

Laura blushed furiously. "I haven't snagged anyone. J.C. and I were just having a quick bite to eat and realized it had gotten late and we both had plans to be at the game."

"So you had dinner and then you came to the game together," Nancy said, her grin spreading. "In my world that sounds a lot like a date."

"Mine, too," the others echoed.

J.C. saw that their teasing had Laura even more flustered. He leaned down to whisper in her ear, "Don't panic. I can handle the talk, if you can."

She turned to him wide-eyed. "But there shouldn't be any talk, not about dating. You don't date at all. I don't date you. I just explained what happened."

"And they're obviously not buying it," he said, impulsively taking her hand snugly in his. "Let's just go with it."

"Go with it," she repeated, her eyes widening with alarm. "What does that mean, go with it?"

"It means tonight you and I are on a date. We'll think of it as an experiment. Maybe I'll discover that I've been wrong to forego a social life since moving to Serenity," he added, though he suspected the opposite was more likely. All the talk might very well reinforce his conviction that he was better off alone.

Laura already looked uneasy. She swallowed hard at his assertion. "This is a bad idea, J.C."

"Not to worry," he consoled her. "Tomorrow we can break up. Happens all the time."

"Not to me. Not in this town."

He winked at her. "Then I'll be your first."

Something in the way she blanched at his choice of words set off alarm bells. No way, he thought. It wasn't possible, was it? Could Laura Reed possibly be as innocent as all that? It should have terrified him, but suddenly he found himself more intrigued than ever.

5

Laura had spent most of the night wrestling with the covers and her confusing thoughts after spending the evening with J.C. To her surprise he'd fit right in with her friends from school. Once the teasing remarks had quieted down, they'd all cheered themselves hoarse as Serenity had managed to prevent a tying touchdown in the final seconds of the game.

Outside the stadium, he'd offered her a ride back to her car, but she'd insisted that Nancy could drop her off. He'd looked vaguely disappointed, which had surprised her after his insistence earlier in the evening that she wasn't to construe his dinner invitation as anything other than a chance to discuss Misty and the problems she was having at school.

On the way to the parking lot by the medical practice, Nancy had had a million questions, which Laura had managed to sidestep fairly deftly, she thought.

"The man just offered to bring you over here himself. What is wrong with you?" Nancy had asked, regarding her with dismay. "I know his company has to be far more scintillating than mine."

Laura had laughed. "Despite what he said at the game, we were never on a date, Nancy. Scintillating doesn't enter into it."

"Well, it should," Nancy told her. "He's the most available bachelor in the entire town, a doctor, no less. The competition has been fierce for years, and you're the first woman I know of, at least locally, that he's been out with."

"Well, I happen to know for a fact that he has a date with a nurse practitioner in the morning," she said, hoping to silence any more uncomfortable speculation about the two of them. J.C. might be a mystery she wouldn't mind unraveling, but it simply wasn't in the cards. One bit of wisdom she'd taken from past experience was an understanding of when to cut her losses.

"He told you he has a date tomorrow?" Linda asked. "What kind of man brags about a date when he's out with someone else?"

"The kind of man who wants to make it clear he isn't on a date with me," she told her. "Do you get it yet?"

Nancy shook her head mournfully. "Well, I say it's just sad. You looked cute together, and there were sparks. I could feel them."

"Because you have a vivid imagination. It's all those romance novels you read."

"True, I want sparks like that," Nancy admitted wistfully. "I have this sinking feeling, though, that I'll never find them in Serenity. You know what slim pickings there are in this town. There are a few decent guys our age, but finding the whole package—intelligence, a sense of humor, good looks and a solid career—that's all but impossible. Those guys get snapped up the minute they cross into the city limits. And now you already have the last man standing in your clutches."

"Will you quit saying that?" Laura begged, though she couldn't argue with Nancy's premise that exciting, stimulating men were hard to find in Serenity.

"Only if I never see the two of you together again, which, if you want my opinion, would be a crying shame."

"Thanks for the input, and for the ride," Laura told her, quickly climbing out of the car. "See you on Monday."

Unfortunately, even though she thought she'd managed to curb Nancy's wild imagination for the moment, once she was curled up in bed, she couldn't seem to stop herself from daydreaming about all sorts of scenarios that could play out between her and an intelligent, thoughtful, compassionate man like J.C. He was everything Rob Jefferson hadn't been. Of course, Rob hadn't really been a grown man when Laura had fallen for him. He'd been an irresponsible bad boy, which had been the allure for the quietest girl in school.

Don't go there, she warned herself. Thinking about the disaster that relationship had become and the repercussions that haunted her still would keep her awake the rest of the night.

After banishing thoughts of both J.C. and her past, she'd finally fallen into a restless sleep around three in the morning, only to be awakened at six by the ringing of the phone.

"Yes, what?" she murmured sleepily.

"Not a morning person, are you?" a man's voice inquired with a hint of laughter.

"Who is this?"

"It's J.C."

"At six o'clock in the freaking morning on a Saturday?" she grumbled, all of the kindly thoughts she'd had about him fleeing.

This time there was no attempt to hide his laughter. "Definitely not a morning person. Good to know. I was hoping to persuade you to go for that run with me."

Sufficient blood finally reached her brain for her to comprehend what he was asking. "You woke me up to ask me to go for a run?"

"That's the invitation," he confirmed. "Breakfast after."

"Was there absolutely anything in our very brief acquaintance to suggest that I run?"

"Nope, but I don't mind if you're a beginner."

It suddenly dawned on her what he really wanted. "You're looking for a buffer to warn off that other woman."

"Congratulations! For that you get a giant mug of coffee to chase away the rest of those cobwebs."

"You're certifiable, you know that, don't you?" She felt totally within her rights to declare that. No sane man made the sort of request he'd just made.

"But you're considering this, right?" he pressed. "What'll it take to push you over the edge? Danish? Croissants? An omelet?"

Since she was awake by now and surprisingly hungry, she gave up the fight. "I'll take the omelet," she said decisively. "With hash browns. And I need an hour to get ready."

"Nobody needs an hour to get ready for a run," he

said. "I'll give you fifteen minutes, twenty if you insist on me stopping to pick up that coffee."

"I insist," she said fervently. "I'm going to need a lot of coffee."

She hung up without waiting for a response or offering him her address. If he couldn't figure out where she lived, so much the better, but something told her he wasn't the sort of man to leave a detail like that to chance.

J.C. pulled to a stop in the alley behind Sullivan's. Half the town knew that sous-chef Erik Whitney was there at the crack of dawn and that he always had a pot of the best coffee in town brewing. Thanks to the occasions when they'd hung out at the gym and the frequency of late-night calls when Erik and Helen's little girl had earaches, he allowed J.C. to take advantage of that from time to time.

"Sarah Beth's next appointment is free if you'll give me three cups of coffee to go," he told Erik.

Erik grinned. "You sound like a desperate man. Late night with the pretty schoolteacher? And exactly how does that third cup of coffee fit in? Sounds mysterious."

"It wasn't that late a night," J.C. admitted, figuring there was little point in denying that Laura was involved. "But apparently by her standards, it's an early morning. I convinced her to go for a run by promising her coffee. Yours is far more likely to impress her than Wharton's."

"Interesting," Erik said grinning. "So, the two of you really are an item? That was the hot topic in here last night, anyway, after your cozy meal together. I suspect there's already a pool going at Wharton's. Grace loves a romance."

J.C. winced. "Whoa! We're just acquaintances," he insisted. "I asked her to bail me out of a jam this morning, and she's gone along with it. I need to hurry, though, before she changes her mind."

"You're in a jam that involves going for a run?" Erik asked with unmistakable confusion. "Do I even want to know? And you still haven't explained the extra cup."

"If you're like everyone else in this town, of course you want to know," J.C. said, amused. "But I don't have the time or the inclination to fill you in. Coffees, please."

Erik handed over the cups. "Okay, but you owe me more than a free office visit for Sarah Beth. My wife's not going to be happy if I come home without details. Then, again, she's getting together with Maddie and Dana Sue this morning. If anything's going on, they'll already know about it."

Sadly, J.C. thought, they probably would.

Laura was waiting outside on the front steps of her apartment building when J.C. rolled to a stop on the street. She walked in his direction, regarding him with suspicion.

"There had better be coffee," she said before even touching the handle of the passenger door.

He held up a cup. "Freshly brewed, as promised."

"Gimme," she said, getting into the car. She took a deep sniff. "I don't recognize this aroma. It smells amazing."

"Sullivan's."

"They're not open this early," she said, regarding him with amazement. "Who'd you bribe?"

"Erik. I promised him his daughter's next office visit on the house."

"Given what doctors charge these days, this is one pricey cup of coffee," she said as she took her first sip. "Oh, my God, it's worth every penny."

He laughed. "That's what I think every time I take advantage of Erik's good nature by sneaking in there before work. I think he considers the coffee to be his version of community service."

"I really do need to get to know him better," Laura said. "Do you think Helen would mind if I start hanging out with her husband?"

"She'd probably string you up a tree," he said with conviction as he pulled up in front of an unfamiliar house.

"Why are we here?" she asked, then remembered. "Ah, the date. Would you like me to escort you to the door?"

"No, I think I'll be safe enough from there to here. Just don't drink her coffee."

"If she's a real runner, she probably doesn't touch the stuff," Laura said. "I'm actually surprised you do."

"Some men have sex to start the day. Since there's none of that in my life at the moment, I drink coffee. Seems to work," he said right before he headed up the walk.

Just as he reached the door, it opened and a woman came out with her red hair pulled high in a sassy ponytail. She was wearing running shorts and a tight-fitting sports top, both meant to display an awful lot of well-toned flesh. Laura glanced down at her sweat pants and ancient T-shirt and sighed. There wasn't a woman in the world who'd buy that she was serious competition for the woman walking her way, talking animatedly with J.C. as if it weren't practically the middle of the night. She might be up at dawn on weekdays, but most Saturdays she indulged herself by sleeping as late as she wanted. Today's was the first Saturday sunrise she'd seen in ages.

In the car, J.C. made the introductions, then headed for the park. As Laura had anticipated, Jan turned down the coffee and stuck to bottled water. J.C. practically gulped down a long swallow of the rejected coffee, then gave Laura an apologetic look. "Did you want this?"

She grinned at his guilty expression. "Not to worry, I'm still savoring the first cup."

"Good," he said and took another long slug of the coffee.

"Careful there," she said, lowering her voice. "You don't want to choke in front of your date."

He glanced at her with a frown. "Was inviting you along a mistake?"

She beamed at him. "More than likely. So far, though, I'm fascinated to see what'll happen next."

Jan turned out to be a perfectly pleasant, intelligent woman who took her running seriously. When J.C. dutifully insisted on staying back with the lagging Laura, she ran on ahead, clearly determined to make it a real workout.

"You could go with her," Laura told him. "I'm not going to catch up. In fact, I'm thinking I wouldn't mind sitting in the shade of that old pin oak over there for a while and enjoying the rest of my coffee. It's a beautiful morning. It finally feels like fall."

He regarded her with amusement. "You really are out of your comfort zone, aren't you?"

"So far, you probably can't even imagine it," she admitted. "I don't sweat. I don't glow. A brisk evening walk is about my limit."

"Then I'm all the more grateful that you made an exception and came along this morning."

"I don't think you really needed my protection. I hope it won't destroy your ego, but I'm not getting the sense that Jan's any more into you than you're into her."

He looked surprised but not displeased by the assessment. "That's what I thought, too, but Debra seemed so determined, it rattled me."

"I suppose you wouldn't be the first couple to be pushed together by an overly zealous matchmaker, but something tells me you're both made of tougher stuff than that."

He met her gaze, his curiosity apparent. "So, just for the record, why aren't you married?"

Laura shrugged off what had been an increasingly touchy subject with her parents the past couple of years. Even though they lived in the Midwest and would probably rarely see her children if and when she had them, they seemed infatuated with the idea of grandchildren. Or maybe they were just eager to make up for the child they'd insisted she give up for adoption when she was barely seventeen, Rob's child. None of that was something she intended to discuss with a man she barely knew. That shameful mistake—the pregnancy—wasn't something she liked thinking about. Nor was relinquishing her child to strangers, even though she'd known in her heart it was for the best. Her mentor back then, Vicki Kincaid, had helped her not only to see that, but to bolster her spirits when she'd been the target of her classmates' cruel remarks.

Instead of going into any of that, she explained, "I work with a lot of women. I don't hang out in bars. Serenity's a small town. There aren't many opportunities for finding someone and falling madly in love."

"Have you ever considered moving to a town where there might be more prospects?"

"Nope. I fell in love with this town the first time I came here for a job interview right out of college. Nothing's changed my mind about wanting to stay here."

"And you're not lonely?"

She leveled a look into his eyes. "Mostly I'm content with my own company. How about you?"

For a moment, he looked disconcerted by the question, then confessed, "From time to time."

"Then let me turn the tables. Why haven't you married? You've admitted people are constantly throwing candidates in your direction."

"None of them stuck," he said. "And I learned a long time ago that marriage isn't for me."

"Trial and error?" she asked, suddenly getting it.

He smiled. "You could say that."

"It must have been a pretty awful breakup."

"You have no idea." He waved her off. "Enough of that. It's depressing." He stood up. "And enough lollygagging, Ms. Reed. We're going to finish this run, even if we have to do it at a snail's pace."

"I can run faster than a snail," she protested, reluctantly getting to her feet and tossing her empty coffee cup into the trash.

"You'll need to prove that before I'll buy it," he said. "Go. You set the pace."

She forced herself to jog along, pushing herself to go much faster than she wanted to but mindful that she'd never break any speed records.

"Okay, you've matched a turtle," J.C. admitted when they'd finally made their way around the lake and back to the car.

"I appreciate the recognition," she commented wryly. "Where do you suppose Jan is?"

"Making her third loop, I imagine," he said. "I know she passed us twice. Didn't you see her wave?"

"You mean through my blinding tears?" she asked, only half kidding.

He nudged her in the ribs as he gave her a bottle of cool water. "Come on. It wasn't that bad. You did it. Accomplishing something new should be giving you a huge adrenaline rush."

She gave him a sour look as she sipped the water. "I'll be sure to let you know when that kicks in."

J.C. was barely behind his desk on Monday morning when Debra came stalking into his office, her expression radiating indignation.

"What were you thinking?" she demanded. "You invite Jan to go for a run, then bring another woman along. Who does that?"

"A man making it clear that he's not interested in anything more than going for a run." He gave her a hard look. "Was she offended?"

"Well, no, but that's not the point. I'm offended."

"I can't imagine why. I took your houseguest out for a run, as promised. We even had a nice breakfast afterward. I paid. She and Laura Reed hit it off. If Jan stays in town, I imagine they'll be friends."

"If I wanted her to make a bunch of friends here, I'd have thrown a party," she retorted. "Believe me, I can do Southern hospitality with the best of them."

J.C. worked hard to stifle a grin. "Jan's a very nice woman, Debra. She's smart, levelheaded and practical. I mentioned to Bill that we ought to look into adding a nurse practitioner. He said he'd be happy to interview her, if she's interested in staying."

"Well, why would she stay now, with you all but declaring yourself off-limits?"

"Because she'd love the job and the town?" he suggested lightly. "Those would be the wise reasons to make such a drastic move clear across the country."

She frowned at him. "You are very annoying."

"Only because you didn't get your way," he said. "Get Laine Tillis into room two, okay?"

"Already done," she said with a sniff. "Just because I'm mad at you doesn't mean I'm not going to do my job."

"Much appreciated," he told her with total sincerity.

That, he hoped, would be the end of her matchmaking... if he was lucky.

The starting bell for third period rang. Laura looked around the classroom and sighed. To her regret, there was no sign of Misty. Just as she was about to finish taking attendance, the door opened and Misty slipped in, hurrying to the very back of the room.

Laura heard a few whispered comments as she passed, but she couldn't make out what was said. Whatever it was, though, put dull red patches of color onto Misty's cheeks. Even from the front of the room, Laura couldn't mistake the sheen of tears in the girl's eyes.

Though she very badly wanted to get to the bottom of those comments, she decided to let it pass for now. She had a hunch one word would send Misty fleeing right back out the door.

Fortunately there was a test scheduled, which guaranteed absolute silence. There was a rustling of papers, a shuffling of feet, but no further whispering.

For the next forty-five minutes, Laura walked up and down the aisles, monitoring as the students wrote their essay responses. In the back of the room, she paused and gave Misty's shoulder an encouraging squeeze.

Misty glanced up at her, her expression filled with such misery that it nearly broke Laura's heart.

"I've finished the test. Could I please leave now?" Misty begged.

Though she wanted to insist that she stay right here until the class ended in another ten minutes, she couldn't bring herself to do it.

"I'll give you a pass for the library," she said quietly.

Misty gave her a grateful look, followed her to the front of the room, then all but ran out the door, leaving Laura to wonder what on earth she was supposed to do to fix this, whatever *this* was.

When the bell rang, she glanced at the students who'd been whispering earlier and picked one at random. "Trish, could I see you for a minute? The rest of you are dismissed. Leave your papers on my desk."

Trish Peterson shifted nervously from foot to foot while her classmates left. Only after the last of them had gone, did Laura meet her gaze.

"I need to go," Trish said. "I have P.E. next period and Miss Wilcox gets really mad if we're late."

"I'll write an excuse for you," Laura said. "Have a seat."

"Did I do something wrong?" Trish asked. "I wasn't cheating, Ms. Reed. I wouldn't do that."

"I know," Laura assured her. "But at the beginning of class, when Misty came in, there seemed to be a bit of a stir. I was hoping you could fill me in on what that was about."

Trish's eyes widened with alarm. "I don't know what you mean," she insisted, though it was obvious to Laura that she was lying. She'd been as chatty as her friends.

"You said something to Annabelle," Laura reminded her. "A couple of the boys made comments, as well. Do you all have a problem of some kind with Misty?"

"Not me," Trish said at once.

"Then who does?"

"No one, I swear it," she said, her gaze darting around.

"I hope that's the case," Laura told her emphatically, hoping to get her point across that whatever they were up to wasn't going to be tolerated. "Because I'd hate to find out you're not being truthful."

"Look, it's got nothing to do with me, okay?" Trish insisted, her expression pleading. "Could I have that note now? I have to go. I'm the captain of one of the volley-ball teams. I really need to be there."

Though she wanted to pursue the subject some more, Laura reluctantly jotted out a note to Pam Wilcox, then waved Trish off. Though the girl had given away nothing, Laura was more convinced than ever that someone in her class was deliberately tormenting Misty and that others were going along with it. She just needed to figure out who, and how bad it had gotten.

Misty sat in the library with her head down on her books trying to keep herself from crying. No matter how hard she'd tried, she couldn't stop thinking about the rude comments the other kids had made as she'd hurried to her seat in Ms. Reed's class. Worse, she knew Ms. Reed had heard them, maybe not the words, but the whispering. What if she started asking a lot of questions? She was already determined to figure out what was going on. If she'd called Annabelle or any of the others on the carpet after class, Misty was probably doomed.

When the bell rang, she was tempted to stay right here. Mrs. Martin, the librarian, wouldn't care if she stayed. She could just show her the pass again and explain she was doing an extra credit project for English.

She was still debating whether or not to risk it, when a shadow fell across the table. She looked up to find Annabelle scowling down at her.

"You need to watch it, slut," Annabelle said.

She spoke in a sneering way that made Misty wonder how half the town could think Annabelle was some sweet little Southern belle. Of course, most people had never seen this mean side of her.

"What's the matter, cat got your tongue?" Annabelle prodded when Misty remained determinedly silent. "You are such a loser."

Enough, Misty thought, squaring her shoulders. "If I'm such a loser, why are you so obsessed with me?" she retorted, feeling a certain amount of pride in having finally spoken up to her tormentor.

"Obsessed? Are you kidding me? You're just an annoyance."

"Is that because your boyfriend wants to go out with me?" Misty asked, knowing she was pushing her luck but suddenly beyond caring.

Color rose in Annabelle's cheeks. Her eyes glittered with fury. "You stay away from Greg, you hear me?"

"I'm not the one making the passes," Misty reminded her. "If you've got a problem keeping him in line, tell him. Leave me out of it."

Annabelle stared at her with momentary shock, then looked for all the world as if she was about to start tearing Misty's hair out. She'd just reached toward her, when Mrs. Martin appeared.

"Girls, you need to keep your voices down," she said, then frowned at Annabelle. "Do you have a pass to be in here?"

Annabelle flushed guiltily. "No, ma'am."

"Then I suggest you get to whatever class you're due to attend before they count you as tardy."

"What about her?" Annabelle asked.

Misty held up her pass. "All nice and legal," she said with a sense of triumph.

Mrs. Martin smiled at Misty, then waved off Annabelle. "Run along."

Only after Annabelle had gone did Mrs. Martin turn back to Misty. "I know perfectly well that pass was for last period, young lady, but it was obvious to me the two of you were having some kind of spat. Knowing how Annabelle can be, I assume she started it."

Misty stared at her wide-eyed. "You're blaming Annabelle?"

Mrs. Martin regarded her with a steady gaze. "Am I wrong?"

For the first time in weeks, Misty felt a tiny shred of hope. Still, confirming Mrs. Martin's guess could lead to the kind of showdown she'd been hoping to avoid. Better just to be grateful for the support and keep silent.

"It was no big deal, Mrs. Martin. Really."

The librarian didn't look convinced. "I'm not sure I believe that, but I'll let it pass. Just promise me that if there is more to it, you'll speak to me or one of your teachers and get it straightened out. Understood?"

"Yes, ma'am," Misty said. "Do I have to go to my next class?"

"Just this once I'll pretend that pass really is for an extra credit English project, just the way you told me when you came in." She gave her a stern look. "Just don't make a habit of this kind of thing, okay?"

"No way," Misty promised readily. "Thank you."

Mrs. Martin smiled at her. "I wish more of the students loved spending time in here the way you do and showed the same respect for the books. You're going to make something of yourself one day, Misty. Don't let anyone steer you off the path you're on to do that."

She walked away and left Misty in tears for the second time in the past hour, but these tears didn't feel nearly the same. They felt good.

6

Laura loved working on the town's fall festival. Right after moving to Serenity, she'd been asked to serve on the organizing committee. It had been her first taste of how eagerly residents of the town threw themselves into these kinds of events. She'd signed up to work on the committee every year since. This year she'd been named the chairperson.

With only three days until the Saturday event, her committee was meeting every evening to make sure all the details were under control. She glanced around her living room at the other women. It was a really good group—Sarah McDonald, who was an on-air talent at the local radio station and married to the station owner; Raylene Rollins, wife of the police chief and owner of Laura's favorite boutique; and Annie Townsend, whose husband, Ty, was a star pitcher for the Atlanta Braves.

She knew perfectly well that the three of them were the younger generation of the group known around town as the Sweet Magnolias, which meant they knew every mover and shaker in Serenity. They could get things done. This year's festival had more official sponsors, vendors and music than ever before. Sarah's husband had even called in a favor to get a couple of up-and-coming country singers to perform.

"Okay, I know you ladies are used to margaritas at your gatherings, but I thought we probably needed to stay stone-cold sober while we go over this final checklist," Laura said.

"I, for one, couldn't be happier," Annie said. "I have no idea how my mom, my mother-in-law and Helen have survived drinking those things."

"Amen to that," Sarah said. "Laura, you need to get together with us and try one." She glanced around at the others. "It would be okay, don't you think so?"

"Absolutely," Raylene said. "The next time there's a Sweet Magnolias margarita night, you're invited. They tend to be spur-of-the-moment when there's a crisis, but we do at least a little planning ahead for a celebration. We'll give you as much notice as we can."

Laura understood that it was a huge mark of acceptance in Serenity to be included with this group of women. The Sweet Magnolias might not be an official organization, but they understood the true meaning of friendship. She was touched that Sarah, Annie and Raylene thought of her as a friend.

"I'd love it," she said simply. "But when your kids are old enough to be in my English class, don't be expecting me to do them any favors."

"My stepdaughter is already in your class," Raylene reminded her with a grin. "Believe me, I hear all about how tough you are. Every time Carrie moans about it, though, she also adds that you're fair and that she's learning a lot. You've even inspired her to keep her grades up, something I think Carter had despaired of accomplishing."

"An outstanding tribute, if you ask me," Sarah said.

"I'll definitely take it as a compliment," Laura said. "Now, let's go over this list before my head explodes just thinking about everything we need to have ready by Saturday. Sarah, how's publicity going?"

"Travis and I have been talking on-air about the festival nonstop and about the musical performances. We've gotten mentions for the singers on the air at country stations all over the region. There have been calendar listings and a couple of stories in the papers, too." She grinned at them. "I predict we're going to be swamped with folks who never even knew Serenity existed before this. I am so glad we decided to move everything over to the high school. We couldn't have managed it all on the town green."

"I'm still taking flak over that from the downtown merchants," Laura admitted. "They say we're toying with tradition and taking business away from them."

"The football field is a few blocks away," Annie said. "There's bound to be an overflow into town and even if there's not, if people have a good time, they'll come back."

"I agree," Raylene said, "and I'm one of those downtown merchants. Sometimes it's important to shake things up."

"And our vendor list?" Laura asked Raylene. "How's that shaping up?"

"Not to toot my own horn or anything, but thanks to all the extra publicity those country performers are getting, our vendor space is sold out. This is going to be the biggest fall festival the town's ever had. We have a really nice balance of people who've come before and people who are new. We'll have food, crafts, art, jewelry, a little bit of everything. One of the farmers is even putting out pumpkins."

Laura turned to Annie. "How about demonstrations? As long as we have that stage set up for the band, are we going to be able to keep it busy the rest of the day?"

"The garden club's talking about planting for fall color," she said, consulting her papers. "I lined up a local chef for a cooking demonstration. That would be my mom, in case you were wondering." She gave them a triumphant look. "And, ta-da, Ty says he and a couple of the other Braves players will come in to sign autographs for an hour in the morning and again in the afternoon." She turned to Sarah. "Can you get the word out about that? Is there still time?"

"Absolutely," Sarah said eagerly.

"This is going to be such a success!" Raylene enthused. "Laura, you're amazing."

"Not me. You all have had these incredible ideas and pulled it together."

"Only because you encouraged us to think outside the box," Sarah said. "Too bad we don't have those margaritas, because this deserves a toast."

"Let's save any toasting until after we've pulled this off on Saturday," Laura cautioned, but even she couldn't contain a grin. "I am so excited."

"Can I change the subject for a minute?" Annie asked. "I know we're all figuratively jumping up and down now, but when we got here, Laura, you looked like you were a million miles away. Maybe it's none of our business, but is everything okay? With you, I mean, not the festival?"

Laura flushed guiltily. "Sorry, just a problem at school. I haven't been able to keep it off my mind for long."

"Misty Dawson," Annie said at once.

Laura stared at her in shock. "What on earth have you heard?"

"I just know Cal's worried about her. He mentioned it when Ty and I were over there for dinner the other night."

"Is the whole town talking about this?" Laura asked worriedly.

"For once, no," Sarah said with confidence. "If they were, I'd have heard something from Grace Wharton. She's the front line of my gossip patrol."

"Thank goodness it hasn't spread to her, then," Laura said.

Sarah's expression turned thoughtful. "Although, now that I think about it, she did mention she found it odd that Misty and Katie were in Wharton's instead of at the football game on Friday night last week."

"But that's it?" Laura pressed.

Sarah nodded. "Grace was actually at the game herself. She only heard about it from the waitress who was giving her a rundown of who'd been in earlier in the evening. Otherwise, if Grace had been there, she'd have a whole lot more information. I don't think the woman intentionally eavesdrops, but I swear she could hear a pin drop in the next county."

"Which makes Wharton's the very worst place ever to tell anyone a secret or do anything you don't want the whole town to know about," Annie concluded. "She's observant, too. I swear Grace knew before anyone when I was struggling with anorexia as a teenager. She picked up on the way I'd just push food around on my plate."

"She spotted the same thing with Carrie," Raylene said. "Carter and I are both grateful that she noticed."

Laura listened to them in amazement. "I'm afraid I'd just dismissed her as a bit of a busybody."

"Oh, she is that," Sarah said with a laugh, "but she is a very well-meaning one and I, for one, love her to pieces."

"For all our grumbling, all of us do," Annie said. "Wharton's is the heart and soul of this town in a lot of ways, and Grace has made it that way for a couple of generations now."

"Thanks for the perspective," Laura said sincerely. She was also grateful that the talk of Grace had managed to steer the conversation away from Misty. As much as she would love input from these women, she wasn't comfortable with drawing even more people into the middle of what could turn into an explosive situation, if her increasingly strong hunch that Annabelle Litchfield was somehow involved proved to be correct.

J.C. usually avoided participating in town events other than the high school games. Though he liked what things like fall festival said about Serenity's town spirit and sense of community, he preferred to keep his volunteer efforts for some of the sports leagues that Cal Maddox, Ronnie Sullivan and others had organized.

This year, though, Ronnie Sullivan had leaned on him to get involved. "My daughter Annie is on the committee. I've promised her I'll be there to help with vendor registration and setup. I need more muscle."

J.C. regarded him warily. "This isn't one of those things that will lead to an even bigger role next year, right?"

Ronnie had merely grinned. "You never know. It's entirely possible you'll have such a good time, you'll be eager to do more."

"Doubtful," J.C. had said at the time.

But when he arrived at the football field at dawn and spotted Laura Reed running around with her hair mussed, a clipboard in hand and a frantic expression, he realized that Ronnie had definitely had a hidden agenda. He turned to the traitor. "So, does Laura have anything to do with your sudden determination to get me involved in town activities?"

Ronnie actually managed to pull off an innocent look. "No idea what you mean," he said. "I thought you two had a thing going. I figured you'd be hanging around all day, anyway. I thought I might as well take advantage of that and put you to work."

J.C. merely shook his head and went off with a woman who'd requested help setting up her tent. "We'll finish this later," he muttered to Ronnie as he left.

But despite his claim of annoyance, he discovered he was enjoying seeing this side of Laura. She might appear flustered and as if she were going in ten directions at once, but she was completely calm as she spoke to everyone and stepped in to solve problems. She was unfailingly smiling, even when she spotted him and faltered a bit.

"This is a surprise," she said. "Who recruited you to help?"

"A very sneaky Ronnie Sullivan," he said. "Anything you need me to do?"

"If Ronnie lured you here, I imagine you should be asking him that question."

"You look more frazzled than he does," he told her. "Prettier, too."

She gave him a startled look. "Are you flirting with me, J.C.?"

Was he? If so, he was as surprised about it as she obviously was. "Could be," he admitted.

A smile played about her lips. "When you figure it out, I'll be around," she told him and dashed off on her next mission.

He stared after her, thinking about why on earth she got to him in a way no woman had for a very long time. Bottom line, though, was that she did. He just needed to figure out if he wanted to do something about it or not.

"You're blushing," Nancy Logan said when she spotted Laura gulping down bottled water as if she were dying of thirst.

"It's warm out," Laura said. "Who thought it would be this warm at the end of October?"

"We're in South Carolina, not the North Pole. It's usually warm this time of year," Nancy said, grinning. "If you're overheated, I think it has more to do with whatever J. C. Fullerton said to you."

Laura frowned. "No idea what you're talking about," she fibbed.

Nancy merely lifted a brow. "Is that so?" she said skeptically.

"I do not have time for this conversation," Laura told her. "If you want to make yourself useful, go over to the PTA booth and make sure all the baked goods are displayed halfway decently. Last time I looked, it was a hodgepodge."

"I'm on it," Nancy promised. "But I won't lose my place in this conversation. We'll pick it up later."

Laura sighed as Nancy left. Her life in Serenity was suddenly a whole lot more complicated than it had been in all of the past ten years rolled into one.

Before she could get too anxious about how that had happened, there was a crisis with the sound system that had her scurrying off to locate Ronnie Sullivan. There were more crises after that, but by ten o'clock all the booths were open, Ty and his baseball buddies were signing autographs for a long line of fans, and people were walking around already with funnel cakes, apple cider and even hot dogs.

"I think we have a major success on our hands," Sarah McDonald said when she found Laura taking a break on the bleachers. "Carter told Raylene that the police are having trouble finding parking spots for everyone who's driving into town. There's an actual traffic jam in Serenity, and it's all because of us!"

"I imagine he didn't sound half as happy about that as you do," Laura said, chuckling.

"Probably not," Sarah said. "He'll manage. That's what a good police chief does, and Carter is excellent."

Laura looked around at the crowds of people. Most seemed to have made purchases at one booth or another.

A couple of the jewelry vendors had people lined up three and four deep.

"You know you'll never get out of doing this festival again," Sarah teased her. "No one will want to try to top this year's event."

"You, Raylene or Annie could easily take it on next year," Laura said.

"But we like working for you. We don't have to think. We just have to do what you suggest."

"You make me sound like some sort of benevolent dictator," Laura said. "That can't be good."

"In this situation, I think the proof of its benefits is staring us in the face. Now I'd better run over to the station and pick up our first group. Travis has them on the air right now, and they're due to start their performance here at noon."

"Thanks, Sarah. You guys have been fantastic."

Minutes later, as she was trying to convince herself it was time to stir and make the rounds again, she saw Misty and Katie on the fringes of the crowd. Misty had that same fearful look in her eyes that Laura had seen far too often at school, as if she'd rather be anywhere but here.

As she watched, Katie leaned closer and said something that almost drew a smile. Then, in a heartbeat, the smile was gone, replaced by utter panic. Laura searched the crowd to see who or what Misty had spotted that had her turning away as if to flee.

It wasn't that difficult to pinpoint the problem. Annabelle Litchfield, Trish Peterson and two other girls from school were heading in Misty's direction. Laura watched as Katie Townsend stood her ground, looking them in the eye and all but daring them to come closer.

Laura was on her feet at once. She forced herself to stroll casually in their direction, ready to intervene if there was so much as a hint of confrontation.

"Hey, slut, how come you're not shacked up with some boy today?" Annabelle called out loudly, clearly intending her remark to be overheard. "Have they all figured out just how lousy you are in bed?"

Laura froze in place for an instant at the ugliness of the taunt. She'd heard way too many comments along that line years ago when word of her pregnancy spread through her school. Suddenly she was that scared, humiliated, seventeen-year-old again, and she knew with every fiber of her being the shame and fear and fury that Misty had to be feeling.

Without giving it a moment's thought, she walked into the middle of the group, turned on Annabelle and leveled a look into her eyes meant to put the fear of God into the girl.

"Enough," she said quietly. "I suggest you girls leave right now."

Trish latched onto Annabelle's arm. "She's right. We should go."

The others waited to see what Annabelle would do. Her face was flushed, and her eyes sparked with anger, but she managed a careless shrug. "Who wants to waste the day at a dumb fall festival anyway?"

Once Laura was sure they were gone, she turned back toward where she'd last seen Katie and Misty, but they'd vanished, as well.

So, she thought, now she knew. For reasons she didn't

understand—and wasn't sure she had to—Annabelle Litchfield was bullying Misty. What she didn't know was whether what she'd seen was the worst of it or only the tip of the iceberg.

J.C. had spotted Laura talking to a group of girls, her expression intent. As soon as the girls had walked away, he approached her. Her expression alarmed him.

"What the hell just happened?" he asked, putting a hand on her shoulder. "Laura, you're shaking."

"I am about as furious as I've ever been in my life," she told him.

"Let's go sit down and get you something to eat. You can tell me."

"I have things I should be doing," she protested.

"After you've eaten and we've talked," he said with just as much determination. "Doctor's orders."

She managed a weak smile at that. "I'm a little old to be getting advice from a pediatrician."

"That's my specialty, not the only medicine I know," he countered patiently, already steering her toward the food booths. "What's it going to be? Hot dog? Corn dog? Hamburger?"

"I really don't think I could eat right now," she argued.

"Ice cream," he said decisively. "Nobody turns down a chocolate-vanilla swirl cone. Sit, and I'll get you one."

He came back with ice cream, corn dogs and fries, plus two diet sodas. She looked at the food and laughed.

"Your patients must love your food guidelines."

"Comfort food," he said. "I just barely managed to turn down the fried-mac-and-cheese balls."

"Thank heaven for small favors." She wiggled her fingers and took the ice cream. "It'll melt if I don't eat it first."

He watched with pleasure as she devoured the cone, then after a thoughtful look at the rest of the selections, reached for the corn dog.

"Are the fries still hot?" she asked as she took her first bite of the corn dog.

He pushed them in her direction. "See for yourself."

Only when she'd eaten half the corn dog and most of the fries did he look her in the eye and say, "Now, tell me what happened back there."

The light in her eyes immediately died. J.C. almost regretted forcing her to talk about it, but he had a strong suspicion she needed to share it with somebody. He happened to be handy.

"Laura, tell me," he prodded when she looked everywhere except at him. "Did somebody say something to you?"

"Not to me," she said. She described the incident between Annabelle and Misty. "I think this rivalry or whatever it is has been going on for a while now. I had no idea that Annabelle was capable of being so vile and mean. It wasn't just the words, though those were horrible enough, it was the way she said it. She meant it to be cruel and she meant to be overheard. She wanted to hurt and embarrass Misty."

"And none of the other girls stepped up to stop her?"

"Only Katie Townsend. She was here with Misty and she tried to warn Annabelle off, but Annabelle just brushed her off like she was invisible. The other girls were laughing until one of them spotted me."

"I had a bad feeling it was something like this," J.C. said wearily. "All the signs of bullying were there."

Laura regarded him with surprise. "Seriously? I mean I've seen kids pushing and shoving on the playground and getting physical in the halls, but this kind of verbal attack is new to me." Her expression faltered and she sighed heavily. "No, it's not. I guess I've just tried to block it from my mind, but that whole incident reminded me of just how deliberately cruel teens can be."

J.C. seized on her slip. "What did you block? Were you bullied?"

She shook off the question. "That's not important. We need to stay focused on Misty."

He knew it was important, though. He debated forcing the issue, but decided she was right about one thing: Misty had to be their immediate concern.

"Bullying happens way too often," he said, his anger kicking in. "Kids pick a target, somebody they think is weaker, and use every weapon at their disposal to make them miserable. Words are often as effective as physical assaults, especially if they can draw in a bunch of other kids to back them up. Sounds as if this is what Annabelle is doing."

She met his gaze. "What do I do now? It didn't happen during school or at a school event. I've not seen or heard anything in school. Do I warn the principal? Talk to Mariah Litchfield? Talk to Misty? Or Misty's parents?" Her indignation was almost palpable. "I wish to heaven I'd heard what was said in my classroom the other day when I first got an inkling about this. I'd have known exactly what to do."

J.C. frowned. "Something happened in class?"

She nodded. She described the whispering that had gone on when Misty had shown up on Monday morning. "I couldn't hear what was said, though. After today, I have some idea, but that doesn't help."

J.C. thought of how critical it was for adults to intervene in situations like this before it was too late. Too often, they looked the other way. At least Laura wasn't likely to do that, not after what she'd heard today. Perhaps even more so, because she'd once gone through something similar himself. Just thinking of that made him want to slam his fist into something.

"Want my advice?" he asked.

"Of course."

"Quietly mention this to a few teachers you trust, ones who'd be in a position to keep their ears open. Gather a little more solid evidence and then the second you all think you have enough, take it to the principal. I assume there's no tolerance for bullying."

"None," she said emphatically. She regarded him with a worried frown. "What about Misty? Should I speak to her about this? Tell her I get it now?"

"It might help if she knows she has your support," J.C. said, wishing he could offer her his, as well. He knew, though, that if she'd been silent so far, she'd only be humiliated if she thought he knew what was behind her desire to get out of school. Not that a little humiliation mattered if it meant helping her, but for now maybe it could be avoided as long as Laura was on top of this.

"Thank you," Laura said. "I did need someone to talk to about this, more than I realized."

"Happy to be here," he said. "And if you ever need

me for backup when it comes to this, all you have to do is ask."

"Thank you for that, too," she said, looking relieved. "Because if this whole thing blows up and I wind up having to take on Mariah Litchfield, it won't be pretty."

He smiled at the image. "I've heard she's a little on the overly protective side," he said, "but in this instance, I don't think she'd stand a chance against you."

In fact, he'd put money on it.

7

"I can't believe Annabelle had the nerve to say something right out there in public like that," Katie said indignantly as she and Misty sat on the back patio at Katie's house after the incident at the fall festival. "At least Ms. Reed heard her. Now if you talk to her, she has to believe you."

Misty stared at her with dismay. "I can't talk to her. The whole thing is too humiliating. If Annabelle gets in trouble, everything will just get worse. They'll go to her mom. She'll raise a stink, and not only I, but Ms. Reed will get torn to shreds all over town."

"Not if Annabelle's suspended or expelled," Katie argued.

"Like that's ever going to happen," Misty said. "Her mama would burn down the high school before she'd let them kick Annabelle out."

Katie grinned. "You don't think she'd really do that, do you?"

"Don't you remember when Mrs. Litchfield went after the teacher back in seventh grade who gave Annabelle a D in physical education? She said her little girl was not meant to sweat, that it was unnatural, and that there must be something wrong with the teacher. By the time she finished with her, half the town thought the teacher was gay or something. She quit before the end of the year."

Katie groaned at the memory. "I do remember. It was awful. Ms. Stevens was really nice, too. The kids tried to stick up for her, but Mrs. Litchfield got so many adults worked up, Ms. Stevens had no choice but to leave."

"And that's who we're talking about," Misty said. "If this turns into a battle between me and Annabelle, who do you think is going to wind up the loser? If there's any mud left that Annabelle hasn't dragged my name through, her mama will find it and try to drown me in it."

Katie stared at her for a second, then giggled. "No wonder Ms. Reed freaks out about you skipping English. You have such a flair for drama."

The last of the morning's tension broke, and Misty giggled, too. "Maybe I've been looking at this all wrong. It's life experience, right? Maybe one day I'll write some mega-seller novel in which a girl who just happens to be named Annabelle gets taken away by aliens."

But even as she smiled at the thought, she realized that by then her nemesis would probably be some superstar singer who wouldn't care two little figs about anything Misty might write. She'd probably just laugh herself silly.

When Misty got home, she found her mother sitting at the kitchen table, a half-empty coffee cup and an untouched plate of scrambled eggs and toast in front of her. Since the same meal had been there when Misty left the house hours earlier, she had to assume her mom was having another one of her down days.

"Mom," she said, giving her shoulder a shake. "You okay?"

Her mother glanced up. "Oh, you're home. How was the fall festival?"

At least she'd remembered where Misty had told her she was going that morning. "It was okay," she said. "You never ate your breakfast. You must be starved. Why don't I fix some grilled-cheese sandwiches and soup?"

"Thanks, sweetheart. I'm not that hungry."

"Where's Dad?"

Her mother shrugged. "He left without saying anything. Maybe he's helping out at the festival."

Misty bit back a sigh. Her mom was still delusional. They both knew that was unlikely. Her dad never volunteered for anything. He was either on a golf course with some buddies, drinking at the nineteenth hole, or he'd hooked up with another woman somewhere.

Misty wondered whether it was her job to try to make her mother face what was really going on. There was no one else to do it. Her mother had made her dad the center of her universe, and his desire for a divorce was killing her. Misty thought the only way her mother would ever be happy was if she snapped out of it, let him go and moved on. Maybe, though, that was a lot harder than it sounded. One thing for sure, she was never getting trapped by a man that way. Love clearly sucked.

As Misty was getting together the ingredients to make the sandwiches, the phone rang. She looked at the caller ID and saw that it was from the Litchfields. Her heart seemed to stop in her chest. That couldn't be good. She let it go to the answering machine.

"Diana, this is Mariah Litchfield," the message began. "This is the third time I've called this morning," she said impatiently. "I really need to speak to you about your daughter. Call me back the minute you get these messages."

Misty sat down hard. She glanced at her mother who looked as if she'd barely heard the words.

"Did you hear that, Mom? It was Mrs. Litchfield. She says she's called before."

"She probably did," her mother said distractedly. "I haven't answered the phone all morning. Why would Mariah be calling me?"

This was the opening Misty should seize. She recognized that. But how could she? Her mother was so lost in her own problems, she couldn't possibly cope with Misty's, too.

"Annabelle and I had words at the festival," she said carefully. "Her mother probably wants to rant that I'm a terrible person."

For an instant she thought she detected a flash of anger in her mother's eyes, but then it died.

"Do you want me to call her back? Is this something I need to handle?" her mother asked halfheartedly.

If only, Misty thought wearily. But she knew there would be no help from her mom. She couldn't cope with this on top of everything else going on in her life.

"I'll deal with it," Misty told her as she put the sandwiches on the griddle.

She only wished she could figure out how.

* * *

Laura feared Misty would cut class again on Monday. Instead, she was there early and sitting in the front row. Laura nodded her approval, then went straight into the lesson. Class ended without incident, though Misty lingered until everyone else had gone.

"Thanks for coming over at the festival on Saturday," Misty said quietly.

"Not a problem. I think I have some idea now about what's been going on. Would you like me to deal with Annabelle?"

Misty shook her head at once. "It'll only get worse if I make trouble for her."

"You know that bullying is grounds for suspension," Laura reminded her. "If Annabelle is guilty of that, she deserves to be punished."

"It's not worth it," Misty insisted.

"If what I heard on Saturday is any indication, then it needs to stop," Laura said just as determinedly.

"You just don't get it. Annabelle's mom will make what Annabelle's doing seem like a picnic. She'll mess up my life and yours before she's through. She's already called my mom to try to make out that what happened on Saturday was somehow my fault."

Laura was shocked. "Do you want me to call your mother and fill her in on what really happened?"

Misty shook her head. "My mom never called her back. She's got a lot of stuff going on. I swore to her it was no big deal."

Laura frowned. It sounded as if Misty wasn't likely to get the backup she needed at home. Thinking of how Vicki Kincaid had been there for her when her parents had been dazed and embarrassed by her teen pregnancy, she immediately asked, "What can I do?"

Misty shrugged. "Nothing, I guess. It helps just knowing you get it. So does Mrs. Martin. She overheard Annabelle last week."

"I don't like the idea of allowing this to continue," Laura told her. "I really think we should report it."

"Please, no," Misty begged. "Once Mrs. Donovan gets involved, it'll get really ugly."

"But it's already ugly, isn't it?" Laura asked gently.

"Not like it could be," Misty insisted. "I can deal with Annabelle." She squared her shoulders, hoping that would give credence to her bravado.

"Not by skipping class," Laura said firmly. "That's no longer an option."

Misty looked taken aback by her firm tone. "Even though you know what's going on?"

"*Because* I know what's going on," Laura told her. "You're not going to risk your future or your grades by skipping class and risking suspension when you're the victim in this."

"Are you sure I can't just transfer back to a regular English class? Maybe Mr. Jamison would let me out of AP math, too. That would make things easier."

"You'd give up everything you worked so hard to achieve and let Annabelle win?" Laura asked. "How would that be fair?"

"I don't care about fair. I just want this over."

"Misty, I might not know how this situation started or how bad it's really gotten, but I do know this— Annabelle isn't going to let it just fade away because you're no longer in the same classes."

Misty sighed heavily. "Probably not," she admitted. "But at least she wouldn't be in my face twice a day with her friends laughing at me, too."

Reluctantly, Laura had to concede she was right. That didn't mean, though, that she would allow a transfer.

"Let's give this some more thought," she said. "I'll bet between us we can come up with a solution."

Misty regarded her doubtfully, but she nodded. "Okay."

"We'll talk again tomorrow."

"Sure," Misty said. "I'd better run. I have Mr. Jamison next period. He's pretty unobservant, but he does notice if people come in way after the bell."

"Would you like a note?"

"Nah. I'm good at sneaking in under the radar."

Or else, despite her very stern warning, Misty intended to spend the next period hiding out somewhere, Laura realized as Misty ran off. She sat back with a sigh, suddenly wishing she could call J.C. and ask if he thought she'd handled the situation as badly as it suddenly felt like she had.

Laura had been on J.C.'s mind ever since Saturday when he'd found her shaken by her encounter with those girls at the fall festival. It was disconcerting how frequently she crept into his head these days. No woman had done that in years. If and when he dated at all, it was the sort of independent, no-strings kind of women who didn't have a vulnerable bone in their bodies. Laura was an intriguing mix of strength and vulnerability. She got to him, no question about it.

And, of course, there was the Misty situation. He couldn't get that out of his head, either.

At three o'clock, knowing that classes were over, he pulled out his cell phone and punched in Laura's cell number, which he'd managed to get from her during the first night they'd gotten together to discuss Misty. It rang several times before she answered.

"Sorry," she apologized at once. "My phone was buried in my purse. I'm not used to listening for it."

"It seems I have a habit of catching you off guard," J.C. said.

"J.C.?"

"Ah, you recognize my voice now. Should I be flattered?"

"You could be, or I could claim I caught a glimpse of the caller ID."

"Did you?"

"No, I was too busy trying to catch the call."

"Look, my last appointment just canceled and I was wondering if you'd have time for coffee, maybe around four-thirty at Wharton's?"

"You're not even trying to bribe me with the good stuff?" she teased.

J.C. laughed. "I suppose I could try to wheedle a couple of cups out of Erik and we could go to the park."

"That might be better than Wharton's, and not just because of the coffee," she said.

"The gossip," he concluded.

"Grace is known for it. Revered, in fact. It might not be a good idea to give her any ammunition to feed the gossip mill."

"Okay, then, I'll meet you at the bench under our pin

oak by the lake at four-thirty. Want anything to go with that coffee? If I'm going to be bribing Erik, I might as well go for broke."

"Surprise me," she said, surprising *him*.

She sounded much more lighthearted than she had on Saturday. Maybe he'd been worrying all weekend for nothing. It could be that she had the situation between Annabelle and Misty in hand by now.

"See you soon, then," he said just as Debra opened his door and beckoned to him. "Gotta go. My next patient's here."

"I don't suppose that was Laura Reed again," Debra said as she walked down the hallway to the examination room with him.

"I don't suppose it would be any of your business if it were," he said lightly.

Her gaze narrowed. "And if I were to tell you that I was thinking of filling that open spot in the schedule at four o'clock?"

"I'd tell you not to do it," he said, earning himself a smug look.

"I knew it," she said triumphantly. "I suppose if I couldn't fix you up with Jan, Laura's not a bad substitute. I wouldn't have pictured you with the quiet, shy type, though."

"Because you never really knew a thing about my taste in women," he reminded her. "You were just tossing candidates my way, hoping one would stick."

"Well, I had to do something," she countered. "A catch like you simply couldn't be left swimming around all alone in the dating pool. It would have been a crime."

"Says who?"

She gave him a wry look. "I think I speak for all the single women in Serenity."

He laughed. "Stick to nursing, Debra. Go with your strength."

"As if I asked for your advice." She nodded toward the examination room door. "Johnny Taylor's just fine, if you ask me. It's his single mama who has a hankering for your special touch." She grinned. "Not that you asked my opinion."

"Duly appreciated, though," J.C. said. Christine Taylor wouldn't be the first single mother to drag a perfectly healthy child in for an unnecessary exam.

Ten minutes later, a beaming Johnny was on his way out with a cherry lollipop, and his disgruntled mother was paying a bill and trying to disguise her disappointment over J.C. showing not one single whit of interest in her.

J.C. grabbed his jacket off the back of his door and slipped out the side of the building. Twenty minutes later, he arrived at the park with coffee and a piece of key lime pie he was hoping he could convince Laura to share with him. He'd brought two forks, just in case.

He found her sitting on the bench along the path near the tree but not under it. She had her face turned up toward the sun, her eyes closed.

"Sneaking in a nap?" he asked quietly as he sat beside her.

"Just enjoying the day," she said, smiling at him but not opening her eyes. "I love it when the air starts to feel like fall. Saturday still felt like summer, but today I'm finally feeling that crisp bite in the air. Makes the sun feel good."

"I brought coffee and pie."

"Ah," she murmured, opening her eyes and turning to him.

The sleepy look on her face gave him a start. Suddenly he couldn't stop imagining what it would be like to wake up next to her.

"What kind of pie?" she asked.

"Huh?" he said, then snapped himself back into the moment.

She pointed at the take-out container. "The pie. What kind is it?"

"Key lime."

"Perfect. It's a favorite of mine." She glanced at the small container again. "Only one slice? Where's yours?"

"I thought you might share at least a bite with me."

She beckoned for the box. "Let me taste, then we'll see."

"Something tells me we need to settle these negotiations now," he said, holding the pie just out of reach. "Once you get a taste, I'm likely to be out of luck."

"Could be," she agreed.

"So, will you commit to sharing?"

She regarded him thoughtfully. "It might be fair since you bought it," she said.

"True."

"But it might be really, really good, and you did say you were bringing it for me."

He smiled as she worked this out in her head. "Also true," he conceded.

"Okay, one bite," she allowed grudgingly.

"Three," he countered.

"Two, and that's my final offer."

J.C. chuckled. "Obviously I'll know better than to get between you and your pie next time."

"Probably wise."

"And I think I'll take my two bites before I hand it over," he said. "Just to avoid any chance of second thoughts."

"I made a commitment," she said indignantly.

"Okay, then, here you go," he said, handing it over and watching as she took the first bite and allowed the tart-sweet combination of the creamy key lime filling melt in her mouth. Watching her savor it was such a turn-on, he almost hated to see it end as she finished her share and gave him the rest. Still, as a matter of principle, he took it. The pie, good as it was, wasn't nearly as satisfying as watching her enjoyment of it.

She took a sip of her coffee, then faced him. "So, why did you call, J.C.? I'm sure it wasn't just so you could feed me pie."

"I haven't been able to get Misty out of my head today," he said, admitting only half of the truth. When she looked skeptical, he shrugged. "Or you. I was worried about you on Saturday. It was clear that you were really taking that nasty incident to heart."

"If you'd heard Annabelle, you'd have taken it to heart, too."

"I'm thinking that it affected you more deeply because it reminded you of something that happened to you," he suggested, seeing the truth in her eyes even as she tried to dismiss the incident.

"Let it go, J.C. It was a long time ago."

"And you've put it behind you?" he asked skeptically. "I'm not getting that impression."

She sighed. "I thought I had, at least mostly. There are some things I'll never forget."

"Such as?" he asked, knowing that the answer probably mattered more than he could possibly imagine.

She kept silent, her gaze staring somewhere off in the distance before she finally faced him with tears in her eyes. "Another time, okay? Please."

He wiped away the tear that slid down her cheek with the pad of his thumb, then finally nodded reluctantly. "Another time," he agreed quietly. "But I won't forget, Laura."

Her lips curved in a rueful smile. "I'm sure of that."

He sat back and forced a more casual note into his voice. "So, how did it go at school today?"

"I finally had a candid talk with Misty," she said. "Oh, she's still pretty circumspect, but at least she's no longer denying that there's a real issue between her and Annabelle."

"That ought to be enough to go to the principal, then," he said, relieved that the matter might soon be resolved.

"Afraid not. Misty's adamantly opposed to it. I have a feeling if I try to force the issue, she'll deny it."

"Why would she do that?" J.C. demanded in frustration. "She has to know this is wrong."

"She knows. She's just convinced that taking this to the principal will make everything much worse." She gave him a weary look. "She could be right. I've heard plenty of stories about Mariah Litchfield and how she works. She's already put in a few calls to Misty's mother. Misty is pretty sure she intends to lay all the blame on Misty."

"It would probably be a good thing to get Diana involved," J.C. said. "Surely she'd come to Misty's defense."

"I'd have thought the same thing, but after talking to Misty, I'm not so sure."

"I know Diana. She's a terrific mother."

"I've always thought so, too, but I think there's something else going on at home. I have no idea what it might be, but I don't think Misty believes she can count on her mother right now."

"What a mess!" J.C. muttered. He drew in a deep breath, then said decisively, "Then it's up to us."

Laura looked startled. "Us? J.C., I know how much you want to help, but you haven't witnessed a thing."

"I've seen how distraught Misty is," he contradicted her. "She wanted to quit school over this. She came to me to get a medical excuse."

"But for all you know, she could have been having a bad day or wanted to quit for no good reason."

"I know the signs of bullying when I see them," he argued stubbornly. Probably far better than she did. He also knew the potential for disastrous consequences if it was allowed to continue.

"And I know Betty," Laura argued. "She's going to want solid evidence, incidents that were witnessed. Not because she won't believe us or Misty, but because she's the one who's going to have to deal with Mariah Litchfield's wrath."

"It just doesn't seem right that so much consideration goes to the girl who's creating the havoc, while the victim's left to suffer."

Laura regarded him curiously. "You've very passionate about this. Does that go beyond Misty?"

He thought about just how personal the issue was for him, but it wasn't something he talked about...ever. Well-guarded secrets were apparently something he and Laura had in common. "I care, that's all."

She didn't look as if she believed him, but thankfully, apparently taking a page out of his book, she let it go.

"Will you be sure to let me know if there's something I can do?" he pressed. "Anything, okay?"

"Of course I will."

"And how about you? You must be as frustrated about this as I am."

For the first time, he saw the weariness and regret in her eyes. "You have no idea, but my hands are tied either until Misty gives me more information or I've witnessed more myself."

"You're not just worried that Mariah would take her anger out on you, are you?"

As soon as he'd uttered the question, he saw the flash of real annoyance in her eyes.

"There's nothing Mariah Litchfield can do to me," Laura retorted. "Nothing that I can't handle. But I've been around the system long enough to know that without solid proof, an accusation like this could do more harm to Misty than it will to Annabelle. Surely you know that, too."

J.C. sighed heavily. "I do, and I'm sorry for even suggesting otherwise. I just find it all so infuriating."

"Believe me, you don't have a lock on that," she said. "We will fix this, though, J.C. Anything else is unacceptable."

He nodded at her strong declaration and knew with certainty that Misty couldn't have a better ally in her corner. He was just frustrated that for the moment, he didn't have that hard evidence she was talking about that meant he could be right there with her.

8

It was after six when Laura finally got home after meeting J.C. in the park. The phone was ringing as she walked in the door. As she reached for it, she noticed she had three messages, a rarity this soon after school. Usually her phone never rang until much later in the evening, if at all.

"Well, well, well," Nancy said when Laura picked up. "Sitting in the park with Doc Fullerton, sharing some little tidbit of food and coffee, right there where all the world could see. Are you still claiming that there's nothing going on between the two of you?"

"That I am," Laura confirmed. "Because it's the truth."

"Then explain why I had four calls on my cell before I could even leave the school building?" Nancy teased. "Every teacher who passed that way going home spotted the two of you, sitting side by side and looking quite cozy, according to every carefully documented and eager report."

"I'm surprised you didn't drive by yourself to check

it out," Laura grumbled, feeling her cheeks flush with embarrassment.

"Oh, believe me, I did. I have to commend the accuracy of the reporting. *Cozy* would definitely be the adjective I'd choose. *Intimate* might be another."

"Two people sitting on a bench in a public park, drinking coffee, constitutes *cozy* or *intimate* in your book? It's pretty obvious we were hardly alone out there."

"Hey, I haven't had a date to speak of in three years," Nancy responded. "Just shaking hands with an available man qualifies as cozy in my book."

Despite her general annoyance at all this sudden fascination with her nonexistent social life, Laura chuckled. "Nancy, you're the one who put out the word that you were declaring a moratorium on all men after your very bitter breakup with Steve. If you want to date, rescind the moratorium."

"I might do that if J.C. had taken a look in my direction, but it's clear he only has eyes for you. It must be that unavailable sign you wear on your forehead. Men can't resist a challenge."

"If that were the case, he'd be chasing you," Laura told her. "I've gone out from time to time. I'm not unavailable."

"Never more than twice with the same man," Nancy countered. "You keep saying there's no point in getting their hopes up when you know the relationships aren't right. It's a mystery to me how you can tell that after two dates."

"I can usually tell after the first one," Laura retorted.

"The second date is so I won't offend them by making a snap decision. I really try to be fair."

"And how do you explain all these dates with J.C.? Aren't you worried about his ego?"

"I'm sure J.C.'s ego is very healthy, and I'm not worried about it because we're not actually dating," she responded with frustration. "Look, I just walked in the door. I'm hungry. I have to figure out if there's anything in the refrigerator to fix for dinner. Pie isn't going to cut it as a meal."

"So that *was* dessert you were having first," Nancy retorted. "My money's on Sullivan's key lime pie."

"Do you have binoculars in your car, for goodness' sake?"

"Nope, just very good vision and strong motivation," Nancy said. "Don't squander this chance, Laura. I mean it. J.C. is a catch by anyone's standards."

Laura thought of his kindness and compassion, his wit and his intelligence. That he happened to be gorgeous was just an added perk. All in all, she could hardly deny what her friend was saying. Nor could she deny those sparks Nancy had claimed to see between them, but she'd learned years ago to distrust sparks. Sparks made people do crazy, irresponsible things. Hadn't she learned that the hard way?

"I suppose if I were interested in casting a line into the dating pool, he would be a great catch," she admitted. "But that's just not how it is between us. He doesn't want to be caught."

"Bet you could change his mind," Nancy said.

"I'm not sure I'm up for the humiliation of being rejected after being so plainly told that he's not interested in getting involved with anyone. Sorry. I'm going to have to pass."

Nancy sighed dramatically. "Foolish, foolish woman. Oh, well, gotta run. See you tomorrow. I'll be the one trying to make you see the error of your ways."

After she hung up, Laura sat down at the kitchen table and thought about the times she'd seen J.C. in recent days. Those blasted sparks had been undeniable. He'd even admitted she'd been on his mind. In some ways that was even more terrifying. What if he decided he was no longer quite so averse to getting involved with someone?

But he'd made such a point of making sure she was aware that he didn't date. She wondered why. His declaration had been pretty unequivocal. There had to be a story behind it. Maybe if she could find out the answer to that mystery, she'd know if he was half as determined to ignore those wickedly inviting sparks as she was.

"You're playing a dangerous game, my friend," Cal Maddox taunted when J.C. showed up at the gym.

J.C. gave him a puzzled look. "Game?"

"With Laura Reed."

J.C. bristled. "What game am I supposedly playing with Laura?"

"The way I hear it from very informed sources, you've been with her quite a lot recently."

"So?"

"There's talk," Cal said, as if that were explanation enough.

"It's Serenity," J.C. said with a shrug. "There's always talk about something."

Cal chuckled. "True enough, but this talk is about

you and Laura being an item. Since I've had the impression for a long time now, based on your refusal to accept any of the blind dates being tossed your way, that you don't want to get seriously involved with anyone, talk is not good."

J.C. finally saw where this was going. And they said women were terrible gossips!

"Are you trying to protect Laura? Is that it?" he asked Cal.

"Well, sure. She's well-liked around town, especially after she pulled off a coup the way she did with Saturday's festival. They'll be talking about this one for years to come."

"Okay, but what does that have to do with me?"

"Not a one of those boosters of hers are going to be happy if she's hurt."

"Ah," J.C. said. "Then let me assure you that I'm not planning on hurting her."

Cal clearly wasn't satisfied. "Because your intentions are serious and honorable, because you have no designs on her or because you think this is just a casual game?" he pressed. "I'm telling you again, if it's just a game, it's a dangerous one. There will be a frenzy. And having been at the center of one myself a few years back, I can assure you, you won't enjoy it."

J.C. regarded him with disbelief. "A frenzy? You can't be serious."

"Oh, yeah," Cal confirmed. "I've already heard some muttering from my wife, who got stirred up by some of the other Sweet Magnolias who were on Laura's committee."

"Muttering?" J.C. repeated, bewildered. This was

probably one of the reasons he was a terrible candidate for another marriage. The workings of the female mind eluded him.

"'Hurt her and die' comes to mind," Cal told him. "Maddie was pretty emphatic about that one."

Since Cal had only the tiniest glint of amusement in his eyes, apparently he was mostly serious.

J.C. shook his head, walked away, then came back. "I met Laura a couple of weeks ago. I've seen her maybe a handful of times, and those weren't even dates. How did this get so crazy?"

"Because you've seen her a bunch of times in less than a month," Cal explained patiently. "The way I understand the logic, an engagement should be imminent. That's the generally desirable Serenity timetable."

"The women in this town are crazy," J.C. muttered.

Cal laughed. "You definitely don't want to say that in public and especially not in front of my wife or the other Sweet Magnolias. You know you're already suspect in that circle because you work with Maddie's ex, right? They have a very low opinion of Bill Townsend."

"So I've gathered, but he's a good doctor," J.C. said, feeling compelled to defend his business partner. "And he's straightened up his life."

Cal nodded. "I can see that, too. The women, however, have very long memories."

"So I'm never likely to get their stamp of approval because of Bill?" he asked, mystified.

"Never's a long time," Cal told him. "But it'll be a process."

J.C. shook his head. This sounded a whole lot more

complicated than his quiet bachelor existence. "Not dating in this town is sounding better and better."

Cal gave him a disappointed look. "If you'd walk away from a great woman like Laura because of a few little hurdles, then you're not the man I think you are."

"Then you're encouraging me to date her?"

"Sure, but only if you're serious," Cal said. "At least I think that's the message I was supposed to convey. I'm a mere man. I could have gotten it wrong."

"Heaven help me!" J.C. declared.

"Yep, that's pretty much what it's going to take," Cal agreed.

As soon as J.C. walked in the door at home, he dialed Laura's number.

Once she'd picked up, he asked, "Have you noticed that people in this town are freaking nuts?"

She chuckled. "I think they'd prefer to be called 'eccentric' or 'quirky.' You've lived here for years. Is there any particular reason you've come to this conclusion now?"

"Cal Maddox lectured me tonight," he reported, indignation creeping into his voice.

"About?"

"You."

He heard her indrawn breath on the other end of the line.

"Me?" she repeated eventually. "Why would Cal be lecturing you about me?"

"Apparently there's some sort of frenzy about the possibility that I'll break your heart."

"I see," she said slowly, then chuckled again. "Sorry,

but that is so typical. Nobody can spend five seconds with someone of the opposite sex in this community without everybody weighing in. I wouldn't be surprised if they're not taking bets at Wharton's."

"Bets? What sort of bets?"

"How soon we'll get married, of course. And, just so you know, it's no quieter over here this evening. My phone line has been buzzing. Apparently sitting in the park was no smarter than going to Wharton's for coffee. There are spies everywhere."

"Well, that's just crazy."

"Of course it is," she said. "But it's one of the things that gives this town its warmth and charm."

She sounded more amused than threatened by all the talk.

"This really doesn't bother you?" he asked, wishing he could get to whatever level of serenity she'd attained over such utter craziness.

"It's embarrassing," she admitted. "But why get worked up over it? You and I know the truth. Isn't that what counts?"

J.C. felt the tension in his shoulders finally start to ease. If she could take the talk in stride, he should certainly be able to weather it.

"Exactly how many calls have you had?" he asked curiously.

"Four from friends at school. Three left messages I haven't returned. One caught me as I walked in the door. She actually knew about the pie. I have to admit, even I was a little taken aback by that."

"Doesn't that rise to the level of stalking or something? It's a little weird."

"She says she's just observant. I don't think we have to worry about stalking till we spot people hiding out in the bushes outside of our homes to see if we're together."

Just thinking about that possibility made J.C. shudder. "Maybe we should get together and talk about this some more, figure out our strategy."

"Strategy for what?" she asked.

"Nipping this gossip in the bud."

"And you think getting together again for any reason is going to help?" she asked, laughing. "Hello! It'll be another sighting. It'll only add more fuel to the fire."

"Then we avoid each other entirely," he concluded, not especially happy with the alternative. Why was that? he wondered.

"That would be the smart way to go, if your goal is to put an end to all the talk," she agreed, though she didn't sound any more enthused about the plan than he was.

"That's not going to work for me," he surprised himself by saying.

"Oh?"

"We have this Misty situation," he said, scrambling for an excuse to cover the fact that he simply didn't want to cut this witty, intelligent, attractive woman right back out of his life. At least not until he figured out why she'd gotten under his skin so quickly.

"That's true, but since it's really a school matter, you don't have to be involved," she said.

"Misty came to me for help. I'm involved," he said, correcting her.

"I could just call you, keep you in the loop," she suggested.

Her willingness to let him off the hook annoyed him.

"Until I'm sure this bullying has ended, I intend to stay on top of this. You're not going to shake me loose that easily, Laura. I'm Misty's physician. I have a responsibility here, one I take seriously."

"Hey, you're the one who was all worked up about a little gossip. I was just trying to figure out a way to put an end to it," she said defensively.

And now she was clearly annoyed with him, he concluded. That's what came from trying to have a simple, platonic relationship with a female. Things always got complicated.

Such as the fact that right this second he couldn't imagine anything he wanted more than to finish this whole ridiculous conversation in bed, kissing her until her indignation gave way to murmurs of pleasure. The image was so clear in his head, he had to swallow hard and try to catch his breath before saying anything.

"J.C., are you still there?"

"I'm here," he said tightly.

"So, what are we going to do?"

"We're going to dinner at Sullivan's tomorrow night," he said decisively. "And this time it *is* a date."

He thought he heard a faint gasp on her end of the line. Good. He'd thrown her for a change.

"I don't believe I heard an invitation in there," she said.

She suddenly sounded all prim and proper. He discovered that tone was a heck of a turn-on. Who knew he'd harbored a secret yearning for an old-fashioned schoolmarm, one who promised to be more complicated than that physics course that had almost cost him his entry to med school?

"Would you like to have dinner at Sullivan's to-morrow?" he asked, trying not to grind his teeth, so it wouldn't sound as if the words were being dragged out of him against his will.

"Dinner would be lovely," she said. "Just one thing."

"What's that?"

"Do you have any idea what you're stirring up?"

He gave the question a moment's thought before an-swering. "In town? Pretty much. Between us? Not a clue."

She laughed. "Okay, then. I guess we're on the same page, after all. Dinner ought to be interesting."

"Oh, it will be," he promised. He just had to remem-ber how this dating thing was supposed to work. These days most of his charm was reserved for getting kids not to bite him when he was giving them their shots. He doubted the same techniques would work all that well on Laura.

Misty had once again fixed dinner, since it seemed apparent that her mom wasn't up to it.

"Soup and grilled cheese again?" her brother com-plained when she called him into the kitchen.

"Hush," she told him, casting a warning look in the direction of their mother.

Jake was thirteen, which made him essentially clue-less, as far as Misty could tell. He just snatched up his sandwich and the bowl of soup and left the table.

"I'm eating in my room," he said on his way out.

Misty sighed, then turned her attention once more to her mother. "Mom, you have to eat something. You'll get sick if you don't."

Her mother blinked and finally focused on her, then glanced at the food. "Oh, sweetie, you didn't need to do this. I would have fixed something."

"When, Mom? It's already after seven. Besides, it's no big deal to heat some soup and make sandwiches."

"But it's not your job to do that," Diana protested halfheartedly. She ate a spoonful of the vegetable soup, then put aside her spoon. She left the sandwich untouched.

"Mom, please, eat some more."

"I'm fine. Don't worry about me. Has your father come home?"

Misty frowned. Wouldn't they know it, if he were in the house? "No sign of him," she said. "He hasn't called, either."

For a moment, her mother seemed to shake herself out of her lethargy. "Speaking of calls, I did have one today from Mariah Litchfield. What exactly is going on between you and Annabelle?"

"I told you the other day, don't worry about it," Misty said. "I've got it covered."

"Not to hear Mariah tell it," her mother said. "There was an incident of some kind at the fall festival?"

"I told you about that," Misty said. "Annabelle and I had an argument, no big deal."

"Are you sure?" her mother asked, regarding her intently. For the first time it seemed as if she truly cared about something other than what was going on in her own life. "You know that I've known Mariah most of my life. I know how she can be when it comes to Annabelle. You don't want to mess with that girl, Misty. It's better to steer clear of her."

"Believe me, I'm trying to do just that," Misty said.

"You're not trying to make trouble for her? That's what Mariah implied."

"No way," Misty said indignantly. She was doing everything in her power to avoid causing trouble. Annabelle was the one who kept pushing and making it almost impossible. "What did you tell Mrs. Litchfield?"

"That I'd have a word with you."

"And now you have," Misty said, unable to keep a hint of bitterness out of her voice.

Her mother gave her a sharp look. "Why do I have the feeling I'm missing something?"

"I have no idea," Misty claimed. "I have homework. I'm going to my room."

For once she was relieved that her mom didn't argue. She didn't even remind Misty to send Jake down to put the dishes in the dishwasher, which meant they'd probably still be on the kitchen table in the morning. Better that, though, than talking about Annabelle for one more minute.

Misty lingered once again after English, hoping to give the other kids time to move on to their other classes. Ms. Reed was pretty cool about it. She didn't even bring up Annabelle for once. In fact, she looked almost as distracted as Misty's mom did these days. Misty wondered what was going on in her life. Funny how she'd never considered what kind of lives teachers lived outside of school.

"Misty, you'd better hurry if you're not going to be late," Ms. Reed said eventually. "Unless there's something you wanted to speak to me about."

"Nothing," Misty said hurriedly, quickly gathering up her books.

She'd no sooner stepped into the hallway than she was surrounded by Greg Bennett and two other guys from the football team.

"So, how about it?" Greg asked, crowding her, a leer on his face. "You've been skipping class a lot lately from what I hear. What's one more time for a little fun? You and me, outside in my car? I promise you'd have a good time."

Misty felt as if she was going to throw up right then and there. "Get out of my face, Greg," she said, drawing on some tiny shred of inner strength.

He only laughed at her. His friends nudged each other, not even trying to hide their own amusement over her pitiful attempt to fend Greg off.

"Who's going to make me?" he taunted. "Not you, that's for sure."

"How about Annabelle?" she suggested, looking him straight in the eye. "Could she make you back off? If she ever developed a spine, that is."

Hoots greeted that comment, which clearly incensed Greg. "Annabelle's got nothing to do with you and me."

"She seems to think otherwise. She seems to think you're her personal property. And I'm sick of taking the fall for you. I'm not after you. I'm not interested in you. I'd be happy if I never saw you again." She glanced at his friends. "Get the message? Pass it on."

She shoved past the three of them and practically ran to her next class. She didn't stop shaking until the period was half over.

She'd pay for that little scene. She knew she would.

Not that Greg would say a word about her rejecting him. His ego wouldn't allow that. But those friends of his were blabbermouths. Annabelle would hear something from them or any one of a dozen kids who'd been passing by. By tonight, she'd be spewing more garbage on the internet.

But, Misty consoled herself, once she'd been called a slut and a zillion ugly rumors had been circulated about all the guys she was supposedly sleeping with, how much worse could things possibly get? At least for once she'd finally stood up for herself. If she could take on Greg—who was just a jerk—and survive, how hard could it be to find a way to deal with Annabelle?

Maybe she'd made a mistake all these weeks by letting herself be a victim. Didn't they say that most bullies were really cowards? She'd assumed there was no way to fight back without making things worse, but maybe there was.

She just had to figure out what it might be. Amazingly, bit by bit, she was starting to feel strong enough to do just that.

9

Laura did her best to steer clear of the teacher's lounge during the day, but eventually she had to stop by for some kind of last-minute meeting of the school's social committee being held right after classes ended.

"I was expecting you in here at lunchtime," Nancy said as soon as Laura appeared.

"I had tests to grade. I ate at my desk," Laura said.

Nancy grinned. "In other words, you didn't want to be bothered with any more of my advice. Not to worry. We have a few minutes now. Jessica and Cal told me they were going to be running late."

Laura regarded her suspiciously. "Did you encourage them to be late?"

"Of course not," Nancy said innocently. "Now, have you given any more thought to what I said last night about dating J.C.?"

Since word about tonight's dinner was likely to spread through town with lightning speed, Laura saw little point in not mentioning it to a woman who was one of her closest friends.

"Some," she admitted.

"Great!" Nancy enthused. "Now we're getting somewhere. You'll need a plan. What's your next step?"

"You really are living vicariously through me, aren't you?"

"You bet," Nancy replied without hesitation. "So far it's been pretty dull, but I have high hopes for the future."

"Then you'll be absolutely thrilled to know that J.C. and I are having dinner tonight at Sullivan's, and he himself has described it as a date," she announced, barely containing a smile at Nancy's stunned expression.

"When did that happen?"

"Right after I spoke to you. Apparently he spent a lot of time yesterday fending off well-meant suggestions, as well. I thought the conclusion would be that we'd go back to our isolated corners and never see each other again." She shrugged, then allowed herself a tiny, satisfied grin. "He came to a different conclusion."

"Well, good for him. He's obviously smarter than I was giving him credit for being."

"He has an M.D. in pediatric medicine," Laura reminded her. "I doubt there's ever been any question about his intelligence."

"There's smart and there's *smart,*" Nancy argued. "I know a lot of exceptionally well-educated men who don't have the common sense of a gnat. My ex was one of them."

Laura welcomed the mention of a very hot-button topic. "Do you really want to talk about Steve? If so, I have some thoughts about it being time for you to move on."

"Now that you mention it, let's not discuss my ex-husband. I am so over him."

Laura had her doubts about that but saw little point in trying to nudge Nancy into facing her grief over the divorce so she could finally get on with her life.

"What are you wearing to dinner?" Nancy asked. "You need something special."

"I just bought a new dress at Raylene's the other day. I wasn't sure I'd ever need it for a date, but I fell in love with it and it was on sale. Adelia Hernandez talked me into it."

Nancy chuckled. "I hope Raylene is paying that woman what she's worth. She could sell ice to Eskimos, as they say. I went in for a scarf and bought three outfits. Used every last dime of my alimony check for last month, but it was worth it. If I ever go anyplace special, I'll look amazing."

"Maybe we should get some people together and go to Charleston or Columbia for a weekend," Laura suggested. "We could go to a concert, have dinner someplace fancy."

"It sounds great," Nancy said. "But something tells me you're not going to have much time for a girls' weekend."

"Please," Laura chided. "I'm going to dinner with J.C., not making a lifelong commitment. I will always have plenty of time to spend with my friends. That's a given. You all mean too much to me."

"Right back at you," Nancy said, then gave her a rueful look. "I hope you'll still feel that way when I tell you that there really wasn't a social committee meeting this afternoon. I knew you were trying to avoid talking to me about J.C., so I called one just for you. Jessica and Cal were never told about any meeting."

Laura regarded her indignantly for an instant, then shook her head. "I'll have to remember how sneaky you can be."

"It's a gift," Nancy said, suddenly unapologetic. "Got what I was after, too. Just keep in mind that I expect a full report on this date of yours tomorrow. Who knows what lengths I might go to for the information? As you've noted, my own life is pretty dull."

"Would you like to come by the apartment at 6:30 for breakfast so I can fill you in?" Laura asked, only half teasing.

"Heavens, no! What if J.C.'s there?"

"J.C. is not going to be in my apartment at 6:30 in the morning," Laura said confidently.

"You never know. I'll meet you at Wharton's instead. Call if you're otherwise engaged."

Laura shook her head at her friend's irrepressible optimism. "I'll see you at Wharton's. Just remember we have to use our 'indoor voices.' Grace has big ears."

Nancy only laughed. "Trust me, by the time we get there, she'll already know the whole story."

Sadly, Laura suspected Nancy was exactly right.

It had been a very long time since Laura had been this nervous before a date. Even though she'd spent a fair amount of time with J.C. recently, there was something undeniably different about tonight. It just proved how the dynamics between two people dramatically changed the instant dating—or the possibility of sex— was introduced. She was still wrestling with how she felt about that. Just a few short weeks ago, she would have sworn she wanted a relationship with real possibilities, but now old fears had surfaced to test that.

Obviously J.C. had his own doubts, as well. He might have invited her out, but she wasn't deluding herself that he'd been entirely happy about it. His reasons for not dating hadn't miraculously faded away. She was fairly certain of that.

When he knocked on her door, she drew in a deep, calming breath, then opened the door with what she hoped was a normal smile and not some sort of nervous, frozen grimace. Her eyes widened when she saw that he was wearing a suit, rather than the more casual khakis and oxford cloth shirt he generally wore to the office. It took his appeal to a whole new jaw-dropping level.

"You look very handsome," she said, hopefully without stuttering.

He grinned. "You look pretty amazing yourself. Is this dress new?"

She frowned at the question. "Why would you think I'd run out to buy a new dress just to go out with you?"

He reached toward her and touched her shoulder. "Tag's still on."

Laura blushed furiously. "Oh, sweet heaven, how did I miss that? Yes, the dress is new, but I didn't buy it for tonight, I swear. I bought it last week, because it was on sale and I fell in love with it and Adelia said it looked good on me." She drew in another breath. "And now I'm babbling on and on about it. Sorry."

His gaze held hers, which should have unnerved her, but instead seemed to settle her.

"Adelia has excellent taste, apparently."

"She does."

"Are you ready to go?"

"Just let me snip off this stupid tag and I will be," she told him.

Fifteen minutes later they were at Sullivan's, where they were greeted by Dana Sue, rather than the hostess. She grinned at Laura. "I saw the reservation and decided to see for myself if the two of you were here together again tonight. It's getting to be a habit. As soon as I saw the reservation book, I stopped off at Wharton's today to place my bet."

Laura groaned. "Way to pile on the pressure, Dana Sue. I'm surprised any couple in this town lasts more than a second with all these interested parties on the sidelines. Shouldn't you be in the kitchen cooking instead of out here meddling?"

"My daughter would never forgive me if I didn't get the latest scoop firsthand. Annie, Sarah and Raylene have become your biggest boosters since the fall festival success. They're already bubbling over with ideas for next year. They're determined to see that you top yourself. I think they'd like to see it take over the state fairgrounds, though that strikes me as overly ambitious."

"It would also defeat the purpose of promoting Serenity, don't you think?" Laura said wryly.

"Well, there is that, too," Dana Sue said. "Let me show you to your table. I gave you a prime spot."

Laura glanced around as they were shown to a table in the middle of the floor. "Where everyone can see us?"

"That's the idea," Dana Sue said cheerfully. "Or I could tuck you into that secluded little booth in the corner over there. I should warn you, though, that choosing that will stir up even more talk."

"I want the corner," J.C. said decisively. "If you have one of those fancy folding screens you could use to hide us from view, all the better."

Dana Sue laughed. "Now that really would stir things up."

J.C. regarded her somberly. "I wasn't entirely kidding."

"Sorry, a secluded booth is the best I can do."

"The booth is fine," Laura said quickly before J.C. decided they should be having dinner in some other part of the state and dragged her back out the door.

As soon as they were alone, she looked into his eyes. He seemed a little panic-stricken.

"Already regretting this plan of yours?" she asked him.

"There was no plan," he said. "The words just sort of tumbled out of my mouth, and here we are."

"We were here the other night and you didn't look like a deer caught in the headlights."

"That was different. It wasn't a date. This is."

"And that changes things," she concluded, knowing it was true. It did change things, whether two people wanted it to or not. Hadn't the very same thought occurred to her earlier?

"Of course it does."

"Then why did you ask me out? You'd already made the ground rules very clear. I certainly wasn't expecting this sudden shift in attitude."

"You suggested we stop seeing each other just to

quiet all the talk around town," he said, then shrugged. "I didn't want to stop."

He looked so thoroughly bemused by his own reaction, she didn't have the heart to keep pushing. "May I ask you something?"

A smile tugged at the corners of his mouth. "It may have been a long time since I've dated, but I do believe give-and-take is part of the evening."

"Okay, then. Why the hard-and-fast rule about not dating up till now?"

"I'm no good at it," he said simply. "Not the dating part, the rest of it."

"The relationship?" she guessed.

"The relationship, marriage, any of that. Fullerton men have really bad track records. It's probably genetic or something."

"You're the medical expert, but I don't think genes have much to do with relationship staying power," Laura said. "Do you know any of this firsthand, or are you relying totally on family history?"

He gave her an approving look. "Cleverly worded," he said. "Yes, I was married."

"And?"

"It didn't last," he said tightly.

"Something you did?"

He frowned at the question. "It must have been."

"You're going to have to explain that. Either it was or it wasn't. Who asked for the divorce?"

"I did."

"Because you didn't love her anymore?"

His scowl deepened. "Do you really need to know every last detail? It was a long time ago."

"And it obviously shaped who you are, at least in terms of how you relate to women, so, yes, being a woman who's sitting here with you right now, I need to know."

"Okay, then," he said, pausing before adding with unmistakable reluctance, "I came home one night after a very long shift at the hospital during my residency and found my wife in bed with the chief resident, who was technically my boss."

He said the words in a burst as if he wanted to get the humiliation out there and over with.

Laura bit back a gasp. "What a lousy thing to walk in on!" She regarded him curiously. "How, in any way, are you to blame for that?"

"I must have been a terrible husband for her to cheat like that. My dad had the same bad fortune with my mom. She was a serial cheater. He just never had the gumption to leave her."

"Thus the Fullerton-men-are-bad-bets theory," she concluded. "Okay, I will allow that you might have made equally bad choices when it came to women, but their behavior is all on them. You didn't turn them into cheaters."

He shrugged. "Maybe we did. I can't speak for my parents' marriage. I was pretty young when things got bad, so who knows how the cheating started. But I was in med school, then doing an internship and then a residency. All of it was more demanding than you can possibly imagine. I was never around."

"Your wife didn't know what it would be like when she married you?"

"She said she did, but I doubt anyone can understand

what it really means to live with a schedule like that until they do. I didn't, even though I saw the med students ahead of me walking around like zombies once they started their internships."

"There you go, letting her off the hook," Laura said, then added fiercely, "You did not deserve what she did."

He smiled at that. "Anyone ever mention this protective streak of yours?"

She nodded. "Absolutely. It's finely honed. Nobody messes with the people I care about."

He looked for an instant as if he might ask if he was one of those people she cared about, but instead he said, "Thus the determination to fix things for Misty."

She nodded, willing to allow the change of topic. J.C. still had the cornered look of a man who'd had about as much personal talk as he could handle for the moment.

"I still don't like what's going on," she told him. "Misty's been in class, but I know things are no better. I can see it in her eyes and in the way she lingers after class to avoid being with Annabelle and her cronies in the hallways. I just wish Misty trusted me enough to let me deal with it once and for all."

"I imagine she's just relieved to know that an adult believes her, that you heard for yourself what she's been living with since school started. Maybe that's enough for now."

"Since when is having an adult stand by helplessly while bullying continues ever enough?" she said in frustration. "I want it to end before things go too far."

J.C.'s expression instantly sobered. "If you ever sense that it's getting out of hand, you tell me, understood? I don't care about school protocol or some kind of evidence that would hold up in a court. This is not going to get out of hand and ruin that child's life."

She was startled by the vehemence in his voice. It wasn't the first time she'd sensed that bullying held special meaning for J.C. Tonight, though, with all of the revelations about his marriage, she judged that his feelings might be a little too raw to pursue yet another touchy subject. She would get to the bottom of it, though. She sensed that it, along with the lousy way his marriage ended, were the keys to understanding him.

And the more she got to know J.C., the more she wanted to know everything that had shaped the man he was now. She just hoped those scars from his past would allow it.

"You need to go online right now," Katie practically shouted in Misty's ear when Misty answered her cell phone. "I can't believe it!"

"What are you so worked up about?" Misty asked, still lost in the fictional world she'd been creating for a story for Ms. Reed's class.

"Just do it," Katie commanded. "You'll see. I'll wait."

"Are you talking about Annabelle's page?" Misty asked, already typing in the link.

"What else?" Katie said. "She's gone too far this time, Misty. You have to tell somebody. This needs to end."

Katie might be dramatic, but she wouldn't get this worked up over nothing, A sense of dread settled in Misty's stomach as the page loaded.

There, front and center, she found a link that, in turn led to even more pictures of some nearly naked girl in very provocative poses. She blinked and looked again.

Even without the identifying comments below, she knew that was her in the pictures, or at least it was supposed to be, she realized, nearly gagging.

How had this happened? Where would Annabelle have found pictures like this? Misty had never been photographed even close to nude in her entire life, except maybe in some embarrassing baby picture taken after a bath. Her parents would have sent her off to an all-girls school in some remote place if she'd ever even considered doing such a thing.

"It's not me," she said in a whisper. "There's no way."

"Well, I know that," Katie said without hesitation. "But she's gone way too far this time, Misty. These pictures will be all over school tomorrow. The site's already had, like, three thousand hits or something. Who knows how many kids at school have printed out copies? Some teacher's bound to see them, and you know what will happen after that."

"I'll probably be expelled," Misty said, sickened by the thought of the whispering and the destruction of whatever was left of her reputation.

Worse was what this would do to her parents. Even though those pictures had nothing to do with her—anyone who wasn't half blind could see that she wasn't built like that—there would be talk.

She sighed heavily. At least she had her answer to her question earlier today. Things *could* get worse.

Misty wasn't in class on Thursday. In fact, she wasn't even in school. Laura checked the attendance records and saw that she simply hadn't shown up. There'd been no call from home, nothing.

She also knew something was up around school. She'd seen the kids huddling in the corridors, whispering and giggling over something that clearly was circulating at warp speed. A terrible feeling in the pit of her stomach told her it had something to do with Misty's absence.

Just as class ended, she noticed Katie Townsend heading toward Annabelle with a glint of real fury in her eyes. Laura automatically headed in their direction to intervene.

"You're nothing but a low-down, lying bitch!" Katie shouted, stunning Laura not only with her choice of words but the venom behind them. Even Annabelle looked taken aback for once. The smug expression she usually wore around school was wiped away in a heartbeat as her friends stared at the two girls with shock, waiting to see what would happen next.

"Okay, that's it!" Laura said. "Katie, Annabelle, we're going to the office."

"But I didn't do anything," Annabelle protested indignantly. "She just attacked me. You all heard her."

"We all did," Laura confirmed. "I think the more important question might be why."

She saw the sheen of tears in Katie's eyes as they neared Betty Donovan's office and knew she was terrified of another suspension. Laura wanted desperately to console her, but the situation was out of her hands. She just wished she had some idea about how it was likely to play out and what on earth had sparked that uncharacteristic outburst.

Betty stepped out of her office, saw the three of them there and motioned for them to come inside.

"Okay, Ms. Reed, why don't you tell me what's going on?" Betty suggested.

"These two had words in my classroom just now," Laura began, only to have Annabelle once again interrupt with a protest that she'd never opened her mouth.

"If anyone ought to be in trouble, it's Katie," she said, still radiating indignation. "My mother is going to be all over you for this."

"I'm sure," Laura said wryly. "I'm hoping, though, that we can get to the bottom of this. Katie, would you care to explain why you said what you said to Annabelle?"

Katie shook her head, staring mutinously at Annabelle. "She knows what she did. She thinks she's some budding superstar, but she's no better than tabloid scum."

Betty regarded her with the same surprise that must have been on Laura's face earlier. "Harsh words, Katie."

"She deserves them and a lot worse," Katie said unrepentantly.

"You may believe that, but we don't know why," Laura told her gently. "Isn't it time we did?"

Katie finally turned to her with a pleading expression. "I can't talk about it, but I promise you it's really, really bad."

Betty clearly had been a principal long enough to recognize they were at a standoff. So did Laura. It was Betty, though, who suggested, "Annabelle, why don't you wait outside for a minute?"

"Why can't I go to class?" Annabelle asked petulantly. "Katie's the one who caused the problem."

"You'll go to class when we've gotten to the bottom

of this," Betty said. "And don't even think about wandering off."

Annabelle shot a withering look in Katie's direction, then stepped outside. Betty made a point of speaking to one of the secretaries, to assure that Annabelle stayed put, before closing her office door.

When she sat back down, she looked from Katie to Laura. "What am I missing?"

"A lot," Katie blurted, then clamped her lips shut.

"Maybe you should tell us," Laura said gently. "Things have obviously gotten out of hand."

"You have no idea," Katie whispered. "But I can't tell. I promised."

Betty turned her attention to Laura. "Any insights you care to share?"

"I think there's some bullying going on, but I haven't witnessed it firsthand, at least not here at school," Laura said, her gaze on Katie, hoping for even the tiniest hint of confirmation. Katie remained perfectly still, her eyes downcast.

Betty regarded Laura with dismay. "You believe Annabelle Litchfield is bullying someone?" she repeated incredulously. "Katie, is that true? Has she been attacking you in some way? Does this have anything to do with why you were caught skipping school earlier this fall?"

"Not Katie," Laura said quietly, her gaze steady on Katie. "I think she's bullying Misty Dawson, but as I said before, I can't prove it."

Betty turned back to Katie. "Is she right?" she asked, her tone far more gentle than anything Laura had ever heard from the tough-as-nails principal before.

Tears spilled down Katie's cheeks. "I can't say," she insisted again.

"But whatever happened just now between you and Annabelle, it was because you were trying to stand up for Misty," Betty guessed.

Katie did give a brief nod at that.

"Okay, then," Betty said decisively as she jotted out a note. "Go on to your next class, Katie."

Katie regarded her with surprise. "That's it? I'm not in trouble?"

"Not unless I hear about another incident like this," Betty told her. "I applaud you wanting to stand up for a friend, but there are better ways to do it. Leave the rest to Ms. Reed and me."

Katie nodded, shot a grateful look in Laura's direction, then practically ran from the room.

As soon as she was gone, Laura looked at the principal. "Now what?"

"Now we try to figure out what that girl out there has been up to. We need to have every single duck in a row before we accuse her of anything."

"I assumed as much, which is why I didn't come to you sooner. I've been trying to get to the bottom of it."

"Oh, we will," Betty said grimly. "For now I'm going to send Annabelle off to her next class. I know she'll assume she's gotten off scot-free, but it's better that than stirring up a hornet's nest before we have our facts straight."

"Because of Mariah Litchfield," Laura concluded.

"Precisely. Frankly, I look forward to tangling with her, if this turns out to be true. She's cost this school system two great teachers. It's about time we're able to turn the tables and give that little entitled, spoiled brat of hers the boot," she said vehemently, then looked chagrined. "Not that you ever heard me say such a thing."

"Not a word," Laura said, grinning.

Her view of Betty Donovan had just done a complete one-eighty. She might be a strict disciplinarian, perhaps a little overly zealous in certain situations, but it was apparent to Laura that when it came to her students and her teachers, Betty had the same sort of protective streak that J.C. had seen in Laura.

10

After she'd left Betty's office, Laura went looking for Cal Maddox. She wanted him to know about the incident between Annabelle and Katie from her before he heard the talk likely floating around school already.

Thankfully she found him in his office between classes. He regarded her with surprise.

"You generally avoid this part of the building," he commented. "To what do I owe this unexpected visit?"

"There was a problem at the end of my AP English class today. Since it involved Katie, I thought you should know." She met his gaze. "Or would you rather I call Maddie and Bill? I never know quite what to do in circumstances like this."

"Why don't you tell me what happened and I'll help you decide? Please don't tell me Katie skipped class again."

Laura shook her head, then described the incident. Though Cal had likely heard far worse in the boys' locker room, he looked stunned when she reported what Katie had said.

"That's not like Katie," he protested. "Maddie would never tolerate language like that."

"Believe me, I get that. So does Betty. She had to be highly agitated to resort to saying such a thing."

"You really think there's an excuse?" he asked, clearly surprised.

She nodded and explained her theory.

Cal listened intently, shaking his head as she described what she'd overheard at the fall festival. "That would explain a lot, wouldn't it?" he said eventually. "I've been teaching for a long time now, and it still astounds me just how cruel kids can be to one another. I always figured boys did the most bullying, but obviously girls can have a mean streak, as well."

"It's shocked me, too," Laura admitted. "And I guess I just never expected it from a girl who's from a good family with all sorts of advantages. Maybe that's the problem, though. Annabelle's gotten away with a lot, and she's come to feel she's entitled to behave however she wants."

"We still don't have all the facts, though," Cal reminded her. "This could be more complicated than we know."

"Oh, I'm sure it is, but with Betty on the case, there's little doubt we'll get to the bottom of it. I have to say I've never seen her quite so furious or determined."

"How was Katie when she left Betty's office? Should I check on her?"

"I think she was mostly relieved that she wasn't in trouble and proud of herself for defending Misty. Still, it wouldn't hurt for you or Maddie to have another talk with her after school. Maybe she'll open up this time, now that she knows it—whatever *it* is—is all going to come out sooner or later."

Cal nodded. "We'll do that. Thanks for filling me in, Laura. And if you need any backup on this, let me know. It makes me sick to think that Misty and Katie have been trying to cope with this on their own, that they haven't trusted any of us enough to ask for help. I know Katie has a good relationship with her mother, and I thought she and I had a good one. It kills me that she was dealing with this and we didn't know."

"Well, they're not on their own anymore," Laura assured him. In fact, the team of people on their side was getting stronger by the minute.

Paula Vreeland knelt in her garden deadheading flowers and snipping dead stalks from the perennials in preparation for winter. Though she had soothing classical music on a nearby radio, the air was frequently laced with muttered curses about the various aches and pains that made doing one of her favorite tasks so uncomfortable.

"Grandma, I didn't know you even knew words like that," Katie said as she slipped into the yard through a back gate, an impish grin on her face.

Paula winced. "Just because I say them doesn't mean you should," she told her granddaughter sternly. "Now come over here and help me up, then go inside and pour us both huge glasses of lemonade. It's much hotter out here than I realized."

Katie helped her to her feet, then gave her a hopeful look. "Are there cookies, too?"

Paula gave her an amused look. "When was the last time I baked anything?"

"Not for a long time, but I know Liz Johnson stops by here on Thursday mornings and she always brings cookies."

Paula laughed. "So, that's why I get these surprise visits on Thursday afternoons. I thought it was because you love me."

Katie embraced her in an exuberant hug. "I do love you," she said. "More than anything."

"Good answer, kiddo. Now get the lemonade and cookies—they're in the jar on the counter like always—while I try to work out some of these kinks from being down on the ground so long."

When Katie came back outside with their snack, she curled up on the chaise lounge in the sun. "How come you're not painting this afternoon? Did you finish the picture you were working on last week? Can I see it?"

Paula shook her head. "I painted over the canvas. I wasn't happy with the way it was going."

The truth was, none of her paintings pleased her these days. After creating amazingly detailed botanical artwork for so many years, after showings all over the world and landing her art in several very prestigious collections, she seemed to have lost something. It was true her vision wasn't what it had once been and her hand was less steady, but she thought it was more than that. Whatever it was, it made painting now more torture than passion.

Katie regarded her with shock. "Grandma, it was beautiful. You could have given it to me, if you didn't like it."

She smiled at her granddaughter. "Next time I paint something, if you like it, it's yours." She studied the usually bouncy teen across from her and thought she detected an unusual hint of worry in her eyes. "Now, tell me what's going on with you these days. How's school?"

Katie shrugged. "Okay, I guess."

Paula frowned. "Something wrong?"

"Not with me. My classes are all good and my grades are okay."

"Then what's the problem?" One of her greatest joys over the past few years was having her grandchildren drop in just like this to share their lives with her. She'd been too consumed with her painting to listen half as attentively to Maddie, and their relationship still suffered because of it. Since Maddie and Cal had married, he'd worked to bridge that chasm, and there had been strides for which she'd be eternally grateful to him.

One thing she'd also learned was patience. When Katie didn't immediately respond, she waited, allowing the silence to linger.

"One of my friends has a problem," Katie admitted eventually. "I've been trying to help her, but I don't really know what to say. And today things went really crazy. I got hauled into the principal's office for trying to defend my friend."

Paula studied her face to try to assess if that was code for saying that Katie herself was the one with the problem. "Tell me," she said neutrally. "I thought you'd been on your best behavior lately since that suspension earlier this fall. You can't afford another suspension."

"I know, but it really wasn't my fault. I had to say

something," Katie said earnestly. "It was the right thing to do."

One of the things Paula admired about the way Maddie had raised her children was that each of them had a well-developed sense of right and wrong.

Oh, her grandson Ty had certainly made his share of mistakes, mistakes that had almost cost him the girl he'd loved for most of his life, but he'd recognized in time that he was on the wrong path. Kyle, thank goodness, seemed steady as a rock, choosing his friends with care. Now here was Katie, as sweet as any mother or grandmother could hope for, in trouble for the second time in a few months. It didn't make a bit of sense.

"Maybe you should let me decide if what you did was called for," Paula suggested with no hint of censure in her voice. "Tell me about it."

"There's this other girl who's being really mean to my friend. She's on her case every chance she gets. She's started some ugly rumors on the internet. There's gossip all over school, but things get really bad because they're both in a couple of classes together. My friend won't even go to those classes anymore."

"In other words, your friend is being bullied by another girl," Paula said, incensed on this child's behalf. "Has your friend reported it to a teacher or to the principal?"

Katie shook her head.

"Isn't there a zero-tolerance policy at school when it comes to bullying?"

"There's supposed to be, but it doesn't always work," Katie told her.

"What about your friend's parents? Do they know?"

"She won't talk to them," Katie said. "I know she needs to talk to somebody, but she's afraid if she tells on this other girl, it will just make things worse." She drew in a deep breath, then added, "And this week it got really, really bad."

"How bad?"

"Somehow this girl, the bully, made up some pictures that were supposedly of my friend. I don't know how she even did it, but they were awful."

Paula stilled. "Pictures?" she echoed, not sure she wanted to know.

"Half-naked pictures," Katie said indignantly. "But it wasn't my friend. She would never, ever do anything like that. Anyone could see it wasn't really her, except for the face, but that didn't stop the pictures from being shown all over school. My friend didn't even show up at school today because she was so embarrassed."

"I'm sure she was," Paula said gently, understanding the depth of her granddaughter's distress. "Have you said anything to Cal? He could probably deal with this. I know he'd want to help."

Katie regarded her with frustration. "He would. He knows something's wrong, and he even asked me about what's going on, but she won't let me tell him anything. Like I said, she's afraid it will get even uglier."

Paula thought she understood now. "But she didn't tell you not to speak to me about it, did she?"

Katie shook her head, looking relieved that Paula got it.

"Want me to speak to Cal or someone else?" she asked, determined to let Katie guide her actions since she'd shown so much faith in her grandmother.

"There's this teacher, Laura Reed. My friend's skipping her class and she seems real worried about it. And she defended me today when we went to see Mrs. Donovan. She made sure I didn't get in real trouble, because she suspects what's been going on. Maybe you could talk to her," Katie suggested hopefully. "But not at school. I don't want my friend to figure out who told."

Paula nodded. "I'll be the soul of discretion, I promise. Maybe you'd better tell me who we're talking about, though. I imagine Ms. Reed is going to want specifics."

Katie's expression fell. "I didn't think about naming names."

"Sweetie, it's okay," Paula assured her. "Between Ms. Reed and me, we'll handle this very carefully. I don't think we can fix it, though, without more than you've given me so far. And didn't you just say that she already has a pretty good idea about who's involved?"

Katie buried her face in her hands. "Misty is so going to kill me," she murmured just loudly enough for Paula to get the one piece of information she needed.

So, Misty Dawson, who'd stopped by here with Katie from time to time, was the target of the bullying. Paula's temper stirred. She was such a sweet, gentle girl, dedicated to getting a good education. Paula had never heard a bad word said against her, though there had been talk around town recently about her parents' marriage being in trouble. Then again, she didn't spend a lot of time on internet sites where malicious teen gossip was likely to be spread.

She stood up. "Let's go inside. I want you to show me some of these posts you were talking about."

Katie turned pale. "I can't. They're really ugly."

"All the more reason for me to see them," Paula said briskly. "The pictures, too."

Katie was slow to follow her into her office, but once there she logged on, made a few clicks and then pointed first to the revealing photos and then to a series of posts on a social-networking site. Paula sat down to read them and once again felt her temper stir. "And you're sure who this *teenidol* is?"

"A hundred percent," Katie said, standing behind her to look over her shoulder.

"And there are more posts like this?"

"Lots of them," Katie confirmed. "I can show you."

"I think I'll just print out these for now," Paula said, tight-lipped with fury. She gazed into her granddaughter's eyes. "Tell me who's doing this."

"Annabelle," Katie said in a voice barely above a whisper.

Paula couldn't hide her shock. "Annabelle Litchfield?"

Katie nodded, then asked, "Now do you blame me for yelling at her today?"

"Not a bit," Paula said, "though it might have been wiser to get me or another adult involved instead."

"I know that," Katie said with evident frustration.

"But Misty wouldn't allow it, even now," Paula realized. "Why on earth would Annabelle hate Misty enough do something like this to her? What can that child possibly have done to her?"

"Annabelle's boyfriend, Greg…" She looked to Paula.

"The football captain? Greg Bennett?"

"Uh-huh. He likes Misty. Or maybe he's just on some kind of power trip because she won't pay attention to him. Anyway, he keeps asking her out, even though she's told him no, like, a hundred times. Everybody in school knows about it, because Greg is too dumb to keep his mouth shut about how he wants to get into Misty's pants."

The words were no sooner out of her mouth than Katie flushed. "Sorry, Grandma."

Paula patted her hand. "Not to worry. At least now I understand the root of the problem. Annabelle's jealous and taking Greg's disgusting behavior out on Misty."

"That's it exactly," Katie said, then threw her arms around Paula's shoulders from behind in an awkward hug. "I knew you'd understand. I just knew it. Can you fix it?"

"Believe me, I'll handle this," Paula said grimly. Annabelle might be her parents' little darling and the pride of Serenity because of her beautiful voice, but a bully was a bully. She wasn't going to be allowed to terrorize Misty another minute if Paula had anything to say about it.

"One more thing," she said to her granddaughter. "Why hasn't Misty spoken to her parents? They should know about this."

"They're probably getting a divorce, and it's really, really bad at home right now. Misty doesn't want them worrying about her. Plus, it's humiliating, you know? The stuff Annabelle is saying is really nasty. Nobody would want a parent to see that, even if they know it's not true."

"I suppose you're right," Paula said.

But the truth was, it was more of a reflection on Annabelle Litchfield and her twisted mind than it was on poor Misty. She could understand, though, why a young woman Misty's age might not be able to make that distinction when she was the victim of such terrible harassment.

Misty hadn't left the house all day. She was pretty sure her mom hadn't even noticed. From everything she'd read online, her mom probably had some kind of depression. She wondered if she ought to call her dad and beg him to do something. Her own efforts to get through to her mom and cheer her up sure hadn't accomplished anything. Who knew what would happen if her mom heard about those pictures supposedly of Misty that Annabelle had posted on the internet?

Every time the phone rang during the day, Misty froze. She worried at first it could be the school, calling to find out why she wasn't there. Then she panicked that it might be another parent calling about the awful pictures. It would be just like some stupid kid to leave them on the screen of their computer or to print out copies and leave 'em lying around for anyone to see.

She eavesdropped at the top of the steps, but so far her mom hadn't even bothered answering the calls. For once, she was glad that her mother was too lethargic to care about who might be calling.

She was just starting to think she'd made it through the day without everything getting any worse when Jake came in from school. Her brother spotted her at the top of the steps and raced up, his face red, one eye bloodied, a scratch on his cheek. He handed her a fistful of pictures. Misty sat down hard, the tears she'd managed to keep at bay all day finally spilling over.

"Is it you?" Jake asked in a voice filled with indignation.

"Are you crazy?" she asked, infuriated that her brother even had to ask.

"That's what I told the guys at school, but they didn't believe me."

"You got in a fight because of me?" she asked. "I'm so sorry."

"It's okay." He gave her a cocky grin. "You should see the other guy." He sat down beside her. "Who would do this to you?"

"You saw the page, Jake. You know who did it."

His eyes widened. "Annabelle? Why? What did you ever do to her?"

"She thinks I want her boyfriend," Misty told him.

"Greg? He's a jerk!"

Misty smiled for the first time all day. "I couldn't agree with you more."

"Have Mom and Dad seen these?" he asked.

"No, and I don't want them to know about any of this. Things are awful enough around here."

"Maybe they could help, though. I think they'd want to."

"You've seen Mom. She can barely get through the day," Misty said. "And Dad's never even here."

"They're gonna hear about this," Jake predicted. "You can't hide it from 'em. They'll be on your side."

Misty wished she was as sure of that as her brother was. "Or they could believe what they see."

"No way," Jake said.

"You did," she reminded him.

"Only for a second," he conceded. "I'm sorry. I shouldn't have doubted you even for that long."

She nudged him in the ribs. "You still fought for me. Thanks for that."

"Nobody talks about my sister the way the guys at school were talking," he said with bravado. "I don't care how many times I get a black eye. I'll always defend you."

Touched, Misty hugged him fiercely until he complained.

"Stop!" he pleaded.

"You defend me, you get hugs."

"Even though my ribs hurt?"

She frowned at him. "How bad did this fight get?"

He gave her an offhand shrug. "Bad enough."

"Are you in trouble at school?"

"No, I waited till I was off school property before I caught up with them. Smart, huh?"

"I guess we'll know when we find out how many calls mom and dad get from the kids you beat up."

He winced. "I never thought of that. Do you think they'll tell? If it were me, I wouldn't want my folks to know that some kid beat me up because I was saying lousy stuff about his sister."

Misty regarded him with surprise. Apparently Jake had both a code of honor and common sense. It gave her a whole new sense of appreciation for a boy she'd mostly thought of as an annoying pest.

J.C. had worked up a pretty good sweat at the gym. He knew he was trying to sublimate the desire to call Laura. Their date had gone a little too well. Not only had he opened up to her in ways he'd never expected to, but the attraction he felt to her had intensified. He'd resisted the urge to kiss her when he'd dropped her off at her apartment, but just barely. Something told him that once he'd crossed that line, he'd be lost, all of his resolve wiped out in an instant.

Glancing across the gym, he noticed that Cal's workout seemed a little more intense than usual, as well. Wiping his face with a towel, he crossed the room.

"Everything okay? You look thoroughly ticked off about something."

"You have no idea," Cal muttered, putting the weights he'd been lifting back onto the stand. "Do you have some time? I'd like to talk this through with an objective outsider. Something tells me you'd be the perfect person."

"Sure. I can spare some time," J.C. said. If it would keep him from going home to an empty house yet again, he could spare a lot of time.

"Let's grab a couple of drinks in the café and sit out on the deck. I don't think anyone's out there. We'll need some privacy for this."

In the café Cal grabbed two bottles of water. "You hungry? Want anything else?"

"Water's good," J.C. said, accepting one of the bottles.

"Put 'em on my account," Cal told the young man behind the counter, then led the way outside.

Dusk had already fallen. Though the air felt more like a humid summer day than late fall, there was a faint breeze stirring the oaks that shadowed the deck. There was the scent of some sort of flower in the air, though

J.C. had no idea what it might be. It smelled nice—a lot like Laura's perfume, now that he thought about it.

"What's up?" he asked when Cal seemed to be lost in thought.

"Just trying to figure out how much of this I can tell you."

"I'm good at keeping secrets," J.C. reminded him. "The whole patient-confidentiality thing is great training."

"Right," Cal said, looking satisfied. "I know you've been worried about Misty Dawson."

J.C. paused before the bottle of water reached his lips. "I have been."

"Well, I think it's about to get really ugly."

Cal described what he'd been told about an incident at school between Annabelle Litchfield and Cal's stepdaughter. "I don't know exactly what set Katie off like that, but it had to be really bad," Cal said. "She's a pretty even-tempered kid."

"And Laura stepped in?" J.C. asked.

Cal nodded. "And apparently knew enough about what's been going on between Annabelle and Misty to convince Betty not to punish Katie."

"How about Annabelle?"

"She's off the hook for the moment."

J.C. was startled. "How can that be?"

"Annabelle's mother," Cal said succinctly. "The principal is not going to mete out punishment to Annabelle until she knows with a hundred percent certainty that Mariah doesn't have a leg to stand on when she leaps to her daughter's defense. I can't blame Betty for that. Mariah's a terror when she's on a tear."

"So I've heard. How'd Laura handle all this?"

"I think it shook her up, but she's steady as a rock. She never once wavered in her belief that Katie was in the right. I have to respect her for that, especially when she knows it's likely to make her Mariah's first target."

J.C. regarded him with real concern. "How bad could this get for her?"

Cal actually chuckled for the first time since the somber conversation had started. "Thought that might be your first worry. It could get bad for a time, but Laura's tough enough and determined enough to weather whatever happens. And if these suspicions about the bullying are confirmed, the whole town would turn out on Laura's side if necessary. We had a few incidents over the years, and the entire community has come down hard on the kids involved. Everyone wants to send the message that being bullied is not just an acceptable part of growing up. It's inexcusable, no matter what form it takes."

J.C. nodded. "Good to hear, and you've just confirmed my impression of Laura. Misty and Katie are lucky to have her in their corner."

Cal gave him a long look. "How about you? Are you lucky to have her in your life these days?"

J.C. thought about denying that she was in his life, but he doubted Cal—or anyone else in town—would believe him. "Yeah, I'm pretty darn lucky, too."

And more aware of it by the day.

11

Laura was completely drained by the time she got home. She'd never been more grateful to have an entire evening stretching out ahead of her with absolutely nothing to do. She'd finished grading tests before leaving school. Her lesson plan for tomorrow was in place. She could soak in a bubble bath, have a glass of wine and a slice of leftover pizza, then crawl into bed with a book.

However, before she'd even glanced through the day's mail, there was a knock on her door. She opened it to find Annie, Raylene and Sarah on her doorstep, laden with bags that seemed to be overflowing with chips and who knew what else.

"Did we have plans?" she asked, knowing perfectly well that they didn't.

"Nope, but I heard from my mom that you'd had a really lousy day," Annie said, "so we're here to offer moral support. It's what Sweet Magnolias do. Mom, Maddie, Jeanette and Helen couldn't make it, but we've pretty well nailed the routine by now. Raylene can almost make Helen's lethal margaritas."

"What do you mean, *almost?*" Raylene said indignantly. "The last ones I made knocked you on your butt."

Annie grinned. "But I'm a lightweight. And I'm not sure knocking us on our butts is supposed to be the purpose. I think they're just intended to create a relaxing buzz."

"Well, I can do that, too," Raylene said, then turned to Laura. "Do you have a blender?"

"Sure."

"Plenty of ice?"

"Yes, but no lime juice or tequila," Laura said.

"Oh, we have the necessary ingredients," Raylene said. "We never go anywhere without being prepared."

"Then let's get this party started," Annie said exuberantly.

Sarah grinned at Laura. "You look a little shell-shocked. Maybe you should just have a seat in the living room and let us do the work. We'll find whatever we need."

Though she didn't doubt for a second that they could easily handle the preparations, Laura couldn't seem to stop herself from following along as they pulled together what looked like an entire meal, plus margaritas, in less than fifteen minutes.

"I cheated," Annie admitted. "Mom made the guacamole. It takes her maybe two minutes. It would take me forever, and it wouldn't be half as good."

"I just bought stuff," Sarah confessed. "Any actual cooking was done by Raylene, so it's guaranteed to be edible. She might not be a chef, and I would never say this in front of Dana Sue, but I swear Raylene's every bit as good as she is."

"Believe me, Mom already knows that," Annie said. "I caught her asking Raylene for a recipe the other day."

Sarah's eyes widened. "Seriously?"

Raylene nodded. "She did," she confirmed, her expression smug. "I'm not allowed to tell which one, because she intends to put it on the menu at Sullivan's. I gave her permission to take total credit for it."

"How is that fair?" Annie protested.

Raylene shrugged. "I'll know. That's what counts. I think it's amazing that your mom, the most celebrated chef in this region, wanted *my* recipe."

Laura allowed the chatter to surround her, feeling herself relax without even the first tiny sip of a margarita. It was enough that these three women had heard something about her lousy day and shown up here to bolster her spirits.

Raylene poured the margaritas into the glasses they'd also brought along, handed them around, then held hers up. "To margarita nights and friends," she toasted.

Laura joined in, took a sip of the drink and nearly choked. "It's a little strong, don't you think?"

"I used Helen's recipe and dialed it back a notch," Raylene argued.

Annie grinned. "Then we have a new lightweight!" she said triumphantly. "I am so glad it's no longer just me."

"Okay, everybody, get some food, then let's have a seat before we fall down," Sarah said, and turned to Laura. "Then you can fill us in on what happened at school today."

"I'm not sure that's a good idea," Laura protested.

"It's okay," Annie said. "I think I already know most

of the details. I'll talk. Laura, you can correct me if I get it wrong. That way you won't be telling tales out of school, so to speak."

Astounded that Annie thought she already knew the details, but not seriously doubting her word, Laura merely nodded.

Once they were all in the living room and had made a serious dent in the burritos, black beans and rice that Raylene had made, along with a lot of chips, salsa and very spicy guacamole, Annie reported what her mother had told her about the incident at school.

To Laura's surprise, none of the women seemed especially surprised to hear that Annabelle Litchfield might be bullying another girl.

"It's that mother of hers," Sarah said knowingly. "Mariah's something else. You know she put the moves on Travis, right?"

Even Raylene and Annie looked startled. "Did you ever tell us that?" Annie said. "When?"

"Fourth of July, after he went on the air and praised Annabelle's rendition of the national anthem during the holiday celebration on the town green. I walked back into the studio, and there she was gushing and practically throwing herself at him."

"What did Travis do?" Raylene asked.

"Not enough, in my opinion. He just thanked her for stopping by. I wanted to rip her hair out. Took me a while to accept that he was being polite and that my reaction might be a little over the top, to say nothing of very bad PR for the station."

"You didn't think Travis was interested, did you?" Annie asked with a frown. "That might have been early on, but everybody knew you were the only woman in town he had eyes for."

Sarah nodded. "I was still having a little trouble believing that back then." She grinned. "Not so much now."

"Well, I should hope not," Laura said. "I still have to fan myself when I hear the two of you on the radio. That man seriously has the hots for you."

Sarah's smile spread. "He does, doesn't he? How amazing is that? And he's *my* husband!"

Annie turned her attention to Laura. "Speaking of men, Mom also gave me a full report on your dinner with J.C. at Sullivan's."

"Do tell," Raylene said with interest.

Laura blushed furiously. "Come on, you guys. It was just dinner."

"But you do like him, right?" Sarah pressed. "I mean, what woman wouldn't? He's gorgeous. He's successful. And until now he'd been determinedly unattainable. How'd you pull off the coup, Laura?"

"By being irresistible, obviously," Annie said, grinning at Laura. "Give the woman some credit. She's as much of a catch as he is."

"Well, that goes without saying," Raylene said. "In fact, I'd say Laura's the bigger prize. J.C. has stayed in practice with Bill Townsend. That's not much of a recommendation."

"Hold on," Annie protested. "Even Maddie doesn't hold that against him. She takes the kids to J.C. and recommended him to me when I refused to take mine to Bill."

Sarah nodded. "Remember, it was Maddie who

pressed Bill to hire him in the first place before her marriage to Bill blew up. She even interviewed J.C. herself and thought he was a good fit for Serenity."

"I still say that affiliation makes him suspect," Raylene said stubbornly. "And if Maddie were being a hundred percent truthful, she'd tell you that, too. I'll bet the only reason she takes the kids to J.C. is because she won't go near her ex-husband, and the only other pediatricians are miles away. No mom wants a doctor for her kids who isn't readily accessible."

Laura listened to them with amusement. "So, does J.C. get a thumbs-up or a thumbs-down?" she asked in jest. "Not that you all have a say. I'm just curious."

"Thumbs-up," Annie said at once.

"I agree," Sarah replied.

"And I'm on the fence," Raylene said. "If Maddie, Dana Sue and Helen were here, I imagine there'd be more thumbs-down votes."

"Helen's jaded," Annie said. "It's all those divorces she's handled. She never forgives any man who's hurt one of her friends the way Bill hurt Maddie. She'd dislike J.C. on the principle of guilt by association. She's still a little cautious around my dad, though since he and Mom reconciled, Helen's tried to forget that she basically wiped the floor with him in the divorce. Dad's made it easier, because he hasn't held a grudge. In fact, one of his favorite sports is getting under Helen's skin."

Laura sat back. "I just love the dynamics in this town."

"How about margarita nights?" Annie asked hopefully. "Are you game for the next full-fledged one?"

"Count me in," Laura said. The margaritas might not

matter one way or the other, but the friendship these women had demonstrated by showing up here tonight was priceless.

J.C. had been calling Laura for hours but had yet to reach her. His conversation with Cal had worried him. He had a hunch she'd taken today's incident at school to heart. Sure, she'd handled it with quiet strength, but the situation was far from resolved. She was bound to be worrying herself sick over Misty. He was feeling pretty stirred up about the latest twist in the situation himself.

When he couldn't stand it another minute, he got into his car and drove over to Laura's apartment. He arrived around ten, just in time to see Annie Townsend, Sarah McDonald and Raylene Rollins emerge from the building. They looked a little wobbly to him, too wobbly to be behind the wheel of a car.

"Good evening, ladies," he said.

"It's J.C.," Annie said exuberantly. "What are you doing here?"

"I came to check on Laura. How about you?"

"We had a margarita night at her place," Sarah said.

He frowned. "A margarita night? What exactly is that?"

"Something Sweet Magnolias throw whenever someone needs support after a tough day," Annie explained, seeming to choose her words carefully.

"So a fair amount of tequila has been consumed this evening," he concluded, fighting a grin.

"A *lot*," Sarah said, her head bobbing like one of those ridiculous dolls.

"I think I've gotten the picture," he said. "How about

I give you all a lift home? Seems to me it would be a shame if the wife of the chief of police got picked up for DUI." He looked pointedly at Raylene when he said it.

"Not driving," she said. "She is." She pointed to Annie, who frowned. "Or is it Sarah? Don't we have a designated driver?"

J.C. shook his head. "Given the universal state of wobbliness I'm seeing here, my guess is no. Come on. I'll take you."

The three women piled into his car without protest. They even managed to direct him to their respective homes. He dropped Raylene off last.

"I take back what I said earlier," she said as she exited the car.

"What did you say earlier?"

"That I was on the fence about whether you were a prince or a jerk, or something like that. Turns out you're a gentleman." Her head bobbed approvingly. "Good for you."

He smiled at the vote of confidence. "Thank you."

"Doesn't really matter what I think," she said. "I'm pretty sure Laura thinks you're a prince. Hurt her, though, and you're dead meat."

"So I've heard," he said. "Good night, Raylene."

He waited until she was safely inside, then drove back to Laura's, uncertain what he might find when he got there. To his amazement, though her eyes were a little bright, she didn't look as if however many margaritas she'd consumed had fazed her.

"You look none the worse for your little party," he commented when she let him in.

"How'd you know about that?"

"I ran into the gals outside and volunteered to take them home. They had no business getting behind the wheel of a car."

"That was so sweet of you," she said.

"Oh, I'm a prince, all right," he said. "At least that's what Raylene claimed the vote had been earlier in the evening."

A blush climbed up Laura's neck and flooded her cheeks. "She told you that?"

"Alcohol tends to loosen tongues," he reminded her. "By the way, she changed her vote. I thought I should tell you that, in case it makes a difference to you."

"Really?"

"She says I'm a real gentleman, after all."

"Wow! Impressive. She was a holdout earlier."

He stepped closer, reaching out to tuck a wayward curl behind her ear. His touch lingered on her flushed cheek. "Did her opinion matter?"

She held his gaze and shook her head. "Not to me."

"I'm thinking I might not want to be a gentleman much longer," he admitted. "What would you think about that?"

She swallowed hard, but she didn't look away. "I'm thinking there might be times when being a gentleman is highly overrated."

He smiled. "Good to know."

"Were you thinking of making such a dramatic change tonight?" she inquired, a breathless note in her voice.

"I was, but the margarita thing has me thinking my timing is really off. I want you to make this decision with a clear head."

She regarded him with disappointment. "Did you really come over here tonight to seduce me?"

"Actually I came because I heard about what happened at school. I tried to call, but never got an answer."

"I let voice mail pick up since I had company," she said.

"Well, it worried me, so I came to check on you."

"Thank you. That was sweet."

He smiled. "Quite a night for me, anyway. First Raylene called me a gentleman and now you think I'm sweet."

"Don't let it go to your head. I'm sure you have lots and lots of flaws. I just can't think of any at the moment."

"I think I'll concentrate on the fact that you haven't ruled out letting me seduce you one of these days."

"No, I definitely haven't ruled that out."

"Another time, then," he said, bending down to touch his lips to hers. He could taste the hint of lime juice, tequila and salt that lingered on her lips, though the kiss would have been intoxicating enough without that.

He'd been right, he thought, as he reluctantly let her go. Now that he'd kissed her, even with just a brush of his lips across hers, he *was* lost. Oddly enough, it didn't terrify him half as badly as he'd expected it to.

"Good night, Laura. We'll talk tomorrow."

As he left, he cast one last glance over his shoulder and saw her with her fingers to her lips, her expression vaguely dazed. Good, he thought. The effect had been mutual.

Laura was surprised when she received a call the morning after margarita night from Paula Vreeland, asking if they could meet for afternoon tea on the patio of The Corner Spa. Paula was a legend in town. An internationally renowned artist, her original works were priced way beyond Laura's budget, but she had managed to buy one print, which hung in a place of prominence on the wall of Laura's little apartment.

Though she thought the spa was an odd choice for a meeting, it was no more odd than the request itself. She had to admit curiosity had gotten the better of her. She arrived fifteen minutes early and found Mrs. Vreeland already there, chatting with her daughter, Maddie.

"Laura, nice to see you," Maddie said. "Mother told me you were coming over. I don't suppose I can sign you up for a membership while you're here? We have special discounts for teachers."

"One of these days," Laura said, looking around with envy at the sunshine-drenched exercise room with its view of a wooded area beyond. Working out here in air-conditioning would be so much nicer than the way too rare, sweat-drenched walks she now took around the park.

Paula gave her daughter a chiding look. "I didn't invite Ms. Reed over here so you could make a sales pitch."

Maddie laughed. "It's part of my job description to reel in new members. Why don't the two of you go out onto the patio. It's quiet out there. I'll bring you something from the café. Anything in particular you'd like?"

"I've heard the fruit smoothies are amazing," Laura admitted. "Could I try one of those?"

"Of course. Strawberry-banana okay?"

"Perfect."

"And I'll just have a glass of sweet tea," Mrs. Vreeland said. "And maybe one of Dana Sue's blueberry muffins."

"Low-fat?" Maddie asked.

Paula wrinkled her nose. "Not if I have a choice," she said at once.

After they were settled at a wrought-iron table on the shaded brick patio, Paula regarded her directly. "I'm sure you're wondering why I called you out of the blue."

"I am curious," Laura admitted, "but grateful, too. I've been dying to meet you ever since I bought one of your gorgeous prints and found out you lived right here in Serenity. Somehow I've never managed to run into you around town."

"Praise *and* a purchase are always great ways to win an artist's heart," Paula said with a laugh, then sobered. "I'm afraid what I have to say is a touchy business."

Laura listened with increasing dismay as the older woman filled her in on what had been going on between Annabelle Litchfield and Misty Dawson. When Paula handed her a computer printout of some of the vicious posts, as well as the nearly naked photos purporting to be Misty, she actually gasped. It was far worse than anything she'd imagined.

"I had no idea," she said. "No wonder Misty wouldn't show her face in my class. I'm surprised she's come to school at all." She sighed. "Of course, she hasn't been there for a couple of days now, and she actually tried to get out of coming at all."

"How did she intend to make that work?" Paula asked.

"She went to J. C. Fullerton and begged him to write

her a medical excuse so she could stay home. He refused, but neither of us had any idea why she was so determined to stay out of school. She wouldn't speak up. It's only been in the past couple of weeks that I've had a real inkling about what was going on. This is exactly the proof I've needed to take this to the next level and get it stopped."

"Thankfully someone brought it to my attention," Paula said. "To say I was shocked would be an understatement."

"So am I," Laura admitted.

Paula nodded. "I thought you would be. Now, what are we going to do about it? It obviously needs to be handled delicately, but there's no room at the high school for this kind of tormenting of a student, especially one as bright and sensitive as Misty."

"I couldn't agree with you more," Laura said.

They both fell silent for several minutes, pondering the next course of action.

Laura eventually gave Mrs. Vreeland a direct look. "I've dealt with all of the parents at one time or another. Mariah Litchfield isn't going to handle this well, is she? I know Betty Donovan was anticipating a full-fledged explosion, even without knowing how bad things really are."

Paula responded with a rueful smile. "Frankly, I fully expect all hell to break loose."

Laura sighed. "I was afraid you'd say that. Then I assume we need to get all of our factual ducks in a nice row before she and Annabelle are confronted."

"Definitely a wise decision," Paula agreed. "If you don't mind, I'd like to stay out of this publicly unless it becomes necessary. Anyone could go online and find this evidence, so I doubt it's necessary that my name be involved."

"I can understand that you want to protect your source," Laura said. "It wouldn't take long for anyone to guess who that source might be." Though Katie Townsend had refused to talk to Cal, she must have gone to her grandmother. Bless her for finding a way to involve an adult without violating Misty's trust.

"But I will come forward if you need me at any point," Paula assured her. "This kind of behavior can't be tolerated. Other than trying to protect my source, I'm perfectly comfortable taking a public stand against it." She smiled briefly. "And there's very little that Mariah Litchfield can possibly do to me. I have no concerns for my reputation, just for my source."

"Understood," Laura said. "I don't think we'll have any problem finding people to stand firm against this once the facts come out." She had a feeling J.C. would be leading the pack, and she intended to involve him at the very first opportunity.

Paula regarded her with approval. "Katie told me you'd jump all over this. She's a great admirer of yours. I can see why."

"Thank you," Laura said, genuinely pleased, not so much by Paula Vreeland's approval, but by Katie's faith in her. "I won't let either of these girls down."

She weighed asking Mrs. Vreeland's advice. "May I ask your opinion about something?"

"Of course."

"You obviously understand how sensitive this situation is, especially with such awful pictures being posted online. I've been hearing talk that Misty's parents are having problems. Normally I'd go straight to them with this, but I don't want to make that situation worse."

"I can appreciate your concern," Paula said, "but do you really have a choice? Once you've taken this information to Betty and she's taken action against Annabelle—suspension, I assume, if not expulsion—the whole town will be talking about it, asking questions and, sad to say, looking online for the evidence. Diana and Les Dawson deserve to be prepared for that. They need to know what's been happening to their daughter before it all goes public, or should I say more public than it is already. Whatever their own problems, I'm sure they'll want to be there for their daughter."

Laura sighed. "My thought, too," she agreed reluctantly.

And unfortunately there was no time to waste. The Dawsons had to be her priority. She'd find J.C. later and fill him in. It was far less important for her to have her own support system in place than it was for Misty to have hers.

"Could we meet here again?" Paula suggested. "I'd like an update on what's happening, if you wouldn't mind. I'm not going to rest well until I know that has been handled and that Misty's safe once more. And I'll want you to let me know if there's any way at all you think I can help."

"Absolutely," Laura said. "And I can't tell you how much it means to me that you and Katie trusted me with this information. I will do my best not to let you down."

"I'm confident of that," Paula said. "Serenity's lucky

to have you here. Not every teacher would be willing to go up against Mariah Litchfield."

Laura couldn't believe that. "Surely not."

"Mariah's the original town bully," Paula confirmed. "Where do you think Annabelle learned her vicious ways? That sweet-as-pie exterior Mariah shows the world to get her way covers up a whole lot of mean. Once upon a time, she had her own dreams of superstardom, but getting pregnant put an end to those ambitions. Not only is she living vicariously through her daughter, but she's filled with anger and resentment. Beware of that, Laura. Even though you're on the side of the angels in this one, you won't come out unscathed."

Laura nodded. "I'm fully prepared for that," she said staunchly, thinking of how Vicki Kincaid had once stood up for her against the name-calling by the other students at her school, and against the small-minded parents who thought a pregnant teen should be banished rather than allowed to complete her education.

Laura prayed she could live up to the example that had been set for her.

12

Laura debated calling ahead to warn the Dawsons she was on her way over but opted instead for just showing up on their doorstep. She didn't want to risk being put off by excuses. Of course, what she couldn't have anticipated was the situation she found.

Misty opened the front door, dismay crossing her face when she saw Laura. "Ms. Reed," she whispered, stepping outside and closing the door firmly behind her. "What are you doing here? If it's because I wasn't in school most of this week, I was sick. I'll have a note on Monday. I promise."

Laura impulsively gave her hand a reassuring squeeze. "It's okay, Misty. I know everything now. I understand all of it."

Misty's eyes widened with alarm. "I don't understand. What do you know?"

"I know about Annabelle and the posts online and the pictures," Laura said gently. "Why don't we go inside and have a talk about it? Are your parents home? We should all sit down and discuss the best way to correct this terrible situation you've been put in since school started."

"No, please," Misty said urgently. "You can't say anything to my mom. She's not well. And my dad's not home."

"You need to call him and ask him to come home," Laura said firmly. "Continuing to ignore this isn't an option, Misty. Once everything is set in motion to punish Annabelle, it will come out. You won't be able to keep it from them. Wouldn't it be better to fill them in now, prepare them? You are not to blame for any of this. You're the victim of a relentless bully."

Tears welled up in Misty's eyes. "What if my mom and dad don't believe that? What if they think I did all those things Annabelle posted? You don't understand, Ms. Reed. They'll hate me, and things are already such a mess here. I don't know how much more my mom can take."

She sounded so scared that for a fleeting instant, Laura wondered if she was doing the right thing. But she knew in her heart she had no choice. The Dawsons had a right to know about something so serious, something that affected their daughter right now, to say nothing of how it might impact her future if she kept missing school to avoid the bullying and taunts of her classmates.

"Misty, I know you want to protect them, but you can't. It's not possible. This will come out." Heaven knew, she'd tried every way she could think of to keep her pregnancy from her parents, but it had been impossible. It simply wasn't something that could be hidden. Neither was this.

"It won't come out," Misty insisted, "Not if you let it

go. I'll come back to school on Monday. I'll stay away from Annabelle. We'll just pretend it never happened. Kids say awful stuff about other kids all the time. We're just supposed to deal with it, right? That's the mature thing to do."

"Misty, this whole situation is so far from right, I don't even know where to begin," Laura said, wondering what messages adults were sending to kids to have them draw such a conclusion. "First of all, what Annabelle's been doing to you is wrong. It's a violation of school policy, if not criminal. I imagine a lot of these posts rise to the level of libel, but an attorney will have to sort that out. I certainly can't ignore it. Second, bullies don't quit unless they're forced to. You shouldn't have to suffer one single second longer."

"But I will," Misty pleaded. "It's okay. I can take it, if it means my mom and dad never have to find out. You don't get how bad things are for them right now."

Laura really needed to understand exactly what was behind Misty's obvious panic. "Let's sit here on the porch for a minute. Why don't you tell me why you think it would be okay to let Annabelle off the hook? What's going on here that makes it so hard for you to go to your parents about this?"

"I told you," Misty said. "My parents can't deal with this. They're gonna get a divorce pretty soon, and my mom's freaking out about it. My dad's not even around most of the time. This will give them one more thing to fight about."

"They're still your parents. They'll want to help you," Laura insisted, praying that was true. Surely they couldn't be so self-absorbed that Misty's problems would seem unimportant?

"But I don't want them to help," Misty repeated. "I can get through this. I'll find a way."

"So far, your way of coping has been to skip school," Laura reminded her. "That's no longer an option."

"Then I'll figure out something else," the teen said with pure bravado. "Annabelle's done her worst."

"If you believe that, let me assure you I think you're mistaken. Here's what I know about bullies. If they think what they're doing is no longer having the desired impact, then they go to another level. Just look at what happened this week. You bravely came back to class. You tried to show Annabelle she couldn't hurt you anymore, and then she posted these pictures."

"But maybe if Annabelle knows how much trouble she could have been in and that I let her off the hook, she'll quit," Misty suggested hopefully. "She could be grateful, you know."

"Do you honestly believe that?" Laura asked.

Misty sat back, clearly unable to defend her position. "Probably not," she admitted reluctantly. "But if she gets kicked out of school because of me, all her friends are going to hate me. They'll all go after me online. They'll corner me in the restroom or in the halls between classes just to torment me. I don't know if I can face any more of that."

"Or they'll realize that nobody in Serenity is allowed to get away with what Annabelle's been doing to you. You'll have helped to send a very clear message to them about bullying."

Misty shook her head. "I don't think it's going to work that way," she said, sounding defeated.

"Trust me," Laura said.

"I do, but..." Her voice trailed off.

"But you're scared," Laura filled in for her.

Misty nodded.

"I don't blame you. But there are a lot of people already on your side, Misty. You have backup now. We're going to put a stop to this. I promise."

Though Misty still didn't look entirely convinced, Laura once again asked to speak to her mother. "Let's get this over with. No matter what else is going on in her life, I know how important you are to her. I think she's going to surprise you."

Misty heaved a huge sigh. "Whatever," she said, but she did lead the way into the kitchen.

Diana Dawson blinked when she saw Laura with Misty. "Ms. Reed, what are you doing here? Is Misty in some kind of trouble in school?" she asked, her expression alarmed.

Laura tried to hide her shock at Diana's disheveled appearance. She'd never seen her looking anything other than her best. Today she looked worn out. She was wearing wrinkled clothes, her expensively styled hair had been left uncombed, her face was devoid of makeup. It was little wonder Misty was worried sick about her.

"Misty's not in trouble," Laura reassured her as she sat across from her at the table. "But there is a problem at school. I thought you and your husband should hear about it from me before things get out of hand."

"It's Annabelle Litchfield, isn't it?" Diana said, sur-

prising Laura and even Misty apparently, given her
faint gasp.

"Mom, do you already know something?" Misty
asked worriedly. "What have you heard?"

"I know that those calls from Mariah weren't about
'nothing,' the way you wanted me to believe," Diana
said. She appeared to brace herself as she met Laura's
gaze. "Tell me."

Laura filled her in without divulging the full extent
of Annabelle's online lies and nastiness. Even so, Diana
showed the first hint of real animation since Laura had
arrived.

"That low-down little twit," she said heatedly, then
turned to Misty. "Sweetheart, why didn't you tell me?"

"The stuff she was saying was too awful," Misty said.
"You already had enough going on with Dad."

"I will never have too much going on to defend
you," Diana said, clearly stirred from her earlier apa-
thy. "What's next?" she asked Laura.

"I'm going to take the evidence I have to Betty Donovan. She'll follow whatever procedures she must to see
that Annabelle is held accountable and stopped."

"Mariah will never take this lying down," Diana predicted. "We can assume that. It will get ugly."

"We could let it go," Misty once again pleaded.

Her mother reached over and covered her hand. "No
way. This will not get swept under the carpet."

"But I'm going to be even more humiliated if everybody in town is talking about this. And what about the
pictures?" she asked plaintively. "Now everybody will
see them."

"I'm going to make a call as soon as I get home to see

what we'd need to do to have them taken down at once," Laura said. "I'll start with Helen Decatur-Whitney, and if she can't handle it, I'll speak to Carter Rollins."

"Carrie's dad?" Misty said, her eyes wide with dismay. "You'll tell the police chief?"

Laura nodded. "I imagine between him and Helen, they'll know what to do legally to put an end to these vicious posts and have the old ones deleted."

"Thank you," Diana said. "And you'll let us know what's going on and what we need to do next?"

"Absolutely." Laura hesitated, then asked, "What about Mr. Dawson? Will you fill him in or should I?"

Diana drew herself up, squaring her shoulders. "I'll tell him. He may not listen to me about much these days, but he cares about Misty and Jake. He'll step up."

"Mom, don't use me to try to drag Dad back home," Misty pleaded.

"It's not about me and what I want this time," her mother assured her. "He'll do whatever it takes to support you. I'm sorry if everything that's been happening here made you doubt that for a single second. Your dad adores you. I only wish you'd told us yourself much sooner. You shouldn't have been facing this alone."

"Jake's kinda helped," she admitted. "He stood up for me at school."

Diana looked startled. "That's how he got the black eye?"

Misty nodded. "It made me sick when I found out he'd seen the pictures, Mom. It was so twisted. That's how I feel about Dad seeing all this. He's going to be totally disillusioned."

"Never about you," Diana soothed her. "Your dad

will understand that it's all lies. It reflects badly on Annabelle far more than it does on you."

Though Misty didn't look entirely convinced by her mother's words, Laura thought she detected the faintest hint of hope in her eyes for the first time in a long while.

By the time she'd left Misty's, it was too late for Laura to reach Helen at her office. She knew the attorney often stopped by Sullivan's to see her husband, the restaurant's sous-chef, on her way home. Helen had even been there when Laura had dined there with J.C. the other night.

Sure enough, she found her in a corner booth toward the back, papers spread out around her and a half-eaten sandwich pushed aside.

"Helen, I'm so sorry to interrupt you, but do you have a minute?" Laura asked.

Helen glanced up, blinked as if to bring herself back to reality, then smiled. "Laura, of course. Have a seat. I'm afraid I was so absorbed by the extent to which my client's husband has been hiding his assets from her that I didn't even see you."

"Are you sure you can spare the time? It's important or I wouldn't bother you."

"I'm just killing time till Erik can take a break. My mother has my daughter for a couple of hours this evening, so it's supposed to be my date night with my husband. Unfortunately, the place is swamped, and he can't seem to tear himself away from the kitchen. Trust me, if you want to spend time with a man on a weekend, don't ever get involved with a chef."

Laura grinned. "At least your loss is the customer's gain. Erik's desserts are pretty decadent."

"Believe me, I am all too aware of that," she said ruefully. "I think I've gained ten pounds since we got married just by sampling all his experiments." She grinned at Laura. "I hear there was a mini margarita night at your place last night. Sorry I missed it, but I gather Raylene has nailed the margaritas."

"They were lethal, if that's what you mean," Laura said. "It was fun, and it was exactly what I needed after a really awful day."

"That's the goal," Helen said, her expression sobering. "I heard a little about what's been going on with Misty Dawson. Anything I can do to help?"

Laura smiled. "That's exactly what I'm hoping you can tell me." She spelled out the situation and showed her the printouts Paula Vreeland had given her. "I understand this is just the tip of the iceberg. The person who brought them to me didn't print out even half of what's online."

Helen's eyes widened as she read through the papers. She actually gasped when she saw the pictures. "You're kidding me! Anyone can see that these pictures have been doctored."

"Of course, but in the meantime, they're a huge embarrassment to Misty, as you can imagine. What can we do to get them taken down as quickly as possible?"

"This is a little out of my area of expertise, but I'll make some calls and see what I can do. I assume you plan to handle this situation at school?"

"I'll call Betty, and I'm sure she'll be all over it first thing on Monday morning," Laura confirmed.

"What about the Dawsons? They should file a lawsuit of their own."

"I think Diana is still reeling, and I'm not sure she's even had a chance to fill her husband in yet. I just left there a little while ago."

Helen nodded. "I'll give her a call and explain her options. How's Misty?"

"Terrified," Laura said frankly. "She thinks going after Annabelle is going to make things even worse for her at school. She's been skipping a couple of classes practically since the beginning of the year because of this. Once the pictures went online, she just stayed home. Unless this is handled well, I'm really worried about the impact it will have on her. So far she's managed to keep her grades up, but not coming to class will take a toll, even on someone as bright as she is."

"She's a junior, right?"

Laura nodded. "And counting on getting into a premier school."

"So her grades this year are crucial," Helen concluded. "Could you arrange for a meeting with Betty Donovan first thing Monday morning for all of us? We're going to want to coordinate what the school's doing, what the Dawsons want and what I'm able to handle."

"About your fee," Laura began.

"There is no fee," Helen said at once, her expression grim. "This one's on me. There's nothing I hate worse than a bully. My entire career has been built on going after men who bully their wives in one way or another. It'll be a pleasure to stop this one."

"Thank you," Laura said with total sincerity. "You really are an angel."

Helen laughed. "I imagine you could find a whole lot of people in this town who'd tell you otherwise."

She began gathering up her papers. "I'm going to tell Erik I have to head home, and then I'll start making those calls," she promised Laura. "I'll phone you as soon as I know anything, and I'll see you at the high school first thing Monday morning. Let me know the time. I'll cancel whatever might be on my calendar if there's a conflict. This is too important to waste a single second."

Laura was about to stand up and head out herself, but Dana Sue approached, her expression somber. "The whole Misty situation is about to come to a head, isn't it? That's why you were talking to Helen."

Laura nodded.

"Anything I can do? We all want to help."

"Just try to keep a lid on whatever gossip you might hear. The poor child's been humiliated enough."

"Will do," Dana Sue promised. "Why don't you stay? I'll bring you the night's special. It's fried catfish, J.C.'s favorite, and I have it on good authority that he's on his way over right now to have it."

Laura lifted a brow. "Good authority?"

Dana Sue grinned. "Okay, I called and told him you were here and looked as if you needed company."

"How did I manage to go so many years in this town flying under the meddling radar?" she asked with a mix of amusement and exasperation.

"None of us ever saw you with the right man before," Dana Sue said.

"And the consensus is that J.C.'s the right one?" Laura

asked. "Even though he works with Bill Townsend? I heard that was a huge strike against him in some circles."

Dana Sue shrugged. "Hey, everybody has flaws. So far none of us have seen any evidence that he shares any of Bill's less attractive traits."

"Then you have thoroughly vetted him?" Laura inquired, only partially in jest.

"Thoroughly," Dana Sue said without so much as a hint that she wasn't dead serious.

"Astonishing."

Just then J.C. appeared. He studied Laura worriedly, then turned to Dana Sue. "Thanks for the heads-up."

"Anytime," she assured him. "I'll send over a bottle of wine. Red or white?"

He glanced at Laura. "White, I think."

Laura nodded.

After Dana Sue had gone, she regarded him with amusement. "Prince wasn't enough. Now you're going for knight-in-shining-armor rushing to the rescue of the fair damsel?"

"I didn't hear you needed rescuing," he said. "At least not exactly. Just that you came in looking pretty intense, then hunkered down in a corner with Helen. It didn't sound as if you were here for a fun rendezvous with a friend."

"True," she confessed. "It's been another perfectly awful day." She met his gaze. "Would you mind if we didn't talk about it right this second? I need to put it aside for a little while before I charge into battle again."

"I'd like to help."

"And, believe me, I'm counting on that. Just an hour

of inconsequential talk and good food and I'll tell you everything."

"Okay, then. Whatever you need," he said. "How about those Panthers?"

She blinked and stared at him, uncomprehending. "Panthers?"

"Carolina Panthers," he explained. "The pro football team in Charlotte."

"I know this will probably change your impression of me, and not in a good way, but I don't follow football beyond the games at the high school."

He regarded her with apparent shock. "Now that is just wrong," he declared.

She grinned. "Does it cut me out of the running?"

He reached for her hand and tucked it into his. "Sorry. Too late for that. You're pretty much at the front of the line." He shrugged. "The only one in it, for that matter."

Despite the miserable day she'd had, she couldn't help allowing herself just the tiniest smile of satisfaction at that revelation.

J.C. saw the faint smile that touched Laura's lips and hid his own smile. It was good to see the shadows in her eyes finally disappear. She'd looked completely undone when he'd first arrived. He owed Dana Sue big-time for having called him. For once he hadn't been appalled by the meddling tendencies of everyone in town.

He'd just left the gym when she'd phoned. Thankfully he'd showered and changed back into street clothes after his workout, so he'd headed directly to the restaurant.

Since Laura seemed momentarily lost in thought, he took his time studying her. Despite the weariness he'd detected, she still had every hair in place, and her clothes were neat as a pin. How did anyone get through a work-day and look that tidy? On some purely male level he wanted to spend a couple of hours mussing her up. As soon as the inappropriate thought occurred to him, he tried to squash it, but the damage had been done. His blood was humming, and it had nothing to do with his own earlier workout.

Whatever she was thinking about, it wasn't the dis-traction he'd hoped to provide.

"You look a little grim," he observed. "Obviously whatever happened earlier is still on your mind. Maybe you should just get it out in the open."

"I suppose it's going to be impossible for me to ac-tually put it out of my head, even for a little while." She met his gaze. "J.C., it's so much uglier than anything I'd imagined."

"So it does have something to do with Misty," he guessed.

She nodded. "I'd already planned to give you a call later. I had to speak to Helen first, and then I intended to go home and call Betty Donovan and then you."

He could see genuine distress in her eyes and im-mediately responded to that and not to the wildly un-expected instinct that made him want to pull her into his arms. "Tell me," he said gently. "You know I want to help Misty any way I can." He hesitated, then asked, "Would you rather not discuss this here? We could change our order to takeout and head over to my place. Or to yours. Wherever you'd feel more comfortable."

She looked as if she were considering the suggestion, then nodded. "You know, I'm sure it would be fine to talk about this here. The booth's pretty secluded, but I would feel a whole lot better someplace else. It may even have been a mistake to say as much as I did to Helen. Do you mind?"

"Of course not. Let me catch Dana Sue and let her know." When he got back to the table, he said, "Our food will be ready in a couple of minutes. Now, let's decide. Your apartment or my house?"

She smiled at him. "Your house? You really are taking a giant leap of faith with me, aren't you? I thought maybe it was off-limits to all women. What if I start getting crazy ideas?"

J.C. laughed. "Your ideas can't possibly be any crazier than mine have been lately. I think I'd like you to come to my place."

"Want to see if I fit in with the leather furniture and giant-screen TV?" she teased.

"Laura, you'd fit in wherever you happen to be," he said with total sincerity.

"Then you're checking to see if my presence gives you a panic attack?" she concluded.

"The only thing I panic about these days is the fact that being with you *doesn't* scare me," he confessed. "That's downright terrifying."

She seemed startled by his revelation but clearly pleased. He looked up then, spotted Dana Sue heading their way and stood. He handed over enough cash for the food, then held out a hand to Laura. "Let's go."

They made the drive to his house in silence. While she wandered around, studying the Paula Vreeland originals on his walls with an awed expression, he put their food onto plates and poured the wine.

"Living room, I think," he said, leading the way. "We'll be more comfortable."

She chuckled. "I got it exactly right. Oversize leather furniture and a giant flat-screen TV. You are so predictable, except for the Paula Vreeland pictures. Those are a total surprise. I'm so envious. I only have one print of hers."

"You like her work, too?"

"Love it. The detail is exquisite."

"Have you met her?"

"Just once," she said. "You?"

"Hey, I'm in practice with her ex-son-in-law, who is not beloved by her. I try to steer clear of her. It's a shame, too, because I'd love to tell her how much I admire her work."

"Then you should. I'm sure she'd love to hear that, despite your unfortunate connection to a man she despises."

J.C. handed her a glass of wine, then took a seat across from her. It wasn't lost on him that, though she wasn't the first woman to cross his threshold in this house, she was the only one who actually looked as if she belonged here. The disconcerting thought rattled his usual composure. One more chink in his defensive armor shot to blazes.

Time to get focused, he decided, hoping to reclaim some semblance of his usual careful distance between him and the sort of messy emotions that always led to disaster for Fullerton men.

"Okay, what have you learned about Misty?" he asked, knowing the change of topic would spoil any intimate mood at once.

Laura described the information she'd been given, then handed over the online posts someone had passed along to her. J.C. read them, his disgust growing. He thought he knew Misty well enough to know that absolutely none of the nasty accusations were true.

"And there's no question that Annabelle's behind this?" he asked.

"From all reports her online identity is well-known to the other kids at school. They were actually passing those pictures around at school today. Why none of the teachers caught a glimpse is beyond me. I saw a few clusters of giggling kids in the halls. I'm still kicking myself for not checking to see what they found so hilarious."

"Any idea why she targeted Misty?"

"It's over a boy, of course. At that age, isn't it always?"

"I guess I'd forgotten what it's like to deal with all those raging hormones, though I certainly see evidence of it in my practice. I'm more likely to see an unplanned pregnancy than something like this, though." He held Laura's gaze. "What's next?"

"I spoke to Helen earlier. She's going to do everything she can to get the posts and pictures taken down. I have no idea how long that might take. I'll go to Betty either later tonight or tomorrow and arrange some sort of meeting on Monday morning." She shrugged. "I guess we'll see where it goes from there."

"I hate to sound harsh, but I have absolutely zero sympathy for Annabelle Litchfield. Whatever they do to her can't possibly be enough."

"That's not the first time this has sounded personal to you," she said, startling him with her perceptiveness.

J.C. tried to fend off more questions. "Okay, yes. I've seen the tragic outcome when something like this spirals out of control. There need to be serious consequences for bullies. I don't care how young they are or how innocent their parents claim the behavior to be. It's wrong."

Laura nodded. "No question about it."

He gave her a thoughtful look. "You sound equally fierce about this. Have you had your own experience with a bully?"

She avoided his gaze but eventually nodded. "Years ago," she admitted.

"I can't imagine anyone picking on you."

She smiled at that. "I was a lot like Misty in some ways, a brainy kid and very shy. The only difference between us is that she's a lot smarter than I was when it comes to getting involved with a jerk."

"Meaning?"

"She knew enough to give Greg Bennett a wide berth. When the hotshot bad boy in school started paying attention to me, I fell for it. I thought I was in love. I thought he was, too." She hesitated, then finally met his gaze. "And then I got pregnant, and he couldn't leave me in the dust fast enough."

J.C.'s anger stirred on behalf of the shy girl who must have been scared out of her wits by an unplanned pregnancy. "What happened?"

"My parents considered sending me to live with relatives out of town, but then they decided that keeping me in school would be a better punishment. They also insisted I give the baby up for adoption." Her eyes shimmered with tears. "So, that's what I did."

"But the other kids made your life hell," he guessed.

She nodded. "If I hadn't had a teacher who stuck by me, I don't know if I could have gotten through it, but she was determined I'd graduate and go on to college, so I couldn't let her down. I figured if she was willing to stand up for me, then I had to stand up for myself."

"And the baby?"

As she shook her head, the tears spilled over, rolled down her cheeks. "I don't know where she is. It was a closed adoption. I pray every day that she's with a loving family, one who'll stand by her if she ever makes the kind of mistakes I did."

"And in the meantime, you're standing by Misty," he said.

"How can I not?" she said simply.

J.C. felt her long-ago pain and sorrow, saw the strength it had created in her and fell just a little bit in love.

"I want to be there Monday," he said decisively. "You'll let me know the time?"

She blinked away her tears, then nodded. "Of course. As soon as it's scheduled. I'm sure you'll be busy with patients. Will that be a problem?"

"Bill will just have to pick up the slack," he said. "This is too important for me not to be there. I want to make sure everyone understands just how serious a matter this is."

"Surely you don't think anyone will try to sweep it under the carpet, do you?" she asked, looking shocked.

"Surely Serenity's not the sort of town to rally around a bully, no matter who it is."

"I hope not, but given who we're dealing with, I think it's best to be prepared for any eventuality."

No matter what, he would not sit by while another child was tormented and the perpetrator was allowed to go free. Once, with its tragic and very personal consequences, had been more than enough. Just like Laura, for his own reasons, he couldn't let it pass.

13

After Laura Reed left, Diana turned to her precious daughter. "I doubt you'll ever understand how terrible I feel about not being here for you while you were going through this. I'm so ashamed that I didn't see how much pain you were in."

"It doesn't matter," Misty said staunchly. "You've had your own stuff going on."

"That's no excuse," Diana told her. "I'm an adult and I'm your mother. I should have seen that something wasn't right. It's my job to protect you and Jake, and I blew it."

"You didn't blow it," Misty said, tears in her eyes. "You're the best mom ever."

Diana smiled at Misty's determined defense. "Maybe once upon a time," Diana said candidly. "But not lately. I'm going to fix this, sweetheart. I promise you. Not just the situation with Annabelle, but all of it. I'm going to pull myself together."

She forced a smile. "Let this be a lesson to you, Misty. Don't ever let yourself be so emotionally dependent on a man that you can't figure out who you are without him.

I wanted so badly for your father to stay that I lost sight of everything else, including who I am as a person. Believe it or not, once upon a time, I had my own goals, completely separate from us as a family. I need to get back to trying to achieve those. First, though, I'm going to get our family back on track."

"Mom, I think it's too late to fix things with Dad," Misty said, her expression hesitant as if she feared saying that hard truth aloud might be too much for Diana.

"I think you're right," Diana concurred. "I just didn't want to accept it. It's up to your dad and me to figure that out, though. And we need to do it now, so we don't go on hurting you and Jake. I guess I kept hoping I could wait him out, that he'd come to his senses and come home." She gave her daughter a rueful look. "Blinders, huh?"

"Pretty much," Misty confirmed.

Diana reached across the table for Misty's hand. "Do you want to talk about this situation with Annabelle some more before I call your dad?"

Misty shook her head. "And I don't want to be here when you tell him."

"You can stay in your room, if you like. Why don't you take some cookies and milk upstairs for you and your brother?"

Misty's eyes widened with surprise. "You baked cookies today?"

The shock on her daughter's face was too telling. Things evidently hadn't been the way they should have been around here for far too long. "I did. I was a little distracted, so they might be a bit brown around the edges, but I think they're edible."

Misty bounced out of her chair and threw her arms around her. "Thank you, thank you, thank you."

"They're just cookies," Diana said, even as she realized that to Misty they were far more. They were a hint that things might be returning to normal, or at least to whatever the new normal might be. It shook her to realize how little her children had come to expect from her.

When Misty had filled a plate with the chocolate chip cookies that had always been her favorite, she poured two glasses of milk, then gave Diana another hug before heading upstairs, shouting for Jake en route.

"There are cookies," she sang out. "Mom baked!"

Diana closed her eyes against yet another potential flood of tears, then determinedly reached for the portable phone and took it outside.

"Les, it's me," she said when her husband picked up. "You need to come over."

"Is this some new trumped-up crisis?" he asked, his tone resigned. "Give it up, Diana. I'm not moving back home."

She drew in a deep breath at his harsh, justifiably suspicious words, then said, "I've finally accepted that, but you do need to come over. There's a problem with Misty and it's serious."

"What's happened to Misty?" he asked, real panic immediately evident in his voice. "Was she in an accident? Is she okay?"

"Physically she's fine, but you're not going to believe what she's been going through on her own, because you and I have been too preoccupied to pay close enough attention to her."

He sucked in a breath, then blurted, "Dear God, she's not pregnant, is she?"

"No, but instead of throwing out possibilities, could you please come over here so I can fill you in on the facts?"

"I'll be there in twenty minutes," he said at once.

Diana turned off the phone with a sigh. Whatever had gone on between the two of them, however badly their marriage had deteriorated, she couldn't deny that Les loved his kids. He might not always know the best way to demonstrate that love, but she knew she could count on him to be there for them. She was the one who had to get used to the idea of living without him.

As of today, though, there was no longer any question that she had to find a way to do just that.

Cookies or no cookies, tonight was turning out to be the worst night of Misty's entire life. Her dad came over after the call from her mom. Even in her room, she could hear them in the living room, fighting like always. When she couldn't stand it, she went to the top of the steps and sat listening. Okay, she knew eavesdropping was bad, but they were fighting about *her*. She figured she was entitled to hear what they were saying.

"How could you let a thing like this happen?" her father shouted. "You say it's been going on since school started. Aren't you supposed to know when your own child is being tormented by another kid? If you're too self-absorbed to pay any attention to what's going on with Misty and Jake, maybe I should fight for custody."

That was the very last straw for Misty. She bolted down the steps and into the living room.

"No!" she shouted at her startled father. "Don't you dare blame Mom. She didn't know because I didn't want her to know. She was already falling apart because of you. I didn't think she could take any more."

Her dad seemed to wilt under the attack. "Oh, sweetie, I'm sorry," he said, reaching for her.

Misty pulled away. "Too late. And what are you sorry for anyway? What happened to me? Leaving us? What? Being sorry doesn't help."

"I think we all need to calm down," Diana said, her tone amazingly strong.

She sounded more like her old self than she had in months, Misty thought, regarding her with shock.

"Let's sit down and talk this through," her mom said in that same quietly determined tone.

Amazingly, her father sat right down on the sofa next to Misty. Her mother settled on her other side.

"Misty, we are both terribly sorry that we've been so caught up in our own drama that we completely missed that you were in trouble," Diana said gently.

"Don't apologize for Dad," Misty said with a sniff.

Her father put his arm around her, and this time she didn't pull away. She let herself lean into him, seeking strength just as she had when she'd run home hurt.

"I *am* sorry, kiddo," he said. "But we know about everything now, and we are on your side a hundred percent. Whatever it takes, we're going to settle this once and for all."

"I just want it all to go away," Misty told him. She tried once again to get some backing for what she thought the best solution to be. "Maybe we could pretend it never happened."

Her dad only hugged her a little closer. "Believe me, I can understand why you'd want that, but you know it would be wrong to let Annabelle get away with this, right? It's not just about you. She could do this to someone else. Bullies don't always pick just one target. It's essential that they learn a lesson and learn it fast."

"But I'm the only one she thinks is after her boyfriend," Misty persisted.

Her mom gave her a questioning look. "And are you?"

"No way," Misty said indignantly.

"Then what makes you think there's not another girl who might accidentally look at Greg the wrong way and get Annabelle all freaked out?" her mom asked. "Or that he's not making a pass at half a dozen other girls right now that she might not know about yet? You're her target today, but it could easily be someone else tomorrow. She has to be stopped. Honey, you do see that, don't you?"

Misty heaved a resigned sigh. "I guess."

"You know your mother's right," her dad said, regarding her mother with approval for the first time in months. "And on Monday morning we'll be right there with you while the principal decides how to handle all this. And your mom says Helen Decatur-Whitney called earlier, and she's handling all the legalities of getting this nonsense taken down from the internet. It could take a little longer than we'd like, but she assured your mom it will be done. Your teacher got her involved."

"Ms. Reed's been really great," Misty said. "Even when I wouldn't tell her what was going on, she let me know she was on my side. She believed in me from the beginning."

"Then I guess we owe her," her dad said.

He stood up then. Misty regarded him hopefully. "Couldn't you stay here tonight?" she pleaded, knowing that now she was the one who was delusional. Staying wasn't an option, even under these conditions.

He gave her a sad look. "It's not a good idea, sweetie. But you can reach me on my cell anytime you need me."

"You're never coming back, are you?" she concluded. She glanced at her mother. "I know I'm the one who said that before, but I was still kinda hoping…"

Her dad swallowed hard. "Sorry, kiddo. I can't do it. We'll still spend lots and lots of time together. Your mom and I will work all of that out."

Misty wanted to hate him for leaving, but how could she? Hadn't she recognized for months now that the marriage was over? It was her mom who'd been living in the dream world. Her mom and maybe Jake, though he didn't say much about it. She was sixteen. She shouldn't act like a baby about it.

She stood up and hurled herself into his arms. "I love you, Daddy."

"I love you more," he whispered back.

When she looked into his face right before he turned and walked away, she saw that his cheeks were damp with tears.

Then she dared a glance at her mom and saw that, though her cheeks, too, were damp, she no longer looked devastated. She looked resigned and, despite that, stronger somehow. She reached for Misty's hand.

"It's going to be okay," she assured Misty. "We're all going to be okay."

As desperately as she'd wanted to, though, Misty couldn't entirely believe her.

* * *

Laura's briefing to Betty Donovan when she reached her by phone on Sunday drew immediate outrage.

"You say there are seminude pictures of this child online, pictures that Annabelle somehow doctored to put Misty's face on them?"

"There are," Laura confirmed. "Helen Decatur-Whitney is working to get everything removed, so I made sure we got copies of every single post and every picture just in case that happened before I could fill you in. Helen has her own copies, and I'm almost certain that she's spoken to Carter Rollins to ensure that the police have whatever they might need in case the Dawsons want to file charges. Helen mentioned something about invasion of privacy, fraud and libel when I spoke to her earlier today. She's discussed that possibility with Misty's mother, too."

"But no one's gone to Annabelle's family at this point?" Betty asked.

"That ball's in your court, at least from the school perspective," Laura confirmed. "Helen suggested we have a meeting tomorrow morning to determine the next step. She thinks we ought to have a plan that takes all aspects of this into account."

"Yes, that would probably be wise," Betty said. "I'll ask Hamilton Reynolds if he wants to be there. As chairman of the school board, he should know what's going on. We're not going to be able to keep a lid on this."

"And J. C. Fullerton has asked to attend," Laura said.

"I'm not sure what he could add at this point," Betty said. "Was including him your idea? I understand you've been seeing him recently."

Laura heard a hint of judgment in Betty's tone. She seemed to have a particularly jaded outlook on the social lives of her teachers.

"J.C.'s involvement has nothing to do with me. Misty went to him to try to get out of school when things first started getting out of hand. She wasn't forthcoming about her reasons, so he and I have been trying to get to the bottom of this for a few weeks now. He's very concerned about the situation and feels he has a vested interest in the outcome. He takes his responsibility as her physician very seriously."

"Okay, then," Betty said, apparently resigned. "Sounds as if we'll have a full house tomorrow morning. Nine o'clock, my office."

"I'll let J.C. and Helen know," Laura said. "You'll alert the Dawsons, or would you prefer that I do it?"

"I'll call them. I want them to know I'm all over this."

Laura hated to bring it up but felt she had to. "What about the Litchfields?"

"Not until we've determined a course of action. I'll make an appointment with them for tomorrow afternoon."

"Will you want me there for that?"

"Let me give that some thought and let's see how tomorrow morning's meeting goes. I'm torn between facing them on my own or bringing in all the backup I can muster," she said grimly.

"I know you didn't ask for my opinion," Laura said, "but I'd opt for the backup."

"Much as I hate to say it," Betty said ruefully, "I'm leaning that way myself. We know Annabelle's going to deny everything, and Mariah's going to leap to her defense. The only thing not certain is whether Mr. Litchfield will prove to be more reasonable."

"All the more reason to have voices of reason right there with you. I've witnessed a few things myself. Helen has the proof in black-and-white. They won't be able to deny that."

Betty chuckled, though there was little humor behind it. "Have you seen the size of Mariah's blinders? None of the designers make sunglasses that big or that dark." She drew in a deep breath. "Not to worry, though. I think we have Annabelle dead to rights on this. If I have my way, tomorrow will be her last day at Serenity High School for a very, very long time."

"Do you think they're going to throw Annabelle out on her sorry behind?" Katie asked Misty in a whisper when she met her outside of school on Monday morning.

Misty shuddered. "A part of me almost hopes they don't," Misty admitted.

Katie regarded her with shock. "How can you say that? Jail's not good enough, if you ask me."

"Because you're just a little bloodthirsty," Misty said, grateful to have such a loyal friend.

"No, because it's what she deserves after everything she's done to you," Katie countered. "I can't believe you still think she should be let off the hook."

"Not because I'm not mad," Misty said. "Or because I think she doesn't deserve it. I just can't help thinking about what her friends are going to do. They could make my life hell for getting her kicked out of school."

"Only if they're idiots like her," Katie said.

"Don't you think they probably are?" Misty said.

"Come on. Who else would fawn all over her? Just idiots who think she'll remember them when she's some big pop superstar."

"As if," Katie said. "She probably won't even admit she came from Serenity. It's not high-class enough for her. I'll bet she even dumps Greg the first chance she gets. He might be the big man on campus here, but he's still from a farm outside of town. She's gonna wake up one day and decide that he's not nearly good enough for her."

"I just wish she'd figured that out because he's a liar and a cheater, not because of who his dad is. There's nothing wrong with being a farmer or a farmer's son, just with being a total jerk."

"Agreed," Katie said. "I guess I'd better go to class. I wish I could come to the meeting with you."

"I wish you could, too. I'm gonna need a friendly face."

"Hey, everybody in there is going to be on your side," Katie reminded her. "You're not on trial. Annabelle is, and she won't even be there this morning, right?"

Misty nodded. But even though she might not have to face Annabelle this morning, she knew there was bound to be a confrontation before the day ended. It scared the daylights out of her.

"I want that girl out of this school and far away from my daughter," Les Dawson declared before Betty could even say whatever comments she'd prepared before the meeting.

Laura regarded the principal with sympathy. She finally had a better understanding of the difficult role of being caught between outraged parents, teachers and the rules. Not everyone always had the same agenda or the same balancing act to achieve.

"Believe me, I totally understand your anger," Betty told Misty's father. "If my child had been a victim of these unconscionable rumors online, I'd be out for blood, too. But there are procedures we have to follow."

"As long as one of them includes kicking Annabelle out of school, I can live with your procedures," Les said. "Otherwise, I'll pull Misty out of school and raise a stink that will tear this school district apart."

"Dad, no," Misty protested.

"Les, I don't think we need to resort to threats," school board chairman Hamilton Reynolds said. "Everyone in this room understands what's at stake."

It was J.C. who interceded, "Maybe we need to find out what the next steps are. Betty, do you have a plan? What has to happen next?"

"Since the majority of the bullying took place online and under a screen name—" she began.

"It happened here, too," Misty said, speaking up so softly it was almost hard to hear her. "In the halls. The stuff she posted was thrown in my face by Annabelle and her friends and Greg Bennett and his buddies."

Betty sighed. "I was afraid of that, but at least there's little question then of who's behind it."

Helen spoke up then. "I've been working with Carter Rollins and a judge. We should have confirmation very soon of who that screen name is registered to. I would be very surprised if it turns out to belong to anyone other than Annabelle. Once that link is established, there will be no way for her to deny that she was behind this campaign to go after Misty."

"I'd like to have that proof in hand before we call in the Litchfields," Hamilton Reynolds said, then held up his hand to fend off an immediate protest from Misty's father. "I know you want this settled immediately. So do I. I also want us to make sure we've covered every legality."

"He's right," Helen said. "Better to take a little extra time now, because once this ball starts rolling, it's going to pick up speed. Mariah Litchfield won't sit by and watch her daughter be tossed out of school quietly, not if she thinks there's even a tiny hint that we haven't crossed every *t* and dotted every *i*. She'll fight like a grizzly to protect her daughter and somehow spin it so it looks as if this is some trumped-up vendetta by a jealous classmate."

"That's absurd," Diana Dawson said indignantly. "She wouldn't dare to try to turn this around and make Misty the one at fault." She winced, shaking her head. "What am I saying? Of course she will! She's already called me once to protest Misty's treatment of Annabelle at the fall festival."

"That's exactly what she does," Betty said, her tone resigned. "And that's why this poor child's behavior is so abominable, because her mother's never held her accountable for a single thing."

"I told you it was going to get worse," Misty said in a small voice. She whirled on J.C. "You should have just given me a note to get out of school."

J.C. gave her a sympathetic look. "We've established that I couldn't do that. And, though it might not seem like it right this second, this situation is going to get a whole lot better. I imagine by Christmas break, you'll have forgotten all about this."

Misty gave him a disbelieving look. "Are you kidding? By Christmas I probably won't be able to show my face here at all, note or no note."

J.C. winced under her scathing scowl. "I'm sorry. You're right. Making things better will take time, but maybe it will help a little if you just remember how many people are on your side. Everyone in this room is here to help you get through this."

"And Katie Townsend has been a rock for you through all of this, too," Laura reminded her. "She won't let you down. I'm sure you have lots of other friends you'll be able to count on."

"Who?" Misty retorted. "Katie's the only one who hasn't been scared off by Annabelle and her crowd."

Betty regarded her sympathetically. "I know it must seem that way, Misty, but it's only because none of us understood what was happening. Every teacher in this school will be on full alert from now on. If anyone tries to retaliate because of what's likely to happen to Annabelle, they will be stopped. You're going to be safe here."

Laura could see that Misty was still skeptical. How could she not be? Up to now the system had failed her miserably. Even she, though she'd been more attuned to the problem than most, hadn't put the pieces together for weeks.

"Misty, what can we do to reassure you?" she asked. "What would you like to see happen?"

"I want us to forget all about it," she said miserably. "Please."

Les Dawson clearly saw his child's unhappiness, but he was already shaking his head. "Not a chance," he muttered. "Helen, I want every action in the book taken in this, here at school, in the courts, whatever it takes. Nobody is tormenting my child and getting away with it."

"Not even if it's what I want?" Misty pleaded.

"Sorry, sweetheart," he said, his tone gentle. "Not even then."

J.C. stood up. "Maybe Misty and I could take a walk, while you all sort this out." He glanced at her. "Would that be okay?"

Looking relieved to have an excuse to escape, she nodded at once. He glanced at her parents and both nodded, Diana's expression full of relief.

"We'll be back in a bit," J.C. said, opening the door and showing Misty out.

Laura looked around and saw exhaustion on every face in the room. She figured her appearance was no less haggard.

"Whatever we decide," she said, keeping her gaze on Betty, "we have to be sure that child is protected from more bullying. I think she's had just about as much as she can handle."

"Agreed," Betty said at once.

"Should we take her out of school?" Diana asked hesitantly. "I know it sounds extreme, but maybe she'd be happier someplace else."

Les shook his head. "Or maybe she'll think she's being punished, even though she's not the one who's done anything wrong."

"But if she'd feel safe again," Diana argued.

Hamilton Reynolds reached over and gave her arm a consoling pat. "I know your first instinct is to protect her, but I think Les could be right. Sending her to another school might send the wrong message to everyone. That said, though, maybe it should be Misty's decision. And maybe we shouldn't ask her until we've dealt with Annabelle and see how that's played out."

"I'm inclined to agree," Helen said. "And I honestly don't think we'll have to wait long. I think we can handle this by the end of the day today, tomorrow at the latest. Betty, I'll call you the minute I know for sure that we have indisputable proof that these posts were made by Annabelle."

"I want to be here when you confront that girl and her parents," Les insisted.

"Not a good idea," Hamilton Reynolds said.

"I'll be here," Helen told Les. "Your interests and Misty's will be protected. You'll have your chance to face the Litchfields when we take legal action."

Diana nodded. "Helen's right. There's nothing to be gained by causing a scene just because we'd like to tear the child's hair out."

Les turned to her with a surprised look. "You, too?"

Diana nodded, a faint smile on her lips. "You have no idea."

Laura saw him reach for Diana's hand and give it a squeeze. Maybe there was no reconciliation in store for those two, but at least they'd found one important thing about which they could agree. From what she knew of disintegrating marriages, it was at least a start toward healing.

14

"Want to take a walk into town to get something to drink at Wharton's?" J.C. asked Misty once they'd left the tense meeting behind.

She gave him a surprised look. "Wouldn't that be, like, skipping school?"

He laughed. "Probably, but you're with me and your principal and parents know it, so I think we can get away with it just this once." He gave her a stern look. "But just this once."

"Got it," she said, then cast a sideways glance in his direction. "I never really left school when I skipped before, you know."

"Really? What did you do?"

"Hung out in a stairwell after the bell rang and did my homework. It was only two classes," she said with a shrug. "At least until those pictures got posted. Then I hid out in my room at home."

"With your mother's permission?"

She shook her head. "I was pretty careful, and she wasn't really noticing a lot of stuff at home then, anyway. She's better now. It's the one good thing about all this. It kinda, like, woke her up or something."

"You know what they say, most clouds have a silver lining," he said.

She rolled her eyes. "That is so lame."

"Probably, but it's actually pretty true. Sometimes, though, you have to look really hard to find them."

When they reached Wharton's, Grace managed to hide whatever surprise she might have felt at their arrival. She was also wise enough not to ask a lot of questions about Misty not being at school. J.C. had no idea if it was a rare display of discretion or if she'd heard what was going on and knew it was best not discussed in front of Misty.

"What can I get for the two of you in the middle of the morning?" she asked cheerfully. "I can still rustle up some eggs or pancakes, if you want them. Or would you rather go hog wild and have ice cream? A burger? A milk shake?"

Misty's eyes lit up, and she looked hopefully at J.C. "A chocolate milk shake would be really good."

"Yes, it would," he agreed readily, giving Grace a wink to indicate he was well aware that he was about to finally break his vow to steer clear of the highly caloric shakes. "Make that two, Grace."

After the woman had gone, Misty gave him a curious look. "How come you're being so nice to me? I kinda put you on the spot when I came to your office, but you don't seem mad about it."

"Because I'm not. I was glad you felt you could come to me, even if I wasn't able to help you the way you wanted me to."

"It's because of me that you and Ms. Reed are dating, isn't it?" she said, suddenly looking very pleased with herself. "That's one of those silver lining things, I'll bet."

J.C. smiled. "As a matter of fact, it is."

"Are you serious about her? Because she's really cool. I wouldn't want her to get hurt."

"That seems to be the general consensus around town, that hurting Ms. Reed would be a really bad idea."

She tilted her head, studying him. "So, do you think you'll get married?"

J.C. knew he should be used to how precocious kids were these days, but it always surprised him when they failed to censor their curiosity. "I'm not sure that's a subject I should be discussing with you," he said, suddenly feeling incredibly awkward and old.

"Because I'm just a kid?"

"No, because it's a topic that Ms. Reed and I should probably discuss before I talk about it with anyone else. And, before you get any ideas, that does not mean it's something we're discussing right away."

"But you haven't ruled it out or anything, have you?" she pressed determinedly. "Because, if you have, you should tell her. You know, so she won't get her hopes up."

J.C. chuckled at her persistence. At least she was smiling for a change, so he was grateful for that much.

"Why don't we change the subject?" he suggested.

"And talk about what? Annabelle?"

"I was thinking more about how you're feeling about school these days."

"Scared," she said without hesitation. "I know I'm

supposed to feel good about all these people being on my side and stuff, but you don't get what kids are like."

"Actually I do, and not just because I'm a pediatrician, either."

She regarded him skeptically. "All grown-ups claim they get it, but they don't. Not really."

"What if I told you that I have some firsthand experience with bullying?" he said. "Would you believe me then?"

"You were bullied? No way," she said with unmistakable astonishment. "Why? Were you a geek or something?"

"It wasn't me. It was my little brother. He had some problems, and the kids at school made his life pretty awful. They were mean right to his face whenever they got the chance."

Her eyes widened at that. "But you stood up for him, right? I mean, that's what brothers are supposed to do. Even my little brother, Jake, stood up for me. He got a black eye because of it," she said, clearly proud of him.

"That *is* what brothers should do," J.C. confirmed. "Not necessarily getting beat up, but taking a stance for someone who's weaker."

"I'm not weaker than Jake," she said indignantly.

"True," he said hurriedly. "But you were the one under attack from a bully."

"What happened with your brother?" she asked, giving him her full attention and leaving untouched the milk shake that Grace had just served.

"It got worse once I wasn't at the same school. We didn't tell our folks, which I realize now we should have.

If the teachers saw what was happening, they didn't intervene the way Ms. Reed has."

"He must have felt so alone," Misty said sympathetically.

"He must have," Jake said, then shook off the memory of the rest. He couldn't bring up the tragic ending. He just wanted Misty to see that *she* wasn't alone. "I told you this so you'll understand just how important it is to me and Ms. Reed and your parents to make sure that you're safe and can go back to being a happy, carefree student again. Whatever it takes, we're going to fix it. Can you try to trust us to protect you? You're not in this on your own anymore, Misty."

She continued to look skeptical. "I want to believe you. But even with all of you, you can't be everywhere. And stuff gets posted online, no matter what."

"I think that will stop once the other kids see how serious this is and what could happen to them," he said. "It goes beyond whatever punishment happens at school. There are legal consequences, as well."

She shrugged again. "I guess."

"And we will be around, Misty. That's a promise," he said with feeling, even though he knew it probably sounded empty to her right now. "Now let's head back over to the school and see what decisions have been made while we were over here playing hooky."

He paid for their milk shakes and they walked back to the high school.

Just outside Betty Donovan's office, Misty grinned at him. "Playing hooky with you is a lot more fun than hiding in the stairwell."

"Well, the next time you feel you have absolutely no

other choice but to skip class, give me a call. Not that I normally condone skipping, you understand."

She grinned. "Yeah, I get it."

"And if you can't reach me, go straight to Ms. Reed."

Her grin spread. "Do you think she'd play hooky with me?"

"I doubt that, but she will help. Believe that, okay?"

"Okay," she said with slightly more confidence.

He hoped she believed him. He hoped she understood that no matter how desperate she got, he—and Laura—intended to be right there as backup for her. She wasn't going to be alone in this ever again. Not the way his little brother had been. He'd let one child down. He wouldn't do it again.

Not unexpectedly, the meeting with the Litchfields got out of hand very quickly, Laura thought as she sat to the side and listened. Annabelle stared straight ahead in sullen silence as Betty explained to her parents in cut-and-dried detail exactly what the school's bullying policy was.

Mariah's gaze narrowed at the recitation. "Why are you telling this to us?"

"Because you need to know that this is serious business. Bullying isn't taken lightly."

But before Betty could describe Annabelle's recent behavior, Mariah whipped around and focused on Laura. "This is all because of you, isn't it?" she said, fire in her eyes. "I heard all about the way you went after Annabelle at the fall festival. I have no idea why you have it in for my daughter, but you won't get away with it. I'll have you fired before the week's out."

Don Litchfield turned on his wife. "Maybe we should hear the rest of this before you go off on some crusade, Mariah. What's Annabelle supposedly done, Betty?"

"Your daughter has an account on a social-networking site," Betty began.

Don looked perplexed. "Big deal. All the kids do."

Betty nodded. "But not all of them use those sites to start ugly rumors about their classmates and to post doctored photos of them posing with virtually no clothes on," she stated, her words matter-of-fact and all the more chilling because of it.

Don suddenly looked a lot less certain.

"You're saying that Annabelle has done that?" Mariah said with outraged disbelief. "You're just as crazy as she is." She nodded in Laura's direction.

Don frowned at her. "Can it, Mariah. I want to hear the rest of this. Betty wouldn't be telling us this if she weren't certain of her facts. Otherwise she'd be opening herself up to a lawsuit for slander." He held Betty's gaze. "Isn't that right?"

"That's a hundred percent right," Betty concurred. "The school system lawyers are all over this."

"Go on," he said tightly.

Something in his tone had Annabelle sitting up a little straighter. For the first time there was a hint of real fear in her eyes. Laura thought she was finally realizing that her game was over, that she'd been caught dead to rights.

"Do you recognize this girl?" Betty asked, holding out the damning photos.

Don's face turned ashen. "It looks like Misty Dawson, at least I think that's her. But it sure as heck isn't her body. She's a skinny little thing."

"They were posted online by Annabelle," Betty told him.

Don faced his daughter. "Annabelle, what do you know about this?"

She shrugged.

He gave her a stern look. "That's not an answer. How did these pictures get posted on your page? Did you put them up there?"

As he waited for a reply, he handed the pictures to his wife. "You want to try to defend this, Mariah?"

Mariah glanced at the pictures and covered her mouth with her hand. She turned to her daughter, her expression slightly frantic as she saw all her plans for Annabelle starting to unravel.

She must be seeing the end of yet another dream, Laura thought with more sympathy than she'd ever imagined having for the woman.

"You would never post filthy pictures like this, would you, sweetheart?" Mariah asked Annabelle, her voice shaky.

Annabelle looked at the floor, not acknowledging the question by so much as a blink.

"Annabelle!" her father snapped, finally grabbing her attention. "Did you do it? And if you tell me you didn't, I'd like to hear a really, really good explanation about how you think it could have happened."

Annabelle gave him a defiant look, folded her arms across her chest and returned her gaze to the floor, remaining stubbornly silent.

Betty stepped in. "There's more," she said quietly. "These are a few of her posts about Misty. There are many, many more if you need further evidence that the bullying has been nasty. And you can see by the dates of the posts that it's been ongoing."

As Don read the pages, his eyes widening with dismay, Betty said, "While you're looking those over, I'd like you to think about what you'd expect me to do if the tables were turned, if this were Annabelle who'd been tormented like this."

Don tried to hand the pages to Mariah, but she waved him off. "I've seen enough, and I don't believe for a minute that Annabelle had anything to do with this," she said with pure bravado. "Someone must have gotten hold of her password and posted those pictures and comments. Why on earth would she bother attacking Misty Dawson?"

Betty glanced toward Laura, indicating she should answer.

"We believe it's because Annabelle found out that Greg Bennett has asked Misty out on several occasions. Rather than blaming Greg, she's taken her anger out on Misty."

Mariah rolled her eyes in disbelief. "Please, Greg knows he's lucky that a girl like Annabelle even looks at him. Why would he cheat on her?"

"Because he can," Laura said. "And so you know, Misty has rebuffed all of his advances, but that hasn't stopped him. And that's only infuriated Annabelle more." She faced Annabelle, who'd finally looked up at the mention of Greg's name. "Isn't that right?"

Annabelle's cheeks had grown increasingly flushed as Laura spoke. She turned on her furiously. "Okay, yes, I hate Misty. She has no right to Greg. He's *my* boyfriend."

"Misty's never been interested in Greg. She's never encouraged him," Laura reminded her gently. "Greg's the one who's pursued her."

Though she looked vaguely rattled by Laura's calm certainty, Annabelle wasn't giving up the pretense of being the victim without a fight. "Well, she has to be sending out some kind of message for him to keep chasing her. She's nothing but a little slut."

Even Mariah finally looked taken aback by the venom in her daughter's voice. "Annabelle, that's enough. You're not helping the situation."

"I've heard enough," Don said, his expression resigned. He faced Betty. "What's next?"

"I have no choice but to suspend her," Betty said. "I think you can expect legal action from the Dawsons. If there's so much as a hint of another incident, Annabelle will be expelled."

Laura thought Annabelle finally looked shaken, rather than defiant, but it was her mother's reaction that startled Laura. Mariah looked genuinely stunned, as if she'd had no idea where this was leading.

"But that will all go on her record," she protested. "Don, we can't allow Annabelle's future to be destroyed by a childish prank."

"There is nothing childish about what Annabelle did," he said. "She's old enough to understand exactly what she was doing. Like Betty said, we need to think about how we'd feel if someone did this to Annabelle. We'd be out for blood."

"But she's our daughter," Mariah argued. "We have to be on her side."

"I'm always on her side," he said. "But sometimes

that means making sure she learns that actions have consequences."

"What if we just took her out of school?" Mariah pleaded. "We could get her into a private school. None of this would have to come out. Wouldn't that be best for everyone?"

"You'd send me away?" Annabelle said, her eyes wide.

"Not far," Mariah said. She rushed on, clearly warming to the idea. "There are excellent schools in Charleston or Columbia. I know it's already late in the fall, but I'm sure we could pull a few strings, find a spot for you somewhere. Don't think of it as punishment, sweetheart. You'll have so many more opportunities. You'll make better friends, the sort of friends who'll last a lifetime, friends from good families with great contacts."

"And where's the money for this expensive private school to come from?" Don asked practically. "Out of her college fund? Then what?"

"I'll ask my parents," Mariah said desperately. "When I've explained, they'll want to help."

Don shook his head. "I'm against this, Mariah. Annabelle needs to stay right here and learn a lesson. You've gotten her off the hook every single time she's done something wrong. That needs to stop."

"We'll talk about this at home," Mariah said, refusing to back down.

"And in the meantime, Annabelle is suspended for two weeks," Betty said. "I'll see that she receives her assignments, so she can keep up with her schoolwork. At the end of the two weeks, we'll see where we stand. If you decide you want to pursue a transfer, let me know."

"Could I go back to my last class now?" Annabelle asked. "You know, so I can at least say goodbye to my friends before I'm banished?"

"I'm afraid not," Betty said. "And you're not allowed on school property until the suspension is lifted. That includes all school activities. You won't be permitted to attend Friday night's football game or to participate as a cheerleader."

The full implication of the punishment finally seemed to sink in. "But Greg counts on me being there," she protested weakly.

"I'm sure he'll manage just fine without you this once," Betty said, her gaze unyielding.

"I guess I'm supposed to live on bread and water, too," Annabelle remarked bitterly.

"It might not be a bad idea," her father muttered. "And I'm going to stand right there while you post a sincere apology to Misty on your page online. Once that's done and had time to circulate, you'll no longer have access to the internet. I believe we'd better take away your cell phone, too, so you won't be texting anyone. Now let's go."

Laura waited until the door had closed behind them before turning to Betty. "That actually went better than I'd anticipated," she said. "Don Litchfield seems like a reasonable man, a really concerned parent who gets what a huge mistake his daughter made."

"Seems that way," Betty agreed. "But I wouldn't do any celebrating just yet. Something tells me Mariah's just warming up."

"Do you think they'll decide to have Annabelle transfer? That could be a real blessing for Misty."

"It could be, but I have my doubts. All those fancy schools Mariah is picturing have the same strict standards about bullying that we have. Once they get wind of why Annabelle's parents are interested in a transfer this late in the fall, they're not likely to welcome her with open arms."

"You don't think if the parents'—or grandparents'—pockets are deep enough, they might look the other way?"

"Possibly," Betty said. "But the side of me that still believes in right and wrong hopes not."

Paula had received a call from Laura Reed asking that their get-together be postponed until five-thirty. She gathered that things were, if not under control, at least on their way to being resolved.

As Paula put aside her paintbrush, frustrated yet again with her inability to get the details on this latest work as delicate as they should be, Katie slipped through the back gate.

"Grandma, it's beautiful," she said, awe in her voice as she came to stand beside Paula.

Paula glanced at her. "You think so?"

"It's so real I can almost smell the scent," Katie insisted. "It's a stargazer lily, right? How do you do that? When I draw or paint, it never looks anything like the way I pictured it in my head."

"It takes years of practice to get it right," Paula told her. "Are you interested in painting?"

To her disappointment, Katie shook her head. "It's too frustrating."

Paula smiled at her. "To do anything really, really

well, you'll face frustration from time to time. That's why I'm often called a perfectionist. For instance, I could show you right now all the things I see that are wrong with this painting."

"No way," Katie protested. "It makes me want to touch it to see if it's a flower instead of a picture. See, it even has that waxy look on the petals and the tiny little spots and that blush of pink. There's even a drop of dew. It's just right."

"Then it's yours," Paula told her. "I'd love for you to have it. Just promise not to let anyone put it in a showing of my work years from now, so some critic can write that I'd clearly lost my touch."

"Grandma, stop saying that," Katie said impatiently. "You haven't lost your touch at all."

Paula smiled at the fierce defense. "Thanks, sweetheart. Now, what brings you by? And on a Monday, no less, when you know Liz hasn't brought over any cookies."

"I wanted to thank you. There was a huge meeting at school today. I think Annabelle's finally going to get what she deserves. I haven't talked to Misty all day, and nobody saw Annabelle this afternoon, but I think that must mean she was kicked out. I know it's because you went to Ms. Reed." She threw her arms around Paula and hugged her tightly. "Thank you so much."

"I just did what needed to be done," Paula said. "And you deserve a lot of the credit for coming to me. Thanks to you I was able to point Ms. Reed in the right direction to get this resolved."

For an instant Katie looked alarmed. "You didn't tell her that it was me who told you, did you?"

"I promised you I wouldn't," Paula reassured her. "But you must know that she probably guessed. You don't need to worry about it, though. I was very impressed with her. She knows the situation requires discretion. And I'm meeting with her shortly so she can tell me how things turned out." She glanced at her watch. "In fact, I'd better get this paint off my hands and head over to The Corner Spa right now. I don't want to keep her waiting."

Once again, lines of worry creased Katie's forehead. "Mom doesn't know about all this, does she? And about what I did?"

"Not from me," Paula verified. "But remember that your mom is married to Cal. I'm sure he's put it all together by now." She tweaked her nose. "And I think you should remember that you could have gone to your mother about this. Not that I wasn't very happy to have you trust me enough to speak to me, but you should understand that you can always trust your mom, too."

"I know," Katie said earnestly. "It was just that I'd promised Misty I'd keep quiet and not tell Mom or Cal, so I needed to find a way to get help without breaking that promise."

"Understood," Paula said. "Do you want a ride over to the spa with me?"

"No. I have my bike. I'll head on home. I want to call Misty and see what happened. I'll get my painting later, if that's okay."

"It's fine. Maybe I'll fiddle with it a little more till it's better."

Katie grinned at her. "Remember what you used to

tell me when I was a little kid and wanted to be prettier? You said it was impossible to improve on perfection."

Paula laughed. "You were exactly the way God intended. This picture…" She shook her head. "Not so much."

"Well, I think it's perfect," Katie said staunchly. "Gotta run, Grandma."

"Okay, then. Be careful riding home."

"Always," Katie said, darting out the back gate.

"And wear your helmet," Paula shouted after her.

"Got it," Katie said, her voice fading as she evidently rode off down the street.

Paula smiled as she went inside. Oh, to have even half that much energy again.

15

Laura wanted nothing more than to head directly home, crawl beneath the covers and sleep for a week to make up for too many restless nights since this situation had come to a head and too much tension today. Instead, she had her promised get-together with Paula Vreeland ahead of her.

News had apparently already leaked out about what had happened at school today, because Maddie Maddox caught her when she arrived at The Corner Spa and pulled her aside.

"I can't believe what I'm hearing," she told Laura. "Is Misty going to be okay?"

"I suppose that depends on what happens next," Laura replied.

"Annabelle's been suspended, though?"

"For two weeks," she confirmed.

Maddie shook her head. "What was that girl thinking?"

"She wasn't thinking, obviously," Laura said. "She was acting out of spite and anger with absolutely no thought to the consequences, either to Misty or to herself."

"How'd Mariah take it?" Maddie asked. "Will she turn on you and Betty?"

"She threatened me early on," Laura admitted with a shrug. "But after all the facts were out there, I think she forgot all about me. Her whole focus is on saving her daughter."

"At least I've figured out why you and my mother were huddled on the patio here the other day. How on earth did she get involved?"

Laura squirmed at the question. Maddie recognized her discomfort at once. "Never mind. I shouldn't have asked. Are you meeting her here again?"

Laura nodded. "I promised to fill her in."

Maddie looked up just then and smiled. "And here she is now. Hey, Mom."

"Maddie, you are not still trying to sell Laura a membership, are you?"

"Actually I'm thinking I should give her a six-month trial membership to thank her for dealing with this mess at school. I may not know all the details, but I do know it's turning out okay because she got involved."

"I certainly second that idea," Paula said.

Maddie grinned at Laura. "What do you say? Six months on the house?"

"Are you sure?" Laura asked, dying to accept but hesitant. "I was only doing my job."

"Nonsense," Paula said. "You went above and beyond and you know it. Don't be modest. It's highly overrated."

Maddie chuckled. "You would certainly know,

Mother. Everything I ever knew about self-confidence I learned from you."

Paula looked surprisingly pleased by the comment. "It's good to know I wasn't quite so terrible as a mother as I'd thought."

"You were never terrible," Maddie protested, looking dismayed. "Just a little caught up in your own world."

"Never a good thing for a mother, no matter the excuse," Paula said, then waved off the discussion. "Water under the bridge. I hope I've made up for it recently."

Maddie gave her an awkward hug. "You know you have. Now, head on out to the patio. It's gorgeous out there, probably one of the last days before it gets to be too chilly to sit outside. I'll bring you something from the café. Laura, will it be another smoothie? We have mango-papaya today. I can personally vouch for it. I had two before I told Susie in the café to cut me off."

"Oh, yes, please," Laura said with feeling. "The last one was fabulous, and mango-papaya sounds even better. I'll need that membership, if I keep drinking those."

"And I want a muffin, full-strength if you know what I mean," Paula said. "None of that low-fat nonsense for me."

"Done," Maddie said. "Head on out. I'll be right behind you."

Once they were seated on the patio and Maddie had brought their snack, then left them alone, Paula regarded Laura with concern.

"You look as if you've had an exhausting day."

"An exhausting *few* days," Laura confirmed. "Knowing how high the stakes were for both of these girls put a tremendous amount of pressure on me to handle this well."

"Then I'm all the more grateful that you're taking the time to fill me in."

"If it weren't for you, it would have been much more difficult to settle this. I'm the one who's grateful," Laura told her with total sincerity. "Here's where things stand."

She outlined the first steps that had been taken earlier. "Frankly, I'm hoping that the Litchfields will send Annabelle away, but we may not know that for a while. Her father seems inclined to keep her right here so she has to face all the consequences of her actions."

"There's a case to be made for that, I think," Paula said. "But it would be easier on Misty, if she were gone. How has Misty been holding up?"

"She's relieved on one level, but she's also terrified there will be fallout, that Annabelle's friends will simply pick up where she left off."

"Surely not," Paula said incredulously, then shook her head. "What am I thinking? It's entirely possible. Children and teens can be incredibly cruel. Lessons at that age aren't absorbed all that readily, either, are they?"

"That's my fear," Laura admitted.

Paula thought about the situation. "You know," she began slowly, "there is one person who might be able to intervene in this. Do you know Frances Wingate?"

"We've met," Laura said, "but she retired long before I started teaching in Serenity."

"Well, she has a very long history with a lot of parents in town. She's well respected for frank talk and for being a tough disciplinarian. I wonder if there's not some way we could capitalize on that respect."

"How?" Laura asked, eager to try anything that might help ease the situation.

"Let me think about that," Paula said. "And I'll speak to Frances. She's had some health issues recently, but I know she'd want to help if she possibly can. I'm thinking she might deliver a real wake-up call at a parents' meeting, get them to take a hard look at what their kids are up to these days, both at school and online. After all, it's the adults who bear some responsibility for letting the kids get away with this in the first place. They allow their children unlimited and uncensored internet access apparently, or something like this could never have happened."

"Talking to the parents would be a great idea," Laura said. "I'll mention the possibility to Betty in the meantime, see what she thinks."

Paula shook her head. "Let me run this by Frances first. I need to be sure she's up to it. I'll call you as soon as I've spoken to her, and we'll go from there."

Laura nodded. "Thanks for thinking of that. Though I'd like to believe this will all stop because Annabelle's been caught and suspended, deep down I know better. It's going to take vigilance to see that things improve for Misty, rather than getting much, much worse."

J.C. had been pacing in front of Laura's since six o'clock. Where on earth was she? He knew she must be worn out from the day's events. He wanted to be here for her, provide whatever support she needed. He'd brought a bottle of wine and planned to order comfort food from Rosalina's, if she'd let him.

It was nearly seven when she drove up, exiting her

car with what looked like the weight of the world on her shoulders. Her expression brightened ever-so-slightly when she saw him.

"I wasn't expecting to find you here," she said.

J.C. gave her a rueful look. "And you're not entirely happy about it, are you? Will it help if I tell you I'm here to offer aid and comfort and then go on my way?"

She seemed intrigued by his response. "Aid and comfort? Explain, please," she said as she led the way into the building and unlocked her door.

"Wine," he began, extracting the bottle from a bag. "Pizza and salad from Rosalina's." He held up their takeout menu. "See, I came fully prepared." He pointed to his last surprise, the one he thought might trump all the others. "And chocolate decadence cake from Sullivan's."

Her eyes widened, and she immediately reached for the box. "Gimme."

Grinning, J.C. held it aloft, out of her reach. "Not until you've had a bath or shower and relaxed with a glass of wine, while I take care of ordering the main course."

"I never considered the possibility before, but are you some kind of saint?"

J.C. laughed. "Hardly, but if my gesture keeps me from being tossed back out on the street, I'll take it as a good sign that I might be on my way to improving my image."

She gave him a curious look. "Was there something wrong with your image?"

"Guilt by association," he said.

"Ah, the Bill Townsend connection," she said. "Of course. I don't think that's being held against you so much anymore. I believe some of the Sweet Magnolias have told you that themselves, have they not? And I happen to know that there are a lot of moms who think you hung the moon." She grinned. "The single ones especially!"

Though she said it lightheartedly, he frowned. "You know I've never gone out with any of them, right? Single moms tend to be vulnerable. That's a bad match for a guy like me who's not looking for permanent."

It was her turn to frown. "Message received."

She turned to walk away, but he caught her by the shoulder and insisted she face him. "There was no intended message for you," he said. He held her gaze, his expression earnest. "Something changed when we met, Laura. I can't explain it, and I'm not entirely sure what's going on with us, but I'm more open to the possibilities than I ever expected to be. Can that be enough for now?"

He waited, his breath caught in his throat. The reaction surprised him. He'd never felt this kind of uncertainty before awaiting a decision from a woman. When he had ventured out on a few discreet dates, he'd been the one in control. Now it was evident that something had shifted, and Laura held all the cards. It unnerved him.

"You're really open to the possibilities?" she asked, studying his face.

"Completely open," he confirmed. "Which is not to say that I'm entirely happy about that. Turning my back on a long-held conviction about relationships isn't easy."

She smiled. "Yes, I can understand how tough it must be to back down even a tiny bit from a stance once

you've taken it. There's all that male pride and determination on the line."

"Something like that," he agreed.

There was more, of course. There was the risk to his
heart, a risk he'd vowed never again to take.

Pleased by the conversation she'd had with J.C. and
feeling surprisingly optimistic, Laura allowed herself
to soak in the tub as ordered, while they waited for the
food to arrive from Rosalina's. There was something
amazingly sexy about knowing that he was just on the
other side of the door while she lay here submerged in
a rapidly disappearing sea of fragrant bubbles.

She closed her eyes and had a sudden image of what
it would be like if the door opened and a stripped J.C.
climbed into the tub with her. She could practically feel
his hands sliding over her body, feel his slick skin next
to hers, imagine his unmistakable arousal.

"Laura!"

The sound of his voice startled her so badly, she sat
up too quickly and sloshed half the water out of the tub
and onto the floor.

"You awake?" he asked, amusement threading
through his voice.

Awake? She was so stimulated she might not sleep
for a week.

"I'm awake," she said in a voice that shook just a
little.

"The food's here. Take your time, though. I've popped
the pizza in the oven on warm."

Suddenly the thought of garlic and cheese and to-
mato sauce had her mouth watering. She realized she'd

missed lunch entirely, and, delicious though it had been, the mango-papaya smoothie hadn't quite made up for it. She was starving. Or maybe it was sexual frustration that had her craving food, all of a sudden.

She scrambled out of the tub, dried herself and mopped up the floor, then pulled on a pair of leggings and a comfortable shirt that barely reached her knees. Though it was something she often wore around the house, she had a hunch it had a morning-after vibe about it that took it a notch above casual to flat-out sexy. With her hair swept up in a careless knot, strands coming loose around her face, and just a touch of lipstick, she had a pretty good idea of J.C.'s likely reaction. Tongue-tied would be nice, especially since that's the way he often made her feel.

When she wandered into the kitchen, she saw that he'd made himself at home. The table had been set, the wine poured and the aroma of the pizza filled the room.

"You are very handy to have around," she said, catching him off guard as he rinsed off the cutting board he'd apparently used to chop a few additions to Rosalina's traditional house salad.

"It's my aim to please," he said as he turned, then blinked. "Holy-moley!"

She smiled at that. "Interpret, please."

"Did we have sex and I missed it? Because that's how you look, as if you just crawled out of my bed."

"Not yet," she said softly, holding his gaze. "And my bed's closer."

Even as the bold words came out of her mouth, she realized this was exactly the moment she'd been hoping for, the chance to shake things up between them, to take the relationship to the next level. It was risky, but what was life without risks? Boring and dull, that's what, and she'd had a whole lot of that for way too long. She absolutely refused to let a long-ago mistake shape her entire future.

A questioning look crossed his face. "Laura? What exactly are you saying?"

"If you can't tell, I must not be saying it right."

"It sounds as if you're no longer hungry for food," he hedged.

She smiled. "I am, but I have this other hunger. It caught me by surprise. How about you?"

He shook his head as if trying to clear it. "You've been surprising me since the day we met."

"And the hunger thing? Where do you stand on that?"

He took two steps until he was right in front of her, then leaned down and touched his lips to hers. "Same page as you, apparently," he said with feeling, then pulled her into his arms for a kiss that was longer, deeper and more amazing than anything Laura had imagined in her bathtub fantasy.

When he released her after what felt like a knee-quivering eternity, she blinked. "For a man who's supposedly out of practice, you kiss really, really well."

He laughed at that. "Shall we see if there's anything else I can remember how to do?"

"I think that's an excellent idea," she said, reaching past him to turn off the oven. "And, remember, I'm a teacher. I know the value of doing something again and again until you master it."

"Laura Reed," he murmured. "You are a tease. Who knew?"

It was her turn to laugh. "Not me, that's for sure. You seem to bring out a side of me I never knew existed." Or one she'd determinedly tamped down until it no longer put her heart at risk.

He studied her. "A good thing?"

She nodded. "Yes. I think it probably is. Scary, though."

"Tell me about it," he said wryly. "Have you tested your limits for tonight, or is that bedroom of yours still an option?"

"Not an option," she said thoughtfully, then grinned at his disappointed expression. "More like a necessity."

He swept her into his arms before she could change her mind and headed down the hallway.

"I knew it," he said, just inside the door. "Frilly, girly decor."

She patted his cheek. "It's okay. I think you're man enough to handle it."

He looked deep into her eyes. "I'll give it my best shot," he said as he lowered her to the bed, then tossed all the pillows aside.

As it turned out, his very best shot was mind-numbingly, impossible-to-catch-her-breath amazing.

It was nearly midnight when Laura looked at J.C. as they devoured the now-cold pizza and warm wine. She was wearing an oversize T-shirt. He was wearing only his boxers.

"I wasn't expecting it to be like that," she told him candidly.

He smiled. "Like what?"

She searched for the right word. "Easy, I guess. Comfortable, as if we'd known each other in some other life and got it exactly right."

He seemed a little startled by her words. "You felt that, too?"

"I kept expecting to wake up and realize we'd made a terrible mistake, reached for something that would change things between us and maybe ruin the friendship we have."

"I think I can safely say we've moved well beyond friendship," J.C. said wryly.

"How scary is that for you?" she asked, studying him with a considering look.

"Not half as terrifying as I anticipated. How about you?"

"I'm a little shaky, but in a good way. Isn't that the way it always feels when you step outside your comfort zone and walk into new territory?"

"What do you see happening next?" he asked.

Laura bit back a smile at the edge of panic he couldn't quite hide. "More of the same," she suggested. "Tonight, tomorrow, whenever."

"And that's all?"

"I'm not rushing out first thing in the morning to book a church, if that's what's worrying you. Nor am I hurrying over to Wharton's to find out who won the pool."

"There's a pool on when we'll sleep together?"

"More than likely, but I was thinking of the one that has us getting hitched. We're not there yet." She shrugged in a casual way she hoped would reassure him. "We might never be there."

Instead of looking relieved, J.C. frowned at her determinedly light tone. "Then this is just a fling to you?"

"No," she said patiently. "I told you I'm up for more of the same. I think that implies something that continues for an indefinite period of time."

"Until someone better comes along?" he prodded.

For an instant, she was taken aback by the bitter note in his voice until it hit her that leaving was exactly what he expected the women in his life to do. It's what his mother had done, what his wife had done. She reached for his hand.

"J.C., tonight was amazing. The past few weeks have been really good. I'm hopeful that there's even more good, possibly even great, and a whole lot of amazing on the horizon. I'm not anticipating an ending before we really get started. You shouldn't, either. That's not to say it couldn't end, but it won't be because I'm not giving it all I have to give. If you can't do the same, then maybe we should write tonight off as just one of those things."

"I don't want to write off anything," he declared, a note of impatience in his voice. He drew in a deep breath. "I'm all in, for the duration."

"Brave man," she praised.

He frowned at her. "Just promise me one thing."

"What's that?"

"When you want out, you'll tell me. You won't let me find out some other way."

She knew he was thinking about the way he'd discovered his wife in bed with another man.

"I promise I will always be straight with you," she said solemnly. "But I can tell you right now that you might have to wait a long, long time before I go any-where, if ever."

He smiled at that, his relief touchingly evident. "Sounds good to me."

Laura was in her classroom after hours the next day when Sarah McDonald came charging in with Raylene and Annie right on her heels.

"You are not going to believe what Mariah Litchfield has been up to today," Sarah said, practically quivering with indignation. "I'd have been here sooner, but I was tied up at the radio station, and then I had to track down Raylene and Annie to see what they'd heard before we came to fill you in."

Laura sighed and set down the pen she'd been using to grade papers. "Tell me," she said, resigned.

"She showed up at the radio station this morning and wanted Travis to put her on the air so she could talk about the vicious campaign being waged against her precious daughter. Want to guess who's at the top of her hit list?"

"Betty Donovan and me, I imagine," Laura said.

"Bingo," Sarah said triumphantly. "I wanted to wring her scrawny neck."

"What did Travis do?" Laura asked.

"Showed her the door, thank goodness," Sarah said. "If he'd so much as cracked open the door to the stu-dio, I'd have wrung his neck, too. He took one look at me and knew it."

"I suppose she feels she has to try to defend her daughter's inexcusable behavior," Laura said. "She's desperate to launch an offensive PR campaign before it's too late to rehabilitate her daughter's reputation. Catfighting that goes to the extreme the way it did with Annabelle is not an attractive trait. I imagine Mariah recognizes that the sympathy is all going to be on Misty's side."

"Don't you dare defend her," Raylene said. "Her next stop was Wharton's, where she tried to put a bug in Grace's ear. I heard every word, just as she'd intended. Everyone in the place did. It was all about how everyone was misjudging poor Annabelle, and Misty was the real culprit."

"Was anyone buying it?" Laura asked, her heart in her throat.

"Not for a second," Raylene said. "Especially not after Grace finished ripping into Mariah for turning her daughter into a spoiled, entitled brat."

Raylene lowered her voice to mimic Grace when she got worked up. "'Mariah Litchfield, absolutely nobody's going to care if that child of yours has the voice of an angel, if she's behaving like the devil's handmaiden. You need to stop this nonsense right now.'"

Raylene grinned. "The whole place erupted into cheers after that. I have to say it made me proud to be a part of this community and glad for Carrie and Mandy's sakes that we're taking a stand against bullying. I'd hate to have something like this happen to either of my stepdaughters."

For a tiny, fleeting instant, Laura almost felt sorry for Mariah. It must be awful to realize that there was little to nothing she could say or do to rescue Annabelle from this mess of her own creation. The town's darling was about to be a pariah at only seventeen. Once again, she wondered if Annabelle wouldn't be better off at a school far from Serenity where she could have her own fresh start.

"Knowing that Misty has all this support is great," Laura said, choosing her words carefully.

Sarah frowned. "Why don't you sound happier?"

"Because Laura's afraid it could wind up with the rest of us getting caught up in doing a little bullying of our own to get even," Annie guessed. "Am I right?"

Laura nodded. "What Annabelle did was horribly wrong. Mariah's just being a mom. She's trying to defend her daughter. I'd hate to see everyone gang up on them."

"How can you possibly take their side?" Sarah asked, her expression incredulous.

"I'm not," Laura insisted. "Far from it. But bullying is bullying. Would we be one bit better than Annabelle if we turn right around and try to demonize her? She needs to be punished, taught a lesson, one from which she'll hopefully emerge as a more thoughtful, considerate young lady."

"Eternal optimist," Raylene said with a shake of her head. "I'm not that hopeful for a major transformation, not with Mariah defending her behavior wherever she can gather an audience."

"And you should hope that the town stays solidly against her," Sarah warned. "Because you and Betty are going to need that support to keep your jobs. Ugly doesn't begin to cover what that woman is capable of doing."

"But the school board has been fully informed about what actually happened," Laura said confidently, though for the first time she felt a little twinge of anxiety. "They're not going to let Mariah target us, or, if she does, I'm certain they'll defend us."

"I'm just saying, it wouldn't hurt to have community support on your side," Sarah said. "Last I heard Mariah was ranting about going to the state, because the local board and the school administration are obviously biased and incompetent."

"It's just ranting," Laura repeated.

"It is," Sarah agreed. "Until she finds some idiot with more power than sense who'll listen."

"Call Helen," Annie advised.

"She's already all over this," Laura said.

"She's all over it for *Misty's* sake," Annie said. "Now you need to be sure she's prepared to defend you."

"That's crazy," Laura protested, still unwilling to believe things would go that far.

"No," Sarah said. "That's Mariah. It wouldn't be the first time she's managed to get her way, even when every single person in town knew she was wrong. You know that, Laura. You've certainly heard the stories. Call Helen. Maybe you'll never need her, but don't let Mariah pick up a full head of steam before you have Helen there to cut her off."

Laura nodded reluctantly. "I'll call her."

Annie held out her cell phone. "Now."

"You really think it's that urgent?"

All three women nodded.

"We really do," Raylene confirmed.

Laura looked into their somber expressions, drew in a deep breath and made the call.

16

J.C.'s thoughts hadn't strayed far from Laura all day, despite the steady parade of patients through his office. He'd just sent the last one on his way when his nurse cornered him.

"I thought you ought to know that Jan accepted Bill's offer today. She'll be moving to Serenity right after the holidays."

J.C. nodded. "Bill and I discussed it before he hired her. I think she'll be a great addition to the practice."

Debra surveyed him with obvious disappointment. "I suppose it was too much to hope that you'd be more excited."

He chuckled. "You know perfectly well that I was never interested in Jan. Nor is she one tiny bit infatuated with me."

"Of course she is," Debra scoffed. "Why else would she be moving here?"

"She told me she was anxious for a change of scenery and being part of a small community. I'm surprised she didn't tell you the same thing."

Debra waved it off as if it were nonsense. "Well, of

course she'd say that to you. Is she supposed to come right out and tell you she's coming because you're hot?"

J.C. nearly choked. "She said that? Jan actually said those exact words to you?" he asked, imagining some very awkward times ahead.

Debra sighed. "Okay, no. I was hoping to give you a little push in her direction." She studied him with a narrowed gaze. "Then there's no doubt? You're actually confirming all the rumors that you and Laura Reed are together?"

"We're definitely seeing each other," he admitted, mostly to end this absurd conversation. "Now I need to get out of here."

"Hot date?"

He rolled his eyes. "Heavy lifting," he said, imagining the workout ahead. Maybe a really hard workout would get the images of *all* these women out of his head, at least for an hour.

An hour later J.C. had barely worked up a good sweat when Cal cornered him, much as Debra had earlier.

"Got a minute?" Cal inquired, his expression somber.

J.C. turned off the elliptical machine and stepped off. "What's up?"

"Let's go into Elliott's office," he said. "I don't want anyone overhearing this."

To J.C.'s shock, he found Elliott Cruz, a personal trainer and one of the gym's partners, there, along with Ronnie Sullivan, who with his wife Dana Sue, were two of the town's business success stories. He'd opened a thriving hardware store on Main Street, and she, of course, owned Sullivan's.

"Why am I feeling ambushed all of a sudden? Did I break a machine or leave dirty towels in the locker room?"

Ronnie chuckled. "You wouldn't be the first, but no."

"I just wanted you to know that there are already some people on this," Cal explained.

"And what is *this?*" J.C. asked, still mystified.

"Mariah Litchfield has officially kicked off her vendetta against Laura Reed and Betty Donovan," Cal explained. "She's out for blood."

The other two men nodded.

"Karen called me to fill me in," Elliott said, referring to his wife, who worked as a chef at Sullivan's.

"And I heard it on the street and from Dana Sue," Ronnie added.

"And as we speak, according to Maddie, the Sweet Magnolias are gathering at Helen's house to launch a counteroffensive," Cal said. "Personally, if I were Mariah, I'd run for my life. I've seen those women in action when they have a cause they believe in."

"Amen to that," Ronnie said.

J.C. felt a moment's outrage on Laura's behalf. "Laura knows?"

"She's at Helen's," Cal confirmed. "I think it was Sarah McDonald, Raylene Rollins and Ronnie's daughter Annie who rallied the troops. They worked on the fall festival with Laura and aren't about to let her get railroaded by the likes of Mariah."

"Annie's fit to be tied," Ronnie confirmed. "I swear I always thought of my daughter as sweet, but when she gets her back up, she's a spitfire, just like her mama." He said it with unmistakable pride.

"Thank heaven for all of them," J.C. said. "I should go over there."

The three men glanced at each other and chuckled.

"Not a good idea," Cal said. "Margarita nights are a no-men-allowed event. What we're thinking is that we should make a few calls, get the husbands lined up, too. I assumed you'd want to help."

"But I'm not…"

"A husband?" Cal said with a grin. "Time will tell. For now, though, your interest in one of the primary targets is good enough for you to qualify."

"Then I'm definitely in," J.C. said. "Where are we getting together?"

"The basketball court at the park," Ronnie said. "We all think better while we're working off a little steam."

"And it keeps us from going off half-cocked and doing something before we've run it past the wives, who are much more civilized about these things than we are," Cal said. "No less furious and determined, mind you. Just a little more controlled. It's actually pretty scary to watch them put a carefully calculated plan into action."

"It's beyond terrifying when they're against you," Ronnie confirmed. "I've been on the receiving end of that. When they're all for you, it's awesome. We're happy to provide all necessary backup."

J.C. nodded. "I can do that," he said. But he also intended to stand front and center when it came to publicly defending Laura and the way she'd handled this extraordinarily difficult situation. Things could have gotten far worse for Misty had Laura not intervened.

An hour after Laura made her call to Helen, every one of the Sweet Magnolias had rallied and gathered at Helen's for margaritas and a strategy session. Laura was a little in awe as she looked around the room at the women willing to go to bat for her. She'd had a few of their children in her classes, but most were here simply because they believed in her. Amazing! It wasn't the first time she'd realized how blessed she was to have them as friends.

"You have no idea what it means to me to know that you are on my side," she told them. "I never would have asked you to back me up."

"You didn't have to," Annie said. "You're one of us. When somebody targets one of us, they take on all the Sweet Magnolias. Right, ladies?"

Margarita glasses were lifted into the air amid a chorus of confirmation.

Tears stung Laura's eyes at the show of support. "Thank you." She turned to Helen. "But do you really think Mariah's threats need to be taken so seriously?"

"I'd rather not take chances," Helen said. "Not that she has a leg to stand on, but if she's the first one out there with a message and she spreads it loudly enough, there are going to be people who believe it, if they haven't already heard the other side."

"We could hold a rally," Sarah said eagerly. "If we do it in the square, Travis and I can cover it live on the radio. That kind of publicity will stop Mariah in her tracks."

Raylene lifted a brow. "Are you sure you're not just a little bloodthirsty because you think Mariah tried to make a move on Travis?"

"I *know* she did," Sarah corrected. "And I might have overreacted just the teensiest bit at the time, but that is not why I think we should do this. We want to get public sympathy on our side, and we need to do it fast. Isn't that what you just said, Helen? This is the best way."

Laura shook her head. "If you all want to hold a general rally against bullying in our community, I'll be there, front and center. But not if this is going to turn into some us-against-them thing. I've told you before, that's its own kind of bullying, and I don't want to resort to it."

"But it could be the only way to counter Mariah," Annie argued. "Fight fire with fire."

"And be no better than Annabelle or, for that matter, Mariah herself," Laura insisted, shaking her head. "No. I won't let you do it. Whatever you all want to do—and believe me, I appreciate so much you wanting to do something—it can't be something that will make the situation worse and maybe even get Misty's name dragged through the mud all over again. We need to remember that she's the reason I got involved in the first place. She's been through enough."

"But you know she's going to want to help," Raylene said, "especially after the way you were so supportive of her."

Maddie nodded. "Diana called me earlier. I know her from the spa and from school because Misty and Katie are so close. She asked me if I'd heard about what Mariah is up to and wondered how she could help. I told her I'd get back to her once we had a plan." She gave Laura a sympathetic look. "I really admire you for thinking about Misty first, but if you ask me, it's time now to worry about yourself. And as much as it pains me to say it, after the ordeal Betty Donovan put Cal and me through, Betty should be doing the same."

"I agree," Helen said. She studied Laura intently. "Are you totally opposed to Sarah's idea?"

She considered the question carefully before responding. "Not if the theme of the rally is an anti-bullying message," she said. "I'd even be happy to speak at something like that. I imagine Betty would, too."

Even as she spoke, she warmed to the idea. Turning to Maddie, she said, "Your mother mentioned she might be able to convince Frances Wingate to speak to the parents about bullying."

Helen's eyes lit up. "That would be awesome. Is she able to do it? Frances is amazing, and there's no one who grew up in Serenity who escaped a knee-knocking, terrifying lecture or two from Frances while they were in school."

"I'll say," Dana Sue said with a shudder. "More than my share, I'm afraid."

"Because you were rebellious," Maddie teased.

"And you were a saint?" Dana Sue countered. "Please."

Helen laughed. "Let's not go there. I think we can all agree that the three of us were thorns in Frances's side back in the day. Bottom line, she'd be the perfect person to remind this entire community of its moral compass. I'm liking this idea of an anti-bullying rally better and better, especially if we can get her help."

Laura turned to Maddie. "Your mother said she'd work on it."

Maddie nodded. "Then she will. I'll give her a nudge, though I doubt it's necessary. She seems to have taken up this cause eagerly. The activist side of her is a new one to me."

"Well, believe me, the situation would still be out of control if it weren't for her willingness to get involved," Laura said, exchanging a pointed look with Helen, who nodded her own confirmation.

"Why don't you see what you can find out from Paula tomorrow, Laura?" Helen suggested. "Tell her about our thinking and see what she thinks the odds are that Frances can help, then give me a call. We need to get right on this. Sarah, how quickly could we schedule something that you could get on the air?"

"We could do it immediately," Sarah said. "But I'd like at least a few days' notice so we can spread the word. We want that square packed with people who totally get that bullying is unacceptable."

Helen nodded. "How about a tentative date for a week from Saturday? If all the pieces fall into place, would that work?"

"It would for Travis and me," Sarah said at once. "I'll make sure of it."

"And we'd have time to rally teachers and parents," Raylene said. "I'll put Adelia Hernandez on that. She seems to snap her fingers and the parents at school fall into line to do whatever she needs."

Helen gave a nod of satisfaction. "Then we have a plan. Laura, are you okay with it?"

"If we can stick to the plan, absolutely," she said. "And if you're looking for speakers who have strong feelings, ask J.C. I think he'd be a powerful advocate for the cause."

"Or for you," Annie teased. "Isn't that right?"

Laura blushed furiously. "Do not go there."

"Then that wasn't him I saw pacing around outside your place last night when I was driving home from work?" Raylene inquired innocently. "Or his car I saw still there this morning? I'm fairly certain he has the only dark green Jaguar in town, but of course I wouldn't want to jump to any conclusions."

Laura sighed at the realization that with such strong support came a complete breakdown of boundaries. Apparently her entire life was fair game.

"Of course you wouldn't jump to conclusions," she said to Raylene, resigned to having such a personal tidbit shared with everyone. "Just please tell me you didn't mention this sighting to Grace."

"Heavens, no!" Raylene said indignantly. "It's only between us girls."

"But Sweet Magnolias have an obligation to be on top of all the hottest gossip in town," Helen declared. "And once in a while it is very satisfying to know things that Grace doesn't know."

"Power to the Sweet Magnolias!" said Dana Sue, lifting her glass.

The faintly slurred comment drew a sharp look from Maddie. "You're cut off. You know one margarita is your limit."

"I know," Dana Sue said sadly. "You know the pitiful truth? I've only had three sips of this one, and I can't even handle that, apparently. It is a sad, sad day."

Annie bit back a chuckle and stood up. "Come on, Mom. I'll walk you home."

Dana Sue's gaze narrowed suspiciously. "Isn't it raining out there? Didn't a cold front move in?"

Annie nodded, her expression determinedly cheerful. "Isn't that great? A brisk walk ought to fix you right up before Dad sees you looped."

Dana Sue looked around unhappily. "What's that line about a thankless child? Something about it being sharper than a serpent's tooth to have a thankless child. It's from *King Lear,* I think."

Laura grinned at her. "Oh, sweet heaven! Not only are you right, but you've just given me hope that the Shakespeare lessons in my class might actually pay off years later. The kids rarely remember a thing beyond final exams now."

Annie rolled her eyes. "I think Mom memorized that one on the day I was born. I've heard it often enough over the years. Good night, all. I'll get the weakling among us safely home."

The gathering broke up after that. Laura was the last to leave. Turning to Helen, she said, "I really don't know how to thank you for everything you're doing for Misty and for me."

Helen smiled. "It's my pleasure. There's nothing I like more than seeing the law used to achieve good for the people who deserve it."

"Very noble," Laura said.

"Okay, maybe I get a kick out of retaliating against the bad guys, too," Helen admitted, a twinkle in her eyes. "Sue me."

"Not a chance. I'd never be foolish enough to go up against you in court."

"I'll talk to you tomorrow then. Let me know as soon as you hear back from Paula."

"Will do," Laura promised.

As she headed home, rather than being terrified about what the future might hold for her teaching career in Serenity, Laura felt amazingly reassured by the knowledge that there were a whole lot of very good people in her corner.

Paula rarely entertained. For years she'd been far too busy with her art, the traveling it entailed and the very insular life she led with her professor husband and Maddie. Only in recent years had she come to understand how isolating that had been for Maddie and how disconnected she'd felt from her own parents. Maddie's tight bond with Helen and Dana Sue had filled the void left by her own family.

Thankfully these days Paula not only made more time for her grandchildren, but for other women, at least the few in her generation with whom she'd made a deeper connection over the years and counted as friends.

After her promise to Laura, she called Liz Johnson, rather than going directly to Frances. She knew Liz would tell her if her idea to involve Frances in this bullying matter was out of the question. Liz, Frances and Flo Decatur were thick as thieves. She knew that Liz and Flo were not only Frances's support system, but her staunchest protectors.

They'd only recently returned from a gambling excursion to Las Vegas that had been covered with outrageous reports on the local radio station. Paula couldn't recall the last time she'd laughed so hard. Though Vegas wasn't her style, she'd almost wished she'd been along, if only to see the three women carrying on so outlandishly. She was half surprised that Flo, at least, hadn't come back wed by an Elvis impersonator to someone she'd met on the Vegas strip.

Tuesday, on her third attempt, Liz answered her call, reacting with surprise to the sound of her voice. "What's this? You emerged from isolation on a Tuesday? I never hear from you before Thursday, and then you only call to verify if I'm bringing cookies over that morning so you'll have them for that sweet granddaughter of yours."

"This time I'm on another mission entirely," Paula admitted. "I need some help." She described the situation, satisfied by Liz's increasingly indignant gasps. "Do you think Frances would be up to saying a few words? I didn't want to ask if it would be too much for her."

"Her memory medicine has been helping," Liz said. "Most of the time you'd never know she has a cognitive disorder. And if I know nothing else, Frances will be as livid about this as I am. You can count both of us in for whatever you need. Flo, too. She likes stirring things up. I wish I still had her energy, in fact. Maybe we can assign her to rally all the seniors in town."

"Would the three of you be able to stop by here tomorrow afternoon?"

"Let me make a couple of calls and I'll get back to you. None of us have packed social calendars these days, so it should be fine. About four o'clock?"

"Perfect. That'll give me time to get in touch with Laura and figure out exactly what's needed and to sneak over to Sullivan's and try to talk Erik into selling me some thoroughly decadent cake. I seem to recall you love coconut with lemon filling. Shall I see if he can whip one up for you?"

"Just thinking about it makes my mouth water, though no one ever made one quite as good as my mother's, rest her soul," Liz said. "I'll make those calls. Unless you hear from me otherwise, you'll see the three of us tomorrow at four."

"Thanks, Liz."

"Don't thank me. There's nothing like a good cause to make me think I'm young again. See you later."

Paula hung up, satisfied. And then she picked the phone right back up and used her powers of persuasion to get that cake for Liz. Luckily, Erik was the kind of chef who responded readily to a challenge. At the mention that no one's coconut cake had ever lived up to Liz's mother's, he was all over it.

"Give me till the end of the day," he told Paula. "I was looking for something new to put on tomorrow's menu as the dessert special. This will be just the thing."

"You're a good man. What do I owe you?"

"Just tell my wife what a saint I am," he said.

"I doubt she needs reminding. Helen was always a smart woman."

He chuckled. "Yeah, but a man can always use extra brownie points."

"Then I'll be sure to pass the word along," Paula promised, shaking her head as she hung up. Aside from her closeness with her grandchildren these days, what she enjoyed most was seeing the unmistakable love between her daughter, Maddie's friends and their respective husbands. Though her own marriage had been solid and exactly right for her, there was something about the open affection among the younger couples that filled her heart with joy.

* * *

After playing basketball with the guys and working out their own strategy for helping Laura and Betty fight Mariah's wrath, J.C. went home, showered, pulled on a pair of sweatpants and sat down to call Laura.

"You doing okay?" he asked the minute she answered. "I hear it's been a tough day."

"You've heard about Mariah and her campaign against me," she concluded.

"The whole thing's ridiculous," J.C. said. "Don't worry about it."

"Even an annoying gnat can make life miserable," she countered. "And something tells me Mariah's a whole lot nastier than an itty-bitty gnat. When I got involved in helping Misty, I didn't expect to wind up the center of attention. Not that it would have stopped me, of course."

He frowned at her oddly resigned tone. "You're not really worried, are you? Because I know the guys have your back, and I thought their wives—those Sweet Magnolia women—were crusading for you, too. Weren't you with them tonight?"

"I was, and they're being really, really great. We decided to hold an anti-bullying rally a week from Saturday. Travis's radio station will broadcast it live from the town square."

"That's great," he said, loving the idea. "Awareness is the key to changing the way these kids behave."

"I hope you'll be that enthusiastic when I tell you that I volunteered you to be one of the speakers."

For an instant J.C. fell silent.

"That's okay, isn't it?" she asked worriedly. "I know how much you care about this, so I thought you'd want to do it."

"Of course I do," he said, wondering if he'd be able to tell the very personal story about why this issue meant so much to him. He knew it was exactly the message that the crowd needed to hear. Maybe he could finally turn what had been a Fullerton family tragedy into something that led to a positive change that might affect the lives of other young people.

"Then why the hesitation?" Laura asked, snapping him back to the present. "Is it because I overstepped?"

He heard the uncertainty in her voice and knew that he was responsible for making her wonder if she had the right to any claim to him or his time.

"You can volunteer me for anything," he assured her. "We're a couple. If you need me, I'm there."

Now it was her turn to fall silent. "We're a couple?" she said eventually.

"Did you think we weren't? I thought the other night sealed that deal."

"But you're so…" Her voice trailed off.

"Cautious?" he said. "No question about it, but since I met you, I've been feeling a little reckless."

She chuckled. "Reckless, huh?"

"Yep. How about you?"

"I was feeling pretty daring myself," she admitted. "At least until I found out tonight that you were spotted at my place."

"Is that such a big deal?"

"It is when your car was also spotted in the exact same spot this morning," she said. "Let's just say I had some explaining to do."

"How is that anyone's business?" he asked, perplexed.

Laura laughed. "You are not that new to Serenity. In

this town, gossip is everyone's business, though I gather the Sweet Magnolias are pleased to have trumped Grace just this once."

"Does it bother you?" he asked, worried that she'd fear potential damage to her reputation over what might be nothing more than a casual fling, not that either of them had defined their relationship that way.

"A little," she conceded. "But I have to admit there's a part of me that is very happy to finally have a social life worth talking about."

J.C. caught the teasing note in her voice and chuckled with her. "Yeah, that's a new one to me, too. It's not half as bad as I expected it to be."

"Just one thing, though, J.C."

"What's that?"

"I'm always going to be more concerned about what you're thinking than I am about what people are saying."

He considered that and thought he heard a faint need for reassurance behind the softly spoken words. "What I'm thinking is that we should continue this conversation in person. Is it too late for me to come over?"

"I think it's the best idea you've had since you called," she said without even the slightest hesitation.

"Then I'll be there in fifteen minutes."

"Great. And, J.C.?"

"Yes."

"Bring your toothbrush and clothes for work."

"And that's the best idea *you've* had since I called."

He had no idea yet where this was going, but getting there was certainly turning out to be an unexpected delight.

17

A week after everything broke at school, Misty stood in the doorway of the kitchen, openmouthed with surprise at the sight of her mother standing at the stove fixing breakfast. It was the first time she'd been up and dressed and looking like her old self in weeks, much less cooking a real meal.

"Pancakes?" Misty said, sniffing the air appreciatively.

"With warm maple syrup, just the way you and Jake like them," her mother confirmed. "Is he up yet? I thought I heard his shower running. You two need to be out the door for school shortly."

"Jake's up," Misty said. She hesitated, then added, "I was gonna ask you, though, if I could stay home today."

Her mother turned away from the stove and studied Misty with a concerned expression. "You feeling okay?"

Misty shrugged.

Diana's face softened with understanding. "You're afraid of what the talk's going to be like at school today," she guessed, then shook her head, her expression filled with regret. "I knew I shouldn't have let you stay home. It's going to be all the harder to go back now, isn't it?"

"Well, duh!" Misty said with feeling. "By now Annabelle's had time to call all her friends and get them on her side. I'll be, like, some kind of pariah." She gave her mother a pleading look. "I know Annabelle getting suspended was supposed to fix things and send, like, this huge message, but come on, Mom. It's bound to be worse than ever. Please let me stay home, just one more day. I'll go tomorrow."

"Sweetheart, it won't be any easier tomorrow. It's always better to face your fears sooner rather than later. Look what happened to me. I refused to admit to myself that your father was going to leave me no matter what I did to try to hold on. I made all of you miserable for weeks, rather than facing the reality and figuring out how to deal with it."

"It's not even close to the same thing," Misty insisted. "Everyone doesn't hate you."

"And no one hates you, either. Annabelle was obviously jealous, and she won't be in school, anyway. And Betty Donovan and Laura Reed are not going to let another student bully you," Diana said with confidence.

Misty rolled her eyes. "Come on. They may be motivated to protect me, but they have their own problems now with Mrs. Litchfield spreading all sorts of rumors about them and threatening to get them fired."

"You're their top priority," her mother said firmly, setting pancakes in front of Misty along with the pitcher of warm syrup. "I truly believe that."

"But they can't be everywhere at once to protect me.

Please, Mom, let me stay home. I'll bet you could get Dr. Fullerton to give me a note."

"I'm very grateful to him for how he's handled all this, but I don't think asking him for a note when you're perfectly fine is a good idea. It didn't work very well last time you tried it, did it?"

"Yeah, but he knows more now and he really gets what's going on at school. Seriously, Mom, way more than you know."

"I'm glad you have his support, but here's how I see it. Your job is to go to school, make good grades and get into your dream college. You can't let this situation ruin that for you. If you do, you'll regret it." She held Misty's gaze. "Do you want a girl like Annabelle to have that much power over your future?"

When she looked at it that way, Misty shook her head. "No," she conceded reluctantly.

"Then going back to school and facing everyone is your only option. I know you're strong enough to do that. You've shown me just how strong you are by dealing with so much on your own."

Misty felt a tiny hint of satisfaction at her mother's praise. "You really think I'm strong?"

Her mom smiled. "The strongest girl I know. Would you like me to drive you to school today?"

Misty regarded her with horror. "And let everyone think I've turned into this huge baby? No way. You just said I'm strong, so how would that look? If you're sure I can't stay home, I'll walk like always."

"I'm sure," Diana said firmly. She gave Misty a stern look. "And don't get any ideas about taking a detour that might take, say, six or seven hours to get you there. Ms.

Reed and Ms. Donovan know they're to call me immediately if you're not in class. We were in touch about my decision to let you stay home. They know that ends today."

Misty regarded her mother with a weird mix of approval and disappointment. "I'm really glad you're getting your act back together, Mom, but you picked a really sucky time to do it."

At the sound of her mom's laugh, Misty grinned, too. Maybe things would be back to normal soon for all of them.

She poked at the pancakes on her plate, which were suddenly tasteless. "Mom," she asked hesitantly, "are you and Dad okay?"

"If you mean are we finally communicating without me wanting to rip his heart out, yes," Diana said in a resigned tone. "But, sweetheart, the breakup of a marriage is tough on everyone, even your dad. It'll take a while for all of us to figure out how this new arrangement is supposed to work. The one thing that should never be in doubt is that your dad loves you and Jake to pieces. He's behind you a hundred percent. If you need him, all you have to do is give him a call."

"I just don't want you to feel bad if I do," Misty told her.

"The divorce is between me and your dad, not you and your dad. You are never to feel bad about loving him or needing him, okay?" she said, pausing to give Misty a hug, then murmuring half to herself. "We're going to be fine. All of us are going to be just fine."

Misty was almost ready to believe it.

* * *

As it turned out, the get-together Paula had planned with her friends had been delayed until Monday. She set Erik's coconut cake masterpiece—a freshly baked one he'd made just this morning to replace the one she'd had to cancel—in the middle of her dining room table, along with a bowl of fresh fruit and her best teacups. She'd had to wash those to get off the dust that had accumulated in the years since she'd last used them.

The collectible chintz cups had always made her smile with their cheery, if mismatched, floral designs. Because of Paula's botanical artwork, Maddie had bought her the first one. She'd found it at a garage sale when she was maybe eight. Each year after that first successful gift, given so tentatively, she'd searched and found a different one for Paula's birthday until there were a dozen or more in the cupboard. Now they were among Paula's greatest treasures.

She wasn't sure what to expect when Liz, Flo and Frances arrived, but she was happily surprised to see Frances looking both strong and suitably indignant.

"The minute Liz told me about your call, I was eager to do whatever I can," Frances told her. "That poor child," she murmured with a shake of her head. "And for it to be someone with all of Annabelle's advantages who's been tormenting her..." She sighed. "I just don't understand young people these days."

"There was always bullying," Liz reminded them. "Back in my day a lot of it came from racial prejudice, but these days with that internet readily available for whatever slur someone happens to think of, well, that's new and downright dangerous, if you ask me. It gives people with all sorts of crazy ideas a platform to spew them out there for everyone to see. No one bothers to separate fact from fiction."

"If you'd seen some of these posts, you'd have been appalled," Paula told her. "Why don't we sit in the dining room while we talk." She winked at Liz. "I have that coconut cake I promised you. I've no idea how it tastes, but it looks pretty amazing. Erik definitely rose to the challenge."

Liz clapped her hands like a child anticipating a favorite treat. "Oh, I can't wait. If it's even half as good as my mama's, you'll have made my day."

When they were settled at the table and tea and cake had been served, the rest of them waited while Liz took her first bite of the moist yellow cake with its fluffy coconut frosting and tart lemon filling. She closed her eyes, a look of pure pleasure suffusing her face.

"Oh, sweet heaven," she murmured. "That's what this is, just heavenly."

"As wonderful as your mother's?" Paula asked, watching her closely, anxious on Erik's behalf.

"Even allowing for nostalgia, which usually has me dismissing all the pretenders I've tried, I'm forced to admit, Erik has done himself proud. This might even be just the tiniest bit better than my mama's, and I would never say such a thing lightly. Is he going to put it on the menu at Sullivan's?"

"He says he is," Paula confirmed. "He thought he'd call it by your mother's name, if you thought that would be all right. What do you think?"

Liz's eyes lit up. "She'd be very honored, and so would I. Adelaide's coconut cake. I love it!"

Catching Fireflies

Flo grinned. "That son-in-law of mine sure does have a magic touch when it comes to baking!"

"He does, indeed," Liz said, closing her eyes as she savored another bite.

"Now that all the cake accolades are out of the way," Frances said briskly, "Paula, I want you to tell me what you want me to do to help young Misty."

Paula explained about the rally this coming Saturday, which both Maddie and Laura had called to tell her about. "Could you say a few words there? Remind the parents about their role in teaching their children how to behave toward their classmates?" Paula grinned. "You know, give them a little come-to-Jesus talk the way you used to."

"Count me in," Frances said eagerly. At Liz and Flo's worried looks, she waved them off. "If I'm having a bad morning, we'll have to reconsider, but this is too important for me not to at least try to say what needs to be said." She turned to Paula. "Can we make my appearance contingent on that, that I'm feeling up to it when the time comes? Or maybe Liz can take over for me." She smiled at her friend. "You haven't lost your touch at rallying a crowd, have you?"

"Oh, I imagine I could think of a few things to say," Liz said. "I'll be happy to step in if needed, but only if needed. You have a connection to these parents, Frances. I'm better known by an entirely different generation, many of whom have died off."

"Then we're set," Paula confirmed, pleased by their willingness to pitch in.

"Now, what about us?" Liz asked. "What can Flo

and I do, beyond me providing backup for Frances if needed?"

"I've already spoken to Helen," Flo said. "She'd like us to make some signs." She gave Liz a sly look. "You're the expert on protest signs. You tell me what to put on them, and I'll make them up. My hand's steady, and I have a whole bunch of bright markers for my granddaughter's art projects."

Paula nodded with satisfaction. "I had one more thought last night. I know the local radio station will broadcast this live, but I think we need to stir things up a bit farther afield. What do you think about me making a few calls to the other media? I still have a few contacts from my various art shows. The individuals may not be the right reporters, but I imagine they can point me in the right direction."

"I say go for it," Liz said. "This isn't an isolated incident or something unique to Serenity. If anything, I'm sure it's a bigger problem in the larger communities. Maybe we can point the way to how things like this should be handled."

"Go, Liz," Flo said. "Still a rabble-rouser."

"And intend to be one until the day they lay me to rest," Liz said proudly.

"Then we have a plan," Paula said, pleased.

The others nodded. "We have a plan," Flo confirmed. "I'll fill Helen in. I have to admit I'm tickled to be part of some crusade she's on. It's not as if I can go to the courthouse and cheer her on when she's handling a divorce, but I want her to know just how proud I am of the stances she takes against all kinds of injustice."

"You *should* be proud of her," Paula said. "I know it

wasn't always easy, but you raised a strong, intelligent, independent woman."

"Who's given me a granddaughter who's the joy of my life," Flo said. "Since I moved back to Serenity to be close to Helen, Sarah Beth and Erik, I count my blessings every single day of my life."

"At our age, just getting up in the morning is one of the biggest blessings of all," Frances said. "Having this cause where we might make a difference, that's just downright amazing."

Paula looked at the three extraordinary women around her table and thought they were the amazing ones. Having them as her friends was at the very top of her own list of blessings.

Laura took one look at Misty's panicked expression when she arrived in class and felt her heart sink. There was little question that things weren't going well on her first day back after the news of Annabelle's suspension had spread. She was torn about pulling Misty aside for a chat. She feared that drawing attention to her would only compound the problem.

Thankfully Misty solved that for her by lingering after class.

"How's it going?" Laura asked her when the other students had rushed off after casting a few disparaging looks in Misty's direction.

"It sucks, if you want to know the truth," Misty said. "Hardly anybody's talking to me. All they do is whisper and point when they see me coming."

Laura regarded her with sympathy. "I know that must

be hard, but it'll get easier. In a few days they'll forget all about you and move on to something else."

Misty gave her an incredulous look. "Like that's ever going to happen with some big rally on Saturday. You might as well put a big sign on me that says Bullying Victim or Big Crybaby."

Laura frowned at her perceptions of herself. "First, you are not a crybaby. I don't want to hear you describe yourself that way. And while you were absolutely a target for Annabelle, only you can allow yourself to be perceived as a victim. That's a mind-set over which you have control."

Misty didn't look convinced, but she was clearly intrigued.

"What does that mean, that being a victim is a mind-set?"

"You can choose how you respond to what other people do," Laura explained. "If you hide out and act ashamed, then not only will people think of you as a victim, you'll think of yourself that way."

"What am I supposed to do?"

"You find a way to stay strong," Laura said, then held up a hand to stop Misty's protest. "I know that's not as easy as it sounds, but you surround yourself with friends who know who you really are. You fight back, appropriately, of course." She gave her a meaningful look. "I think it might even help if you got on that stage this weekend and told your story. Let people hear how what happened affected you. Take back your self-esteem by speaking out for others. Keep this from ever happening to anyone else." She shrugged. "Just a thought. It's up to you."

Misty seemed to consider the idea, but her expression remained skeptical. "You really think what I say could make a difference?" she asked.

"Absolutely, and it's a way to show everyone—yourself included—just how strong you are." She studied Misty, gave her some time to think it over, then asked, "What do you think?"

"Will you be on stage, too?"

"Me, Dr. Fullerton, Mrs. Donovan, Frances Wingate," Laura confirmed. "Maybe Hamilton Reynolds from the school board."

"What if the kids start heckling me?" Misty asked worriedly.

"What if they do?" Laura said. "It'll say more about them than it does about you. And I imagine the crowd won't tolerate it for more than a second. If anything, any hecklers will be proving just how important a rally like this is. You know Dr. Fullerton and the rest of us won't allow it to get out of hand. We'll be right there with you."

"Can I think about it?" Misty asked eventually. "It would be good to feel strong and in control again. I'm just not sure I'm ready to stand up in front of a crowd like that. Public speaking's never been my thing. I want to throw up when I have to give a book report in class."

"Think about it for however long you need," Laura told her. "And no matter what you decide, it's okay."

"You won't be disappointed in me if I say no?"

"Not a chance. I just think this is a great opportunity for you to move forward." Laura reached in her desk and drew out a notepad with her name printed on it and wrote a note for Misty's next class. "Here you go. Now run along to your next class. And anytime things get tough around here, come find me or go to Mrs. Donovan's office. No more hiding in stairwells, okay?"

Misty regarded her with surprise. "How did you know that's where I was?"

"Lucky guess," Laura admitted. "I'd looked practically everywhere else in the building. Now you've confirmed it, so you've blown your cover. If you skip again, it won't take me more than a minute or two to track you down."

"Maybe Mr. Jenkins will let me sit in the closet with the mops," Misty said, her expression thoughtful, but a twinkle in her eye.

"Don't even think about it," Laura said sternly. "Now run along. I'll see you in class tomorrow."

Misty was almost to the door when she turned and ran back to embrace Laura. "Thank you," she murmured, then raced off, her cheeks flushed pink.

Laura stared after her, tears welling up in her eyes. Over the years she'd wanted desperately to believe she was making a difference in the lives of the kids she taught, a difference as powerful and lasting as the one Vicki Kincaid had made in hers. Now, with Misty and this terrible situation, she honestly felt she could say she had, at least with one student.

J.C.'s day had been filled with frustration. Two parents had the audacity to bring up what had happened to "poor Annabelle" and expressed outrage that she'd been suspended over something they considered to be so minor. To their shock, he'd delivered a stinging lecture on the possible consequences of bullying that had sent them scurrying off looking chagrined.

He was about to write his notes in the file for his last patient of the day when Bill walked into his office.

"Exactly what did you say to tick off Delilah Jefferson and Jane Trainor?" Bill asked. "Debra says they left here muttering about switching to a doctor in Columbia."

When J.C. started to respond, Bill held up a hand, a grin spreading across his face. "She also told me they deserved every word you said."

J.C.'s quick rise of temper cooled. "I suppose that's something," he said, appreciating his nurse's support. He explained about both incidents. "I couldn't let what they said go unchallenged. If that bothers you, I'm sorry, but this is one subject about which I intend to take a stand."

Bill nodded. "I gather half the town is taking a stand on one side or another. I talked to my son last night. Ty says Annie's smack in the middle of planning this rally on Saturday."

"And I'm one of the speakers," J.C. said.

Bill nodded slowly. "Something tells me I need to be there as a show of support. I may not have seen anything as extreme as what's gone on with Misty Dawson, but I see kids all the time starting in grade school who suddenly don't want to go back. They develop stomachaches and every symptom known to man to avoid having to go to school. It can almost always be traced to some other kid picking on them, stealing their lunch money or knocking their books out of their arms and pretending it's an accident."

J.C. regarded him with surprise. "I don't suppose you'd want to speak on Saturday, too. Maybe if these parents hear just how early bullying affects their children's lives, they'll take it more seriously and pay more attention to the signs. This whole business of thinking it's just part of growing up is nonsense."

"I couldn't agree with you more about that," Bill said, looking thoughtful. "Okay, sign me up, if you think it'll help to have another perspective."

J.C. grinned. "It'll help. Since we want to keep the rally fairly short, the more speakers we have, the less each of us will have to say."

"When have you ever been short-winded when it's a subject you're passionate about?" Bill taunted. "You spent a full hour trying to convince me we needed to hire Debra's friend as a nurse practitioner. Her credentials alone would have been enough to convince me."

"I figured you already knew we needed the help," J.C. countered. "I just wanted to be sure you had all the data you needed to support making the decision and spending the money." He gave Bill a long look. "You know, there could be another benefit to having you get up on that stage on Saturday."

"What's that?"

"It might make you a real hero in your daughter's eyes. Katie was the one who made sure Misty got the help she needed. Not that anyone's mentioned that to me directly, but all roads point in that direction."

Bill stiffened ever-so-slightly. "Katie and I have done okay since the divorce."

J.C. regarded him doubtfully. "Seriously? How many times has she put you off when you had plans? I know you've mentioned it to me on several occasions."

Bill shrugged, though his expression said he was anything but indifferent. "She's a teenager. None of them want to spend time with a parent."

"Maybe that's all it is," J.C. conceded. "But just in case, this couldn't hurt your cause. She may have been, what, just six when you left Maddie? But now she's old enough to understand everything that happened back then, and she may be a whole lot more sympathetic to her mother."

Bill winced. "I know you're right. She's even made a few comments, and, just as you guessed, she has been pulling away. It tears me up that I ruined my relationship with my kids for an affair that wound up going nowhere. Now I have a son in Tennessee I hardly see and three kids here who spend as little time with me as they can manage. I never thought my life would turn out like this. Let that be a lesson to you, J.C. When you have someone incredible in your life, do not do something stupid and thoughtless to ruin it."

J.C. nodded, thinking of Laura. "Advice I'm doing my best to heed." He regarded Bill curiously. "Do you think Delilah Jefferson and Jane Trainor really will take their kids over to Columbia to see other doctors?"

Bill shrugged. "So what if they do? Their loss, not ours."

J.C. admired the cavalier attitude but still felt the need to reassure his partner. "I'll do my best not to chase off any more patients, okay?"

"While I'd appreciate that from a business perspective, when it comes to saying what needs to be said,

I don't ever want you to hold back," Bill said clearly. "Understood?"

"Understood," J.C. said. "And appreciated more than I can say."

18

Laura made it a point to go outside after school and linger where she could be seen by the students as they walked to the parking lot or headed home on foot. She noted that Betty Donovan and several other teachers were visibly scattered outside the school, as well. The usual clusters of chattering students seemed to break up quickly and move on.

Satisfied that they'd done what they could to ensure there would be no torment of Misty, at least on school grounds, Laura was about to return to her classroom when she saw Diana Dawson heading her way.

"Do you have some time?" Diana asked.

"Of course, come on inside. Were you here to pick up Misty?"

Diana gave an exaggerated roll of her eyes. "Are you kidding? She'd rather die than have me wait outside for her."

"They do develop a healthy independent streak at this age, don't they?" Laura said with a laugh.

"You say independent streak. I say aversion to all things parental," Diana replied. "You should have seen her expression when I offered to drive her over here this morning."

"I can imagine," Laura said.

As soon as they were settled in her classroom, Laura asked, "Was there a particular reason you wanted to see me, beyond being worried about Misty, of course?"

"I came to thank you for being so quick to spot what was going on with my daughter. I'm very sorry to say that I was so lost in my own misery, I didn't realize how much trouble she was having. I can't forgive myself for that."

"You shouldn't blame yourself," Laura consoled her. "I know parents are supposed to see and hear everything, and I truly do believe they have a responsibility to pay attention to what's going on with their kids. That said, I also know just how good kids are at keeping things from their parents. I know Misty was doing her best to deal with this on her own, because she didn't want to upset you. She found what she thought was the best way to handle it."

"Skipping classes," Diana said with a shake of her head. "What was she thinking?"

"It was a terrible solution," Laura agreed. "But it's exactly what caught my attention. Students as smart as Misty generally have no reason to skip a class unless there's some other problem. I'm just sorry it took me so long to pinpoint what that problem was."

"If I wasn't to blame, then neither were you," Diana said fervently. "I think what really woke me up to what lousy parenting I was doing was realizing that Misty was trying to avoid upsetting me." She regarded Laura with dismay. "My daughter's job isn't to protect *me*. It's mine to see that she's safe and happy."

She gave Laura a plaintive look. "Is she now, do you think? Safe and happy, I mean?"

"Not entirely," Laura said candidly. "It was tough for her today. She stayed behind when my class ended. She told me the kids were whispering behind her back. I tried to convince her that will pass, but she's not quite ready to believe it when all the evidence is to the contrary."

"I tried to tell her the same thing this morning," Diana said wearily. "She wanted to stay home from school one more day. Maybe I should have let her."

She looked so lost, Laura patted her hand. "Don't second-guess yourself. I think sending her to school was exactly the right thing. A few days off last week was understandable, but longer would just have made coming back that much harder."

"That's exactly what I told her," Diana said.

"The whole staff kept a very close eye on things today. There may have been a few whispers which unquestionably upset her, but no one was openly ganging up on her. We will stay on top of this, Diana. I promise you that."

"Thank you," Diana replied, then straightened up, her expression determined. "Now, tell me what I can do to help you with Mariah Litchfield's vendetta. Whatever you need, consider it done."

"Thanks," Laura said. "Just be there for the rally on Saturday. I tried to convince Misty to say a few words about this experience. I think it might help her to reclaim her self-esteem if she feels she's in charge of her life again and can speak out to help others who are being bullied. You could encourage her to do that, if you agree."

Diana nodded. "I do agree. Bullying needs to have a face and a voice. Who better than Misty, if she feels up to it? I won't push her, though. I can't do that."

"I wouldn't expect you to," Laura said. "She's a great girl, Diana. You and your husband have done a wonderful job with her. She's smart and ambitious, and there will come a time when this will just be a small, unfortunate blip in her life."

"I hope so," Diana said. "Teenagers take things so seriously. Everything's life or death to them. It scares me when I think how easily a good kid's life can be derailed by an incident like this. This could so easily have turned into a tragedy."

Laura understood her distress. "But it didn't," she reminded Diana. "Misty has a lot of support. She's going to be fine."

Unfortunately, even as she spoke the confident words, she worried she might be tempting fate just a little.

After a frantic week of preparations for Saturday's rally on the town green, by Friday Laura was exhausted and stressing out. J.C. took one look at her when he picked her up and shook his head.

"We're skipping the football game," he announced, his jaw set determinedly as he anticipated an argument.

She gave him a halfhearted one. "We can't," she protested. "I should be there, if only for appearances' sake. Besides, you love going to the games. And we promised Cal and Maddie we'd meet them there."

He handed over his cell phone. "Call and tell them

we're not coming," he said. "You need a break from everything related to that school, if only for tonight."

She frowned at him. "When did you turn so bossy?"

"It's a tactic I usually reserve for my most stubborn patients," he admitted. "It seemed appropriate tonight."

"I'm not some six-year-old who won't take her cough syrup," she grumbled, but she did make the call to Maddie.

"J.C.'s apparently made other plans for tonight," Laura told her, then listened, a smile breaking across her face. "Yeah, that's what I told him." She glanced pointedly at J.C. "No, he hasn't told me how he's planning to entertain me, but it better be good."

She was grinning when she disconnected the call.

"I suppose Maddie had a few ideas about how I should keep you occupied," he said. "It seems she usually does."

"Oh, yes," Laura said. "Mostly X-rated."

J.C. chuckled. "I could get behind that. How about you?"

"I'm not so sure yet. I'm a little annoyed by your presumptuousness."

"No, you're not. You're relieved not to have to sit in the stands and listen to the people around you taking sides."

"Okay, yes," she finally conceded. She regarded him curiously. "Are you as shocked as I am that there are people who actually believe Annabelle's punishment was too harsh?"

"Sadly, no," he said. "I've dealt with a few of them in the office since this happened."

"You're kidding!"

"Nope. It never ceases to amaze me how some parents can fail to take something like this seriously. One father, who brought his son in for a shot, then berated him when he cried, said kids these days need to toughen up. He says we're raising a generation of sissies." He shook his head. "Just the kind of message an impressionable boy needs to hear from his dad."

"How old was his son?"

"Four," J.C. responded wryly. "Guess you can't start too young with the stoicism in some circles."

"Good grief. What did you say?"

"That life has plenty of hard knocks that can't be avoided, but children deserve to be protected and kept safe from this kind of nonsense for as long as possible or at least until they're old enough to know how to handle it."

"How did he take that?"

J.C. shrugged. "He was the third parent of the week to threaten to take his child to another doctor."

Laura regarded him with dismay. "J.C., I'm so sorry."

"Why? Because I spoke my mind and some idiot couldn't take it? That's life, too." He gave her a chagrined smile. "Fortunately Bill thinks we've got too many patients as it is. He figures being abandoned by a few of the impossible ones isn't a huge loss."

"Good for Bill Townsend. That's just about the first totally admirable thing I've ever heard about him."

"He's not the complete jerk some people think he is," J.C. said, feeling compelled to defend Bill. "Cheating on Maddie the way he did and parading his pregnant girlfriend around town was wrong, but no one is sorrier about that than Bill is. It cost him everything. He realized way too late that he was still in love with Maddie, but by then she was with Cal. His girlfriend recognized that he'd never truly love her the way he did Maddie and left him to move back to Tennessee with their child. His relationships with each of his kids has suffered. I'm not suggesting that he's some kind of a saint, just that he paid a heavy price for his mistake."

"I guess I hadn't thought about it from that perspective," Laura admitted.

"I doubt those Sweet Magnolia friends of yours would encourage that slant. From what I hear they're loyal to their own and not very forgiving of anyone who messes with them."

"They are that," Laura confirmed. "When I first moved here, I didn't make a lot of friends outside of the other teachers at school. Being around the Sweet Magnolias, thanks to getting to know Annie, Sarah and Raylene on the fall festival committee, has been a real eye-opener. I envy them those deep, lifelong friendships."

"I thought they'd made you one of them," he said. "Obviously they consider you a friend."

"They do, and it's incredible to have their support, but they have all that history together. I'll never have that. With no siblings and my parents living in the Midwest, I don't have one single person around here who knows my whole history and can talk about shared experiences from the past. Having that is such a blessing." She hesitated, then added, "Not that there aren't some parts of my past I'd just as soon forget. And some, I fear, that will never leave me."

Eager not to dwell on the child she'd never know,

she studied him. "What about you? Who knows your whole life story?"

"My life story's not that interesting," he said. "And there's a whole lot of it that's best left in the past. Now, then, how about a quick dinner at Rosalina's before the game crowd pours in? Seems to me pizza or pasta are great comfort foods. I'm pretty sure it's the aroma of all that garlic that does it."

She gave him a knowing look. "You're not getting off the hook that easily, J.C. The second you hedge about your past, you only make me more curious. However, since I am starving and pizza sounds great, we'll postpone my inquisition until after dinner."

He grinned at her. "If I play my cards right, you will have much more intriguing things to focus on by then."

She chuckled. "Okay, that could work, too."

Laura had to admit she'd given very little thought to Misty, tomorrow's rally or even J.C.'s secretive past during the course of the evening. J.C. had done an excellent job of distracting her. Time and again, in fact.

But now, stretched out next to him in his king-size bed, she yawned and propped herself up on one elbow. "Okay, my turn," she said lightly.

He gave her an amused look. "Seems to me you've had a few turns already, but okay," he said, reaching for her.

"Not that," she said, playfully slapping away his hand before it could start working its magic once more. "I want to hear about you. Just one thing I don't know will do for now, but it better be good. You won't get away with telling me you hate broccoli or love mystery novels."

"Boy, you're setting the bar awfully high. I usually don't talk about the important stuff until the fifth or sixth date at least."

"Fifth? Sixth? Date? Chance meeting? Who's really been counting what's official and what's not?" she asked blithely. "Talk to me."

J.C. rolled onto his back and stared at the ceiling. For several minutes, she thought he might not speak at all, that she'd overplayed her hand.

"You know the biggest secret in my past," he said eventually.

"About your wife sleeping with your boss," she said. "I know that shaped your attitude toward women and relationships, but it didn't define who you are, J.C. Not entirely, anyway. I don't think anybody is shaped by just one event." Since he obviously wasn't volunteering information, she decided to probe for what she really wanted to know. "What were your parents like?"

"They were—are—basically good people. We don't have a lot of contact anymore."

Laura frowned at the admission. "Why is that?"

"We just don't. People grow apart, at least we have."

"Are your parents still living in the town where you grew up?"

He shook his head, his expression guarded as if he feared she might keep digging until she hit on some truth he didn't want to reveal. That only encouraged her to press on.

"Where are they?"

"My mother eventually left home, permanently, I

mean. She left more than once chasing after some man or another before that. I thought I'd explained about the cheating. Anyway, she traveled all over, but she eventually moved to Charlotte, North Carolina, to be closer to her sister. My father's in Tampa."

Laura frowned. "But you didn't grow up in either Florida or North Carolina, did you?"

"No. I was raised in Charleston."

She struggled to put the pieces together from the tidbits he was revealing. "Are you not close to your mom because she left your family?"

"That's part of it, I suppose. I saw what her leaving that last time did to my dad. It broke his spirit. The going and coming home had been terrible enough, but knowing it was final, that she was never coming back?" He shook his head. "He was never the same after that."

"Which makes you stronger than your father," Laura said. "Losing your wife didn't break you."

"No, it just left me bitter and determined to avoid all future entanglements," he said wryly, then glanced at her. "Until you. Somehow I couldn't resist you. I'm still trying to figure that out. How'd you sneak past all those well-honed defenses of mine?"

"Maybe the why and how don't matter," Laura said. "Sometimes fate just steps in."

"Maybe, but fate has a way of being unreliable. It can take things away just as quickly as it brings them into your life," he said, an edge of cynicism in his voice that suggested he still didn't entirely trust what was going on between them.

"Do you still think I'm going to abandon you?" she asked.

He shrugged. "It's always a possibility."

Laura felt the pain behind that admission. She wondered how much time it would take before he believed in her, in *them*. Or, because of his mother's treatment of his father, would he always have this nagging doubt that would hang over their relationship and keep it from flourishing?

Misty stared at the words she'd written earlier and wondered what on earth she'd been thinking when she'd agreed to speak at tomorrow's rally. How was she supposed to stand in front of all those people and reveal the shame she'd felt at the terrible things Annabelle had posted online about her? Getting through it had been hard enough. Reliving it in public might be more than she could do.

Her mom, Ms. Reed and even her dad had agreed, though, that talking about it might give her some kind of catharsis or something. As much as she trusted all of them, she thought they were being a little optimistic. Nothing was going to make her life better, not until she could go away to college and forget all about Serenity and Annabelle and stupid Greg Bennett.

She hadn't told a single soul—not even Katie—that Greg had been more and more persistent now that Annabelle wasn't in school to catch him trying to hook up with Misty. He'd cornered her in the hallway half a dozen times during the week, making her squirm with his disgusting suggestions about what he'd like to do to her. Thankfully all the teachers seemed to be hanging out in the halls between classes and after school. Whenever one of them had moved close, Greg had taken off, his smirk firmly in place. He was such a jerk! She still couldn't believe this whole mess had happened because Annabelle, who was otherwise pretty smart, hadn't recognized that.

Once more she looked at her notes for tomorrow, then crumpled up the paper and threw it in the trash. It landed right there with her first dozen attempts. When her cell phone rang, she grabbed it, relieved to have an excuse to take a break. She saw Katie's name and smiled as she answered.

"Boy, am I glad you called," she told her friend. "I've been trying and trying to write something for tomorrow, but everything I put on paper seems stilted and stupid. I'm thinking it's a bad idea for me to try to do this."

"No, it's not," Katie said. "If anything, it's more important than ever."

Something in Katie's voice alarmed Misty. "What do you mean?"

"There's something online. I'm not sure who posted it, but it was somebody from school. I spotted it on my page and when I looked around, it was all over."

Misty felt her heart actually sink in her chest. "How bad is it?" she asked.

"Pretty bad," Katie said.

"More pictures?" she asked, a catch in her voice. Those had been the worst, most degrading of everything Annabelle had done.

"Uh-huh, and not like last time," Katie said, her voice filled with sympathy. "These are worse, like they came from some porno site or something. There's no way anyone could believe they're you, but that's what it says."

Tears leaked out of Misty's eyes as she managed to whisper, "Where?"

"Go to my page. I wanted you to see them before I printed them out for Helen and Ms. Reed. Then I'll get Kyle to take them down. I called him to come home from school as soon as I saw this. He'll be here any minute and he knows how to pull stuff like this down. I've already posted a message about how phony they are and how disgusting the person is who put them up."

Misty knew that wouldn't be enough to stop the circulation of the pictures, though. This kind of thing could take on a life of its own. She was probably lucky someone hadn't decided to take it a step further and fake a video. Even a post that was taken down in minutes could go viral.

Her hands shook as she logged on to her computer and went to the social-networking site. One glimpse of the pictures made her gag with disgust.

"Oh, Katie, don't let Kyle see them," she pleaded, figuring this would just about doom that secret crush she had on Katie's brother. It wasn't much of a crush, because he was older and didn't even know she was alive. Unlike Katie's other brother, Ty, who was this major sports superstar, Kyle was quieter and a bit of a nerd. But he had a wicked sense of humor that made Misty laugh. "Please, Katie. I'll never be able to look at him again."

"Misty, it'll be okay," Katie said. "Kyle was as furious about this as I am. The minute I told him, he said he was heading home. He knows this isn't you and, most of all, that it isn't your fault. I pity whoever did it, if he figures out that part."

Misty was surprised it wasn't obvious. "It wasn't Annabelle? You're sure?"

"Not unless she's started some other page and online identity. Her old page is completely gone. I checked there first. I don't know enough about technology to figure out where this started, but maybe Kyle will."

"How am I supposed to even show my face tomorrow, much less speak?" Misty asked wearily.

"You'll do it because you aren't going to let these idiot bullies win. If you need me to, I'll stand on that stage right beside you. I can get some other kids to do the same thing. We'll present a united front, so everyone knows you're not in this alone."

"I know you're trying to help, but the truth is I *am* alone," Misty told her, feeling utterly defeated. "That's my name linked to those awful pictures, not yours or some other girl's. No matter how many times I tell people it wasn't me, that image will stick in everyone's head."

"It won't," Katie said with feeling. "We won't let it. But you have to speak tomorrow and show everyone how strong you are, that you're not going to let this destroy your reputation."

"I don't feel strong," Misty said miserably. "I know I didn't entirely believe it would be over once Annabelle was caught and suspended, but everyone kept saying it would be. I let myself start to hope they were right. Now, this. How am I supposed to go through this again, especially when I don't even know who's behind it this time? All I want to do is crawl into bed and hide."

"I'm telling you Kyle will figure out who did this, or the police will. The second I show these to Helen, you know she's going to be all over it. And Chief Rollins will be, too. His sisters are in school with us. I know he's terrified that the same awful thing could happen to Carrie or Mandy, so he takes it personally. I heard him tell Helen this wasn't happening in his town, not on his watch."

Misty almost managed a smile. "You almost make him sound like some sheriff in the Old West."

Katie giggled. "I guess in a way that's what it's like around here. Chief Rollins considers every single crime like an attack on him. He's fair, but he doesn't even take misdemeanors lightly. I heard my mom, Dana Sue and Helen saying that they'd have been locked up for sure if he'd been in charge when they were teenagers. They got into mischief all the time."

Misty actually chuckled at the image of the three women locked up. "Helen would have hated not being able to wear her stiletto heels in jail," she said. "She has a shoe wardrobe that's the envy of every woman in town. One pair probably costs as much as all my school clothes last fall."

"Yeah, Helen does love her Jimmy Choo's."

Surprised that she'd been able to find anything at all to laugh about, Misty sighed. "As bad as this is, I'm glad you told me, and I'm even happier that you're my friend."

"Always," Katie told her. "Now, I think I hear Kyle downstairs. Let me get him on this right now. I'll call you back after he's handled it and after I speak to Helen, okay? Or do you want to come over? Maybe hang out for a while?"

The thought of facing Kyle after he'd seen the pictures online was way too depressing. "Not tonight."

"But I will see you at the rally tomorrow, right?" Katie said.

When Misty didn't immediately answer, Katie prodded, "You have to be there, Misty. And you have to speak. You'll regret it if you don't. I'll come to your house and go with you, okay?"

"Okay," Misty agreed reluctantly.

With Katie's warning about regrets still ringing in her ears, Misty hung up, then threw herself across her bed. Her friend was probably right. She would hate herself if she didn't stand up for herself.

She just wasn't sure she could face the humiliating prospect of having everyone staring at her, wondering if just maybe she really had posed for those sick pictures online. If even a single person believed she could do anything like that, she thought she might very well die of embarrassment.

19

Cal and Maddie had just finished cleaning up the kitchen and putting their two little ones down for the night when Kyle walked in, his expression dark. Maddie gave him a questioning look.

"Were we expecting you tonight?" Maddie asked, giving him a fierce hug. "Not that I'm not always happy to have you come home from college."

"Katie called me," he explained, looking from his mother to Cal, his expression puzzled. "She hasn't talked to either of you about what's going on? I thought for sure she would."

Maddie frowned. "Not a word. What is it? Why would she call you, rather than telling us?"

"Something to do with Misty," Cal guessed, his anger stirring. "And it's online. She wants you to fix it."

Kyle nodded. "She filled me in on what's been happening and on tomorrow's rally. Someone's apparently not taking it well."

"What does that mean?" Cal asked.

"They posted fake pictures of Misty online, worse than the previous ones, if Katie can be believed. It shook her up. She asked me to help her take them down. I got in the car and headed straight home." He gave Cal a distraught look. "I can't believe some pervert is doing this to a nice girl like Misty. Who would do such a thing?"

"We all thought the obvious suspect had been neutralized, so to speak," Cal said. "Either she's foolish enough to keep her vendetta going or someone's acting at her behest."

"At the moment, that hardly matters," Maddie said. "Can you do what Katie wants? Can you take them down?"

"Shouldn't Helen see them first?" Cal asked.

"I think Katie was going to call Helen and print them out for her before I got here," Kyle said. "Helen can probably get a court order under the circumstances, but I may be able to get them down faster."

"As long as Helen's okay with it, do it," Maddie said at once. "Even if Katie's already called her, I'll get her over here."

Kyle nodded and headed upstairs.

Cal looked at his wife. "This makes me sick to my stomach and I haven't even seen the pictures."

"What it makes me is livid," Maddie said. "I keep picturing Katie being in the same situation, and I want to rip out the heart of whoever is tormenting Misty." She regarded Cal with dismay. "Could Annabelle possibly be doing this? She's already in a world of trouble."

Cal shook his head. "I honestly don't know. I know Mariah has raised Annabelle to feel entitled and a little above everyone else in Serenity, but I thought her father was trying to keep her grounded in reality, especially now with so much on the line."

Maddie nodded. "I'd better make that call to Helen. Do you want to check on the kids, see if there's anything you can do to help?"

"On my way," he said, then paused to give his wife a kiss.

"What was that for?"

"Just to let you know how glad I am to be married to a woman who's such an incredible mother of such terrific kids. Katie's not only smart, she's mature beyond her years. And she's learned what it is to be a good friend from watching you, Helen and Dana Sue."

"I know Bill's their father," Maddie said, "but you've had a lot of influence in the way all of them have turned out. Credit where credit's due, okay?"

Cal winked at her. "Let's see if we can keep getting it right with the little ones. We have a long way to go with them."

Upstairs he found Kyle at work on Katie's laptop while Katie paced around the room, chewing on one of her nails. She regarded Cal with alarm.

"You know?" she asked.

He nodded. "You could have told your mom and me, but I'm glad you called Kyle for help. The important thing is to deal with this, and you did all the right things."

To his surprise, Katie threw her arms around him. "I've wanted to talk to you from the very beginning, but I couldn't."

"I know you made a promise to Misty. You did the best you could, and your mother and I are very proud of you for figuring out a way to help Misty and remain loyal at the same time."

"I still felt kinda sneaky," she admitted.

"But you knew it was too much for you and Misty to handle on your own. It takes real maturity to recognize that and act."

She gave him a pleading look. "Don't look at the pictures, okay? It's awful enough that Kyle has to see them."

Cal understood her embarrassment on her friend's behalf. "You made printouts for Helen?"

"Uh-huh, and she's coming over. As soon as she says it's okay, Kyle will take them down. He thinks he can do it, right, Kyle?"

"I can do it," he said grimly. He glanced up at Cal. "Now that I've seen the disgusting things, I'm even more anxious to get my hands on whoever posted them in the first place."

"I think we all would like a chance to have a little come-to-Jesus talk with that person," Cal admitted. "Any idea who it might be?"

"I'm working on it," Kyle said.

"Anything I can do?" Cal asked.

Kyle nodded toward his sister. "Get her to go downstairs. Having her standing over my shoulder makes me nervous. I don't like her seeing this stuff."

"I've already seen it," Katie protested. "Besides, I'm not looking at the pictures. I'm trying to see what you're doing so I can fix it myself next time."

Kyle gave Cal a pointed look. "Please."

Cal put a hand on Katie's shoulder. "Come on. I think I heard Helen drive up. You can come downstairs and fill her in before she comes up to take a look for herself."

Katie nodded at last. "Okay," she grumbled, then

scowled at her brother, "but I want step-by-step instructions."

"Yes, mini-crusader," Kyle said. "I'll see what I can do."

"Do you promise or are you just trying to pacify me?" Katie asked.

Kyle shook his head ruefully. "You probably don't want an answer to that."

"Jerk," Katie muttered.

"Pest," Kyle responded in kind.

"Enough," Cal said, smiling at the familiar bickering. For all of it he'd heard from these two over the years, he knew with every fiber that they had each other's backs. Kyle coming home on a moment's notice was proof enough of that.

Laura paced behind the stage that had been set up on the town green.

"She'll be here," J.C. said, knowing she was worried about Misty. She had been ever since Helen's call the night before to report the latest bullying incident.

"Maybe she shouldn't be," Laura said. "I know I pressed her to do this and Diana backed me up, but that was before those pictures turned up online last night."

"Your reasoning is just as valid now," J.C. said. "I'm not saying it will be easy for Misty to face all these people, but if she does it, I think she'll feel so much better about herself. Taking a stand for herself and against bullying will send a message to this town."

"I know the town needs to hear the message," Laura said. "I'm just not sure Misty's the one who has to deliver it."

"Who better?" J.C. countered. "And we're all going to be right here on stage with her. She won't be alone. Trust me, she's going to feel empowered for having done this."

Laura obviously remained unconvinced. "She's only sixteen, J.C. She must be devastated to think even one person might believe she actually posed for those pictures."

"She's strong enough to do this," he repeated. "And she'll be even stronger once she does."

He looked out over the crowd just then and spotted Misty and Katie circling around the fringes, heading toward the stage. The two girls were deep in conversation. Misty seemed to be lagging behind, but Katie kept urging her on.

"Here she comes now," he told Laura. As he spoke, he noticed the whispers building as people spotted Misty. For the first time, he felt a faint stirring of dread. Maybe he was the one who was wrong. Maybe this had been a terrible idea. Everything that had happened had taken a toll on Misty. What if this turned ugly and became the last straw for her?

Frowning as the whispers spread, he turned to Laura. "Maybe you were right. Maybe she shouldn't do this."

Laura regarded him with surprise, clearly taken aback by his sudden change of heart.

"Listen to them," he said, nodding toward the growing crowd. "Something's stirring them up."

But then Misty was beside them and he couldn't say more. He forced a smile. "You doing okay?"

"Scared to death," she said.

"It's okay if you want to back out," he said. "We have other speakers."

She shook her head. "No," she said firmly. "Everybody was right. I need to do this." She glanced at Katie. "You're going to stand right there with me, though, right?"

"I won't budge from your side," Katie promised.

"And we're all going to be on the stage, too," Laura reassured her.

Just then the microphone crackled to life. Sarah McDonald welcomed everyone to the live broadcast of the Serenity Rally Against Bullying. "You all already know why we're here today. We intend to take a stand against something that eventually affects just about every child. Bullying can take many forms, from the toddler who snatches away shovels from the other kids in a sandbox or pushes another child off of a swing to something as offensive as what's been happening recently to one of our high school students. We're here to let everyone know that none of that is acceptable in our community, that we're a town where people treat each other with respect and dignity."

Her comments drew mostly cheers and applause, though J.C. noticed that a few people looked on silently.

Sarah continued, "Now I'd like to introduce a woman who taught many of you to always be on your best behavior, Frances Wingate."

Frances looked frail but determined as she approached the podium. She looked out over the crowd. "I see a lot of people here today who spent time in my classroom over the years. I'm here today to talk about how ashamed I am of you."

Her words drew a shocked gasp.

"Yes, you," she continued, her tone stern. "These

are your children who are engaging in these disrespect-
ful, despicable acts against other children. I don't know
much about how the internet works, but I do understand
that it can be a tool for cowards, a way to torment another human being. And that's what's happening right
here in Serenity, with your blessing."

She gazed out over the crowd. "Oh, I hear some of
you saying you didn't put up those posts or that your
children would never do such a thing, but do you know
for a fact that they didn't? Do you monitor what they
do online? I'll wager you don't. Far too few parents do.
And unless you happen to be one of those few who does,
then you're responsible. You!" she said sternly, looking
from face to face in the increasingly silent crowd. "You
let this happen. You can fix it."

Once more, she seemed to be looking every indi-
vidual in the audience straight in the eye as she added
fiercely, "And I expect you to do it."

With that, she turned and walked back to her seat and
sat down heavily. It took a moment, and then thunder-
ous applause broke out.

J.C. leaned over to whisper in her ear. "You've given
me a tough act to follow."

She gave him a shaky smile. "Oh, I think you've got
what it takes."

Laura gave his hand a squeeze. "I know you do."

J.C. approached the podium with trepidation. He
began by talking about the kind of incidents he and
Bill saw in their practice, the evidence of the toll bullying took on even the youngest children.

"We all act as if it's no big deal at that age, that kids

need to toughen up. I was told that just this week by a parent. Well, here's the way I see it."

He drew in a deep breath, cast a quick glance at Laura, then said, his voice wavering despite his best attempt to control it, "Bullying cost my little brother his life."

Blinking back tears, he continued, "Stevie was a great kid. He was slower than other kids. He struggled in school, though it took years to figure out exactly why. His classmates were calling him a dummy by first grade. They never chose him for their teams at recess. He wanted so badly to be liked, to be normal, just like everyone else. He had a smile that could light up the world, but, day by day, year by year, that smile faded and the light in his eyes died."

He let that sink in, then said, "When I realized what was happening, I did everything I could to protect him. I had more bloody noses and black eyes than any kid in school. My parents and teachers thought I was a trouble-maker because I never told what was going on. Neither did Stevie. For a while things even got better."

He paused. "And then I went to high school, leaving my kid brother on his own back in middle school, struggling to fit in, being beaten down emotionally a little more each day." He heard the collective indrawn breath of the crowd and let the silence go on before adding, "Until he couldn't take it anymore. Stevie hanged himself after school one day. He was thirteen years old." J.C.'s voice broke. "Thirteen. Look around you at the children you know who are just barely starting adolescence. Try to imagine the amount of pain a child that age must have been in to take his own life."

Like Frances, he tried to look every single person in the crowd directly in the eyes. "Thirteen," he said again at last. "The kids in Serenity deserve more from us."

Even through his own tears, he saw tissues come out of purses as he spoke. As he walked back to his seat, Laura was on her feet, enveloping him in a hug. Misty joined her.

"I knew," Misty whispered, tears streaming down her face. "You didn't say all that, but I knew the story didn't have a happy ending."

"No, it didn't," J.C. said, then gave her a hug. "But this one will. No matter what I have to do to see to it, Misty, this one will."

Laura was devastated by J.C.'s revelation. No wonder he'd taken what was happening to Misty so seriously. He'd lived the horror of bullying and seen just how tragically it could end.

What she couldn't understand was why he hadn't told her sooner. Just when she thought they were close, when she'd convinced herself they had a real shot at the future, she realized he was holding yet another part of himself back.

This wasn't the time for thinking about any of that, though. Bill Townsend was speaking now, adding a voice for even the youngest children who were victimized on playgrounds or in classrooms. He'd be followed by Helen and Chief Rollins. Then it would be Laura and Betty's turn to explain how the school intended to handle not just this incident, but any further bullying incidents.

Each of them kept their remarks short and to the point. As Misty's turn to wrap up the event came closer,

Laura kept a careful eye on her. She seemed to have drawn some kind of strength from listening to J.C. There was a determined set to her jaw and a spark in her eyes that had been missing when she'd first arrived at the town green.

Since Laura was to introduce her as she wound up her own remarks, she turned to Misty before she rose. "You ready to do this?"

Misty nodded. "I can do it."

"Of course you can," Katie said loyally.

Laura said a few words, then expressed her pride in Misty's willingness to come forward and talk about what had happened to her and how it had affected the way she looked at herself, at the town and the future.

No sooner had she finished her introduction than she noticed a restlessness on the fringes of the crowd. She realized then that many of the students from the high school had gathered back there, united for reasons she feared might not be good.

Anticipating a problem, she lingered by the podium next to Misty and Katie, drawing a concerned look from J.C. She gave him a faint nod toward the edge of the green. Obviously picking up on her warning, he slipped over and spoke quietly to Carter Rollins, who immediately left the stage.

Misty had barely opened her mouth to speak, her voice quavery but determined, when the first jeer rang out. "Hey, girl, is this you? Can you do me like that?"

A picture was waved in the air, a grainy, but devastatingly recognizable blowup apparently of one of the doctored photos that had made its way online the night before.

Misty's voice faltered as people looked around.

"Whoa, girl! Who knew little Goody Two-shoes looked like that with her clothes off?"

At the second shout, Carter's men moved in and started taking teens into custody. The entire crowd erupted with cries, some directed against the teens, some against the interfering police officers.

Misty's face had turned beet-red. Tears welled up in her eyes as she fled the stage.

"Go after her," J.C. shouted at Laura. "I'm going to help Carter round up those jerks."

Laura found Misty sobbing in the alley behind the radio station, Katie at her side. Sarah McDonald reached them before Laura did and pulled Misty into her arms. "Don't you shed one single tear over those idiots," she soothed. "Not one single tear."

"But now everyone's seen the pictures. Even my mom and dad. They were there in the front, but they still saw them. They must think I'm awful."

"Your parents will never for a second believe those pictures are real," Laura consoled her. She glanced at Sarah. "Will you stay with them? I'll go look for Diana and Les."

"No," Misty pleaded. "I don't want to see them."

"You need to see them, and they need to be with you. They must be worried sick about you right now."

"We'll be inside the station," Sarah said, looking to Misty for agreement. "You'll be safe in there. We can keep the doors locked, check before we let anyone inside."

Misty sniffed and nodded agreement.

Laura took off in search of the Dawsons. She found

them by the stage looking frantic. Les looked as if he wanted to break a few bones. Only Diana's command that he stay focused on Misty seemed to be keeping him calm.

"Where is she?" Diana demanded when Laura approached. "Did you find her?"

"She's at the radio station. Sarah took her and Katie inside."

"Thank God," Diana murmured. "Les, are you coming?"

He looked toward the commotion still going on across the green. "I'd rather…"

"Beating some kid to a pulp might give you temporary satisfaction," Diana said. "I wouldn't mind throwing a punch or two myself, but Misty needs us." She latched on to his arm and shook it. "Did you hear me? Our daughter needs us."

Les sighed. "You're right. Let's go."

Laura let them head over to the radio station on their own, then found Helen in the crowd.

"How much worse can this get?" she asked the attorney.

"A whole lot worse before I'm done," Helen said grimly. "Thanks to Kyle Townsend, I have a pretty good idea of who was behind those latest pictures. Carter's going to follow up and, if I'm right, suspension from school will be the least of what happens to some of these kids. I'm taking a whole slew of them to court. Apparently Annabelle was just the instigator. There were a few kids just waiting in the wings to escalate this."

She gave Laura a weary look. "It's going to get uglier before it gets better. Do you think Misty will be able to handle that?"

Laura thought of the shaken, sobbing girl she'd left with Sarah and wondered about that. "I honestly don't know," she said. "How much can a girl her age handle before it breaks her?"

"I'm almost ready to suggest to the Dawsons that they let her transfer to a school somewhere else," Helen said. "I'd pay for it myself just to get her away from this. At the same time, I hate for Misty to feel like she has to leave her home because of what someone else has done."

"Unfortunately, I think maybe at this point, she'd be eager to go," Laura said. "But I agree with you, it would be a crying shame. Is it too late to push to have Annabelle transferred out of this school system?"

Helen nodded. "More than likely. I'm not saying that shouldn't happen. It probably should. I just don't think that's going to fix things. Too many other kids will be right here unless I can manage to make examples of all of them. At this rate, half the senior class should probably go."

"That would certainly cause an uproar," Laura said, trying to imagine it.

Helen nodded. "Something tells me an uproar is what it's going to take to turn this around."

"Is there anything you need me to do right now?"

Helen shook her head. "I'm heading over to the police station next."

Laura nodded. "I'll check on Misty. If you run into J.C., tell him I should be home in another hour or so."

Helen hesitated. "Did you know what he was going to say today?"

"Not a clue," Laura admitted. "My heart ached for him when I heard what happened to his brother."

"That's a heavy load of guilt for anyone to carry all these years," Helen said.

Laura was startled by her assessment. "Guilt? J.C. didn't do anything wrong. He tried to help."

"Doesn't matter," Helen said. "Whatever he did wasn't enough, and I know how men's minds work. The guilt of not doing enough can eat away at them for years to come."

"Voice of experience?" Laura asked.

Helen nodded. "Erik had his share of baggage when we met. It still surfaces from time to time. Keep an eye on J.C. Something tells me he'll need you today more than he'll ever admit."

Laura watched her go, her thoughts in turmoil. She'd felt sick for J.C. as he'd spoken, but not once had she imagined him blaming himself for his brother's death. Of course he did, though. Anyone who cared as deeply as he did would take something like that totally to heart. Even more than his wife's betrayal, *this* is what had shaped the man he'd become, the direction his life had taken. She even wondered if he'd become a pediatrician simply to be a first line of defense against signs of bullying.

What she didn't know was how she'd ever convince him that the guilt shouldn't be his burden.

20

The police station was chaotic. J.C. tried to stay out of the way, but he had no intention of leaving until he was sure the hooligans who'd taunted Misty were, if not behind bars, at least charged with disturbing the peace or whatever else Carter could think of to throw at them. He imagined Helen had a few ideas along that line she was eager to share. He'd never seen her looking more ferocious as she huddled with the police chief.

Eventually she headed his way.

"You okay?" she asked him. "I know what you said today couldn't have been easy, but I think it had an impact, J.C. I really do. I saw the shock on people's faces when they realized the sort of consequences this behavior can have. There's a tendency to dismiss it as childish mischief, but we both know it's a lot more than that."

"Obviously it didn't faze those boys," he said ruefully.

"Because they're young and stupid," Helen said succinctly. "Just wait till Greg Bennett and his cronies figure out they're about to be suspended from the football team for the rest of the season over this. Betty can hardly wait until Monday morning to haul them into her office for that announcement. Amazingly, the coach is backing her up a hundred percent. I knew Cal would have, but the football coach is usually a lot more focused on winning than he is on what's right."

"Some things are more important than a winning season," J.C. said grimly.

"Unfortunately, not being able to play is likely to kill Greg's chances for a college scholarship," Helen said. "I have little to no sympathy for the boy, but that's going to be tough for his folks to accept. They were so proud that he'd be their first to get into college."

"What's next?" J.C. asked. "Is there anything I can do here?"

Helen shook her head. "Carter has things under control and the prosecutor will be here shortly to do all the official paperwork and determine the charges. I'll also be conferring with him about bringing criminal charges against the person who posted the latest pictures online. I'll be in court first thing Monday to file a civil case, as well."

"Do you know who did it?" J.C. asked. "You're a hundred percent sure?"

Helen nodded. "It was Greg. It was his way of standing up for Annabelle, if you can believe that. He thought it might take the heat off of her. I'm not entirely convinced that Annabelle herself didn't put him up to it. That is one twisted relationship. If I were Mariah, I'd get those two as far apart as possible."

"Do you think the Litchfields will transfer Annabelle to another school after this?"

Helen nodded. "I don't think they're going to have a choice. Betty and Hamilton Reynolds were talking about a formal expulsion hearing earlier. The school board will hold an emergency meeting on Monday."

"That could be best for everyone," J.C. said.

"Only if Mariah accepts it graciously," Helen warned. "I'm not convinced she's capable of that. If anything, she's going to be more furious than ever with Laura and Betty." She met his gaze. "That reminds me, Laura said to tell you she'd be at home. She'd like you to come by."

J.C. nodded. "I want to see the Dawsons first, then I'll head over there."

Or not, he thought. He wasn't sure he was quite ready to see the pity in Laura's eyes when she looked at him. It had been there after he spoke. It was the same look he'd seen time and again after Stevie had died. It was usually accompanied by a bunch of platitudes that didn't mean a thing, that his brother's death was a terrible tragedy, but that none of it was his fault.

Nonsense. He'd known what was happening to his brother and he hadn't stopped it. If that didn't place the blame squarely on his shoulders, then what would?

Laura was beside herself. There'd been no sign of J.C. on Saturday afternoon. Nor had she heard from him that evening or today. When Helen had called to give her an update on the charges pending against the various students involved in the previous day's debacle, she made herself ask about J.C.

"He didn't come by?" Helen asked, clearly surprised. "I passed along your message and he said he was going by the Dawsons first and would head to your place after that."

"I haven't heard a word from him," Laura admitted. "Maybe I should go over to his place to check on him."

Silence greeted her words. "Maybe not," Helen said eventually. "Yesterday was obviously very emotional for him. He laid himself bare before the entire town, told something he's apparently never revealed to anyone in town before, an obviously painful part of his past. I spoke to Bill briefly, and he said J.C. had never even mentioned it to him. He probably needs to regroup."

"But what does it say about us that he doesn't want my support while he does that?" Laura said wearily. "Maybe I've been kidding myself that we're actually building a strong relationship here."

"I don't know J.C. all that well, but I know a little bit about men who feel guilty about a tragedy, even when that guilt isn't justified," Helen said. "They're terrified that the people they love will think less of them."

"That's ridiculous!" Laura said.

"That's male pride," Helen countered. "Give him a little time, Laura. He'll come around. At least, that's my advice. You're free to ignore it. Until Erik, my track record with men wasn't exactly a shining example of what healthy relationships were meant to be."

Laura chuckled at the honest statement. "I'll take that into consideration."

"J.C.'s a good guy," Helen said. "That much I do know. I wasn't always sure of it, but now I am."

"I know," Laura said softly. She'd already recognized that he was one of the best. And he'd come along when she'd almost given up hope of finding real love, the kind that would weather any storm.

On Monday morning, Laura didn't have a second to spare for thoughts about J.C. The halls were erupting with angry chatter as the news leaked out that a number of the football players had been suspended from playing for the remainder of the season, including Greg Bennett. To her regret, the blame for that was being placed not where it belonged—on the young men themselves—but on Misty.

She debated with herself, then decided to address the situation in her first class. Maybe she could diffuse the situation at least a little.

"I've heard a lot of talk this morning about what happened on Saturday and about the fallout," she began, only to draw hostile stares from many of her students. "Let's talk about it." She looked into each grim face. "And let's do it politely."

"It's all because Misty Dawson is not only a little slut, but a crybaby," one of the girls said snidely.

Laura held her gaze. "Which part of *politely* didn't you understand? Students in my classes don't call each other sluts or crybabies or anything else that's intended to deliberately hurt them. That's bullying. Have you learned nothing from what's been going on recently? Words can wound people. Actions can wound people. And yet I look at you and some of you clearly still think it's one big joke. Annabelle Litchfield is being transferred to another school because of this. Greg Bennett is likely to lose his college scholarship because he can't play ball the rest of the season. What about any of that strikes you as funny?"

"It's not funny," Jeb Hightower said. "It's wrong. I hope Misty can't sleep because of what she's done to them."

Laura regarded him with shock. "Hold on. Misty was

the victim, not Annabelle or Greg. She was targeted on-line and right here at school with vicious rumors and lies designed to humiliate and embarrass her."

"What makes you think they were lies?" Jeb said, looking around with a smirk. "A picture's better than a thousand words, right?"

"And a fake picture says more about the person who created it than it does about the person supposedly in it," Laura corrected, though she could see that she wasn't getting through to them. They were intent on defending their friends and demonizing Misty. How on earth was she supposed to turn this around? Could it even be done?

"Does anyone here have a different perspective?" she asked hopefully.

Sally Washington, a shy girl who rarely spoke unless called on, raised her hand tentatively. "I think maybe they don't get it," she said, nodding toward Jeb and Hailey who'd spoken out first, "because nobody's ever picked on them."

"Or because they were born bullies, too," Tim Rogers dared to say, shooting a defiant look at Jeb. "You started stealing lunch money from the littler kids back in first grade. You did it just because you were bigger and you could."

"And, Hailey, you never speak to anyone who isn't pretty or popular," Sally added, apparently gaining strength from Tim's accusations. "It's like the rest of us don't even exist. At most we're an annoyance in your perfect little world. I'm tired of it. If you don't like me, fine. I don't need to be your friend, but I'm a person and you should at least be polite to me and the other kids who aren't as popular as you."

Sally's declaration stirred a few others to echo the same thoughts, and suddenly the tide turned ever-so-slightly. Hailey, Jeb and a few others were on the defensive and had perhaps their first taste of feeling what it was like to be disparaged and ridiculed publicly.

Jeb continued to look defiant, but Hailey actually looked shaken. Her eyes filled with tears.

"I didn't know," she whispered. "I honestly didn't know how it felt to have people say hateful things."

Laura held up a hand to stop the discussion. "I think what happened in here just now is really, really important. I hope all of you will think about it before you speak disrespectfully to or about another classmate. Sally got it exactly right. You don't all have to be best friends, but you do owe it to each other to be courteous and respectful. Sally and Tim, thank you for speaking up. And, Hailey, I'm proud of you for taking another look at what you've been doing."

When the bell rang, she dismissed the class, feeling the tiniest bit more optimistic.

But as soon as she stepped into the hall, she saw Jeb immediately align himself with his buddies, overheard the same old rallying cry in Greg and Annabelle's defense. And knew that the risk to Misty was far from over.

J.C. was glancing at his next patient's file, when Debra stepped into his office. "Laura Reed is on the phone for you. She sounds upset."

Though he'd spent most of the weekend avoiding her, he knew that couldn't go on forever. He nodded. "I'll take it. Let Mrs. Hodges know I'll be in to check Liza in a minute."

Debra nodded, then retreated and closed the door behind her. J.C. picked up his phone.

"Is everything okay?" he asked at once. "Is Misty in school?"

"No sign of her," Laura said tersely. "I'm really worried, J.C., and not just because she didn't show up. I guess that's understandable under the circumstances, but the talk around school isn't good. The kids are taking sides. Some of them, especially those who've dealt with their own instances of bullying over the years, are firmly on her side, but the others, I don't know, J.C., their attitude scares me. I think they want revenge of some kind. They see Annabelle and Greg and the others who've been suspended as the real victims."

"Unfortunately, I suppose that's not really surprising. Have you heard about any specific plans for retaliation?"

"No, but I have to wonder just how much more Misty can take. I called Diana before I called you, and she says Misty's been locked in her room most of the day. She won't talk and she won't come out. I can tell that Diana's starting to freak out just a little. I have a terrible feeling some of what I'm hearing here at school is spilling over onto the internet and Misty's aware of it."

"I can't say I blame Misty for wanting to hide out or Diana for being scared," J.C. said. "I'm sure my story about Stevie probably didn't help matters. I meant it to be a warning to the perpetrators of how tragic things can get, but I imagine Diana can't shake that image. I should have thought of that."

"It was a story people needed to hear," Laura said

with conviction. "Don't beat yourself up for sharing it. And I didn't call to make you freak out over Misty, either. I'm just wondering if we shouldn't go over there."

"No question about it," J.C. said. "I was there for a while on Saturday, and Misty seemed to be holding up okay, but I have no idea what's been happening online since then. It makes sense to check on her. I'll pick you up the minute school's out."

"Thank you," Laura said.

"No thanks necessary."

"Yes, there are. You didn't make me feel like an idiot for worrying."

"Are you kidding me?" he said incredulously. "It's because you care so deeply that I fell for you." He heard her faint gasp of surprise and almost smiled. That was definitely a conversation they needed to have soon. Things between them deserved some clarity, which he imagined had been in short supply the past few days with him steering clear of her, rather than turning to her for comfort.

"I'll see you soon," he told her. "We're going to find everything is just fine when we get there."

Despite the staunch words, though, he was a wreck for the next couple of hours until he could leave to pick up Laura. It took every ounce of restraint he possessed not to jump in his car and head straight over to the Dawsons. He did allow himself to make a quick call to Diana, who said Misty had emerged long enough to eat some soup. That was reassuring enough to get him through the rest of the afternoon.

Still, thoughts of Stevie were never far from mind. All those years ago, he'd managed to convince himself his brother was coping okay. He'd been so caught up in his own activities in high school, he'd left Stevie to fend for himself.

He'd realized just how mistaken he'd been when he'd come home one day to find his brother had hanged himself from the light fixture in his room. He was barely breathing when J.C. got to him. J.C. had done everything in his power to resuscitate him as he'd waited for the paramedics, but it had been too long. Though Stevie had clung to life with the help of machines for a few more days, his parents had eventually made the horrendous decision to let him go. None of them had ever entirely recovered. His mother had left for the final time soon after.

Those days had changed J.C. forever. He'd chosen his medical specialty of pediatrics with an eye toward being alert to all signs of bullying affecting his young patients. It still killed him that he hadn't spotted it sooner in Misty's case.

Though he told himself she was fine a hundred times as the clocked slowly ticked off each interminable minute, he still found himself at the high school at two, rather than three. Laura regarded him with surprise.

"Can you get away now?" he asked, unable to hide his sense of urgency.

She took one look at his face or heard something in his voice and immediately nodded. "Give me two minutes to get someone in here to cover my class."

Not until they were in his car did she reach for his tensed arm, resting her hand there until he slowly relaxed.

"Did you speak to Misty?" she asked.

He shook his head.

"Diana?"

"Yes, and she even said Misty had eaten a little soup for lunch."

"Then what spooked you? Were you thinking about your brother?"

"How could I not?" he asked angrily. "I should have done more. He died because I didn't protect him."

"No, J.C. What happened was a tragedy, but it wasn't your fault. You were, what, eighteen when he died, even younger when you had to start protecting him? You couldn't have understood then how lost and alone he was feeling."

"Maybe not, but I did know what was happening. I just turned into some self-absorbed jerk and convinced myself he could handle it. I forgot all about my own brother," he said, his tone filled with the self-loathing that was never far away whenever he thought of Stevie's death.

As they pulled to a stop in front of the Dawsons' house, Laura forced him to meet her gaze. "Have you ever let down another child?"

"There have been patients I couldn't help," he said.

"But not for lack of trying, right? Just as you're doing everything possible for Misty. We both are. This situation is going to get better, J.C."

"How can you possibly be so sure of that?" he asked.

She smiled then and the ice around his heart seemed to melt just a little.

"Because you and I will see to it," she told him. "I have that much faith in us, in you."

For the first time in years, J.C. actually felt as if he just might be the kind of man who was worthy of such unquestioning trust.

When Misty heard a car outside and glanced out her bedroom window, she saw both Dr. Fullerton and Ms. Reed walking toward the house. At the sight of them, she panicked. Leaving her room, she raced down the stairs to beat her mom to the door.

"You're not here to make me go back to school, are you?" she demanded when she opened it. "Please, don't try to force me to go. I can't. All of Annabelle's friends hate me now, and just the way I thought it would, it's getting uglier online. Now the other kids are posting mean things, too. Today's been worse than ever."

Dr. Fullerton's gaze narrowed. "What do you mean?"

"Everybody hates me now," Misty said, near tears.

"Let me see," Ms. Reed commanded.

Misty regarded her with dismay. "Do I have to? They're pretty disgusting."

"We need to see them," the doctor said. "It's okay, Misty. We're not going to believe them. Have a little faith in us. We both know the kind of person you are."

She knew if they went online themselves, they'd be able to find the sites on their own, so she finally sighed and showed the posts to them.

"I just don't understand how this could keep happening now that the court's involved," Misty said miserably. "Surely Annabelle's parents wouldn't allow it, and the other kids should be smart enough to see how severe the punishment is. Look at what's happened to half the football team."

"It's not Annabelle," J.C. said, after studying the posts. "I'd bet money on that."

"But that's her screen name," Misty argued. "She'd stopped using the page, but today it was back up."

"I have a hunch she's given someone else access to her account," J.C. said. "Laura, you read papers all the time. I imagine you look to see if an essay sounds as if it was written by the student who turned it in. What do you think?"

Ms. Reed glanced at the posts and nodded. "There's definitely something different about these."

Misty was completely thrown by their reaction. "Are you sure? How can you tell?"

"An expert would have to compare them, but there's a difference that seems apparent to me," Dr. Fullerton insisted. "Laura, do you have anything more specific?"

Ms. Reed studied them with a thoughtful expression. "There's a different vocabulary for one thing, and the grammar isn't quite the same."

"But who?" Misty asked, then sighed. "I guess there are plenty of kids who really hate me now. It could be any of them."

"Or it's not a kid at all," Dr. Fullerton said, looking angrier than Misty had ever seen him.

Misty blinked at him. "You don't think it could be Annabelle's mom, do you?"

"She would have access to the computer," Ms. Reed said, though she looked as stunned by the possibility as Misty was. "I just can't see Mariah resorting to this, though."

"Okay, then what about Greg Bennett?" Dr. Fullerton asked. "He's one angry kid. He's lost a lot. It wouldn't surprise me a bit if he figured out a way to retaliate. And Helen says he's the one who was behind the pictures posted right before the rally."

Misty stared at him in shock, then stood up, practically shaking with fury. "That does it," she said furiously. "One bully was bad enough, but I will not allow a creep like that to freak me out." She looked at her English teacher. "I'll be back at school tomorrow and I'll be in class."

Both adults seemed startled by her announcement. Misty understood their reaction. She'd been a shaky mess when they'd gotten here. In fact, for weeks now she'd acted as if the things being said about her were true and she had a reason to hide. No more. She was done with that.

Maybe it was standing on that stage on Saturday after all that had given her a different perspective. Even though things had gone horribly wrong at the rally, she'd seen a few people look at her with understanding and sympathy. Some people had gotten it, just the way Ms. Reed had said they would.

Just walking onto the stage and facing the crowd had taken more courage than she'd ever imagined she possessed. Now she would draw on that strength and face the kids who'd made her life miserable. They were the ones who should be ashamed of themselves, not her.

Ms. Reed smiled at her. "Misty, I could not be more proud of you."

"Me, too," Dr. Fullerton said, then grinned. "Want a ride to school?"

"Nope," Misty said decisively. "I'll go with my friends. I still have some, despite what's happened.

They'll back me up." She gave Ms. Reed a knowing look. "You know they will."

The teacher smiled. "Yes, you have some very good friends. They've just been waiting for you to say you needed them."

"And one of them took matters into her own hands. I know that, too," she said. "I know Katie's been feeling guilty for ratting me out to her grandmother, not that she's admitted that she did it, but come on, who else would talk to Mrs. Vreeland? It's about time for me to tell her she did the right thing. I haven't been willing to admit that before."

"I know she'll appreciate that," Ms. Reed said. "And if you need any extra backup at all tomorrow, you can count on me."

"You two have been great through all of this," Misty told them, then gave them a sly look. "So when are you going to go out on, like, a real date instead of pretending that you're together all the time because of me?"

To her amusement, Ms. Reed blushed and even Doc Fullerton looked flustered. She laughed.

"You two are so busted," she told them. She grinned at J.C. "There's that silver lining thing, doc. The one you were trying to convince me is always there."

He looked a little embarrassed, but he nodded. "No question about it, Misty. No question at all."

Misty wondered if maybe she hadn't found her own silver lining, as well. It turned out she just might be a whole lot stronger than she'd ever imagined. Tomorrow would tell.

21

"So, are we going to let a teenager call us on being a pair of chickens?" J.C. asked Laura as they left Misty's.

"You're the one with the lousy track record who wasn't interested in dating," she reminded him. "I've dutifully kept from labeling whatever it is we have been doing."

"Maybe it's time that stopped," J.C. said. "Earlier today I was thinking maybe we should have some clarity about what's going on here. Put our cards on the table, so to speak."

"I certainly stress clarity in my students' essays," Laura said. "It might be nice to have some coming from you." She gave him a considering look. "Unless you're still not ready for that kind of conversation."

J.C. smiled at that. "Willing to let me off the hook?"

"If need be," she said. "I've discovered lately that I'm incredibly patient."

"What if I admit that I'm starting to see the error of my ways? Not dating, at least right out there in the open and calling it what it is, isn't really working all that well for me anymore. You deserve better." Feeling vaguely bewildered, he added, "And it seems I want more."

To his relief, Laura gave in readily. "Then I wouldn't say no to another dinner at Sullivan's," she said.

"With not a single mention of Misty all evening?"

She held his gaze. "I can do that. Can you?"

He laughed. "I guess we'll just have to give it a try and find out."

Unfortunately, getting through the evening without the subject of Misty coming up proved to be impossible. Most of the patrons at Sullivan's fell silent when J.C. and Laura entered. Then, one by one, many of them approached to offer a few words of support, both for Misty and for J.C. and the pain he'd suffered years ago on losing his brother.

Uncomfortable with all of the attention, he saw no graceful way to make his excuses and leave, but Laura clearly guessed some of the emotional turmoil he was going through.

"I'll be right back," she said, giving his hand a squeeze and hurrying off in the direction of the kitchen.

When she returned, she was carrying a huge take-out bag. "Dinner," she announced triumphantly.

"How'd you pull that off?"

"I told Dana Sue what was going on out here and said we needed to leave. She put two meals together in no time, along with dessert and a bottle of wine." She grinned. "Best of all, it's on the house. She flatly refused to let me pay her. She said she owed it to us because our dinner plans were interrupted by her intrusive customers."

"I should thank her," J.C. said.

"Call her later," Laura urged. "The kitchen's a mad-house. Only for you would I have risked going in there uninvited." She shuddered dramatically. "I'm lucky to emerge without battle scars."

J.C. chuckled. "It couldn't have been that bad."

"Trust me, it was downright dangerous."

When they were seated in his car, he turned to her. "Thank you for recognizing that I was about to come unglued at all that well-meant sympathy in there."

"I doubt you would ever come unglued," she said, "but I could see that you were uncomfortable. Now, shall we go to my place or yours for this feast?"

"Yours," he said at once. "I stared at my walls way too long over the weekend. I need a change of scenery."

"Okay," she said, "but the rules are back in effect. No talk of Misty, bullying or anything related to it."

J.C. nodded, then gave her a wicked look. "What *will* we do?"

Regarding him with amusement, Laura tapped on the bag of take-out containers. "Dinner," she replied at once.

"I'm a fast eater."

"Then we can negotiate over dessert for what comes next," she teased. "I have some thousand-piece puzzles if you're interested."

He looked into her eyes and held her gaze until the color rose in her cheeks. "The only puzzle I'm even re-motely interested in is figuring out Laura Reed and why I can't seem to stay away from you," he said quietly.

A slow smile spread across her face. "Then that's what we'll work on."

J.C. laughed. The end of the evening definitely

promised to be a lot more intriguing and potentially satisfying than the beginning.

Laura closed her eyes and savored a bite of Erik's triple-layer red-velvet cake. When she opened her eyes, she found J.C.'s gaze locked on her lips.

"Do you have any idea of how amazing that is?" she murmured.

"Hmm?"

She gestured toward the cake. "That," she said. "It's heavenly. Moist, delectable sex on a fork."

"What?" J.C. asked, blinking. "Did you just compare that cake to sex?"

She nodded, grinning. "It's pretty darn close."

"Lemme see," he said, motioning for her to share a bite.

She pulled her fork and the cake out of reach. "You have your own slice. This is mine."

"But if you let me have just one taste of yours, I might be persuaded to leave that other slice here for you."

"An intriguing offer," she said, studying him. "How do I know you'll do that?"

"It will take a certain amount of persuasion," he told her thoughtfully. "I'm thinking a few kisses for starters, then we'll see where that leads."

She blinked, then chuckled. "You want to exchange actual sex for cake?"

"The way you were talking it would be a fair exchange. What do you think?"

"I think you're nuts," she said flatly, then shrugged. "But okay." She offered him a taste of the cake. "Incredible, right?"

"Not bad," he said, then gestured to his lips. "A kiss for comparison."

Accepting the challenge, she leaned forward and touched her lips to his. He cupped a hand behind her neck and pulled her closer. What was meant to be a casual dare of a kiss turned into something deeper and far more compelling. She was pretty sure there was steam rising by the time he released her.

"No comparison," he said, looking into her eyes. "That was *way* better than any cake ever made."

"You have a point," she admitted, setting the plate aside and reaching for him. "The cake can wait."

She was pretty sure it would still be spectacular for breakfast.

J.C. walked into the kitchen the next morning and found Laura at the table wearing nothing more than his shirt, a cup of coffee in front of her along with the last few crumbs of the cake. The second slice, if he wasn't mistaken.

"Was that on your mind all night long?" he inquired.

"Not all night," she said with a grin. "You kept me pretty entertained most of the time."

"Pretty entertained?" he repeated with a quizzical look as he poured himself a cup of coffee. "Not exactly the rave reviews I was going for."

She laughed. "Okay, it was a stellar performance. You drove every other thought completely out of my mind."

"Better," he said, leaning down to kiss her before peeking into the refrigerator. "Eggs? Bacon?"

"Sorry, not in this house. I have some bran flakes."

J.C. shrugged. "That'll do."

When she started to get up, he pushed her back down. "I can track down a bowl, cereal and milk. You stay right there and look fetching."

"Fetching?"

"My shirt becomes you. Come to think of it, are those bowls on a high shelf? It might be fascinating to see what happens if you have to reach for them."

She grinned. "You wish. Get your own bowl."

When he'd poured the cereal into a bowl and doused it with milk, he settled across from her.

"We never did have that clarity conversation last night," he said.

"That's okay."

He shook his head. "No, it's not. I owe it to you to be honest about what I'm thinking."

"Are you thinking that being good friends and having incredible sex isn't a clear enough message?"

Startled, he met her gaze. "Is that all you want from me? Friendship and an occasional roll in the hay?"

She frowned at his sharp tone. Reaching for his hand, she said, "Hey, that's not what I was saying at all. I just meant that what we have right now is good. It doesn't need a label. I'm comfortable with where we are, if you are."

"Well, I'm not," he said, surprisingly irritated by her willingness to settle for what she'd made to sound extremely casual.

"Okay," she said quietly. "Then clarify."

"Look, you know I wasn't looking for a relationship," he began.

"Abundantly clear," she confirmed. "Almost from the very first words you ever said to me."

He scowled at her snippy tone. This clearly wasn't going the way he'd intended it to. "I'm trying to tell you that things have changed for me. The fact that I'm attracted to you is hardly a shock, I'm sure, but it's a whole lot more than that. I like you. I really like you. And I enjoy being with you."

"Still sounds a lot like friends with benefits to me," she said, "which was all I was suggesting earlier."

"We are not friends with any damn benefits," he retorted, exasperated because she was making this all but impossible. "I'm falling in love with you, which you might know if you'd actually listen, instead of coming up with all these smart replies of yours."

She blinked, though he couldn't be certain if it was because of his tone or the import of what he'd said.

"You're falling in love with me," she echoed softly, looking stunned.

"Yes," he said, his own tone softening. "Don't ask me how it happened, because I really thought I was immune."

"Can you get vaccinated for that?" she asked, her tone lighter.

J.C. chuckled. "Not that I know of, or, believe me, I would have." He reached for her hand and twined her fingers through his. "I can tell I've caught you completely off guard, and it's not as if I'm asking you to tell me you're madly in love with me or anything like that. I just wanted you to know, it's serious for me. More serious than I was expecting."

With her free hand, she caressed his cheek. "It's way more serious than I was expecting, too."

"So we're both committed to whatever this is?" he asked, wanting to be sure.

Smiling, she nodded. "I'm committed to whatever this is."

J.C. sat back with a sigh. For the first time in years, he felt an amazing sense of contentment steal over him. Apparently, when the right woman came along, commitment wasn't half as terrifying as he'd been thinking all this time. If only there weren't this nagging thought in the back of his mind that even something that felt so right could still end very, very badly.

Laura was in the middle of a test with her second period class when one of the secretaries from the office came in. "Mrs. Donovan wants to see you right away. I'll stay here and monitor the class, if that's okay."

Laura nodded. "They're taking a test," she said, then raised her voice, "so there's to be no talking."

"Got it," Cathy said. "Leave 'em to me."

Since Laura knew she'd actually been a drill sergeant in the army before retiring to Serenity with her husband, she figured Cathy could control a roomful of teenagers.

In the office, she found Betty with Helen. They were looking at a thick sheaf of papers.

"Uh-oh," Laura said nervously. "What's going on?"

"Mariah's claimed to the school board that you both should be fired," Helen said, her voice tight. "It's all ridiculous, of course, but she's managed to get it on the agenda for this afternoon's meeting. I think what she really wants is to create such a stir that the board won't be able to deal with Annabelle's expulsion. It's a delaying tactic, nothing more, just the way she managed to wrangle a postponement to get the meeting pushed over to today, rather than yesterday, when Ham originally had scheduled it."

"But we'll still have to defend ourselves," Betty said wearily. "Which will take time."

Helen shook her head. "Not to worry. I'm all over this. I've already spoken to Hamilton Reynolds, who's fit to be tied. Yes, he can't afford to sweep this under the rug, but I imagine he can wrap up the discussion in about ten minutes, tops."

Betty gave her a wry look. "He certainly put me in my place quickly enough when I brought up those charges against Cal several years ago." She shook her head. "Looking back, I don't know what I was thinking."

"You had a few bitter parents who thought Ty Townsend was getting preferential treatment from Cal because he had a relationship with Maddie," Helen consoled her. "Maybe you went overboard trying to soothe their ruffled feathers, but that's over and done with. Everyone in town knows you're a good principal. They also know Laura's one of the best teachers at the high school. These charges of Mariah's are nonsense, especially this notion that you two had some kind of vendetta against Annabelle. The suspension of all those boys for bullying pretty much makes mincemeat out of that argument."

"What do you need from us?" Laura asked.

"Not a thing," Helen said. "If Mariah wants me to produce all those posts Annabelle put online to prove that she was, in fact, bullying, so be it. They were coming out in court sooner or later, anyway. As a mother, though, I'd have thought she'd prefer later, after tempers in town cool down a bit. The content of those posts doesn't reflect well on Annabelle or on Mariah's parenting."

"This is mostly about the transfer," Laura guessed. "Remember what Don said, that getting Annabelle into some private boarding school would cost money they don't have. If Mariah couldn't find the money, then she's clearly not one bit happy about having to drag Annabelle over to another district for classes every day. She's probably grabbing at any straw she can think of to keep her here."

"Not an option," Betty said flatly.

Helen confirmed it. "The transfer's already been approved. Ham put through the paperwork this morning. The Litchfields can choose a different school, but Annabelle won't be staying here."

Laura regarded her worriedly. "Without even a public hearing? Could Mr. Reynolds do that on his own?"

"Certain circumstances allow him to act in the best interests of the district," Helen explained. "And, frankly, he was furious that Mariah managed to get the meeting delayed. He made calls to the other board members after the prosecutor and Chief Rollins explained to him what they felt was in the best interest of the community. Every board member backed him up after what they saw at Saturday's rally. Every single one of them has privately expressed to me how dismayed they were by what happened. They'll still take a formal vote this afternoon. That will tidy up any legal loose ends."

"If I weren't still so outraged with Annabelle for what she put Misty through, I'd almost feel sorry for her," Laura said. "She's just a teenager, and this could change her life."

"Hopefully for the better," Helen said, undeterred by any hint of sympathy. "Today's board meeting is in the auditorium at four o'clock. Can you both be there by 3:30 in case there are any last-minute surprises or details we need to go over?"

"Absolutely," Betty said. "Are we going to need character witnesses or anything like that?"

"I'll handle that," Helen said. "I'll have a couple of people on standby just in case, but I promise you I don't think they're going to be necessary."

Laura hoped she was right. She'd never in a million years anticipated things going this far just because she'd been trying to protect one student from another's bullying.

J.C. had listened quietly as Helen explained why she needed him to attend that afternoon's emergency school board meeting.

"You've got to be kidding me," he said incredulously when she was finished. "Mariah has actually gone through with this? When the meeting was postponed, I thought she'd had second thoughts."

Helen shook her head. "She's not the sort of woman to go down without a fight," she said wryly. "This is her last-ditch attempt to turn her daughter into the victim of some terrible conspiracy."

"That's absurd!"

"Well, of course it is, but it's hard to ignore someone who's shouting not only in your ear, but making phone calls to every media contact she has in the region. The school board has no choice but to address these charges and formally take whatever action they feel is warranted."

"Action? Seriously?" He raked a hand through his hair. "How did this get so completely turned around?"

"Stop fretting," Helen soothed. "There will be no action, except maybe recognition that Betty and Laura acted totally appropriately. If I were on the board, they'd get an award."

J.C. nodded. "What kind of testimony do you need from me?"

"Just back up Laura and Betty that this was a serious situation. I'll only call you if I need to, but we have to be prepared."

"Oh, I'm prepared," he said grimly. "Who else are you calling?"

"I've spoken to Diana Dawson. She's eager to speak out. When Misty overheard our conversation, she volunteered. I think she'd be the most compelling witness of all, but I won't use her unless I absolutely have to. The poor kid's been through enough."

"If she wants to do it and you need her, call on her," J.C. advised. "Every time she has a chance to stand up for herself or someone else, she gets a little stronger."

"I hadn't thought of it that way," Helen admitted. "I'll trust your instincts then. See you this afternoon."

By the time J.C. walked into the school auditorium, he'd worked up a full head of steam over the absurdity of this entire gathering. Sure, there were a million and one legal reasons things had to be conducted this way, but he considered it a colossal waste of time when the outcome was preordained.

No sooner had he walked in, than Laura caught a

glimpse of him. She broke away from the group with whom she was speaking and headed his way, a frown on her face.

"What are you doing here?"

"I'd have been here anyway, but Helen called me," he said, pressing a kiss to her cheek. "You okay?"

"She says I will be," she replied, though her hand in his was like ice. "I'm trying to believe her."

"You can," J.C. said with confidence. "Nobody's going to get railroaded here today."

They were joined by Diana and Misty.

"I'm so sorry you've been put in this position," Diana told Laura.

"Me, too, Ms. Reed," Misty said. "But don't worry. We've got your back."

Laura frowned at Misty. "I thought you were coming back to school today, young lady."

Misty grinned at her mother. "Told you she was going to be ticked."

Diana flushed guiltily. "After I spoke to Helen about what was happening this afternoon, Les and I decided Misty needed another day away from this atmosphere. Hopefully tempers will have cooled down and things will be back to normal later in the week."

"I think that was very wise," J.C. told her approvingly. He nudged Laura in the ribs. "Right?"

Laura smiled weakly. "Of course it was. Sorry, it just makes me so mad that Misty is missing classes because of this."

"I'll make up all the work," Misty promised. "Katie's bringing over all my assignments later. My grades are not going to suffer, I swear it. Remember what I told you. I'm done letting those jerks mess up my life."

"Okay, then," Laura conceded. "I guess I can't ask for more than that."

Helen joined them then. "Let's head down to the front row. I want all of you close by, in case I need to call you up on stage. I still don't think it will come to that, but I'd like to be prepared."

As they walked to the front of the auditorium, J.C. kept Laura's icy hand firmly in his grip. Once they were seated, he leaned closer to whisper, "This is going to turn out okay. Believe that."

She gave him a surprisingly shaky look. "I want to."

"Did you not see how much support you have in this room?" he asked incredulously.

She blinked and shook her head. "What do you mean?"

"The place is packed. People are waving signs in support of you and Betty. I detect Liz and Flo's hand in that. They're handing them out at the door, and Frances looked to me as if she's whipping people into a frenzy in the hall outside. Every one of the Sweet Magnolias is out there, too. They have quite a rally going on, in fact."

"How did I miss all that?" Laura asked.

"I'd like to think it was because you couldn't take your eyes off me," J.C. teased, "but I imagine it had more to do with being scared out of your wits."

"I'm not scared," she retorted, then sighed. "I'm terrified."

He lifted her hand and kissed her knuckles. "Don't be. I'm right here. Just squeeze my hand if you get nervous."

She gave it a tremulous squeeze.

"There you go," he said.

"It didn't make me any less nervous," she confessed as the microphone on the stage crackled to life.

He leaned closer and sealed his lips over hers, lingering just long enough until he felt a hint of heat in her skin. He smiled as he moved back. "Better?"

"Sure," she said with a shaky grin. "Now Mariah can come after me on a morals charge."

J.C. laughed. "Good. Your sense of humor's intact. I was getting worried."

"I wasn't joking."

"Well, you should have been. You're a great teacher, and everyone in this room, with the possible exception of Mariah, knows it. By the time we all get through, the board will think you're a saint."

"Unless they saw that kiss," she grumbled, but at least this time her eyes were sparkling.

22

Hamilton Reynolds banged his gavel down so hard, it looked as if it shook the table. The sound drew startled gasps, then silence as the crowd waited for the drama to unfold.

"I see we have a full house," the board chairman said. "Too bad more of you aren't here when we conduct our regular business." He looked pointedly around the auditorium. "Now, it seems we have two issues before us for this emergency session. The formal expulsion of Annabelle Litchfield and countercharges from Mariah Litchfield that principal Betty Donovan and teacher Laura Reed were engaged in some sort of conspiracy against Annabelle."

He sighed heavily. "I suppose we have to deal with the latter before we can vote on the expulsion."

He glanced into the audience. "Mariah, do you have legal representation here?"

"No," she declared in a ringing voice. She stood up, marched up to the stage and turned to face the crowd.

"Address me and the rest of the board," Ham commanded. "You're not at some political rally."

"Oh, don't get all smug and righteous with me, Ham Reynolds," she said. "You're no better than the two of them. I'm considering forcing a recall vote to get you out of office, too."

"Do your worst, Mariah," he said calmly. "Now say what's on your mind. And keep it to facts you can substantiate. I won't tolerate character assassination of these two fine people."

Mariah blinked at his words. "So much for impartiality," she grumbled. "Obviously I'm wasting my breath talking to the likes of you."

"I told you that you could have your say. Now don't make me lose patience and change my mind."

It was obvious to Laura that the crowd was getting restless as the exchange dragged on with no real evidence being laid out for the board to consider. Instead, Mariah was on a rant about adults picking on her sweet little girl who'd never squashed a bug, much less attacked another human being.

"It must be totally obvious to everyone in this town that Annabelle would never do the sort of mean-spirited things she's been accused of," Mariah summed up. "She's a good girl, and her reputation's being ruined by these two petty people. I've a good mind to file a lawsuit for slander once we get through these proceedings." Despite Ham's earlier warning, she turned back to the crowd. "I ask you now, are these really the sort of people you want educating your children?"

A loud chorus of "yes" exploded throughout the auditorium, leaving Mariah clearly stunned. She was about to flounce off the stage, when Helen rose and walked up to join her.

"Not just yet, Mariah," she said quietly. "Since you've been up here doing a bit of slandering of your own, let's make sure we get the facts on record."

Mariah blinked and turned to Ham. "Can she do this?"

"I believe she can," he said, then glanced at the other board members who nodded in assent.

"Mariah, I know you've always taken an active interest in Annabelle's singing, is that right?" Helen asked. It was more statement of fact, since it was something no one in town was likely to question.

"Well, of course. She has an amazing voice. Everyone knows that."

"Agreed," Helen said. "But what about her school work? Do you monitor that, make sure her grades are up?"

"Of course," Mariah said. "Not that she'll need a college education with the career that's ahead for her, but she wants to go, so, yes, we pay close attention to her grades."

"I thought so," Helen said, smiling. "All reports say she's always been a good student." She glanced down at some notes, though Laura had a hunch Helen already knew exactly what was written there. "Now, how closely do you keep an eye on her online activities? Do you have access to her social-networking account, for instance?"

"Of course not," Mariah said indignantly. "Children deserve to have privacy just like the rest of us. It's in the Constitution, for heaven's sake."

Again, Helen smiled. "Then you can't say with a hundred percent certainty that Annabelle never posted the bullying taunts that appeared on her personal page and then circulated to all of her friends, can you?"

"I'm telling you she wouldn't do that kind of thing," Mariah said.

"And while your faith in your daughter is admirable, I have here pages and pages of posts that say otherwise. I also have statements from the police, the prosecutor and the website administrators confirming that this is Annabelle's site and that her screen name and password were used for these posts. I can read them one by one, if you'd like. We can let the board decide if the posts rise to the level of bullying that is justification for immediate expulsion in this school district."

Mariah seemed to deflate before their eyes. She'd obviously been counting on her counteroffensive to take the heat off her daughter and turn it onto Betty and Laura. Now that the strategy had failed so miserably, she looked a little lost.

"She's a good girl," she whispered, though it lacked her earlier conviction.

"I think up until this incident she probably was," Helen said more gently. "This was a wake-up call, Mariah. Rather than viewing this as an unjust punishment, view it as an opportunity for Annabelle to have a second chance. There's already a lot of national attention on this case, mostly thanks to you. Let's resolve this quietly so your daughter and Misty Dawson can move on with their lives."

By now there were tears on Mariah's cheeks, and she was shaking uncontrollably. Helen put an arm around her and walked with her off the stage. It was so quiet in the auditorium, Laura was pretty sure they could have heard a pin drop.

Hamilton Reynolds cleared his throat. "Okay, then, first things first. Does anyone up here see any need to discipline Betty Donovan or Laura Reed for the actions they took to protect Misty Dawson?"

"I vote for a commendation," Bernice Walker said fiercely. At a look from Ham, she grinned. "Oh, I know, it's supposed to be a motion. Well, I'm making it."

"Second," Trent Ayers said.

Ham gave a nod of satisfaction. "Any discussion?" He looked around but the other board members were merely nodding acquiescence. "Okay, then, all in favor?"

The commendation was approved unanimously.

"Now to the expulsion," he said. "Do I have a motion for that?"

It, too, was quickly approved by a unanimous vote.

Laura finally let out the breath she'd been holding. J.C. gave her hand a squeeze. "I told you it was going to be all right."

"You told me, but anything could have happened in here," she said.

"Not with Helen on the case," he said, then stepped aside as well-wishers came to surround her.

The Sweet Magnolias were first in line. Laura was enveloped in hugs from Sarah, Raylene and Annie, then from Maddie, Jeanette, Dana Sue and Karen Cruz.

"I think a celebratory margarita night's in order," Annie declared.

Sarah immediately shook her head and nodded toward J.C. "This is an occasion for a coed gathering, if ever there was one."

"My house, then," Raylene said. "I baked lasagna this morning just in case."

"I can bring salad," Dana Sue said. "And some killer guacamole, since it wouldn't be a true Sweet Magnolias gathering without that."

Helen joined them just then. "I just got off the phone with Erik. The dessert's covered."

Laura looked around at them, feeling oddly choked up at yet another display of such loyalty. "Are you sure?"

"Of course we're sure," Sarah said. "You're one of us, aren't you? And this is what we do to celebrate."

"I'll round up all the guys and let them know," Annie offered, then rolled her eyes. "And the kids."

"I think we should include Frances, Flo and Liz," Karen said hesitantly. "Would that be okay?"

"Of course," Maddie said at once. "They have Senior Magnolia status with us."

Laura looked over at Betty, who was standing with a couple of other teachers but basically seemed pretty alone. "Would it be okay," she began with a glance toward the principal.

Everyone looked to Maddie for a response, since she'd been most affected by Betty's attack on Cal several years earlier.

"Oh, why not?" Maddie said. "I'm married to the best man on the planet. I can afford to let bygones be bygones."

Helen draped an arm over Maddie's shoulders. "What a woman!" she teased.

"That's me. Generous to a fault," Maddie said. "What time is this party starting?"

Raylene glanced at her watch. "It's nearly five now. How about six-thirty?"

Everyone quickly agreed, then went off to handle their various assignments. Laura turned to J.C. "You are coming, aren't you?"

He looked hesitant.

"Hey, what about all that talk about going public, admitting we're a couple, not that it'll come as a huge shock to anyone."

"But this crowd?" he said, looking oddly shaken. "They're liable to take the news and run with it."

"Run with it where?" she asked, bewildered.

"Straight down the aisle," he murmured, then looked sheepish. "Overreacting, huh?"

"Just a little. We're tougher than them. Nothing goes on between us unless we want it to. We've done okay so far with that philosophy, haven't we?"

"What I want is a little privacy and a very long night with you in my arms," he said.

She warmed to the comment but held firm. "First you have to play nice with our friends."

"How long?"

She grinned. "Until you can persuade me there's more intriguing entertainment at home."

J.C. chuckled. "I imagine I could persuade you of that before we ever leave the school building, if you'll join me for five minutes in a broom closet."

"Ambiance, sweetie," she teased. "You'll have to do better than surrounding me with mops, water buckets and wet rags."

He gave her an endearingly solemn look. "I swear, you won't even notice they're there."

"Not gonna happen," she repeated.

But she couldn't seem to shake the thought that it might be fun to let him try.

The party at Chief Rollins's house was turning out to be a lot more fun than Misty had anticipated. For a long time now, she hadn't expected to feel normal or to hang out with other kids ever again. When Katie had suggested she, her mom and Jake come tonight, Misty had initially declined, but Maddie had joined them and pretty much insisted. She'd noticed that Mrs. Maddox generally seemed to get her way. She hoped her own mom would be forceful like that one of these days. She had been once upon a time, and it seemed to Misty as if she'd been getting stronger during this ordeal, just as Misty herself had.

Even though it was great being included, the house and backyard were packed. There was barely room to turn around, especially with some huge addition being built onto the back of the house and construction stuff all over.

Mrs. Rollins's lasagna had been enough to feed a small army, but the men had insisted on throwing hamburgers and hot dogs on the grill anyway, so there were all these great aromas in the air, right along with more laughter than Misty had heard in a very long time.

She was sitting all alone in a chair beside this really cool garden, when Katie and Mandy Rollins joined her, along with a girl named Lexie, who apparently lived next door. She was Mandy's age, just fourteen, so not on Misty's radar much before tonight.

"I'm really sorry about what's been happening to

you," Lexie said, then blinked shyly, her expression crestfallen. "Is it okay to say that? Would you rather I not even mention it?"

"It's fine," Misty said. "Thanks."

"Not just at school," Lexie said, emboldened to go on. "I mean the divorce thing. My mom's going through that, too. It really sucks."

"It definitely sucks," Katie confirmed.

Mandy gave all of them a sympathetic look that was tinged with wisdom. "You know what's worse? Losing your mom and dad in a car crash and knowing you'll never ever see either one of them again."

Lexie, clearly a kid who took everything to heart, gave her a horrified look. "Of course it is. What was I thinking? I am so sorry. Sometimes I forget why you're living here with your brother and Raylene."

"It's okay," Mandy soothed. "Most of the time I don't think about it so much. Carter's the best big brother and guardian in the world, and Raylene's been amazing. Still, they're not my mom and dad, you know?"

Lexie gave her an impulsive hug, her cheeks still pink with embarrassment. "I'm sorry," she whispered, looking stricken. "It's just that my mom gets so down sometimes, and my dad's being such a jerk, I forget that there are people who have it a lot worse."

"Pain is pain," Katie said. "That's what my mom always tells me. She says my feelings are valid because they're my feelings." She grinned. "And then she proceeds to tell me why I'm completely crazy for feeling the way I do."

"Do you think moms have some book or website they go to so they can find stuff like that to say?" Lexie asked. "I'll bet we've all heard the exact same things all our lives."

"Don't even mention websites to me," Misty said. "I may never go on my computer again."

"Yes, you will," Katie said, nudging her in the ribs. "How else will we keep in touch when you're off at some fancy Ivy League college and I'm back here at Clemson?"

As soon as she and Katie started talking college plans, the younger girls took off. Misty watched Lexie with a frown as she piled a plate high with food.

"She's pretty skinny. She can't possibly eat like that all the time," Katie noted worriedly.

"Maybe she missed lunch today," Misty said, not seeing anything that unusual about it. Jake ate like that all the time, especially since their mom had been erratic about getting meals on the table. She thought she recognized the signs of hunger rather than something more dire, the way Katie obviously thought she did.

"I don't know," Katie began.

Misty interrupted. "Stop fretting. You heard her talking about her mom being a wreck because of the divorce. Maybe her mom's been too caught up in that to cook very much. My mom sure has been."

Katie's expression brightened. "That's probably it. Let's get some lasagna before it's all gone. And then brownies. Erik's are amazing."

As they went to get food, Misty spotted her mother deep in conversation with a couple of the other women. She looked happier than Misty had seen her for a long time. And Jake was over the moon hanging out with Coach Maddox and the men.

Tears filled Misty's eyes. It had taken a really awful crisis to get them to this point tonight, but she had a hunch that this was another of those silver linings Doc Fullerton had been talking about. With all these people backing her up, maybe she'd never feel quite so alone ever again. Her mom and Jake, too.

J.C. had been given the dubious honor of helping out at the grill. Apparently it was a duty usually guarded protectively by Erik, but he was held up at Sullivan's tonight. Cal had immediately enlisted J.C. to take his place.

"I haven't done a lot of grilling in my time," J.C. reluctantly admitted, eyeing the huge gas grill with a certain amount of trepidation, and maybe a little awe, if the truth be known.

"You watch. You flip," Cal said as if it were mind-less work.

Of course, that didn't explain why Erik thought it needed a master chef to do it well, but J.C. was forced to take Cal at his word, especially since he was lining up burgers in one row and hot dogs in another at a rapid clip.

"So, you and Laura," Cal began as he placed the meat on the grill. "It's finally getting serious? You're openly dating these days?"

J.C. thought of his earlier comment to Laura about this crowd being dangerously addicted to marriage.

"I'm not sure *serious* is quite the right word," he equivocated.

Cal regarded him with a hard look. "But you're sleep-ing with her, am I right?" At J.C.'s unmistakably shocked reaction, he waved his long fork dismissively. "Hardly a secret, J.C. I warned you about that a while back."

"So you did," J.C. said, not sure if the regret he felt was for not listening back then or for showing up here tonight. "You going to call me out, demand to know my intentions?"

Cal chuckled. "Not me, man, but take a look around. There are lot of women here who'll have your hide if you mess with her. I've warned you about that before."

"Define *messing with her,*" J.C. requested, though he was pretty sure he understood Cal's definition.

"Break her heart. Toy with her affections. Sleep with her, then dump her." He lifted a brow. "You follow me now?"

J.C. nodded. "I think I've got it."

"And?"

"I will do my best not to break her heart," he said and meant it. It was far more likely that she'd wind up breaking his, though he'd started to have hope that maybe this time things would turn out differently.

"She's a strong woman," Cal said with admiration.

"The strongest," J.C. confirmed.

"Smart, beautiful, caring."

J.C. chuckled. "I don't need a resume of her attributes, Cal. I can see them for myself."

"Just thought I'd put in a good word, in case you've been sitting on the fence."

"I don't do much fence-sitting," J.C. told him. "I'm either in or out."

His gaze searched the yard until it fell on Laura and lingered, watching the smile blossom on her lips when she caught him staring.

"And you're definitely in," Cal concluded happily, watching him. "Good to know."

Yeah, J.C. thought. He was definitely in.

Misty had been worrying all night about finally walking back into school and facing yet more stares. Sure, once she'd found out Greg Bennett was likely behind the latest online posts, it had made her plenty mad, but she was a long way from being brave enough to confront him.

"Are you sure you don't want me to drive you to school today?" Diana asked.

"No way," Misty said.

"How about I take you over to Katie's? You can walk from there with her."

Misty knew she probably ought to do this all on her own, but she seized the lifeline her mother had thrown. "Let me call and ask if that's okay," she said at once.

As soon as she got Katie on the phone, she told her what was going on. "Could my mom drop me off at your house?"

"Of course," Katie said at once. "How about this? Let me make a couple of calls. I think we should show up in force. Let Greg see that you're no longer alone, that you're surrounded by friends who'll stand up for you. He's such a jerk, it probably never occurred to him that anyone would choose you over him."

"Maybe nobody else will want to get involved," Misty said worriedly.

"Leave that to me," Katie said with confidence. "I've been telling you all along that a lot of people have been on your side. They've just been waiting for a signal from you that you want their help. Be here in fifteen minutes, okay? We don't want to be late."

"We're leaving now," Misty said, glancing at her mom, who smiled and nodded.

"I gather Katie has a plan," her mom said.

Misty grinned. "Katie always has a plan. I think she was born to fight for the underdog. She'll be a mini-Helen if she decides to go into law. Or maybe even president. She's smart enough."

"So are you," her mom said loyally.

"I haven't felt smart for a while now, but today?" She shrugged. "I almost feel like my old self again."

There were half a dozen kids already waiting at Katie's by the time they got there. As the group walked toward the high school, more kids fell into step with them. By the time they reached the high school, there were maybe twenty kids surrounding Misty, clearly eager to face down Greg or anyone else who dared to taunt her.

Just inside the building, Misty spotted Greg with a couple of the teammates who'd been suspended from the team along with him. He looked as if he were going to get in her face, but her friends moved en masse to block him.

Misty worked her way between them until she was facing him. "No more," she said quietly. "This is over."

"Not even close," he said with what seemed more like sheer bravado than real conviction.

"Don't you get it yet?" she asked. "You've lost way more than I have. Sure, you tried to ruin my reputation and I almost let you get away with it, but you've lost your scholarship and your whole future." She held his gaze. "Tell me the truth, Greg. Was it worth it?"

Then, holding her head high, she walked right past him and down the hallway to her first class, her friends right there with her.

She was shaking by the time she reached her classroom, but Katie reached for her hand and gave it a squeeze. "I am so proud of you. You looked him right in the eyes, Misty. That took real guts."

"I was shaking," Misty admitted.

"Doesn't matter. In fact, I think that's what courage is, being scared and doing what needs to be done, anyway."

Misty gave her a hug, then smiled at the others who were still standing guard around her. "Thank you, all of you."

"Hey, it could have been any one of us," Susie said quietly. "In fact, at one time or another, it probably has been."

To Misty's surprise, Hailey, a friend of Annabelle's who'd never even given her the time of day before, separated herself from the crowd. Looking nervous, she met Misty's gaze.

"I just wanted to say I'm sorry," she said in a whisper. "For everything."

Before Misty could absorb the wonder of that admission, Hailey was gone.

The warning bell rang then and they all scattered. Misty walked into her classroom and for the first time in months felt the knot in her stomach finally ease.

Laura was still a little flushed and giddy from an incredible, passion-filled night when she was called into Betty's office the next morning.

After a precious few moments of pleasantries, Betty inquired, "Do I need to remind you that we have a very strict morals clause in our contract with our teachers?"

Laura stared at her. "Excuse me?" But even as the words left her mouth, she put two and two together. "Let me guess. Mariah Litchfield was on the phone to you first thing this morning because she spotted J.C.'s car at my house."

"Correct," Betty said.

"And after everything that's gone on, you can't see that for the attempt at retaliation it is?"

"Of course I can," Betty said impatiently. "I told her I'd bring it to your attention and I have."

Then to Laura's surprise, she grinned. "Under the circumstances, I wouldn't worry too much about it. The school board is very impressed with how well you and J.C. handled the whole thing with Annabelle and Misty. That much was evident at the emergency board meeting. You could probably get away with just about anything right now, and I'm in a pretty generous and forgiving mood myself these days."

Laura thought of what they'd discovered on Friday. They were still awaiting confirmation from Chief Rollins's sources before tackling the latest situation.

"Well, you might want to prepare them for the possibility that it's not over just yet," she said, then filled Betty in on their suspicions about Greg Bennett, not only stirring things up at the rally, but taking over where Annabelle had left off online.

"Oh, sweet heaven!" Betty murmured.

Laura held up her hand. "I think Misty wants to tackle this one on her own. She's back in school today, and she fully intends to deal with Greg in her own way. Let's give her that chance. She needs to feel in control of her life again."

"You've got her back?" Betty asked.

"Absolutely."

Betty nodded. "Then we'll see how it goes, but expulsion is not out of the question, even if he is captain of the football team. I would have thought he'd understand that after seeing Annabelle get sent off to another school and being suspended himself from playing for the rest of the football season."

"Hopefully it won't come to that," Laura said. "But it was good to see Misty walk in here this morning with her head held high and her friends around her."

Betty gave her a surprising smile. "And it was nice to see you walk in here today with some color in your cheeks. I hope it works out for you and J.C. He's a good guy."

"Yes, he is," Laura said. "But it's still early going."

After the past few days, though, it already felt as if they were a whole lot closer to forever.

Still, she knew his history and his conviction that Fullerton men were bad bets when it came to lasting commitments. She had no idea if he'd ever be able to take the kind of leap of faith required to claim the future she was starting to want. Then again, she'd managed to overcome her past. Surely a man as smart and sensitive as J.C. could do the same.

23

After the post-school board celebration at Carter and Raylene's house, J.C. knew he'd finally been accepted by the Sweet Magnolias, for better or worse, he thought, given their penchant for meddling.

Still, he was pleasantly surprised when town manager Tom McDonald and his cousin Travis approached him and invited him to join the entire Sweet Magnolias crowd for Thanksgiving. Tom and Travis had befriended J.C. early on, even before the other men, because they hadn't been around during the tense days of Maddie's divorce from Bill Townsend.

"And bring Laura along, of course," Tom told him. "I'm sure the women are planning to invite her, but just in case, I want you both to know we'd love to have you there. You two seem to have the Sweet Magnolias' stamp of approval these days. Young, attractive vigilantes for social justice and all that. As town manager, I can't tell you what it means to have people like the two of you in this community. I'd like to attract more young professionals just like you."

"Bill's just hired a nurse practitioner who'll be joining us soon. I think she'll fit right in with your view of what Serenity can become moving forward," J.C. said. He gave Tom a wry look. "As for that stamp of approval you mentioned, is that really a good thing?"

It seemed to him it came with a lot of pressure. He'd seen that in the speculative glances directed at him and Laura the other night at Raylene's, to say nothing of Cal's pointed cross-examination, obviously at Maddie's behest.

Travis laughed at his skepticism. "It's definitely a good thing," he insisted. "Have you not heard the way Maddie and Helen have been singing Laura's praises for how she handled the whole bullying incident? Your contribution has not gone without notice, either. You got a lot of points for the way you opened up at the rally. And the way I hear it, they're crediting you for getting Bill to speak, as well. That did a lot toward redeeming him in their view."

"He wanted to be there," J.C. said. "And I know he felt every word he said very deeply. I hope they'll finally give him the credit he deserves for turning his life around after messing up so badly."

Travis held up his hands. "Not up to us. If it were, it would be a nonissue, but we take our cues from our wives when it comes to this sort of thing. I'm not going into battle against the full fury of the Sweet Magnolias. Helen, in particular, scares me to death."

J.C. laughed. "She has that effect on a lot of people."

"And yet no one can deny that she's the best friend ever," Tom said. "We've all seen that side of her."

"Indeed," J.C. agreed.

"Back to Thanksgiving," Tom said. "You have to come. The tradition is to do this at Sullivan's because the crowd keeps growing. Dana Sue and Erik do most of the cooking, the turkey, stuffing and so on, mostly because nobody wants to try to outdo them in the kitchen. Even so, all the wives contribute a dish or two. There's enough food for an army."

Seeing no gracious way to get out of it, J.C. finally said, "Okay, count me in. And I'll check with Laura and let you know."

"So, how serious are you two anyway?" Travis asked. "You've looked pretty tight every time I've seen you together. Sarah's convinced there will be a wedding by spring."

J.C.'s nervousness rocketed off the charts. "What is it about this town that everybody thinks they deserve inside information on every relationship in Serenity?"

"The pools at Wharton's are a big incentive," Travis said, clearly not joking. "That money adds up fast."

J.C. turned to Tom. "Surely there's some law around here about gambling."

"Oh, I'm sure there is," Tom agreed. "Do you want to tell Grace about it? Besides, I think all this meddling is part of our civic charm." He grinned at J.C. "So, answer the question. How serious is this?"

J.C. thought of how quickly and hard he'd fallen for Laura despite every well-honed defense mechanism in his arsenal. "I think maybe she ought to know if it's serious before either of you do."

Both men hooted at the evasive response.

"Oh, boy, he's down for the count," Travis exulted, giving his cousin a high-five. "Told you so."

J.C. gave him a resigned look. "I don't suppose I could convince you to keep that to yourselves, could I?" He might be down for the count, but he still wasn't sure what he intended to do about it.

"You want us to keep a secret from our wives?" Tom inquired with feigned horror.

"Yes," J.C. said flatly.

Travis's gaze narrowed. "For how long?"

"Until Thanksgiving," J.C. said on impulse.

The date seemed appropriate. He'd been fighting the depth of this attraction for a while, but that was the past talking, not the present. Maybe it was time to leave the past where it belonged—behind him—and lock in the biggest blessing to ever come into his life.

Laura debated long and hard with herself before coming to the conclusion that there was one last thing she had to do to put the entire bullying incident behind her. In the spirit of Thanksgiving and with her heart open to forgiveness, she found herself driving over to the Litchfields' on the day before the holiday. She'd heard that Annabelle would be going away to a small girls' school in Charleston right after the long Thanksgiving weekend.

She rang the bell on the brick Colonial house and waited nervously. It wouldn't have surprised her to have the door closed in her face, but when Mariah opened it, she merely stood there in openmouthed shock.

"You!" Mariah said. "How dare you come here after what you've done?"

"Could we talk?" Laura asked. "Please."

For a moment, it looked as if Mariah would shut the door, but instead she eventually stepped aside to allow Laura to come in.

"Come to gloat?" Mariah asked as she showed the way into a living room that had been carefully designed as a showcase rather than a room to be enjoyed. There wasn't a speck of dust on any surface. Every picture hung precisely straight on the walls, and not one single object seemed out of place. All gleamed from recent polishing.

Laura sat on the edge of an antique Queen Anne sofa chosen to reflect status, rather than for comfort.

"I'm so sorry you think that's the kind of person I am, that I would come here to gloat about what has been a tragedy for so many young people in this town," she said.

"Then why are you here?"

"To see how you and Annabelle are coping with all this. No matter how it seems to you, I know how much you love your daughter and how devastating all of this has been to your plans for her future."

Rather than responding to the olive branch Laura was attempting to hold out, Mariah's gaze narrowed. "Annabelle's future is not over, not by a long shot, despite your best efforts to destroy her."

Laura sighed. "I never wanted to destroy anyone, Mariah. I wanted her to wake up and realize that what she was doing to Misty was wrong. I wanted you to see that young people need guidance, not a free pass. Everyone in Serenity has always shared your dreams for

Annabelle. She's amazingly talented. But that doesn't mean she's better than everyone else or that her actions don't need to have consequences. I honestly hope she's going to be a better person because of what's happened."

"Really?" Mariah said scathingly. "That's what you hope?"

"It is," Laura said, holding her gaze with an unblinking gaze of her own.

Suddenly Mariah seemed to crumble before her eyes. She buried her face in her hands. "I had so many dreams for her, so many hopes," she whispered tearfully. "I know everyone thought I was pushing her, making her do this to make up for my own dreams getting shoved aside when I got pregnant, but it wasn't about that at all."

"Tell me," Laura said, honestly wanting to understand.

"From the day Annabelle first stood in church and sang a solo, I knew she had something special. She was better than I'd ever dreamed of being. We all heard it, and she was only eight years old. From that moment, I've devoted myself to making sure she had everything she needed. I had no idea it could go so terribly wrong."

Laura regarded her with compassion. "Few parents completely understand how fine the line is between supporting and loving their children unconditionally and giving them carte blanche to do whatever they want to do. I may not be a parent, but I struggle with discipline every single day in my classroom. I need my students to follow the rules, but I also want them to understand why those rules matter, to get that I'm not just being vindictive or arbitrary."

Mariah nodded, her expression filled with sorrow and regret. "I don't talk about this ever, because there's no point, but maybe it will help you to understand just a little." She drew in a deep breath, then said, "My father was an incredibly tough disciplinarian, at least that's how he saw his actions. He used a belt to keep us kids in line."

Laura winced as she heard the pain in Mariah's voice.

"He said it was because he loved us," Mariah said wryly, "but it was hard to believe that with welts on our backsides more often than not. I vowed I'd never be like that. I wanted Annabelle never to doubt for a single second that I loved her more than my own life."

"You've proven that," Laura assured her. "And you're not the first parent to go to an opposite extreme from the way they were parented."

"But I think it's clear that leniency wasn't the answer, either. You should hear the conversations Annabelle's father and I have been having about that these past couple of weeks. He'd been warning me for a long time I was too easy on her, but I couldn't see it."

"Then perhaps this has been a wake-up call that will turn things around for all of you," Laura said. "Maybe you could focus on being grateful that it came in time and before any real lasting harm came to Misty or, for that matter, to Annabelle."

Mariah didn't look entirely convinced, but at least the hostility that had been in the air when Laura arrived was gone.

"Thank you for coming by," she said at last. "It took

real courage and grace to do that. I'm not sure I'd have done the same."

Laura smiled. "Who knows? You might have surprised yourself."

At the door, she held out her hand, waited perhaps a beat too long until Mariah took it. "Happy Thanksgiving, Mariah."

"Happy Thanksgiving to you, too," Mariah said. There was even a hint of real sincerity behind the words.

As Laura walked away, relief washed over her. This sad chapter, she hoped, was finally closed.

Thanksgiving morning in South Carolina didn't always have the cool, crisp weather that Laura had grown up with in Iowa, but the skies were blue and the air balmy. She returned home from a church service and coffee hour to find J.C. pacing impatiently in front of her house.

"Where have you been?" he asked.

"Where do a lot of people usually go on Thanksgiving morning?" she retorted.

He winced. "Church. Of course."

"Is there a reason you're here so early? I thought you weren't picking me up to go to Sullivan's until two o'clock."

"There's something I wanted to talk to you about before that," he said, following her inside, where he continued to pace.

Laura regarded him with curiosity. "Is something wrong? You seem particularly agitated this morning."

"I need coffee," he said. "Do you have any coffee?"

"I can make some."

He waved off the offer. "No, don't bother. I'll have water."

He charged off to the kitchen. Laura let him go. He obviously needed time to compose himself, though she couldn't imagine why.

When he came back into the living room, he sat down next to her on the sofa, then popped right back up.

"You and I," he began, then stopped.

Laura had seen plenty of nervous kids in her classroom trying to work up the courage to do an oral report. It was usually best to nudge them along.

"Yes," she said. "You and I…"

He shook his head as if she'd snapped him back from some faraway place. "I never thought I'd be doing this again," he said, making absolutely no sense.

"Doing what?"

He looked her in the eyes, his expression charmingly bewildered. "Proposing."

Laura couldn't seem to keep her jaw from dropping. "*That's* what you're doing?"

He nodded. "Making a real mess of it so far, huh? You can't even tell what I'm up to. How pitiful is that?"

Even though her heart was pounding and she was trying valiantly to keep from shouting yes, she managed to look him in the eye. "Is that what you really want to do, to propose?"

He nodded. "I never expected this. You, me. Falling in love." He groaned. "I am so sorry. This is such a disaster. I should probably wait, start over another time. Take you out for a romantic dinner or something." He frowned. "We've never even had a romantic dinner, not really. Why would you want to marry a man who hasn't even courted you properly?" He raked his hand through his hair, leaving it charmingly rumpled. "What is wrong with me?"

She smiled. Beamed, in fact. "You're doing just fine," she assured him. "And, believe me, there is nothing wrong with you. I've tried to find something, just so I could protect my heart in case this went nowhere." She shrugged. "But, sorry, J.C., no flaws. I haven't found a one."

"I could list them, you know, in the interest of fair disclosure and all that."

She barely managed to contain a chuckle. "Or I could make it easy on you and just say yes."

He blinked at that, took a step back, then came closer, his gaze narrowed. "Did you just say yes?"

"I did, unless you've changed your mind and decided not to ask, after all. You seem to be trying really hard to talk yourself out of it."

"But I wanted to do the whole romantic, down-on-one-knee thing," he protested.

She stood up and moved into his arms. "This was better. This was you being sweet and sincere and scared to death. Seems to me any sane person committing to forever ought to be scared to death."

"But you did it without even a blink of the eye," he noted.

"Because I've wanted this since the first day I walked into your office and you warned me off," she said. "Just shows how perverse I am. I've always been drawn to the unobtainable. There was a time when that didn't work out so well, but this time?" She smiled at him. "This time I think it's going to turn out exactly right."

He picked her up and spun her around until she was dizzy. "I just knew today was going to be the luckiest day of my life," he said. "Now all we have to do is undergo a cross-examination by half the town. They're all going to have something to say about this, you know. Maybe we should skip Thanksgiving dinner and celebrate right here, by ourselves."

"Not a chance." She looked into his eyes. "Anybody in that crowd who hates your guts or knows any deep, dark secrets?"

"Absolutely not," he said, frowning.

"Ditto with me," she told him. "I think we're good to go."

"Have I mentioned that I love you, Laura Reed?"

"No need," she told him. "It's been in every word you've said and everything you've done for weeks now. It just took you a while to figure that out."

He laughed. "Having you around to read my mind is definitely going to make my life a whole lot easier."

"And having you in my life is going to make me happier than I ever expected to be. I think that makes us a pretty good team."

He held her gaze, then said quietly, "We're going to be unbeatable." His expression sober, he added, "One more thing."

"What's that?"

"You've never said that you'd like to find your child, but I think I know you well enough to understand that not knowing where she is has been eating away at you.

If you want to make an effort to find her, to make her a part of our lives in whatever way she'd like to be, that's okay with me. I'll do whatever I can to help you."

Laura blinked back tears at his words. He'd just touched on so many raw emotions. "I don't know, J.C. Maybe she won't want to know me," she said voicing her greatest fear.

"You won't know until you've tried to reach out. And what I know with absolute certainty is that she'd be the luckiest girl in the world to discover that she has a biological mom who was brave enough to give her up."

So many times over the years Laura had thought of trying to find her child, but she'd thought it would be selfish. And maybe she'd been just a little bit afraid of what she'd find—a young woman who wanted no part of the person who'd given birth to her, then given her away. Perhaps now, with J.C.'s love and support, she could risk that.

"Thank you," she said softly.

He tucked a finger under her chin and looked deep into her eyes. "You never have to thank me for loving you and wanting to do anything and everything that will make you happy. From here on out, there's nothing in my life that will matter more."

She smiled at that. "You know what I'm going to be most grateful for today?"

"What?"

"That all the other single women in this town somehow missed what a catch you are or were scared off by your warnings to stay away."

J.C. chuckled. "You weren't scared off, were you? Not even a little bit."

"I had a few uneasy moments," she admitted. "But I think I knew from the very first day that you were going to be worth every risk I took. Turns out I was right."

"I'm glad you think so," he said, then cut off the conversation with a kiss that took her breath away.

"Oh, yeah," she murmured, when she could speak again. "I was really, really right!"

* * * * *

Questions for Discussion

1. Laura Reed feels passionately about being a good role model and mentor for her students because she once had a teacher who played that critical role in her life. Have you ever had a mentor or friend whose advice and support made all the difference for you in a difficult situation? Explain what happened.

2. If you're a parent, how attuned are you to your child's behavior and signs of possible bullying? Do you believe bullying is ever innocent, acceptable or just part of growing up?

3. What is your local school's policy on bullying? Is there not only a policy, but an active program to prevent bullying? If not, should there be?

4. Has your community experienced a tragedy related to bullying? What actions were taken as a result? Should more have been done?

5. If a teacher or neighborhood parent reports that your child has bullied another child, what is your first reaction? Like Mariah, do you instinctively defend your child, or do you keep an open mind?

6. What is the parent's responsibility in preventing bullying? Do you pay close attention to what your children are doing online? Do you feel children, especially teens, have a right to privacy, or is it more

important to monitor what's going on in their lives? How do you balance those things?

7. In the story, J.C. has been through a lot. Which incident do you think did the most to shape the man he is today—losing his brother, or his wife's betrayal? Has there ever been a defining moment in your life that shaped who you are?

8. For a time, Misty's mother is so lost in the pain of her divorce that she stops paying close attention to the needs of her children. Have you ever been through such a difficult time that nothing seems to matter beyond your own pain? What were the circumstances and how did you overcome that?

9. Mariah Litchfield seems to be using Annabelle to live out her own lost dream of being a singer. Have you known parents like this—men or women—who live vicariously through their children and seem to take their successes or failures too personally? Do you think that's good for either parent or child?

10. Paula Vreeland feels she's losing her touch as an artist and is frustrated that her current works don't measure up. Are there things you once loved doing that as you age you no longer do as well? Did you give them up in frustration or find a new way to enjoy them?